501

D0234298

The Darkness Inside

The Darkness Inside

JOHN RICKARDS

PENGUIN BOOKS

PENGUIN BOOKS

Published by the Penguin Group
Penguin Books Ltd, 80 Strand, London WC2R ORL, England
Penguin Group (USA) Inc., 375 Hudson Street, New York, New York 10014, USA
Penguin Group (Canada), 90 Eglinton Avenue East, Suite 700, Toronto, Ontario, Canada M4P 2Y3
(a division of Pearson Penguin Canada Inc.)
Penguin Ireland, 25 St Stephen's Green, Dublin 2, Ireland
(a division of Penguin Books Ltd)
Penguin Group (Australia), 250 Camberwell Road,
Camberwell, Victoria 3124, Australia (a division of Pearson Australia Group Pty Ltd)
Penguin Books India Pvt Ltd, 11 Community Centre,
Panchsheel Park, New Delhi – 110 017, India
Penguin Group (NZ), cnr Airborne and Rosedale Roads, Albany,
Auckland 1310, New Zealand (a division of Pearson New Zealand Ltd)
Penguin Books (South Africa) (Pty) Ltd, 24 Sturdee Avenue,
Rosebank, Johannesburg 2196, South Africa

Penguin Books Ltd, Registered Offices: 80 Strand, London WC2R ORL, England

www.penguin.com

First published 2006
1

Set in 11.75/14 pt Monotype Garamond
Typeset by Rowland Phototypesetting Ltd, Bury St Edmunds, Suffolk
Printed in England by Clays Ltd, St Ives plc

A CIP catalogue record for this book is available from the British Library

Acknowledgements

As always, many, many thanks to my editor Beverley Cousins, and to everyone else at Penguin for everything they've done – you're all absolute stars. Thanks also to Luigi Bonomi for all his help, as ever.

Many people helped this book along the way, but special mention has to go to Otis Twelve, Bryon Quertermous and Sarah Weinman for giving me a good kick when I needed it most.

And to Rachel for everything.

'To be left alone, and face to face with my own crime, had been just retribution.'

– Henry Wadsworth Longfellow

Prologue

'You're a nice guy, Alex.' That's what people say to me at parties. They look at me and they see what they want to see, make their own assumptions. Good points and bad points. Quiet, friendly, but a little withdrawn. A hint of strength that comes from the jobs I've had, present and past; no such thing as a spineless Fed. Yet there's nothing there to envy. No riches, no grand life to make them feel small.

They see me as non-threatening, which is why I'm only ever 'a nice guy', never anything more.

It's usually said with a hint of pity in the eyes or in the voice.

They judge everyone on acquisitions – the house, the car, the pretty wife, the three kids and the mortgage – and I come up short on all counts. My Bureau career dead for six years now, doing all right in the private sector, but *it's not the same, is it?* I live in a small apartment, alone. No wife and kids, and I'm not looking for them, not any more. My best hope for family bliss was torn from me a year ago and I accept that there'll not be another.

Certainly not another like it.

The people at parties would like me to keep trying, of course. Get out, get down, get laid. Get a life.

Settle for second best. 'You're a nice guy, Alex,' they're thinking. 'But you're going to end up alone and dead with little to show for it. What a waste.'

That's what they think when they tell me I'm a nice guy at parties. I know it, but I smile and nod anyway, and we talk for a while longer, and eventually I go back home to my empty life and I exist for another day.

I wonder what those people would say if they could see me now – in a trash-strewn alleyway, police lights flashing in the streets beyond, and every cop in the city hunting me for murder.

Chapter One

'RELATIVES CALL ON FALL RIVER KILLER TO BREAK SILENCE,' the headline reads. Dense columns of text fill much of page five of the *Boston Globe* beneath, along with the same mugshot of Cody Williams the media's used in every story written about him since his arrest seven years ago. Hair tied back in a ponytail, pulling his forehead taut and snapping his skin to attention, white in the photographer's flash. Heavy eyes staring contemptuously forwards. A faint sneer on cracked lips.

Looking at it, I feel a hollow, queasy sickness. The same sense of pursuit, dislocation, something invisible closing in behind that's been with me since the story about Williams' inoperable pancreatic cancer broke.

Since he became news again.

Since the past came back to threaten the present.

I don't read the *Globe*. If someone hadn't left a copy in the foyer of the building my agency shares with several other companies, if I hadn't picked it up for something to skim in the elevator, trying to shake the chill of the fall morning outside, I would never have seen the article. Not until the story's inevitable regurgitation on the TV news later in the day, anyway.

The families of several alleged victims of convicted murderer Cody Williams have pleaded with him to break his silence and reveal the location of their remains. Their request follows reports that FBI agents have recently attempted to persuade the 'Fall River Killer' to talk. Williams is currently serving a life term in Ashworth prison for the murder of serial rapist Clinton Travers in Hartford, CT. Although he never stood trial for their abductions, he is widely believed to have been behind the disappearances of seven girls over the course of a single year in the southern Massachusetts, Rhode Island and Connecticut area.

In an open letter to Williams, the relatives of those girls whose bodies have never been found ask him to give up their locations before he dies. 'Don't leave us forever wondering where they are. Let us bury our loved ones properly,' the letter reads.

Williams has always maintained his silence regarding the location of his alleged victims. In the seven years since his arrest, the remains of three girls – Kerry Abblit, Joanne Tilley and Abbie Galina – have been found in stretches of remote woodland. The bodies of Marie Austen, Brooke Morgan, Katelyn Sellars and Holly Tynon, all believed to have been killed by the Fall River Killer, have never been located. Williams was recently diagnosed with terminal pancreatic cancer and doctors say . . .

The lift doors slide open and I walk through reception and into our office, home to Robin Garrett

Associates, licensed private investigators, and a bunch more besides. A single large, utilitarian space. White walls, deep-red carpet. Steel shelves and filing cabinets, catalogue office furniture. Like most open-plan workplaces staffed by fewer people than they could comfortably fit, it feels like converted factory space, not a purpose-built office building a few blocks from Kenmore Square. Bright morning light slanting through the windows, the artificial tang of metal and plastic from the clutter, the all-pervasive electrical hum from the computers and the coffee machine.

Rob Garrett, my boss and friend, looks up from his screen. Early forties, a few years older than me, close-cut brown hair now liberally shot with grey. 'Morning, Alex,' he says. 'Had a good few days?'

I nod and sit at the desk opposite. 'Yeah. I didn't do anything much.'

'No?'

'Cleaned the apartment, caught up on a few things I'd been putting off.'

'You're right, that doesn't sound like anything much.'

'Didn't have much else to do.' I shrug. 'How were things here?'

'Fairly quiet. You didn't miss a lot. The kids are dealing with most of the bread-and-butter stuff that came in. Oh, and Sophie stopped by to let us know what hours she's available to work around her lecture schedule.'

'As busy as she was last semester?'

'That's about the shape of things. Although it looks like a cushy number compared to what I can remember of college.'

'Back in the day.'

He nods. 'Back in the day.'

'Listen to us, like a couple of old men,' I say, grinning. 'Did you trace McKean's ex-wife?'

'I paid a visit to her place in Portland on Thursday.' He chuckles. 'I don't know why his lawyers think she'll help his defence – she didn't say very much about him that *I'd* want repeated in a courtroom.'

'She was full of happy reminiscences and fond memories of her dream marriage, huh?'

'I get the impression she'd be happy to see him spend a few years in jail, yeah. Something of a vengeful streak to that woman. But I guess that's their problem, not ours. I posted the bill to them this morning.'

'I don't blame her for not wanting anything to do with him,' I say, dropping the *Globe* on to the nearest stack of paper.

'Yeah, nasty piece of work.' He leans back and flicks his eyes in the direction of my desk. 'You had a couple of calls on Friday. There's a note about one of them stuck to your monitor.'

I tug the Post-It off and run my eyes over Rob's scrawl. As I do so, he continues. 'I told them if it wasn't life-or-death urgent, they'd have to wait until you came back today.'

'They didn't push it. Guess it can't have been life-or-death urgent then.'

'Special Agent Downes, I think her name was. It's on the note.'

'Tanya Downes. From the Bureau's Boston field office.'

Rob nods. 'You know her?'

'No. After my time.'

'She said they needed to talk to you about Cody Williams.'

My heart sinks but I try to hide it. 'Did she say why?'

'No.' Rob frowns. 'You don't exactly sound raring to go.'

'How much do you know about Williams?'

He glances at the *Globe*. 'Only what I've seen in the news. I'd left the Bureau by the time he came along.'

'I was one of the agents working his case.' I sigh hard, swallow my unease and reach for phone.

'Yeah?'

'I was kind of hoping I'd never have to think about the guy ever again, that's all.'

When I eventually get through to Tanya Downes we briefly exchange pleasantries, but otherwise she's all business and wastes little time. 'I take it you've seen the press reports on Williams.'

'They say he's got cancer and could die anytime from weeks to months.'

'That's right.'

'I was planning on holding a party when it finally happens.'

'We're being pressured by the families of four of his victims to get him to talk and give up the places he hid their bodies before he checks out,' she says, ignoring my remark.

'Yeah, I saw their letter to him in this morning's paper.'

'How do you suppose he reacted?'

'He probably pissed himself he was laughing so hard,' I tell her. And I can almost picture him doing it. 'Cody Williams was never the sort to repent on his deathbed.'

'That's more or less been my experience of him as well. The letter, though, was more of a publicity tool.'

'Publicity for who?'

'By making it public, we hoped to increase the pressure on him to tell us what he knows. Privately, at the families' request, we've been talking to him in prison for the past week or so, in the hope of getting something useful.'

'With no luck.'

Downes pauses for a moment, then says, 'No. He's told us nothing about the locations of the victims.'

'The thudding sound you might be able to hear in the background is my jaw dropping from the sheer volume of surprise I'm feeling right now.'

'*However*, he *has* intimated that if he were to talk to anyone, it would be the agent who first spoke to him at the time of his arrest. Which was you, wasn't it?'

'Yeah.'

'So we want you to come out to Ashworth and speak to him for us. Try to make him see the pointlessness of taking his secrets to the grave.'

'Go to the jail to appeal to Cody Williams' better nature.'

'Or whatever you think will play best, of course. The doctors can't give us a definite timescale for his condition, so we're assuming we need to work as fast as possible. Obviously,' she continues before I can raise it as an objection, 'the Bureau will pay whatever reasonable fees your agency wants to charge.'

I think of all the reasons I have for refusing. I think of Cody's smug satisfaction. I think of the way it felt to stand helplessly by while he committed his crimes. While he killed those kids.

I think of all the lies.

'I don't know about all this, Agent Downes.'

'You don't know if you can succeed?'

'I don't know if I want to share the same air as Williams.'

'It'll be good publicity for your company, especially if you pull it off. A media spotlight can only be good for business.'

'You mean this whole thing will be good publicity for the FBI,' I reply, frowning. 'You can have the local SAC or some spokesperson handing out soundbites about helping the community, victim support. The caring, sharing face of today's Bureau. And you can't afford to let this slip away from you.'

'Conversely,' she says, as if I hadn't said a word,

'if it became known that you refused to help, I imagine the bad publicity would seriously damage the reputation of both yourself and your company.'

'Is that so, Agent Downes?'

'I doubt the families would think very highly of you either.'

'You forget that I was the one who got the guy that killed their kids. Of all people, they'd be the ones most likely to understand why I wouldn't want to set eyes on a son of a bitch like Cody Williams again.' I try to keep my temper in check. 'Let's face it, Agent Downes, the Bureau needs this far more than I do, so don't try threatening me with talk about public opinion. You're the ones who can't afford to get crucified in the media if you don't come up with the goods.'

The line goes quiet for a moment before Downes says anything further. From her tone, I guess she's decided to abandon that line of argument. 'I'm sorry, Mr Rourke,' she says.

'Alex. Calling me Mr Rourke makes you sound like my dentist.'

'I wasn't trying to coerce you, Alex, just pointing out the facts. I do understand why you might not want to speak to Williams. Really, I do. I know that it wasn't long after his case that you had your, uh . . .'

'Breakdown. A couple of months after his conviction, that's right.'

'And having spent a short while in the company of Williams, I'm inclined to agree with you that he is a son of a bitch and the sooner he checks out the better. But the families of his victims deserve one more chance to find out what happened to them, and time is running out. If there's any chance we can persuade him to speak to us, we've got to try, for their sake. We'll pay you well for your time, and don't forget the benefits – or otherwise – of that media spotlight.'

I rub my eyes, thinking long and hard. I can see Rob watching me across the room, although he's trying to make it look like he's reading something on his computer screen. My senses are swamped by memories long locked away.

I can smell the rancid sweat on Williams' skin the first time we met, see the hunger and the mocking light dancing in his eyes. I can hear his easy denial of his crimes, the undertone that says he's lying, and that he knows I'm aware of it and is enjoying it immensely.

'OK,' I say, much to my regret. 'I'll do it.'

'Thank you, Alex.'

'Here are my conditions, though. Firstly, I'll work on this until I exhaust all the possibilities I can think of. When I say I'm all out of ideas, or I'm fed up with the whole thing, my job is over. I go in there and Williams tells me to go fuck myself, I can walk away.'

'That's no problem.'

'Secondly, you're going to have to clarify the legal position here.'

'What do you mean?'

'Williams was never convicted of anything apart from the murder of Clinton Travers and the attempted kidnapping of Nicole Ballard. We had to drop the charge of murdering Kerry Abblit for lack of evidence, and we could never make cases against him for the others.'

'But we know it was him,' she points out.

'You, me and everyone else knows, but that's opinion, not legal fact. Williams isn't going to incriminate himself by revealing the locations of four murder victims if he thinks he could end up in court. And I don't want to go through the process of testifying again. If there's going to be any kind of legal proceedings arising out of these interviews, I'm not going to be involved.'

'That's fair enough. We're still working out the details, but we already had those concerns in mind. No one's too bothered about trying to get him into court – he'll have died in jail before any case comes to trial. It's likely that the interviews will be planned in such a way that nothing you learn in them would be admissible, so trying to bring murder charges would be a moot point. Good enough?'

'Yeah, I think so.'

'When are you available to start?'

'Tomorrow.'

'Excellent. I'll arrange the details and then call you with a time when we can meet to go over everything beforehand. See you then.'

I put the phone down and pinch the bridge of my nose. Rob waits a few seconds and then says, 'So, what's the deal with Williams?'

Chapter Two

Skip back just over seven years.

Purple-white lightning shears through the thick bank of black cloud overhead as rain pounds against the windshield of our Lincoln Town Car. The oppressive, cloying heat that surrounded Providence on my arrival from Quantico has given way to an explosive summer thunderstorm. Agent Jeff Agostini from Boston Field Office cranks the wipers up to full speed and swears under his breath, easing off the gas a little to adjust for the slick highway surface. Winds buffet against the window beside me.

'Blazing sunshine back in Virginia, huh?' he says, half shouting over the storm. He's a young guy, younger than me. Well-built, looks like he works out regularly, for fitness rather than bulking out, eager and sharp-eyed. Close-cut blond hair and a sharp, aquiline nose. I haven't known him for long enough to judge his qualities as an agent, but he's hardly shut up since we left the airport.

'That's right. This'll blow itself out before the afternoon, though, I reckon.'

'Maybe so, maybe so.' He taps his index finger on the wheel like it's in time to some unheard music running through his head. 'First time in New England?'

I shake my head. 'I was born in Maine.'

'Heh. Northerner, huh?'

'Yeah.'

'You come back here much?'

'Last time I was in this part of the country was a series of rapes in Hartford, Connecticut, a few months ago.'

'Rapes, sure, I heard about those. You get the fucker?'

I glance at him. He's driving with one hand on the wheel, the other gesticulating for emphasis on almost everything he says, but despite the constant energy boiling off him, he doesn't seem overly worked up. Must just be his way, I guess.

'Not yet.'

'Yeah, but I heard you had a suspect.'

'That's right.'

'Some guy you brought in for questioning, I heard. I think someone was talking about that at the office.'

'Yeah, we had a guy,' I say.

'Was it at the office? No, no. Saw it on TV.'

'He wouldn't talk, and the cops haven't nailed him on the evidence. Not yet.'

He nods vigorously. 'Some of them are real hardasses like that, yeah. Had one guy we brought in on one of the first cases I worked after the Academy. He was running guns and all sorts of shit in through Boston Harbour. Two years ago? Eighteen months ago?' He pauses, fingers still drumming on the hard plastic of the steering wheel. 'When did the Steelers take the Cowboys to the cleaners? Broke their quarterback's leg, beat them by nearly fifty clear points.'

'No idea.'

'Anyway, whenever. So we have this guy with a warehouse – not just, like, a truck or something, but a fucking *warehouse* – full of serious military hardware. We have half a dozen people who claim they work for him. And, ha, we've even got a dozen Haitians he'd shipped in for some side deal with someone. They're happy to testify that he was the one giving orders to the men who took them out of the container they were kept in on the way up from Florida. We're still getting the forensics, but we've got the guy by the balls, right?'

'Sounds like it.'

'By the *balls*. And would he talk? Not a bit of it.'

'Not even to cut a deal?'

'You got it. He kept claiming he was just renting out this warehouse to some people he'd never met and the whole thing was nothing to do with him. Even after the forensics came in. He was just a landlord to the mob, or some shit. He was as innocent as anything.'

I nod. 'And he was dead in the water when the case came to court.'

'Jury took less than an hour to decide. Sent down for a whole lotta years. And the look on his face, like he couldn't believe it. I'm telling you, man, I laughed for days at that.'

As the strip malls on the outskirts of Providence begin to thicken and intensify, a sure sign that we're nearing our destination, Agostini takes his eyes off the road long enough to look down at the case wedged between my feet. 'Is there anything you want to know that wasn't in the reports?'

'I don't think so,' I yell back, as another sheet of lightning wracks the sky. 'You've got three missing kids so far, all between the ages of twelve and thirteen. The last one, Holly Tynon, went missing, believed abducted, some time late yesterday.'

'From right here in Providence. The first two, Kerry Abblit and Katelyn Sellars, were from Fall River and Springfield, across the state line in Massachusetts.'

I nod. 'Yeah. And there's been no sign of them since, and no suggestion they were running away from home.'

'Right, right. No way were these runaways,' he says, conviction, determination running through his voice.

'It's been two months since Abblit went missing and around four weeks for Sellars. Information on what happened to both of them is sketchy.'

'Sketchy. Yeah, you could say that.'

'No one saw it happen, and there's nothing in the way of physical evidence to work on.'

'Yeah, and both city police forces were seriously thorough in canvassing for information, did a shitload of door-to-door, but there's been nothing much of any use so far.'

'Nothing helpful on suspicious vehicles at the first two disappearances?'

'Uh-huh,' Agostini says. Tap, tap, tap from his fingers. 'That is, we have a bunch of, like, possibles, but both happened in urban areas, so there were a lot of vehicles around. We could try tracking every car and truck and shit that was around at the time and still be working on it by the time we retire, you know?'

Into houses now, residential areas, highway beginning to blend with the town's road network. A news van passes us, heading in the other direction, wholly out of place in this suburban landscape. Above, the storm continues to pound away.

'OK,' I say, running through the facts more for my own benefit than for Agostini's input. 'So Holly was last seen at around 9 p.m. yesterday, leaving a friend's house to walk home, a journey of just under a quarter of a mile. A couple of people living on the same street as her friend remember seeing her pass by.'

'Yeah, they were the last ones we know that saw her.'

'For the moment. We might get lucky when this thing hits the evening news. Jog a few memories. At around 9.45 p.m. Holly's parents called her friend, but she'd left well before then. They then phoned other friends to see if she was with any of them, gone somewhere else on her way home. When those calls drew a blank, her father, John, went out to check the route between the two houses, to see if he could find any sign of her.'

'And he finds jack shit.'

'Right, nothing. At around ten-fifteen, they call the police.'

Agostini nods. 'And forty-five minutes later, the cops contact us, and as this is a child abduction, we contact you NCAVC guys. Speaking of which, isn't there, like, supposed to be another agent here with you?'

'Bert Drury. Went down with serious food poisoning this morning. Hospitalized and out of action for the time being.'

'Seriously?'

'Seriously. They didn't tell you?'

'No, but I've been kinda busy, so I might have missed it.'

'Well, you're working with me on this case. For now, at least. Have you had anything from Behavioural Analysis yet?'

'Not so far as I know. Last I heard they were still working on it.' Tap, tap, tap. 'I'm partnering you on this?'

'That's the plan.'

'Cool. Because I really hope we get this fucker before he snatches any more kids.'

'You got kids of your own?' I ask.

'No, this kind of thing just gets to me, you know? I guess you work on these cases a lot, though.'

'I guess so. But you never get used to it. Not when it's kids. Trust me on that.'

Agostini swings the car into a street of pleasant identi-kit suburban housing. Upper-end blue-collar or non-management white-collar family homes. Tidy, compact front yards. Boxy but reasonably attractive buildings. A block of small stores and a gas station down one of the side streets we pass. And up ahead, two more news vans and a couple of patrol cars belonging to Providence PD. No TV crews out filming; they're probably sheltering from the rain.

We pull up next to one of the cop cars and climb out. The Tynon house looks exactly the same as all the others on the block. If it wasn't for the vehicles crowding the road outside, I wouldn't have given the place a second glance. There's no sign of the rest of the street's residents; like the news teams, the storm must be keeping them indoors. That, and fear. Something has invaded their quiet neighbourhood and taken one of their own. I inhale deeply, drawing in as much of the clean, rain-washed air as I can.

Agostini looks oddly at me as he scrunches his neck, trying to draw his head down into his suit collar to protect it from the elements. I turn away from the street and follow him up the driveway to the house.

The uniformed cop who answers the door checks our ID, then points us through into the living room. There, a man and woman sit with their hands clasped together, saying nothing and staring at the far wall. Their skin is pale, eyes sunken and dark. A second man is sitting on the far side of the woman, one hand resting on her shoulder as he looks up at the two of us. From the sad, uncomfortable look on his face, and a hint of a resemblance, I guess he's Mrs Tynon's brother, here to support her.

Just as he leans towards Mrs Tynon's ear to speak, someone taps me on the shoulder and I turn to see a detective in suit and tie, his badge on his belt. He looks us up and down and says, 'I'm Detective Hall. Glad you could come.'

We shake hands briefly, then he slips past us and goes to speak to the family, hunching down to their level so he doesn't have to raise his voice. No one likes breaking such an uncomfortable silence too badly, not if they can avoid it. 'Mr and Mrs Tynon,' he says. 'These men are from the FBI. They're here to help us look for Holly.'

The brother keeps his eyes lowered, but man and wife crane their necks round to look at us. Both look haggard, emotionally battered. Some people react to the presence of the Bureau in an investigation with renewed hope, an indication of the efforts being made on their kids' behalf. Others see it as a sign to expect the worst. Forensic techs in plastic coveralls on the evening news. Body bags or tactfully covered stretchers. Lonely collections of flowers left by strangers.

'Mr and Mrs Tynon,' I say, making eye contact with both. I see no renewed hope there. 'I'm Special Agent Alex Rourke, and this is Agent Jeff Agostini.'

'What happened, Agent Rourke?' she asks. 'What happened to our little girl?'

'That's what we're going to find out, Mrs Tynon. Between us, Providence Police Department, Rhode Island State Police and a dozen other departments in New England, we're going to find out. Whoever's responsible for taking Holly, he won't get away with it, I promise.'

I don't know if her husband picks up on some uncertainty in my reply or not, but he drops his eyes and says, half-croaking, 'You're here because of the others.'

Agostini glances at me.

'Bill's wife heard them talking about it on the news,' Tynon continues. 'Those other two girls, the ones in Massachusetts. They're saying it's the same guy. The same as got our little girl.'

I decide to go with the truth. 'We don't know that, but there is a possibility, yes. Just as there's a possibility that something totally different happened to Holly. It's our job to find out for certain what happened and get her back for you if we can.'

Stop there, and pause as I catch sight of the framed family photos on the mantel at the far side of the room. Holly, smiling at me from behind the glass. Preserved, like a butterfly in a case. Next to the pictures are a couple of sporting trophies from some school tennis competition. A tiny model of a clarinet; maybe she was learning to play the instrument. Fragments of a life preserved in miniature. Part of me wants to warn her parents, to soften the inevitable blow. To tell them that in child-kidnap cases of stranger abduction for sexual purposes where the child is not released after the initial offence, ninety per cent are dead within twenty-four to thirty-six hours of the abduction.

Mrs Tynon opens her mouth and says in a quiet, clear voice, eyes blank and hollow, 'Did you find out for certain what happened to the other girls, Agent Rourke?'

That seventy-five per cent are killed within the first three hours.

'Did you make the same promises to their parents? In all those weeks, do you even know where those children are?'

That chances are, she'll never see Holly alive again.

'My daughter is dead, isn't she, Agent Rourke?'

Chapter Three

'Cody Williams was one of the worst pieces of human filth I ever encountered in the Bureau,' I tell Rob. The look in Marie Tynon's eyes, blank and dead and utterly bereft of all hope like a light behind them had suddenly been switched off, forever burned in my memory, rises to the surface once more. No parent should outlive their own child. To miss out on seeing them grow and bloom. Not to see the outcome of years of love and attention. No parent should have all that torn from them in an instant by a total stranger.

'Yeah, I saw what he was supposed to have done on the news.'

'I worked a bunch of cases involving kids,' I say. 'But he was the worst by far. The news doesn't show how bad he was.'

'What's his story?'

'He grew up in New York State but ran away from home at thirteen. Nothing to do with the parents, as far as we could make out.'

'No history of abuse or anything?'

'No abuse, that's right.' I nod. 'We never found out much of what happened after he ran, but I got the impression that he'd hung around with some strange people.'

Rob raises an eyebrow. '"Strange?" You mean like serious headcases, or "strange" as in a little eccentric? Or people with weird lifestyles?'

'He never said. But occasionally he'd mention something, some little thing he'd done or that might have been done to him, and you'd get an impression. Some indication of the way he'd grown up in his teens. And the things he considered normal . . .'

'Bad?'

'Tell me about it. But despite that, he had no criminal record or anything like that. He just surfaced again in Fall River maybe a year before Kerry Abblit went missing, out of nowhere. He was twenty-two.'

'That's young for one of these.'

'Now he's almost thirty, he's young to be getting cancer, too. Just a shame he couldn't get it any younger. Anyway, he worked as a delivery driver for a specialist auto-parts firm, driving rare or imported spares to repair shops and private owners all over southern New England.'

Rob nods. 'Giving him a truck or a van and a reason to travel almost anywhere.'

'Exactly. I don't know at what point on his travels he decided to start snatching young girls, but he certainly had plenty of opportunity. We never could find out for sure what, if anything, started him off.' The remembered scent of the man assails me once more. 'From what he said in my interviews with him, I know the son of a bitch enjoyed the whole thing. He was smart, though, and never gave away anything that could be tied conclusively to any of the crimes, certainly not if we didn't have the bodies.'

'Which is why he was never charged.'

'Right.'

'Not with the kids' murders, anyway,'

'Thing was, I *knew* it was him as soon as I first talked to him. Everything about the guy screamed "child murderer". He must have known we didn't have the proof to make a case stick.'

'How did you get him in the end?'

'Arrogance,' I say, trying to brush off the question. Thinking about Williams again is making my skin itch. 'He committed a murder he couldn't hide, well outside his usual victim range. Then one of the girls he tried to grab managed to fight him off, and she ID'd him. We got him, just too late. The cancer can't kill him soon enough, if you ask me.'

Rob raises his eyebrows but decides not to ask any further questions. He's just gone back to looking at his screen when the door swings open and Simon Bisley, one of our younger staff, walks in. He's a college drop-out, but a talented one, and he seems to enjoy the job. Early twenties, with a shock of bleached blond hair and a thin goatee beard in his natural ginger-brown colour. His eyes are red-rimmed, and his shirt looks like he slept in it.

'Good night, was it?' Rob asks.

'Yeah, you could say that.' The rasping croak from a throat that saw one too many drinks last night.

'So who is she?'

He rubs his head and smiles to himself. 'I've got no idea what you're talking about.'

'Come on, kid. All that time emailing and sending text messages. Don't even try to claim that was work.'

'I plead the Fifth.'

Rob chuckles. 'Oh, and we had a call yesterday from a girl who didn't leave her name, looking for you.'

'All right, but what makes you think I saw her last night?'

'I'd be very surprised if that shirt you're wearing had just come from the closet,' I chime in.

'And you haven't shaved.'

Simon shrugs. 'Maybe I overslept.'

'Maybe you did, but I doubt it. So who is she?'

'Maybe I was tending my sick mother at the hospital all night and didn't have time to neaten up before I came to see you two slave-drivers.'

I laugh.

'Hey, I have a mom. It could happen.'

'Come on, Simon. Names, places, details. It's not as though girls are interested in you, well – ever,' Rob says, grinning. 'Not everyone is blessed with my good looks and charm, after all. So you must be dying to brag.'

Simon shakes his head. 'You guys are worse than my parents, you know that? Her name's Eve.'

'And?'

'And I'm not saying anything more, not about last night, hangovers, the shirt, the lack of a shave, nothing. A gentleman does not discuss such things.'

'You kids,' Rob says.

Next day, I wait on the doorstep of my apartment building for Agent Downes, smoking. I've managed to cut down to ten a day or so. Probably not long before I quit altogether; that's the way the world is. Early morning sunlight slants across the street in front of me, glittering from under the far edge of a bank of black cloud that covers most of the sky. A cold day, with the promise of rain. I should be thinking about the interview ahead, preparing questions, strategies. Instead I'm trying not to think of the events of seven years ago.

A red Pontiac Bonneville pulls up by the side of the road, and Tanya Downes waves me over. I have to move a bulky box file out of the way before I sit down. The car smells of air freshener and seat fabric, bitter and chemical. The radio is on at low volume, tuned to what sounds like one of Boston's talk-only stations.

'Good morning, Alex,' she says, as she slips the Pontiac into gear. She's dressed in a deep-blue trouser suit, crisp and clean. Dark hair in a neat ponytail, mouth set in a businesslike smile. She reminds me of a schoolteacher, the sort you get in movies, who cracks down on troublemakers in her class while simultaneously showing the kids the joys of poetry or classical literature. The stereotypical teacher, not the real thing.

Not quite what I expected from our phone conversation. For one thing, I thought she'd be older, my age at the very least. For another, she seems to be friendlier in person. A body language thing, I guess. Or she's making a deliberate effort to get on my good side.

'Hi.'

'All ready for today?'

'As I'll ever be. What's in the box?'

'In there you'll find a copy of the case files on all the missing girls, as well as Williams' other crimes – Nicole Ballard and Clinton Travers – and everything we've been able to learn about the bodies that we've found since his conviction.'

'Some light bedtime reading, huh?'

'I thought you might want to refresh your memory, just in case there's anything there you can work with to persuade Williams to talk.'

I nod, glance down at the file. 'Thanks.'

'You can hang on to that until you're done working with us. It's not as if there's anything in there we need for the time being.' She smiles. 'You're not quite as I imagined you, you know.'

'You must have seen photos.'

'They never tell the whole story.'

'And you must have read my file.'

'I did, but like the pictures, it's all out of date. You've changed since your Bureau days.'

'I guess I have.'

'You've lost the regulation suit for one thing.'

'That's the private sector for you.' I shrug. 'How

long have you been with the field office here in Boston? I thought you'd be older.'

'Maybe I am. They can do wonders with skin creams and the right diet these days.'

'You'll have to tell me your secret.'

'You're big into women's skin cream?'

'Can't get enough of it.'

She laughs. 'I've been at the field office for a few years now. With a bit of luck, I'll be able to make SAC before too long.'

'Onwards and upwards.'

'I don't see anything wrong with wanting to make the most of my career, Alex. Besides, if I could climb into the upper echelons I might be able to do some large-scale good. Make my mark on Bureau policy.'

I refrain from passing judgement on her chances of having much of an effect, and on the impression her words engender that she sees fieldwork as just a stepping stone on the path to glory. Instead I say, 'I was never any good at playing Bureau politics in Washington myself.'

'It is a little like wrestling sharks naked, or so I understand. But then your speciality was very much investigative work.'

She glances at the box file, and I give it an experimental heft to show willing, but leave it closed. It's heavy, solid-feeling. I already know most of its contents from the original investigation and trial; hell, I wrote some of the reports that must be in there. The only additions of note I can think of would be scene reports and examinations of the bodies of Kerry Abblit, Abbie Galina and Joanne Tilley.

'The three girls you've found so far,' I say to Downes. 'What's the story with them?'

She purses her lips, thinking. 'Joanne Tilley was the first to be found, nearly five years ago. She was buried in woodland not far from Ware in Hampshire County.'

'Quite a way from where she went missing.'

'Right. Her remains had skeletonized, but the medical examiner's office identified her from dental records. There didn't seem to be any clothes or remaining possessions with her.'

'No scraps of material or anything like that?' I say.

'None at all.' She shakes her head. 'The remains were disturbed when a nearby tree fell in a storm, hauling up its root system en masse. No animal activity, but they had been moved a little by the tree and the rain. We couldn't be certain, but it looked like she might have been strangled.'

'Yeah?'

'As I recall, there might have been other injuries, but it was impossible to say whether they occurred pre- or post-mortem.'

Joanne Tilley was a sweet, quiet child. A huge Disney fan. She dreamed of becoming a veterinarian at a zoo or wildlife park when she was older. On Sundays she liked to go to her grandmother's house with the rest of her family. Her favourite food was butterscotch.

Outside, it's still dry, but I can see from the swaying

trees, already changing colour with the fall, that the wind has picked up. My breath leaves vapour bursts on the glass.

'Was there any indication how Williams would have dumped her in that location?' I ask. 'Parking lots or access roads he would have had to use, that sort of thing?'

'Two. A parking lot and a fire break, both around half a mile away from the dump site. At the time she was found, we checked for old reports of suspicious activity or vehicles in the area from the time before Williams' arrest.'

'I'm guessing you found nothing.'

She nods. 'Nothing at all. Although we weren't really expecting to. It would've been nearly impossible to get anything we could pin on Williams without knowing exactly when she was dumped.'

'Barring an old report of someone seeing him waltzing from his van with her body tucked under one arm, shouting his name to anyone within earshot.' I smile. 'And there's not exactly much chance of that.'

'Not exactly, no.'

'Carrying a girl's body half a mile, he would probably have used a bag, or wrapped her in fabric or plastic. But there was no fibre evidence of any kind?'

'Nothing. Either we missed it, or everything was moved or destroyed down the years, or when the tree fell.' Downes takes her eyes off the road long enough to glance at me. 'Is this important for the interview with Williams?'

'The more I know about him already, the less I'll have to persuade him to give up, and I don't really have time to read the entire file now. Which vic was found next?'

A truck flashes past, heading north back to Boston. The garish yellow text on the side looks like 'BODY PARTS', but I guess I must've misread 'AUTO'. Other traffic is relatively light, even though it's leaf-peeper season. The wrong kind of weather to be ogling the foliage.

'Kerry Abblit,' Downes replies. 'She had a similar burial some way from where he must have parked his vehicle. She was found in marshland a few miles south of Fall River, not far from Horseneck Beach, about six months after Joanne Tilley. It looked like a combination of erosion and animal activity uncovered her. Again, the remains were skeletonized.'

'Strangled?'

'Strangulation was the most likely cause of death, yes.'

Kerry Abblit could be trouble at school, but she was just free-spirited, her parents said. She had dozens of friends and was a secret fan of the old jazz albums her dad collected. She had a pet mouse called Till.

'However, there were also signs that she'd been injured before death, possibly beaten. A broken arm, blunt trauma to the skull. We had more luck with trace evidence than we did with Tilley. There were half a dozen or so dark synthetic fibres with her bones.'

'But they didn't match any samples taken from Williams' van or house,' I say. When Agent Downes looks at me, I add, 'Because you would have charged him with her murder by now if they had.'

'That's right.' She smiles. 'I see your time away from the Bureau hasn't slowed you down.'

'A few years older, a few grey cells less than before, but yeah, I can still make intelligent guesses, chew my own food, go to the bathroom without help.' I flash her a quick grin and say, 'So the fibres came from whatever her body was carried in, or something used to tie her or hold her in place, or from wherever she was taken before or after death.'

'Some sort of carpet was the probable source, according to forensics. But there were too few, and they were too old, to say for certain. But if they were, then most likely they'd have come from where she was kept or from the vehicle used to carry her.'

'So he stashed her somewhere else while he was beating the hell out of her.'

'Unless he had another vehicle.'

'We never found any indication that he had a second vehicle. But another property is possible, I guess. A derelict house, maybe even a cheap motel somewhere.'

Downes raises her eyebrows. 'Wouldn't that be too public?'

'Not necessarily. I worked on a case once with some guy who was on the run for . . . something. But as he was hopping from state to state, he was picking up hookers, taking them back to wherever he was staying and beating them to death.'

'No one noticed?'

'You'd think someone would hear screams or something, but these were *very* cheap motels and not usually especially crowded. They'd only find the victims when they cleaned the rooms after he left. A dead girl in the bathroom. Four or five states he did this in, until we caught up with him some place in Louisiana. Got there before he left town again. He decided to shoot it out with the police rather than surrender, as I recall, and took a bullet to the head as a result. Suicide by cop. But it goes to show – you *can* commit murder in a public place like that without anyone noticing.'

We pass a signpost pointing left for MCI-Ashworth. Downes makes the turn, on to a narrower and quieter road than the main highway.

'Anyway, so then you found Abbie Galina,' I say.

She nods. 'We were hopeful after Abblit that we were going to turn up all the body dump-sites fairly quickly. The first two showed up only six months apart. I know the families were optimistic.'

'But Abbie was found a couple of years after the other two.'

'Two years, yeah. It was the same deal as the others. She was buried in the countryside, not too close to road access, to minimize the chances of discovery, but not far enough away to be too difficult to manage.'

Abbie Galina had a difficult childhood, struggling with a

*life-threatening illness in her first two years. But she had
recovered fully and was a healthy, happy girl who had started
showing signs of a real talent for art.*

'They were all buried naked, as far as you can tell?'

'Right.'

'So what happened to their clothes and personal
possessions? I know we never found much at Williams' home when we searched it. There was a piece
of jewellery that had belonged to Kerry Abblit –
which he claimed he bought at a yard sale – but no
sign of everything else.'

Downes shrugs. 'They were probably thrown away
in the trash or burnt. Williams might let you know
for sure if you can get him to play ball.' She rolls her
eyes and for once her businesslike façade cracks a
little. 'Oh, crap.'

The prison complex looms up ahead, a blocky
structure of red brick, tall and ominously unfriendly
in the gloom. Huge and secluded. Twin high fences
topped with razor wire surround the facility. One
main building divided into a number of wings and a
couple of smaller structures to make up the rest of
the complex. On the grass near the gates and the
main parking lot is a scattered gathering of people,
some bearing placards. There are a couple of news
vans parked nearby and camera crews are out and
about, getting crowd shots or prepping for thirty-
second anchor spots. The only placard I can read
from here has the words 'LIBERTY BEFORE
DEATH' emblazoned on it in bright red letters.

'I'm sorry, Alex. I was hoping we could avoid this,' Downes says apologetically.

'Cody Williams has *supporters*?' I ask, raising an eyebrow.

'People are suckers for anything that can be painted as a "hard-luck case". '

'But Cody Williams . . .'

'Yeah.'

'Shit.'

'Yeah.'

As we pass the knot of protesters, heading for the gate into the main parking lot and not the separate visitors' one, I see many of them turn to look at our car. Most of those gathered here look depressingly normal – middle-aged, white- or blue-collar, or younger and more colourful student-types. None of them look like the freakshow crowd you get at such protests in the city; I guess the jail is too far for them to drive. A couple wave their placards, but only half-heartedly, unsure of our identities or purpose. I find myself shaking my head. Small-minded 'crusaders' without the first idea about the man they're crusading for. I want to jump out and yell Cody's crimes and character at them until they get the message, to shake them by the shoulders and ask them what the hell they think they're doing. But I can't. Camera crews turn to see what the commotion is about, and my heart sinks. I only hope they've lost interest before we leave the car to head inside the prison complex.

'How can they possibly support him?' I ask. 'He's a multiple child-murderer.'

She shakes her head. 'Never convicted. He's in jail for one attempted abduction and the murder of a serial rapist. Paint it right and they can make him look like a tragic vigilante who went over the edge. One of his fan websites claims he was trying to protect Ballard by abducting her.'

'People believe *that*?'

'People are idiots.' She shrugs.

'You could have mentioned his fan club when you were offering me the job.'

Downes says nothing as she swings the car into an empty space and pulls up. We sit in silence for a moment, gusts of wind rippling against the windows. The prison blocks out the view ahead of us, a solid wall of brick, final and absolute. Then I drop the box file in the passenger footwell and look across at her.

'Best get moving,' I say.

'You're not taking the file?'

I shake my head. 'No point, not this early in proceedings. Today isn't likely to be about details.'

As I step out of the car, I glance back at the gates and the knot of protesters. I can see some of the TV cameras pointed in our direction and I quickly turn away. Downes locks the car and leads me towards the entrance without paying any attention to the crowd behind us.

'Remember what we've agreed with Williams and his attorney,' she says, as we hurry across the parking lot. 'Whatever he says to you doesn't have to be admissible, so don't give him a Miranda warning.'

'I can't anyway – I'm not in law enforcement, remember.'

'True,' she says. 'But don't worry about anything like that. Williams also doesn't want any recordings made of your conversation, and no witnesses to overhear what he says. Think of it as an informal chat.'

'An informal chat, right. Nothing more.'

'You'll be meeting in the visiting room, because he feels safer, knowing it's not likely to be wired in any way.'

'I'd prefer it if he was a little on edge. If he's totally confident in his security, he'll be harder to break down.'

'His conditions. And we have to abide by them, because if he decides to clam up, there's nothing we can do. Basically, he's calling the shots here. We just have to hope he really does want to talk to you.'

I nod. 'Right. Who else is going to be around?'

'The guard on duty and I can watch through the door glass, and there's CCTV covering the room. No sound, though.'

'He's not worried about lip-readers?' I'm only half joking.

'Chances are he'll face away from the camera,' Downes replies, as we step into the building. I'm not sure, but I think she's only half joking as well.

Inside, we're met by a woman who identifies herself as Deputy Superintendent Alia Shaw. Maybe a couple of years older than me, about my height. Blonde hair cut short. A long, haughty face to match a severe brown trouser suit she wears like body armour.

'Special Agent Downes, Mr Rourke,' she says, extending a hand in greeting. In her other, she holds visitors' badges for the pair of us. 'Welcome to MCI-Ashworth. I know Agent Downes has visited our facility before, but have you, Mr Rourke?'

I shake my head. Inside, the prison feels like a hospital. Sterile walls and smooth floors, a slight curve to almost every edge, just to take the sharpness off. All in an off-cream colour. I guess all this is supposed to soothe people, dull the brain into utter passivity until it turns into so much grey sludge. Lobotomies without the surgery. Why they have it in the administrative part of the complex as well as the prisoner sections, I don't know. The air smells of acrylic and air-con.

'We're a medium-security facility with maximum-security systems,' Shaw says, as she leads me down one of the multitude of interchangeable corridors. 'We've only been fully operational for ten years.' She smiles. 'Your tax dollars at work.'

'Really?' I ask, feigning interest. The sound of raised voices reverberates dully in the distance before fading out again. 'Solving the overcrowding problem, huh?'

'That's about the shape of it.' She shepherds us through a set of locked doors to the right, nodding at the guard stationed there. We swing left and through what looks like a waiting room. Up ahead, a twin set of barred barriers either side of a security station, and beyond the trap a hospital-style door through which I can see the orderly collection of tables and chairs that make up the visiting room. The lights are either off or turned down low and the room is gloomy.

'This is Outer Control,' Shaw says. 'You'll have to leave most of your personal items here for security reasons. I'll provide you with one of our debit cards, so if you want a coffee or anything you can get it from the machines in the visiting room.'

I drop my wallet, keys and scant pocket clutter into the box provided by the guard on duty.

'You're not going in, is that right, Agent Downes?' Shaw says.

'That's correct. I'll be watching through the door from here.'

Shaw turns to the guard and says, 'Tell them to show Williams in.'

A grating, mechanical buzzing echoes across the dim emptiness of the visiting room. A door on the far side opens, the bright electric glare beyond temporarily flooding the area with light, picking out everything in sharp relief. Silhouetted against the blue-white glow are two men, one of them a guard with his hand on the other's shoulder. A flash of the second man's long, unkempt hair, bouncing against his shoulder as he shuffles forward. No more than five and a half feet tall, ragged, wiry figure hidden behind a prison uniform slightly too large for him. Eyes that catch a stray reflection from the windows high up to the right, glittering in the gloom as he sits and his escort turns to leave.

'For Christ's sake, Clive, turn some lights on,' Shaw says to the guard next to us.

A flicker from two of the fluorescents inside, strobing the prisoner below, picking everything out in crystal detail. Lank curly brown hair. Hooded eyes and sallow skin. Blank expression. Grey sweatshirt stamped with the DOC logo over a rumpled white shirt turning yellow at the corners. Manacled hands resting on the table, fingernails bitten and ragged.

A second buzzer, and the door in front of me opens. Cody Williams looks up and smiles crookedly.

Chapter Four

'I want to start by walking Holly's route,' I say to Detective Hall and Jeff Agostini once we've left the Tynons alone and retreated to the kitchen. 'It should only take five minutes. I'll go talk to the friend she was with and her family. What are their names?'

'Tina Aitken is the girl Holly was friends with,' Hall says. 'Cole and Natasha are her parents.'

'Tina, Cole, Natasha. Right.'

'What do you need to ask them?'

'Nothing specific. Have you spoken to them?'

Hall nods. 'Yeah, I have.'

'Any chance the father did this? It's best to start close and work outwards in my experience.'

'No,' Hall says, shaking his head. 'He was watching TV with his wife between the time Holly left and the time John Tynon called him to see whether she was still there.'

'In which case, all I want is just to get their stories first-hand and to get a look at the neighbourhood. There's a chance Holly wasn't grabbed by a complete stranger, but by someone who lives locally and might have seen her on the journey home.'

'You think that's likely?' Agostini asks.

'No. Possible.'

'Possible, right. It's just, like, hard to imagine the

fucker who'd do something like that living somewhere like this, you know?'

'It's always hard to imagine it happening anywhere,' I say. 'But it happens.'

Hall nods. 'Yeah, it happens. Even here. Although this is the first we've had in years. What'll you be looking for, Agent Rourke?'

'I'll just run my eyes over the neighbourhood, see if anything stands out. I'll see if Tina can think of anyone Holly might have gone to meet.'

'It's ground we've already covered, but I guess there's no harm in seeing if anyone's remembered anything more. Is there anything you need us to do?'

'You've checked her route with K-9 units, is that right?'

'Earlier this morning,' Hall says. 'The weather hasn't helped, though.'

'No trail?'

'Some, but it was confused and we couldn't get a clear abduction point. The handlers say her traces may have faded out a couple of blocks from the Aitkens', but they weren't certain. We've had forensics take away anything they could find from the kerb and roadside at that point.'

Agostini drums his fingers on the kitchen worktop. 'You have any luck with that?'

'No. Nothing promising anyway.'

'In that case,' I say, 'keep on trying to trace anyone Holly might have gone to see, or anywhere she might have gone on her own. If she's just with a boyfriend or something and hasn't caught the news, I'd be very happy.'

'Probably too young for a boyfriend,' Hall says.

Agostini shakes his head. 'Hey, my kid sister had her first crush when she was, like, ten.'

'It doesn't matter. There's no boyfriend that we know of.'

'No?'

'No.'

'Well, in addition to that, get anything you can dig up on traffic in this area last night. Vehicles, drivers, anything and anyone we can put in the right place at the right time. Particularly the point where her scent trail went cold. Keep us posted on anything interesting.'

'Sure,' Hall says.

Agostini looks at me. 'What about me?' he asks. 'What do you want me to do?'

'Drive up to the Aitkens' house and wait for me there. We'll need the car. If you don't mind the rain, you can walk back to meet me on the way. Once we've spoken to them, we'll play it by ear. See what comes up.'

'What do you think our chances are?'

I don't answer him. Let the silence do the talking.

'Shit,' he says.

Step back outside and the storm hasn't let up at all. Driving pellets of rain slice through the air like buckshot, slapping into the jacket of my suit with considerable force. Agostini looks at me like I'm crazy again as I wave away the offer of an umbrella. In the wind, it wouldn't hold up anyway. I pass the news vans and leave the sad gathering of vehicles outside the house behind.

The neighbourhood feels closed off or abandoned, like

the streets in some disaster movie after the killer plague's hit and everyone but the lone survivor is dead. The houses look like mostly family residences; people with similar jobs, similar lives. Similar times for going out and staying home. The small yards are pleasant, but boxed-in. Most have hedges, or a couple of small trees, or a fence, something to form a barrier between each residence and the public street. Even down cross-streets I don't see any bars, clubs, late-night malls or anywhere else local to go after work. At nine on a week-night, I doubt there'd be anyone much out at all. People who have to go out of their way to catch a movie or get drunk tend to make a night of it if they can. Otherwise, they stay indoors and watch TV. Crime-free neighbourhood too, and I doubt anyone gives a second glance to traffic on the streets.

Holly Tynon's abductor chose his area well. If he deliberately chose it at all, I remind myself. Maybe he was just passing and got lucky.

The spot where the K-9 teams thought her scent might have gone cold is fairly obvious — at least to me, now I know what to look for. Despite the rain, it's easy to see the five-yard stretch of gutter by the roadside swept clean by forensics techs looking for any kind of trace evidence. Twenty-five feet or so from the nearest intersection, right where a car that had just made the turn would stop, the exact spot. I picture the driver pulling up, asking for directions, asking the time, offering a ride. Hitting Holly, knocking her out so she won't scream for help. Pulling a knife. Pulling a gun.

My cell phone rings, Agostini's number on the screen. I hit the 'call' button and say, 'Yeah?'

'Alex, I've just heard from the cops. They've found Holly Tynon's wallet in a park a mile or so away. Whereabouts are you?'

'The likely abduction site.'

'I'll come pick you up.'

Less than a minute later, Agostini's Town Car stops next to me, and I hop in, noticing for the first time that I'm utterly soaked. He glances at me once, then pulls away from the kerb and heads north without passing comment.

'Did they say anything about it?' I ask him. The route we're taking runs past the Tynons' house. It could be that the abductor came this way as well.

'Only that someone out jogging spotted it and called the cops. I don't know if they moved it or not before they called it in.'

'They were out running in *this*?' I gesture at the water sluicing down the windshield.

'Must take it fucking seriously.'

'You've got that right.'

He gestures at my dripping-wet suit and smiles. 'You're hardly in a position to criticize.'

I let the remark pass without comment, instead eyeballing the grey-smeared houses and storefronts as they pass by. Lightning snaps like a flashbulb in the sky, but more distant now, over to the right. The storm seems to be moving away and the rain is easing off.

We hang a left and pull up next to a low earthen bank

topped with an arrow-straight stand of trees. Two police cruisers and a forensics van are parked just ahead, and a uniformed cop in a rain slicker stands on the sidewalk, presumably there to shepherd the curious away.

'What's the situation?' I ask, flashing my badge at him.

'Been on the scene for forty-five minutes or so,' he says, and wipes water from the end of his nose. 'Crime scene unit confirmed it was the Tynon girl's wallet ten minutes ago. They should be on their way over by now.'

'Have you started canvassing for witnesses?'

He nods. 'Sergeant Griffin's been in contact with Detective Hall. I think they've got that in hand, sir. But I'm just here to keep people out of this part of the park. They haven't told me everything.'

'Sure. Thanks, Officer.' I'm about to walk off, into the park, but turn back and look at him. 'Have they marked out a route it's OK to follow?'

'Yes, sir.' He points to a gap between two of the trees. 'They've left a taped trail on the path that enters the park just over there. One of the first things they did.'

I breathe an inward sigh of relief. If they've kept as much of the area as possible around the wallet clear, hopefully we'll have some shoe impressions we can use. The last few specks of rain hit my face as Agostini and I cut through the grassy bank on the marked gravel path, then the wind blows dry and fresh.

The park isn't huge. An uneven swathe of green a few hundred yards across, rising and falling. Trees and stands of bushes dot its surface, breaking up its shape, blurring its edges. The far side looks artificially flattened, used

47

for ball games maybe. The right is bordered by a small stream that winds away to the south-east. A line of yellow tape runs down the path we're on to a beech a few yards from a couple of forensic technicians in coveralls and a uniformed cop. As we get closer, one of the techs steps over the tape, holding a plastic evidence bag. His counterpart stays in place and seems to be marking out possible impressions for later examination.

'Special Agent Alex Rourke,' I say when we reach them. 'What have you got so far?'

The first tech holds up the bag. Holly Tynon's wallet, battered pink nylon bearing an equally battered depiction of Piglet from Winnie-the-Pooh. Cheaply made, and starting to show threads. Seen a lot of use, I guess.

'Jack's starting to examine the ground for impressions. I'm going to run this back to the lab and we'll get it fully checked over,' the tech adds.

'Any prints or fibre?'

'Not that we could find out here. We'll know more later.'

I nod. 'Have you confirmed that it is actually Tynon's?'

'Yes. We opened it – in the bag, of course, to catch any trace evidence – and it's hers all right. Library card from school. Only coins inside, no notes.' He lowers the bag. 'It looks like it was thrown away, most likely from the path.'

'Impressions?'

He shakes his head. 'It doesn't look like we're going to get much on shoe prints. You see that clump of bushes over there?'

I follow his outstretched finger. 'Uh-huh.'

'It could be whoever did it was aiming for those, but it fell short or hit the tree on the way. Which means they probably did it after dark; they'd have seen where it landed otherwise.'

'Is there any way of telling for sure how long it's been there?'

He shakes his head. 'Not possible, especially with the storm.'

I think for a moment, weighing up the possibilities. 'OK, thanks,' I say to the tech and let him continue. I turn to the cop. 'Is the entire park sealed off?'

'I think so, sir,' he says. 'We've got guys on most of the entrances.'

'Check to make sure.' To Agostini, I add, 'Jeff, get hold of Detective Hall. Tell him to be extra careful about local house-to-house and canvassing. Make sure his officers note anything at all that seems weird or suspicious.'

'Anything weird. Gotcha.'

'Anything at all.'

Agostini nods vigorously. 'I'll tell him.'

'Do it. This guy could be a local.'

Chapter Five

'Long time no see, Agent Rourke,' are the first words Cody Williams says to me once the door behind me has closed and we're all alone in the visiting room. His voice is throaty and a little raw. Still pretty strong, although his tone remains low for the moment. He sounds pleased to see me. Probably knows this is his last time in the limelight and aims to enjoy it as much as possible.

'That's right.' I stay standing a couple of yards in from the door, don't move to sit opposite him. No sense letting him get comfortable.

'You still chasing the bad guys?' He examines his fingernails.

'More or less, yeah.'

'And now you've come back to see little old me.' He glances back up, looks annoyed that I haven't moved at all, and adds, 'Now you sit down here with me right now or I'm going back to my cell.'

I stay where I am. 'First I want to know if you're actually willing to tell me anything or not. If you just want to play a few conversational games, relive old times and generally dick me around for a few hours, then I'm leaving. It's not worth my time or effort. If you're willing to give up information, then I'm willing to stay. But only if you're willing.'

'You'd quit? What would you say to all them crying families then? What would you tell them?' He sneers, then breaks off into a fit of wet coughing. The disease or the treatment, I don't know. Makes repeated hacking noises, then spits out a great wad of yellow phlegm on to the floor next to him with every sign of satisfaction. 'I read that letter they sent to the newspapers. They're still all so fucking wet-eyed over a couple of little whores. "Waa! Waa! Where's our little baby? Waa! Waa."' He sniggers at his own joke. 'With them like that, and it being on the news, what would your bosses say to you, you walked out of here with dick to show for it?'

'That doesn't bother me.'

'You don't like me, do you, Agent Rourke? You never did. Even that first time we spoke, I could tell you'd have been happy to kill me right there.'

'What's to like, Cody? In all the time I've spoken with you, all through the trial, all the TV spots and column inches I've read about you, I've never heard of one single decent thing you've ever done or one redeeming quality you've ever possessed. Now are you going to play ball, or do I get to go home?'

He nods, slow and jerky like a marionette. 'Yeah, I think you and I might come to an understanding. Sit down.'

I hesitate for a moment, then get a cup of lukewarm coffee from one of the vending machines in the corner before heading for the seat opposite Williams. Up close, I can smell the rancid sweat cloying beneath his prison uniform, catch the faint whiff of body chemistry gone badly wrong. His eyes are rheumy, but sharp, although his movements aren't as fast. A couple of small sores next to his bitten lips. Yellow teeth.

'OK. Where do you want to start?' I ask him.

'I'll tell you about the girls.'

'The four that haven't been found yet?'

He smiles and shakes his head. 'All of them.'

'I don't need to hear about them all,' I say, trying to work out what he's up to. 'I told you I didn't want you to waste my time, Cody.'

'Have you sneaked a microphone or some shit in here, Agent Rourke?'

'No. What would be the point?'

'No?'

'No.'

'I guess that's a shame, some ways.' He shuffles in his seat. 'You see, I never told anyone my story, how I did what I did, or why. I wanna do that before I die, y'know?'

'If you want me to get a tape recorder in here for you, it's no problem.'

'No. I don't want to do that whole "memoirs" shit. I'd like this to be just the two of us, what with all the history between us. What we've both done.' Williams smiles again, breathes in noisily. 'That way, you can listen to it all, and then you can decide what you want anyone else to know. Like an editor, right?'

'Or a priest.'

'Yeah, exactly,' he says, and I finally think I under-stand why he's doing this. He wants to get back at me, the only way available to him.

If he tells me everything he can remember about the killings, every time I have to speak to one of the girls' relatives, telling them where we're going to find the bodies, I'm going to have to keep the rest of what he says buried. Every sordid detail will be kept forever fresh for me, and everything I don't reveal means another half-truth, another lie. I don't know if Williams is aware of the protesters outside the gates, but whenever I hear someone calling for his release, the full knowledge of his crimes will surface in my mind, knowledge no one else possesses. Not only that, but some could see him as cooperating with the authorities and he could win extra perks as a result.

Son of a bitch.

But I've been down this road before. Williams apparently doesn't know that I'm no longer an FBI agent and that once our interviews are over, I'll have nothing more to do with him or his case. All I have to do is find out where the last four of his victims are buried, then I walk away.

'OK, let's get this over with,' I tell him. 'How about we start with Katelyn Sellars. She was the earliest victim we haven't found.'

'I'd rather start with the Abblit girl. She was the first of all.' He smirks, coughs again. Another gob of rancid mucus hits the floor. 'Funny, I only know the names because I heard them on the news. And in interviews with you and the cops, of course. Names don't matter. Who they were doesn't matter. Only thing that mattered was what they could be, y'know?'

'No, I don't.' I sigh, cross my arms. 'I guess we're talking about your fantasies here, right?'

He laughs, phlegmy and wet, making his shoulders shake and setting his lank hair dancing. 'Yeah, I guess we are. You wanna hear about them? Do you? I could tell you all about them. You got kids yourself?'

'No, I don't, and forget about trying to get a reaction out of me. I've talked to more freaks like you than I care to count. Assuming any of the other cons here would even give a child-killer like you the time of day, you must've heard plenty yourself. Do they shock you any more? Or are you just bored by the stories and the people who tell them?' I lean forward, rest my elbows on the table, look Williams in the eyes. 'So you're a sick fuck. You know it, I know it. Big fucking deal. Let's get to the point here, Cody.'

'But that was the point for me, Agent Rourke,' he says, smiling. He leans in closer and I can see a strand of spit in the corner of his mouth that stretches white with every word, somehow always holding itself together. 'Don't you want to hear how I fucked her? How I made that little bitch scream for me?'

'No, I don't.' I stand and walk towards the door, not even giving him the satisfaction of a black look. My hand is touching the door when Williams starts laughing again behind me.

'I'm sorry, Agent Rourke. I'm just joking with you. Couldn't help it. Come back and we can talk properly.'

I glance round to see him smiling at me. 'Properly?'

'Sure. Come on. Don't you feel you owe it to me?'

'OK, talk. But any more screwing around and I'm gone for good.'

'Whatever you say.'

I return to the table and sit warily in the chair. 'Why are you doing this, Cody? What are you getting out of it?'

'What do you mean?'

'Is it so you can get one last thrill, going over your old crimes, knowing you won't be touched for admitting them? Explain it to me. I can't figure out if this is just a personal power trip, or you're hoping for a release before you die, or what.'

Williams leans back in his seat. 'Why ain't important, Agent Rourke. Don't worry about it. Important thing is that I can tell you what you need to know. You and those whining fucks who wrote the letter. And I'm going to start with the Abblit girl.'

'If that's what you want,' I say, folding my arms. 'Shoot.'

'I remember that day real clear.' Williams drops his eyes, withdraws into an inner world. From the ease with which he makes the transition, and the way he licks his lips at the images in his head, I guess he's done this a lot over the past few years. And enjoyed it every time. 'It was hot, sun shone all day. Hardly a cloud. I had to take a delivery to some guy out past Pittsfield in the morning. I was already thinking about it, even then. You know how you wake up some mornings and you'd just love to get laid?'

I stay silent, so he continues. An old classic of interrogators – give them an uncomfortable gap and they'll usually fill it for you. 'So I'm checking out the chicks on the way to this guy's house, and it's summer so they're letting it all show, and while I'm there we talk about girls and stuff. What we like, what we don't like. I head for home and I figure, yeah, today's the day I get a girl.'

Williams looks back up, smiling faintly, old hunger burning in his eyes. I try not to listen too hard to what I know is coming next.

'I was almost home when I saw her,' he says. 'The loveliest thing you ever set eyes on. Her hair was so dark, looked black in the evening. I just fell in love with her face, though. So pretty.' The smile broadens and his fingers flex involuntarily, perhaps reliving the feel of Kerry Abblit's face held in his hands. 'I had to have her, y'know? I pulled up the van a little way ahead, next to this factory building they'd converted into offices. No one had bought them yet, though, so I knew there wouldn't be anyone inside to see. I just stood on the sidewalk with a piece of paper in my hands, looking like every other delivery guy checking addresses, until she walked past. Got my hand over her mouth and hauled her back through the van's side door. I had to knock her on the side of the head a couple of times to show her I wasn't going to fuck around. That didn't spoil things too much. Got her tied up tight, then hit the road again.'

His eyes refocus on me for a moment before drifting back to his memories. 'I couldn't take her home, I knew that, see. Too risky. So I drove out of town, looking for someplace quiet, all the while with her waiting in the back, like she was calling to me.' He laughs damply, once, and shakes his head. 'Fuck, man. You know what it's like when you just want some privacy – seems like everyone follows you around and you can't get away. Must've taken me an hour to find some place to park the van, away from people who might've seen or heard. Man, I had a fucking hard-on like you wouldn't believe by then.

'Oh, but you didn't want to hear about that, right?' Williams says, glancing at me.

I lock eyes with him coldly, flatly. Keep my arms folded. Say nothing.

Disappointment washes across his face. His mouth takes on a slightly petulant, unfairly put-upon pout. 'Anyway, I kept her for a day or two, but eventually she just broke, so I had to get rid of her. So I wrapped her up in cloth and buried her near the beach a couple of nights later. Shame the bitch didn't last longer.'

I let the room fall silent, making sure Williams has finished. I uncross my arms and say, 'What kind of cloth did you wrap her in?'

He laughs. 'Why the fuck would I remember that?'

'Come on, Cody. Your memory seems pretty clear

to me. You must've replayed the whole thing plenty of times in your mind over the years. So tell me, what kind of cloth did you wrap her in?'

'That's all you're going to ask? You don't want to know why I took her, what I was thinking when I did?' He sighs and slouches back in his seat, apparently baffled.

'I'm not asking that because there's no point,' I tell him. 'There's no rational thought process there. So one day you're feeling horny and decide to do something about it; rational thought would have said to get a hooker, or go try your luck with the women in the nearest bar. But you didn't. Rational thought would have told you Kerry Abblit was a thirteen-year-old girl and that what you were about to do was so far off the scale that you barely class as a human being any more. But you did it anyway. I don't understand that and I never will, nor will anyone else. You're a fucking alien to me. No point trying to figure you out if it's impossible. So, yeah, all I want to know is what kind of cloth you wrapped her in.'

Williams flicks his hair out of his eyes. 'There ain't that much different between us, Agent Rourke.'

'Yeah, *right*.'

'It doesn't take much to turn you into me. And in any case, you and I have got other similarities.'

I say nothing.

He coughs a couple of times, then sniffs hard. Another rattling noise from somewhere inside his throat. He swallows. 'The cloth was a kind of beige.

An old sheet I was saving for rags in my garage. Anything else? You already found her, right. How much more could you want to know?'

'Nothing that comes to mind.'

'Then I guess we're done for today.' He splutters again. 'I'll tell you about one of the others tomorrow.'

Without saying another word, I leave him sitting alone in the empty visiting room. The door swishes shut behind me and once again I'm standing in the slightly synthetic air of Outer Control, away from his poisonous presence. I want a bath, a long one. I want to get drunk and forget about the guy. Agent Downes swings off her chair behind the security desk and says, 'How did it go?'

'OK, more or less.' She must have seen me come close to leaving early on in the interview, but she didn't mention it, so neither do I. 'Williams seems to be willing to give up as much detail as we want — at least for the time being.'

'Really? That was quick.'

'It's not as good as it sounds. He wants to talk about all the victims, not just the four we're interested in, so I guess I'll have to put up with another couple of days of him reliving past glories before we get anything immediately useful.' I run my hands through my hair. 'Did he explain to his lawyer at all why he suddenly agreed to do this? I know he wasn't playing ball with you; why change just because it's me he's talking to?'

She shrugs and rolls her shoulders, working some

life back into them as we make for the exit. 'No idea,' she says. 'Probably because you worked on the case originally, so he knows you're going to understand what he's talking about. You interviewed him before – maybe you impressed him.' She smiles at me.

I raise my eyebrows and say nothing as we turn in our visitors' badges and leave the sterile prison and its lukewarm, recycled air. I know for a fact that Cody isn't doing this because he's impressed by me.

Far from it. Cody hates me. With good reason.

Outside, iron-hard specks of rain fall sporadically from the sky, whipped by the wind into darts of icy water. The protesters are still standing on the far side of the gates, most of them now huddled in raincoats and ponchos in various garish colours, although the last of the news crews is loading up their van for the journey home. A middle-aged man in a raincoat half-heartedly shakes the 'LIBERTY BEFORE DEATH' sign at us as we pass. Hardly anyone else bothers to make the effort.

When we reach my apartment in Boston, Downes says, 'Are you going to be OK handling this on your own for the next few days?'

'Should be, yeah. Does Ashworth know I'll be coming and going like this?'

'They do. You're cleared with the prison for as long as you need.'

'OK. I'll be in touch once I've got anything or if something comes up.'

Wave briefly to Downes as she pulls away from

the kerb, then unlock the front door and step into my apartment. The place is on the small side and I haven't tidied in a while. Coffee table covered in papers, magazines and other clutter. Plain mantel over an old setting for a fire or heater of some sort, now long gone. TV wedged into one corner. An ageing sofa and a totally mismatched armchair. I drop the bulky FBI case file on the last of these and go make a cup of coffee before I start reading.

I skip over the paperwork for those victims whose remains have already been found and concentrate on Marie Austen, Brooke Morgan, Katelyn Sellars and Holly Tynon. It feels strange, looking back on reports I wrote all those years ago. Some of the details have faded from my memory, but I can still remember how I felt when writing each one. Tiny associations with every page, paragraph, scribbled notation. Fragmentary windows into history, jumbled and confused like a dream.

Early evening and I'm still working my way through the stack of papers and photographs when the phone rings.

'You're at home, aren't you, Alex?' Rob asks. 'Turn on the news.'

I fumble for the TV remote. 'What's on?'

'You are,' he says.

Chapter Six

Five weeks past the discovery of Holly Tynon's wallet in the park and the investigation is stalled. We've found nothing more, and despite Providence PD's best efforts we haven't turned up any useful leads. I've interviewed dozens of potential witnesses and long-shot suspects, both for Holly's abduction and the previous two cases. So far, we have a few scraps of information to go on, none of it useful. A guy who thinks he may have seen a white van, unknown make or model, in the area of Katelyn Sellars' disappearance, no other details and no one comes forward. Someone's neighbour acting funny around the times of the disappearances; turns out he's having an affair with a married woman, and we discount him. By now, everyone knows she's dead, and even her parents rarely ask the cops for any news. I've got used to living out of a motel and hoping for a break – a body, a witness, anything – frustrated inactivity and the sense of going in circles building with every day of little progress.

Then eleven-year-old Brooke Morgan goes missing from Auburn on the outskirts of Worcester.

'What exactly do we know?' I ask Agostini, who's managed to beat me to the scene.

We're standing in a leafy, pleasant street lined on one

side by a sprawling privet hedge bordering a churchyard and on the other by a community hall. Red brick houses a hundred yards or so further along. Road packed with police vehicles and, back behind a taped-off boundary area, a couple of spectators.

'One of the neighbours said he was driving home from the store and saw a girl who could have been Brooke talking to a man next to a white or cream-coloured van of some sort.'

'He couldn't get a make?'

'Apparently not. The cops spoke to him for a while, they said.'

'Not even a vague idea?'

Agostini shakes his head. 'Just the colour.'

'Shit.'

'Maybe it's for the best. I mean, how often do these guys say, "I saw this and I saw that and it was a car like this", and it turns out to be nothing but bullshit that their eyes or their brains have got all screwed up inside? I'd rather look for, like, a white van than a white Ford van and find out it wasn't one of them after all but another make, you know?'

'We should have a word with him ourselves too, just to be sure.'

'He's over there. Told him not to go anywhere yet.'

I nod. 'Good.'

'Anyway, he didn't see what happened to her – apparently he was back at the intersection,' Agostini jerks a finger behind us, past the church, 'and traffic cut off his view. When it cleared, she was gone and the van was pulling away. He hadn't seen any sign there was a struggle or that she'd got in the van, so he didn't think much about it.'

'When did he report this?'

'As soon as word got out she was missing. The cops say he's feeling real guilty about not trying to get a better look, or trying to stop the guy.'

I find I don't care much about the witness's feelings, one way or another. 'Too late for feeling guilty.'

'Yeah. She's been gone about five hours now.'

'What did he see of the kidnapper?'

'Nothing much, not from that distance. He couldn't even tell us the guy's build or clothing.'

'Was he sure it was a man?'

Agostini scratches his neck. 'That's what he says, although I doubt he's as certain of that as he claims. I don't think he saw dick apart from the van.'

'How about the girl? Was he sure it was her?'

'What do you think?' He raises his eyebrows. 'About as certain as he was about the man. Some goddamn witness.'

'Yeah.'

'But the cops checked as soon as they hit the scene, asking after other kids in the houses down here. None of them talked to anyone in a van this afternoon, so I think we can assume that was our girl.'

'OK. What are our chances of getting any kind of physical evidence?'

'They've got forensics on the way. There's nothing immediately obvious here, but we could get lucky.' He gestures at the roadside. 'Maybe shoe impressions on the verge . . .'

'Something small he might have dropped . . .'

'Yeah, anything like that. What do you reckon on the van? Whole nine yards?'

I think for a moment, watching a uniformed cop walk up the drive to the Morgan family home. In a way, I hate these moments in an investigation. The early hours, where you have the best chance of breaking the case, and also the best chance of making one wrong move that screws the whole thing up, and then you have weeks of getting nowhere and another dead girl on your conscience.

'It's about the only lead we've got, so yeah. Get as much detail on it as we can and start trawling. We'll have to get the local and state police to give us anything they have on traffic stops, minor reports, anything involving light-coloured vans of any kind from today in this area. The same with the cops in Fall River, Springfield and Providence. Any vehicle we can tie to the areas of the disappearances at the right times.'

Agostini glances at me. 'They didn't get anything on traffic reports before. How much are we likely to get this time?'

'We didn't know the vehicle before. It might jog a few memories – a cop remembers a white van with a loose fender that he thought about stopping but didn't, that sort of thing. Whatever we can turn up.'

'Sure. Check for owners?'

I nod. 'All light-coloured vans registered to anyone

living within two miles of any of the abductions. Same with commercial vehicles, but we might have to handle them differently than domestic owners.'

'That's going to be a long list, Alex.'

'No shit.'

'We'll have to start eliminating people from it as soon as we get further information,' Agostini says.

'Yeah, and there's no guarantee the guy we're looking for is local to any of these crimes. It just seems likely that he would've been for at least one of them.' I think of Brooke Morgan again, and the knowledge that every decision I take could mean the difference between life and death for her. If she's still alive, in that lucky twenty-five per cent. 'Let's get what we can from this scene. This is as fresh as we're going to see, so let's make the most of it. But now I guess I'd better go and speak with the family. Do the usual questions.'

'Right. I'll go talk with that witness, see if he's remembered anything more. Don't hold your breath though.'

Joe and Andrea Morgan are dead-eyed and still in a state of shock over their daughter's abduction, made worse by the knowledge that she really has been snatched by someone and isn't just lost. I pass a couple of uncomfortable minutes in their house in monosyllabic conversation with them; we do nothing to encourage each other and I leave again, hoping privately for some instant breakthrough that will allow me to return Brooke alive, just to alleviate their despair.

We don't get one.

Examination of the abduction scene yields mixed

results. On one hand, they corroborate the witness's story; we find clear shoe impressions from a child and a man with a pattern that seems to match the idea that Brooke was standing close to her abductor, talking, at a guess, when she was snatched. The man's prints look like cheap boots or heavy shoes with no markings on the soles. The cops try to get a closer match to a particular brand. There are no clear tyre impressions by the roadside, so nothing on the van.

We also have a couple of pieces of trash that may or may not have come from the abductor's vehicle. A Mars wrapper – no prints, no saliva – and, much more interesting, a piece of plastic shrink-wrap backed with paper that looks like the packaging for a syringe. No sign of the needle itself. There's a partial print on the plastic, which we run eagerly through the AFIS system only to draw a blank. Whoever owned this, they don't have a record. As it could just as easily belong to a diabetic or a junkie as to the abductor, I also know we can't rely solely on the print. We need more, and we're not getting it.

Our list of van owners gives us a huge number of 'possibles', many of whom are eliminated by the cops over the next couple of weeks as they are contacted and their alibis checked. I decide to have Agostini and I handle the interviews with many of the remainder personally, just in case anything workable comes up. Most of them are self-employed manual workers, delivery drivers or unemployed, with either no idea what they were doing at the times we're interested in, or no one to corroborate their whereabouts. After a while, their faces, voices, homes begin to blur and become indistinct.

A brick two-storey with a bare front yard.

'I was off work with flu that day,' a stocky guy with a beard and big glasses says, voice a nasal whine. 'Must've been like that for three or four days, I think.'

A small apartment near a river.

'You should ask my neighbours. I see them pretty often. They might remember seeing me.'

A blocky family home with wooden siding in need of repair.

'I was driving roofing supplies out someplace near Beckett.' A bald man with a prominent nose. Shrewish wife waiting in the kitchen for us to finish. 'I've got the work schedule; the customer might be able to say when I was there, if that's any help. I heard about what happened. You any closer to catching the guy?'

Dreary apartment building that smells like old coffee.

'So am I a suspect or something? Shouldn't my lawyer be here?' Stick-thin guy well into his fifties. He shrugs. 'It doesn't matter, I guess. It's not like I've done anything. Come on in.'

A scruffy little office above a thrift store.

'No, I was at my sister's place in New Hampshire. But I've seen this case on the news, and I've got a theory you might be interested in . . .'

Another anonymous small house in Fall River.

'Yeah?' says Cody Williams. 'What do you want?'

*

His home is a narrow two-storey house with a square patch of slightly ragged greenery that passes for a front yard. A few shrubs, some flowers, starting to grow rampant. An unmarked white van sits on the driveway. When Williams – a wiry guy with long curly hair tied back in a ponytail, fit physique beneath a grey T-shirt, but pale to look at – opens the door, a wash of warm stale air, moist and acrid, washes past him. Slick skin reeking of old sweat. More ancient scents embedded in the fabric of the house itself. My nostrils recoil, but I try not to show it.

'Mr Williams, I'm Special Agent Alex Rourke, and this is Agent Jeff Agostini.' We hold up our badges. 'We need to ask you a few routine questions, if you have a few minutes.'

One side of Williams' mouth twitches into a smile. 'This is about that kiddie thing, right?' His choice of words jars. 'I've seen it on the news. Then someone from the cops called about the van, asked where I was.'

'That's right, Mr Williams. All we're doing is asking people a few standard questions, just to eliminate them from our lists.'

'You guys the only two they got working on that? I kinda figured there'd be more of you. I mean, where're we at now, four of them girls gone? Five?'

'There's a lot of cops working on this too, Mr Williams.'

'A lot, huh?'

'Yeah.'

'And all they've got for you two to do is ask "routine questions", Agent Rourke? With all them pretty young things still missing?' Another twitch of the mouth. A thin strand of spittle stretches between his lips.

'That's not all we've got.' I shake my head slightly but keep my eyes fixed on Williams. I can feel my heart moving up a gear. If this guy can't give us any answers, if he's still a potential suspect by the end of today, I make him for the abductions. 'This is just what we're doing today. Just talking to people.'

Williams shrugs. 'How long's this going to take?'

'A few minutes, nothing more. Can we come in?'

'We're best talking here, Agent Rourke. I've been doing some work on the house. Place is a mess and there's dust all over.' I can't tell if he's lying or not.

I look at Agostini, and he takes out a notebook. To Williams I say, 'How long have you owned your van, Mr Williams?'

'A couple of years.' He sniffs. 'I use it for work mostly.'

'What do you do for a living?'

'I deliver car parts for Drill Hall Collectors' Autos.' Defiant tone in his voice. Like we're kids playing Twenty Questions, and he wants me to use up all twenty without guessing what he's thinking of.

'Is that here in Fall River?'

He nods. 'Yeah.'

'Where do you deliver to?'

'All over. Wherever the customers live. Everywhere from New Haven to Manchester.'

'You do these deliveries every day?' I say.

'Not every day, no. Sometimes I have time off, or I work at the auto shop. But most days I have to take

70

something somewhere. Sometimes I help with installation as well.'

'Been doing it long?'

Williams shrugs. 'About a year.'

'Nice job?'

'It has its good points.' He smiles faintly, knowingly.

'Did you have deliveries to do on May twenty-first?'

He looks like he's thinking for a moment. 'What day was that?'

'A Tuesday.'

'Lessee . . . that was the same day as the first of them, wasn't it? No, I can't remember. Should do – the last guy asked as well. I'll have to check my work book.'

'You do that,' Agostini says.

Williams ducks back into the house, leaving the two of us alone for a moment. I glance at Agostini and raise my eyebrows, flick my eyes at the place Williams had been standing. He looks back and shrugs almost imperceptibly. Then our suspect returns.

'Yeah, I had a delivery that day, Agent Rourke. Lunchtime, I had to run some engine spares out to a customer out past Pittsfield on Route 7.'

'And you left there at what time?'

'Dunno. Got home early evening, at a guess.'

'Could we have this customer's name and address?' Agostini asks from behind me.

'Sure.' Williams hands over a scruffy notebook open to a page full of spidery writing. 'It's right there.'

'You live here alone, right?' I ask.

'Yeah.'

'Is there anyone who might be able to confirm when you arrived home?'

Williams shrugs. 'I doubt it. I hardly know my neighbours. No reason they'd remember.'

'OK. How about June twentieth?'

'I dunno. What does it say in there?' He gestures at the notebook.

Agostini flicks through until he finds the right page, squinting to read Williams' scrawl. 'Empty. There's no entry for it,' he says.

'Then I guess I was doing nothing. Maybe I was working at the auto shop. You'd have to ask my boss there.'

'OK, we will. July seventeenth?'

Williams looks at Agostini, who skims forward a few pages. 'Nothing again,' he says to me.

'There you go, Agent Rourke. Nothing again.'

'August twenty-third?'

'Some place called West Boylston,' Agostini says. 'Two in the afternoon.'

'I don't suppose you remember anything more about it, do you?' I ask Williams. 'Since it's so recent and everything.'

'Off the top of my head, Agent Rourke, I don't think I remember a thing about it.'

'Is that so?'

'I do a lot of these jobs, you know. Must've been just the same as all the others. I don't think about them much.'

I glance at Agostini, who flashes a look back and then

hands the notebook to Williams. The suspect nods but doesn't say anything.

'Thank you, Mr Williams,' I tell him. 'We'll be in touch if we need anything more.'

'Before we go, I don't suppose I could ask a favour?' Agostini says, matter-of-factly. 'I couldn't use your bathroom, could I?'

Williams smiles again, lines of spittle stretching out once more at the corners of his mouth, white against his teeth. 'I'm sorry, Agent Agostini. Afraid my bathroom's full of junk at the moment, where I've been working on the house. Until I put everything back it can't be used.'

'No? Well, thanks anyway.' We turn to leave.

'You be sure to tell me if you find anything out about them girls,' Williams calls after us. I can hear a smirking tone, a hint of enjoyment he can't seem to keep from his voice. 'It's such a shame to see something bad happening to such pretty kids.'

As we walk down the driveway and the door to the house closes behind us, I say to Agostini, 'What did you see in that notebook?'

'Just what he said – a list of jobs he's had to do.'

'Nothing more?'

'Not that I saw.'

'Did you get a look at any of the ones on the days around the abductions?'

Agostini grins. 'Yeah, but I need a map. I don't know where they are. You think it could have been him?'

I look back at the house before climbing into the car. No sign of movement from inside, but I can imagine

73

Williams standing in the musty interior, watching us. Staring through one of the windows, smiling crookedly. 'Yeah, I do. I sure do.'

The disappearance of Abbie Galina two days later only confirms my suspicions.

Chapter Seven

'The FBI began last-ditch efforts to persuade Fall River Killer Cody Williams to reveal the locations of four of his victims today, calling in the former federal agent who handled the original case in a bid to make him talk. Although he was never formally charged, Williams is alleged to have killed seven girls in Massachusetts and Rhode Island. Only three have ever been found.'

Cut to footage taken by one of the news crews at the prison this morning. Camerawork at distance, showing me and Downes walking into the jail. Someone at the station must have recognized my face, done their research.

'Former FBI Agent Alex Rourke, seen here entering MCI-Ashworth prison earlier today, led the investigation into the crimes, interviewing Williams several times and testifying at his trial.' Cut back to studio. Briefly bring up a pair of still photos. 'Mr Rourke retired from the FBI not long after Williams' conviction for murdering serial rapist Clinton Travers and the attempted abduction of thirteen-year-old Nicole Ballard, and now works as a private detective in Boston. Mr Rourke was brought in by the FBI's local field office thanks to pressure from relatives of the missing victims who want the chance to give their loved ones a proper burial.'

Cut away again, this time to a man just into his fifties. Dark sweater, contrasting iron-grey hair. Square glasses. He's standing in front of what must be his yard, a neatly kept square of green lined with shrubs. Joe Morgan, Brooke's father. I still recognize him.

'We just want to give our daughter the peace she deserves,' he's saying. 'I can't ever forgive Cody Williams for what he did, but it'd at least mean he was showing some repentance for it before he died. By keeping silent for so long, all he's done is kept our grief fresh. It's time we all got to move on.'

Back to the studio. A brief 'No comment so far' from the FBI and the coverage moves on to another story.

'They didn't waste any time, did they?' I say to Rob, as I lean back in my seat.

'Do you think the exposure is going to give you any problems?'

'I doubt it. I'd guess a couple of calls from journalists – I'm in the phone book, easy enough to find. Maybe a few through to the office as well. But that should be it. And as I'm not saying anything except through the Bureau, and only when I've got something from Williams, they shouldn't be too much hassle.'

'If you say so. I'll field anything that comes into the office. Are you going to be in at all over the next couple of days?'

I think for a moment, then say, 'Yeah, almost certainly. It depends how talkative Williams is tomorrow and what he says. If it's anything like today, he won't use up too much of my time.' And I'm just fine with that, I add to myself. The less the better.

'In that case, I'll see you soon. Take care.'

Hang up and leave the TV on. Make a cup of coffee, skim through the channels, the remaining papers and photos in the Williams file abandoned for the time being. I've made something bearing a passing resemblance to dinner when the phone rings again. I pick up, half-expecting some journalist who's just caught the news.

'You're a fucking asshole who's going to burn in hell.'

I think about hanging up for a moment, then say, 'What?'

'You heard me,' the unidentified woman says. 'Harassing an innocent man while he's dying. Keeping him locked away without any genuine evidence. You're nothing but scum.'

I sigh. 'Lady, you have no idea what you're talking about. Cody Williams is the most unpleasant human being I have ever met, and the thought of him rotting in hell for what he's done keeps me warm and happy at night. Goodbye.'

I hit 'end' and drop the phone in its cradle.

The same thing happens twice more before I unplug the phone after reaching the inevitable conclusion that people are idiots.

'Leave the poor man alone! Just like the government — can't even let a man die in peace!' *Click.*

'You framed him, you and the FBI.'

'What?'

'He didn't kill Clinton Travers. Why would he? And he was trying to protect that poor little girl, probably from someone like you! So you fixed things to send him to jail. But God knows what you did, Mr Rourke, and you'll get what you deserve.' *Click.*

Once I've stopped these interruptions, I continue to channel-surf and attempt a fresh look at the rest of the information on Williams and his victims, but I can't concentrate and end up heading for bed with a chunk of it still unread.

Next day I drive back out to MCI-Ashworth, once more under grey skies. The crowd outside the prison gates is larger than before; the newcomers probably saw the protest on TV and showed up to get their faces on the news. In addition, a second, smaller gathering has clustered a little closer to the main highway. This group of a dozen or so have a couple of placards with them, one of which reads 'CHILD KILLER ROT IN JAIL' in bright red letters. Williams' supporters further along shout and jeer from the roadside, some moving closer to the 'Vette to vent their spleen in full while I wait for the gate to open. I can't make out any of their words; I've got the Chicago Kingsnakes cranked up on the stereo for just this occasion. None of them look happy, though. A couple of TV crews film this one-way

78

exchange of views. I let it all slide past me as I enter the comparative tranquillity of the prison complex.

This is how it goes for the next two days. The news cameras don't bother turning up again, but the protesters keep up their vigil, although the numbers begin to fall away. Each day I arrive at the jail we go through the same pointless face-off with the same lack of results.

Inside, Williams keeps talking. The two of us alone in the empty, hollow visiting room, he recounts the abduction and murder of Abbie Galina and Joanne Tilley. Broken here and there by wet, hacking coughing and signs of his obviously weakening condition, he runs through both crimes. Very little difference to what happened to Kerry Abblit. I'd rather he talked about something helpful, but he'll only tell me what happened to the victims who have never been found after reliving what happened to the ones we know about. I let his eager ramblings about the girls run their course with minimal interruption and bury my disgust.

Abbie Galina played Titania in her last school production of A Midsummer Night's Dream. *She had a rapidly growing collection of music and wanted to be a DJ when she grew up. She was throttled and buried in straggly woodland.*

In the evenings I leave the phone off the hook. Now and then my dreams are plagued by flashes of dead children.

Joanne Tilley was on the under-thirteens swimming team and also enjoyed gymnastics. She'd spend her Saturdays shopping at the local mall with her friends. She used to enjoy skateboarding, but a badly broken arm seriously dented her confidence. Cody broke it again, before strangling her with electrical cable.

Then, on the fourth day, I find a letter waiting for me when I leave for the prison. Handwritten address, Providence postmark.

Dear Agent Rourke,

The FBI told us they were hoping to persuade Cody Williams to tell them where we might find Holly's remains before he dies, but they never said they would be asking you to speak to that man again. After the work you did to catch him and the evidence you gave at his trial, we wouldn't have asked you anything more. We had thought we'd managed to put the whole thing behind us, knowing she'd never be coming back to us and that we had to move on. Strange how we still cling to any hope of news after all this time. Now we are both praying that you can learn what we need from him.

We've seen those people protesting on the news. We can't believe it or understand it. Please don't let them get to you, Agent Rourke. You were always good to us while you were looking for Holly and the man who killed her. Please keep trying, for us.

Good luck and God bless,

John and Martha Tynon

I read the letter through, then toss it on the coffee table. Head for the jail under the cold sunshine of fall in Massachusetts. Swallow it down. Try not to get caught up in it.

Williams greets me with a long, ragged clearing of his throat. This time, he doesn't manage to hawk up any phlegm but only makes dry gasping noises, mouth opening and closing like a fish, before getting himself under control. Once he's finished, he says, 'So who do you want to talk about today, Agent Rourke?'

I grab a coffee from the machine and sit down opposite him. 'Well, we're out of people we already know about. So how about we start with Katelyn Sellars? She was the first of your victims we still haven't found.'

'Well, it ain't necessarily so that we're out of people we know about. There's at least one other we both know.' He smiles faintly, wolfish. 'But sure, let's talk about that Sellars girl.'

'You picked her up on her way to school, right?'

Williams smirks. 'Yeah. I had to leave early that day, driving all the way to Albany. You got a photo of her? For old times' sake.'

'No.'

'Too bad. She looked real fine that morning. Good enough to eat. Black school trousers. Them little white socks. Just lovely.'

I sigh, try to hurry him up, get to the point. 'You snatched her in the usual way? The lost delivery driver routine. Bundle her into the van.'

'Yeah. Her mind must've been elsewhere 'cos she hardly knew it was happening. Hadn't even started trying to scream by the time I had her in the van and the door shut again.' He runs the tip of his tongue over his bottom lip. 'I took her away, had to stash her before we got to Albany.'

'Where did you stash her?'

'That doesn't matter, Agent Rourke. She wasn't there long. Some place off the highway.'

'You moved her again afterwards?'

Williams picks at one of his ragged fingernails. 'Sure. Ain't no good doing all this if you've got no privacy. There's a house near Lake Stevenson. People I used to know sometimes used it for fishing or getting drunk. Abandoned for ages, and I guess none of them had been back there in years. So the place was ideal. I took her there. Kept her there for a while, a couple of days.'

'Could you mark it on a map if I gave you one?'

Williams shrugs, thinks for a moment, looking down at his hands. 'Maybe. Might take a while for me to figure out what's what. Leave a map with me and maybe I can find it.'

'After you'd kept her there for a few days, then what?'

'She was in a bad way by then and I had a load of work on, y'know, I had a lot of deliveries and things to do. She was just a nuisance, pretty fucked up by that time. So I strangled her, right there on the floor.' There's no emotion in his voice at all. He might as well be reading a weather report. He really doesn't care, doesn't feel a thing. The only hint of anything deeper comes after a brief pause, when he adds, 'It was strange, seeing her lying there. She'd looked so perfect, walking down the street. Didn't seem like the same girl.'

Katelyn Sellars was in the Girl Scouts. She had a crush on a guy in the grade above her called Jack. She had dreams of becoming a fashion designer and moving to Europe.

'You dumped her body?'

'Yeah.'

I frown. 'Where?'

'Took her out and buried her not far from the shore, maybe a mile from that first girl.'

'You don't remember more exactly than that?'

Williams shrugs. 'Hey, she was a piece of meat.'

'If this shit is all you've got to tell me, Cody, then as far as I'm concerned we're finished here.'

'Easy, Agent Rourke. I'm thinking about it. You've just got to give me time to remember back to these things. Bring that map tomorrow, that should help. It ain't easy, especially not now.' He coughs, something wet rasping at the back of his throat. I'm certain he's just doing it for effect. 'But all this talking about old times is making it clearer, and that's helping some.'

I remain unconvinced that he's telling the truth. 'Really?'

'Yeah. We should talk more. How about we talk about Clinton Travers while I'm trying to remember what I did with them girls? You could tell me all about him, and maybe while I'm listening and thinking back, something'll shake loose.'

The room darkens, the air becoming thick and cloying, as Cody's intentions become clearer. We have our shared past and the ties that bind us, and now he's pulling them anew. I wonder how far he'll go with this.

'There's nothing to talk about,' I say. 'We can stick to the girls and nothing else. I'll have the map with me tomorrow. Between then and now, you think hard. If I don't get some clear answers from you soon, these conversations will be over for good.'

I stand and make for the door. Behind me, I hear him give a satisfied little sigh. 'Oh, come on, Agent Rourke,' he whispers just loud enough to hear. 'Let's talk about what happened to Travers.'

I don't look back.

Chapter Eight

It's March, four months before Holly Tynon failed to come home. Hartford, Connecticut, and a rapist committing attacks with alarming frequency and regularity. The cops decided they wanted help, and turned to the Bureau. Technically, it should have been the Behavioral Analysis Unit's baby. But while they did a large chunk of the initial analysis work, they were too busy with other cases to provide operational support in the field with the investigation and suspect interviews, so it was passed to me.

'I was jogging. Before breakfast. Just like I always do,' the woman is saying. Thin-lipped, fighting to concentrate and stay focused. Red eyes and the creased brow above them showing just how much emotional strain she's under. Her hands, clasped around the coffee cup, play and fiddle with each other incessantly.

Naomi Carson, the detective with Hartford PD heading the investigation, gives her a warm, understanding smile and says, 'You were near the river?'

'I like to run there,' the woman, whose name is Mary, says. She's the rapist's ninth, most recent victim. The only one he's snatched in daylight so far. 'I always go jogging there. Unless it's raining. Or I've got to hurry to get to work.'

'So you jogged from your home . . .'

'I jogged from home and I'd almost got as far as the river. I was by that . . . that row of stores on Henry Street. That one that sells all the chocolates and things. And then I felt a . . . his hand . . . I . . .'

'It's OK, Mary,' Naomi says softly. 'He grabbed you?'

She sniffs and nods. 'From behind me. I didn't hear him. He had his hand over my mouth . . . and he dragged me back . . . He had a knife. He held it by my neck. There's an alleyway behind the stores. He dragged me back there . . .'

'And that's where he attacked you.'

Mary gulps. 'He put something over my eyes. Like . . . like a bag or a blindfold. I thought he was going to kill me. I thought I was going to die. He kept saying I was a . . . a . . . bitch. All while he was . . . And then, then he left. When he finished.'

Naomi nods. 'What happened when he left?'

'He took the thing he had over my eyes and said he'd kill me if I looked. He . . . said he knew where I lived. Then he ran back down the alley behind me. I think he had a car somewhere. Maybe. I . . . I heard one start up not long after.'

'Did you get a look at the man?' I ask, calm and gentle. 'Do you remember anything about his appearance?'

'I . . . I did, not very much – he was running away – but I did.' Mary gulps again. 'He had a black ski mask. Like a bank robber. And he had a dark blue jacket, and dark jeans, I think. And I saw his shoes. They were like work boots or something. The ones with the thick soles. I saw them as he was running.'

'Was he wearing gloves at all?'

She nods. 'Yes, sorry, yes. He had gloves.'

'How tall was he?'

'Tall. Taller than me . . . six foot, maybe? And he was big. He was a big man.'

Naomi smiles. 'That's really good, Mary. That's a big help to us. Do you remember anything else about him?'

'I . . . I don't know.' Mary thinks for a moment. 'Yes, I saw his hair. Sticking out underneath his ski mask. It was dark, black or brown. Yes, dark. But . . . no, that's it. I can't think of anything more.'

'That's OK, Mary,' I tell her. 'You've given us a lot to go on. Thank you.'

She looks at me. 'Will . . . will you catch him?'

I smile. 'You've got the whole of Hartford PD *and* the FBI looking for this guy. We're going to catch him, Mary. He won't be able to hurt anyone else.'

Months later, I'll hear an echo of these words in the promise I make to Martha Tynon. There's so much I've failed at.

Nine women raped, at a rate averaging one attack per week. Same MO each time. A hand clamps over the mouth, and they're forced at knifepoint to a nearby sheltered spot. The rapist blindfolds them, possibly using the sort used by people to help them sleep, before he makes any move around from behind them. He says hardly anything, except to call his victims 'bitch' or 'whore'. The attacks are short and brutal. He rapes them, often beating or slapping them about the face and head, then leaves with a final warning that he knows who they are and where they live. Hartford is normally a fairly quiet city, and the whole place is on edge. The crimes have been front-page news since well before local law enforcement requested our help. The media coverage doesn't seem to have bothered the attacker. Which means for every week this investigation takes, another woman is likely to be raped.

It's after duty hours, and I'm sitting with Naomi Carson in a bar down the road from police headquarters. All-red interior, comfortable seats, more mirrors on the walls than regular establishments. I don't know its official name, but Naomi tells me everyone calls it 'the Bordello'.

'Do they serve you at the table, or do you have to ask for a private room?' I ask her.

She laughs. The joke's poor, but it's been a stressful day. Naomi's a couple of years younger than me, not bad to have made detective. Short blonde hair, no jewellery. Except for witness interviews, she usually dresses in T-shirt and jeans, the former generally short enough to show off a little midriff. I guess she's making the most of it while she can.

'It could be worse,' she says, as the drinks arrive. 'There's a bar not too far from here called the Slaughterhouse.'

'Nice. An old meat warehouse or something?'

She shakes her head. 'Nope. No one knows why it's called that, but that's the way it's been for as long as anyone can remember.'

'You'll have to show me it sometime. It'll be nice to have someplace to celebrate when we nail this son of a bitch.'

'If we do,' Naomi says.

'If?'

'So far, he's picked on lone women, all but one after dark. Approached from behind very quietly, never lets them get a look at him until they're in post-attack shock.'

'Except for the first one.'

'Yeah, except then. But she only got a tiny glimpse when he slapped her face during the assault. Back before he started using the blindfold.'

'True,' I concede. 'And she didn't give much to go on.'

'Let's see if I remember it right: A broad-shouldered white guy wearing a ski mask. Uneven teeth. Stubble just visible on his top lip. Too dark to say what colour his eyes were. Tall, probably. Breath that stank of alcohol. That's hardly a big deal. We could pull in every alcoholic in town with that description.' She gestures around at the bar, although the place is practically empty. 'He uses a condom, and we've found no sign of pubic hair or other readily traceable evidence. Zip at the scenes, apart from four condom wrappers with no prints or other identifying traces on them.'

'It's not much.'

'Alex, this guy could move out of town tomorrow and we'd never find him and never know who he was.'

'It's not much *yet*. All we need is one break, one lead on one suspect. You know how these things work.'

'Nine victims down, and we've got nothing to go on.'

I can't help but agree. When I came to Hartford, the BAU had just finished its report on the rapist. And that was sketchy as hell, which I guess may have influenced their decision to pass on the fieldwork. They suggested looking for a white male, mid-twenties to early forties. Physique and dress of a manual labourer or former manual labourer. Quite possibly with a history of violent crime, given his lack of nerves and the efforts he made to avoid leaving usable evidence behind. Probably lived alone, as the timing of his attacks would arouse suspicion from a spouse or loved one. Some kind of recent personal trauma that triggered the first attack, most likely involving a woman – a divorce or relationship break-up, for instance. The first rape seemed less planned than the later ones – no blindfold, for instance. Lived in Hartford for some time, very familiar with the city.

Nothing, in fact, that the cops here didn't already know for themselves.

We have a quiet couple of drinks in the Bordello, let talk turn to other things outside work. Small stuff. Time filler. Then Naomi apologizes and says she has to go.

'I've got to get ready for a gig,' she tells me.

'A gig?'

'Yeah. As in musical performance.'

I raise my eyebrows. 'Seriously?'

'I've played violin since I was in high school,' she says, grinning at my surprise. 'There's a few of us play as a kind of folk-blues band. Only local, bars and such.'

'No shit. I'm a blues fan myself.'

'You should come along,' she says. 'The Glasshouse, starting at nine. I'll keep an eye out for you.'

I smile and watch her leave.

*

The next day, one of the investigative team manages to identify a car caught on CCTV a couple of blocks from Mary's attack. There was next to no traffic at that time of the morning, so we home in on this as a workable lead. The car belongs to an ex-con called Clinton Travers. Travers has a couple of convictions for assault with a deadly weapon – a knife – and assault and battery, unarmed this time. A third conviction for armed robbery was overturned on appeal, and he's been implicated in a number of other crimes. He finished his last parole nearly a year ago and was last known to be working in a machine shop and living with his then girlfriend, Angelina Lewis. Even better, his build and features all match what we know about the rapist.

Naomi and I go to speak to Angelina, now sharing an apartment with a friend. Almost the first thing she says is, 'Is this about them rapes?'

For a second, I'm convinced we've got him. That she has concrete information we could use on Travers.

'Why would you say that, Ms Lewis?' Naomi asks.

'Clint's got a record, I know that. I figured you'd be looking at anyone with a record as a suspect. He's a violent son of a bitch, I know that for sure.'

I curse inwardly and try not to let it show, while Angelina tells us all about her ex-boyfriend.

'I walked out on him about a week after New Year,' she says. 'Told him I was fed up with him, and that Macy was waiting in the car for me outside, that she'd call the cops if he did anything.'

'He was violent towards you?' Naomi asks.

'Yeah, sometimes he'd knock me around. If he had a bad day or he thought I'd been too friendly with someone else.'

'Why'd you stick with him?'

'He could be nice the rest of the time. I think he really cared for me, in his way. And he always apologized and shit afterwards, like it was going to be the last time.'

'But it never was?'

'I guess not. But I felt sorry for him, some ways. Hard to get a decent break when you're an ex-con. But it got too much in the end.'

'How did he take it when you told him you were leaving him?'

She frowns. 'Strange. First off, he started shouting, asking if there was another guy. Flexed them fists like he was going to hit me, but didn't. I just yelled back that it was him that was the problem and it wasn't anything to do with anyone else. So he shouted some more, called me a fucking bitch and stuff. But then, when I was about to walk out, he just started crying. Burst into tears. Begged me not to go. But I did, and I haven't seen him since.'

'When was this, Angelina?' I ask.

'January twelfth.'

The night of the first rape. We apply for a search warrant.

Chapter Nine

When I get back to my apartment from MCI-Ashworth, I slump into a chair and call Agent Downes. My landline's voicemail is showing half a dozen messages, but I ignore them for now.

'Williams has started talking,' I tell her once the formalities are out of the way. 'He says he buried Katelyn Sellars on Horseneck Beach about a mile from Kerry Abblit. I'm going to take him a map tomorrow to see if he can pinpoint where exactly.'

'That's great, Alex. How reliable do you think he is?'

I think for a moment before answering, back to the last words he said to me before I left. 'I think he's willing to tell the truth.'

'But?'

'But he likes playing little games. So as long as I can keep him on track, I'll hopefully be able to get everything you need out of him.'

'Have those people outside the prison given you any trouble?'

'No, not really. Harmless idiots, most of them. Some nasty messages on my phone and in my email, but nothing much else.'

'Good. Don't let them get to you, Alex. We all

want you to do well. The SAC even had Deputy Director Woods on the phone yesterday to find out what progress we were making.'

'The publicity machine's in full swing, then.'

'Don't sound so disappointed,' she says. 'We'll all come out of this looking good if we get a result.'

'If Williams really does play ball. If he's just jerking me around, we might still end up with nothing. Don't forget that.'

'I won't.' She sighs quietly. 'I'd better go. Keep me posted.'

'Sure,' I say. 'Goodbye, Agent Downes.'

'Tanya. Goodbye, Alex.'

I've barely hung up when the phone starts ringing again. I think about ignoring it, but as there's a chance it's something important, I pick up.

'Yeah?'

'Mr Rourke? I'm sorry to call you at home like this, but I've not had much luck with your office.' A man's voice. Deepish and a little nasal. No one I know.

'Who is this?'

'Will Holden. I'm a journalist with the *Boston Herald*. You probably won't remember, but I covered the original disappearances as well as the trial.'

'Sorry, Mr Holden. Nothing to say.'

He dives in quickly before I can put the phone down. 'That's what your partner's been telling me.'

'Remind me to thank him for doing so.'

'Look, just give me a minute for a couple of quick

questions and then I can stop bothering you. If you're lucky, the other papers will pick up what you tell me for their own coverage and they won't have to hassle you to do it.'

'I can't give you any details.'

'You don't need to,' Holden says. 'Be vague . . .'

'I'm good at vague.'

'. . . Is Cody Williams cooperating with the questioning, how confident are you that he'll help, how it feels to be back on the case, that sort of thing.'

For a moment, I think about the protesters gathered outside Ashworth. I think about the anonymous voices calling to tell me I'm going to hell, that I'm hounding an innocent man, that I'm a hero. I think about fielding questions at the scenes of abductions, outside family homes, on the steps of the courthouse. I remember how it all felt, all of it.

Eventually, and picking my words carefully, I say, 'OK. Williams and I have had some productive informal conversations. So far he seems to be co-operating, and I hope that he'll be able to shed light on what happened to those girls. I expect that anything I learn will be passed on to the families and others by the FBI in due course. I can't comment on what he may or may not have said so far. That's for the FBI to do, not me.'

'You said "informal". Does this mean he's not being questioned in any official legal capacity?'

'That's right. I'm not in law enforcement any more, and he isn't being questioned under a Miranda warning

95

or other legal structure. I'm the only one speaking to him, and our conversations are not being recorded in any way, as he requested. None of what he says is admissible evidence and, as far as I'm aware, there will not be any further court cases arising from what he tells me.'

'And how does it feel to be back on one of your old cases?'

'No comment on that,' I tell Holden.

'No?'

'Is that it?'

'I think so. Thanks a lot, Mr Rourke. I appreciate your time. I'll let you know through your office if we get anything back on this.'

'Sure.'

I hang up and head into the kitchen. A glass of water, a cup of coffee. Something to wash through me, clear my head. Leaning against the black marble-effect work surface, taking slow mouthfuls of water from a tall glass, I stare blankly at my reflection in the kitchen window. Gaunt, hangdog eyes. Lifeless. I realize I miss ordinary human contact. Speaking with Rob or the 'kids'. Friends. Acquaintances. Nothing like that for what seems like ages, and it's left a hole.

I grab my coat and leave the apartment. But not before I snatch up the bundled FBI file on Williams' case. The curse of the job – may as well take some reading matter with me.

*

Mochi Noodle Bar on Preston Avenue is busy, but not too busy to be short on seats. I grab a place at a table near the counter and drop the file in front of me. The place smells of steam and a dozen different spices. Lime-green walls, carpet to match. Decade-old pop music plays from a stereo near the fridge, barely audible over other diners' conversations, a couple in what I think is Cantonese, and the clatter of people eating. From the back I can hear the metallic rattle of Danny Cheung cooking. His wife, Sally, weaves her way over and smiles.

'Hiya, Alex. How are you?'

'I'm OK. How about you and Danny?'

She nods, ponytail bobbing, and gestures at the folder on the table. 'We're fine, thank you. Are you busy today? Looks like you've got a lot of reading to do there.'

'Some,' I say. Either she hasn't seen the news or she's deliberately avoiding the subject. I'm glad, either way. 'Skimming, mostly.'

'Right, right. So what can I get for you today?'

I rattle off an order and she vanishes out to the kitchen. Comes back to place a beer in front of me, then leaves me to my reading. I start by checking what Williams has already told me against what we know from both the original investigation and the later discovery of the three sets of remains, trying to judge whether he's being completely honest or not.

Katelyn Sellars did indeed go missing on the walk to school. With the number of her fellow pupils heading in the same direction and the other morning traffic, we had a very narrow timeframe for her disappearance, five minutes at most. This fits with Cody's snatch, grab and drive away explanation. No preamble. No stalking her beforehand. No one remembered anyone suspicious hanging around in the days before she vanished, which again fits. No reports of his van in the area, but then as soon as he hit any kind of major street he'd have been lost in the usual morning rush. So far, so good.

As I eat dinner and finish another beer, I flick back through the others he's told me about, checking what we have on paper against what Williams told me in jail. Reading the scene report for the discovery of Kerry Abblit's remains, I hit a sour note. Only a slight one, possibly the result of a failing memory or his illness, but something he may also have invented just for kicks. Williams told me he wrapped Kerry's body in an old beige sheet for burial. Forensics found no sign of the sheet, and the only fibre evidence was a small number of what may have been dark carpet threads, synthetic. Which didn't match any of the materials in his house or van; all were checked. He said he parked up some place quiet to have his fun and – I rack my brain – then kept her alive for a couple of days. I wonder if he held her at the old lake house he said he left Katelyn at, and why he didn't mention it before. Presumably, that's where the fibres came from. If the place was carpeted.

I make a note to ask him about it first thing

tomorrow. If he's been lying about any part of his actions, it throws everything he says into question. I wouldn't put it past the son of a bitch.

Say goodbye to Sally, wave to Danny through the swing door to the kitchen, and make my way back home under a cloud of mixed emotion.

A blaze of white turns the rain into a field of stars for a brief second. Water turns to blood, oily black in the darkness, as everything falls away and I begin to choke.

I awake on the couch, TV still playing the channel I left it on last night. Pain at the base of my neck, teeth on edge. I shower and have my morning coffee, watching the news, before heading out to MCI-Ashworth once more. On the way I pick up a copy of the *Herald*. Buried a couple of pages into the interior is a more or less word-for-word repeat of what I told Holden the previous evening, along with some refresher case background and a mention of the ongoing protests. Not a bad piece, and I find I don't care if the FBI disagree.

In the visiting room, Williams is waiting as usual, and he doesn't look well. A wheeled drip-stand next to him is hooked into a vein on the back of his hand. His eyes are hooded and red, and I guess he slept very little last night. Every so often he rubs at his mouth and smacks his lips as if he's thirsty, but he doesn't ask me to grab him anything from the machine.

'Rough night?' I say, trying not to reveal the fact

that I think he deserves it. Williams knows it anyway, and I feel no sympathy towards him at all, but there's still some automatic mechanism inside that enforces a certain degree of civility towards a dying man. I hate myself for it.

Williams shrugs his slumped shoulders. 'Guess I'm getting used to them by now. Who'd you want to hear about today? That Providence girl's next, right?'

'Yeah, she is. But first I want to go back to Kerry Abblit for a moment,' I say, hoping I'm not about to put the skids on finding out what happened to Holly or the others. I don't think I could face the parents again if I did.

'What about her?'

'You said you had her for a couple of days before she died.'

'Uh-huh.'

'Did you take her to the same place as Katelyn Sellars? That house by the lake?'

He thinks for a moment before shaking his head and blinking twice. 'Yeah. Yeah, the house. Why?'

'What's the floor of the house like?'

'What the fuck's that got to do with anything?'

'When they found her body there was no sign of the sheet you say you wrapped her in. But there were carpet fibres, and they weren't from your van or your house. I'm trying to understand where they came from.'

Another pause. 'Yeah, the house had carpet in it, I guess.'

'Guess?'

'Yeah.' Williams must know I'm not convinced, as he continues, 'Or I might have got that confused with one of the others. There was a lot of them, and it was a long time ago, y'know? Shit, I don't remember half the things I did last week, especially not now. And they were worth dick once they were dead. Why'd I care?'

I lean forward, rest my hands on the table. 'So how can I be sure that what you tell me in here is correct?'

'You don't forget *that* stuff, what happens before they die,' he snaps back. 'But anyways, I guess you'll just have to trust me and we'll see what we can do, OK? Now you want to talk about that Providence girl, or do I go back to bed?'

I sigh, give him a moment to cool down, then say, 'Sure. Tell me about Holly Tynon.'

'I picked her especially,' Williams says. 'Knew what I wanted to get, kind of girl I was looking for. Been driving around for a while, no luck. But then I saw her coming up that driveway. I got around the block double-quick, managed to head her off at the corner. I didn't have time to set anything up, so I just stopped with a street map leaning on the wheel, opened my door and asked her over for directions. Hauled her in and shut the door fast, just as she started making noise and fighting. She soon shut the fuck up when she saw the knife. Made that little bitch blow me while I was driving along, since she was in there.'

He cracks a leer at the memory, eyes going wide and black for a moment. Breath laced with the rotting scent of dying body chemistry, the ammonia smell of failing organs, the acid bite of a system in collapse, washes past his cracked lips.

'Why'd you bother ditching her wallet?'

'I had to stop so I could get her all tied up safe in the back of the van. I figured since there was that park right there, I might as well get rid of anything that was obviously hers while I had the chance. No sense doing it when I got home. People would know where she ended up. Little mistakes always get you caught, my daddy used to say. And I thought it might throw you off the trail a bit. Y'know, not being sure where she was headed. Waste a bit of your time.'

I can imagine him doing it for just such a reason. An extra little dig at the people hunting for him. I don't believe his dad ever said anything of the sort. His dad knew him well before he became the monster, not since. 'What then?'

'Same as usual. Kept her until she wasn't any fun any more. Then I got rid of her.' A smile flickers across his face for a moment. Then his features sag back into their usual hollow slump. 'I had to break her legs and shit to fit her in a bag. I didn't want to be too obvious this time – I nearly got found out by someone driving by when I was taking the body of that other girl out of the van – so I stuffed her in a gym bag.'

'Where?'

'Woods, some way down the road from Worcester. I wrapped her up in tarpaulin and buried her well off the nearest trail.' He catches my expression. 'Rutland State Park, I think. Or Moore.'

His mouth twitches a couple of times, but he stays quiet and seems to have finished.

'Again, could you be more specific?' I say.

'You got that map? I can help out with the other one while I'm at it.'

I unfold the map and lay it on the table along with a pencil. Williams gazes at it for an eternity, with only the occasional movement of his head to show that he hasn't slipped into a trance or fallen asleep.

Eventually, he marks two small circles on it and looks back up. 'There you go.'

The map's a decent scale, but even so, each circle must cover half a square mile of ground, and I tell him so. 'Can't you narrow those down? Those areas will take forever to search.'

'I wouldn't know. Never looked for a body myself.'

'You must be able to remember the route you took to get to the burial sites.'

Williams shrugs. 'Some of it, yeah. The rest, I'd probably have to see them again to know for sure.' He jiggles his drip line. 'And that ain't so easy now. It's not going to get any easier either.'

'So think harder.'

'I'll try to. Of course, there's still a few things unresolved between us, and they're causing me some distraction right now. You have anything you'd like to get off your chest, just to clear the air, you feel free.' He waits for me to speak, but I say nothing, my resolve to stick to talking only about the girls just as strong as ever. I won't give the leering son of a bitch the satisfaction. 'Otherwise, you leave me this map and I'll keep on thinking through this afternoon and tonight, and I'll see what I can do. Best hope it doesn't take too long – I can't have that much time left.'

When I leave, the first few regular prison visitors are already waiting in Outer Control, all of them women. A couple of them look at me strangely, perhaps trying to work out what I'm doing here. As I'm beginning to wonder the same thing myself, I can't offer them any clues, and merely trudge past them with hardly a sideways glance.

From the 'Vette, I call Tanya Downes to fill her in on developments. 'He's given me rough locations for two of the bodies. I'm trying to persuade him to be more specific, but it looks like he might drag his heels here.'

'Why?' she asks.

'I'm not sure. It might be that he wants a chance to walk over the scenes himself, pick them out by hand.'

'A "last breath of free air" thing?'

'Something like that,' I say, watching the tiny knot of protesters in the distance. This morning's fresh news story has sparked a little revival in their numbers. 'Or he's angling for another concession that he's going to spring on me some time in the next couple of days.'

'Well, let me know if he asks for anything more. He'll die there in Ashworth, and nothing is going to stop that. That will not change, Alex. But if all he wants is a more comfortable cell or better food, something of that nature, we might be willing to play ball. Don't tell him that, though. His help should come for free if possible.'

'Sure.'

Her tone relaxes. 'Changing the subject, I've been wondering if you'd like to go out for dinner some time.'

'Uhm . . .' The question catches me completely off guard, leaves me reaching for an excuse to say no. And I can't think of one, not without stretching out the silence beyond the time when it'd become clear that I was lying just to avoid it. 'Yeah, sure. Uhm . . . when?'

'I'm free for most of this week. I'll give you a call.'

'OK.'

When I get home there's a piece of hate-mail mixed in with the usual junk and bills. I throw it in the trash without bothering to read it. I'm not in the mood to deal with other people's anger. They think they're doing right, but they know jack. I know how it feels, but I don't want to think about it. I want to be reminded of better, simpler times.

It takes me almost an hour to dig out a trio of old photos of myself that I want to see again, slightly faded prints of me as a newly graduated field agent. Young and fresh-faced. Crisp suit. Proud grin. I can still remember how I felt when they were taken, but the memory is a little dim now, fogged by the passing years, how far I've come, the places the journey has taken me, the things I've had to do.

I don't know whether to feel sad about that or not.

Chapter Ten

Early Saturday morning, and a cold, clear day outside smells like frost. My nerves are tingling slightly. Like a soldier waiting for the order to attack. Strange, but I guess I just want us to get the guy quickly and cleanly.

Two blue-and-whites accompany Naomi's plain sedan across town to Travers' place. Flashes streak against passing buildings from the single blue bubble strobe on its roof, the 'Kojak light' most unmarked cars carry.

'What's on the warrant?' I ask her.

'We can search his house, car and person, looking for anything pertinent to the investigation, including clothing, weapons and personal effects, so we can look just about anywhere for what we need, given how easy it all is to hide. We haven't been able to get a warrant for a DNA sample, though.'

'No?'

'The judge said the evidence against him so far was too thin to allow it. But if there's anything physical there, we should be OK to take it.'

'It's not like we've got any DNA to compare it to, I guess.'

'Not yet, anyway,' she says.

We cruise through nearly empty streets. A smattering of people out early, but not many. My breath mists the window.

'How likely is it that Travers is going to give us trouble?' I ask.

'Not very. He's pretty much a career criminal, so he should know the drill by now. My main worry is that he'll see us coming and try ditching anything incriminating. Hopefully, he'll still be in bed when we arrive.'

I nod. Unconsciously check my gun in its shoulder rig. 'Let's hope so.'

We pull up outside an ugly brick apartment building, one of an identical row of similar structures. Dwellings on four storeys, the last of them firmly embedded in the slope of the roof. Curtains mostly still shut. Half a dozen steps up to the front door, a second set leading down and to the side to the entrance of the basement apartment. The scent of stale steam coming out of a heating vent somewhere nearby.

'Travers is on the first floor,' Naomi says.

Through the front entrance and up the cheap-carpet-tiled stairs inside, trailing in the wake of four uniformed cops. By the time I reach Travers' door, it's already been forced open and Naomi has started ordering him around in the hallway of his apartment.

'Mr Travers, I'm Detective Naomi Carson with Hartford PD, and this is Special Agent Alex Rourke from the FBI. I have here a warrant to search these premises as well as your vehicle and personal effects. Your cooperation would be appreciated. Hopefully, this won't take any longer than it needs to.'

Travers runs his eyes over the piece of paper in Naomi's hand. He's a tough, beefy-looking guy with a mop of untidy black hair and a couple of tattoos on his right arm. Faded grey T-shirt and boxers. 'Car keys are on the table in the living room. Car's parked out back.' He moves to the side of the corridor to allow the cops past and looks me up and down. 'Never met a Feebie before,' he says. 'Guess I must've done something special to have you guys after me.'

I don't give him a reply, just push through and on into the apartment proper, leaving one of the uniforms to babysit him. The place is gloomy and untidy. Curtains closed, heating on. Overly warm and with an acrid, musty smell that sticks in the back of my throat. A small kitchen off to the left with a smattering of dirty crockery. Ahead, the living room, with a collection of ratty furniture, a TV, a coffee table covered in junk, and a couple of stacks of videos in one corner and shelves littered with magazines and a half-dozen or so paperbacks. Well-used ashtrays, an empty beer can, coffee mugs. The magazines are mostly old porno titles. *Red Hot Cheerleaders* and *Down 'n' Dirty Amateurs*. I can't tell whether they would've been here when Angelina lived with Travers, but they look well thumbed.

A pair of doors leading off the living room open on to an equally untidy bedroom covered in discarded clothes, and a cramped bathroom. Amongst the clutter on the bedroom floor I can see a pair of heavy brown suede shoes. A puffy dark blue jacket is hanging from the back of a chair. I point them out wordlessly to Naomi and continue to look around the apartment as the police team slowly begins to sift through its contents. Looking through one of the back windows, I can see down into the parking lot at the rear of the building. Two more cops have just started searching his grey Toyota Camry.

Travers never seems to lose his cool throughout the search, treating the whole thing with a laid-back contempt and speaking as little as possible. Once we've gone over the living room, he sits down and watches TV, doing his best to look like he's ignoring us until we're finished.

We leave with his shoes, jacket, several pairs of pants and three hunting-type knives in plastic bags. We haven't found the ski mask or the blindfold and I know, as I'm sure does Naomi, that unless we're very lucky, we don't have enough to arrest him. Unless we can find something that ties Travers or his clothing to one of the victims or the scenes specifically, it's all circumstantial.

As the last cop files out, I take one final look around the living room, then make for the door. Travers follows to show me out. 'So long, Mr Feebie,' he says, as I step into the hallway. He leans closer and smiles, dropping his voice slightly. 'It's kinda fun when you get to see the cops looking in all the wrong places, for their bad guys, I mean. You ever wonder if this sort of thing just encourages people? You know, when they know you're not getting it right?'

'What?'

'I'm just thinking out loud.'

'That's got to be a first.'

'I'm thinking, what if, like, this guy you're after might have heard about all this here, and be thinking that he can get away with it now, if you ain't found nothing. Makes you wonder, doesn't it?'

'Not really.'

'Hell, if he could see you guys he might get tempted by that pretty detective of yours. She's real cute. Doubt she'd want to go out for a drink or something? Heh.'

'I doubt it.'

'You could ask.'

'Could, but won't. Goodbye, Mr Travers.'

He closes the door and leaves me outside, digesting his words. His implied taunts. The suggestion – unprovable and inadmissible – that we got the right guy, we just couldn't find the evidence. And that he knows we can't take him down. Or it might just be an ex-con's joke at the expense of law enforcement. A sly 'fuck you' to his old enemies.

Don't judge yet, I tell myself. We could get lucky with the clothes.

Outside, in the car, I tell Naomi, 'We need to keep him under surveillance. Twenty-four hours a day. Constant watch. When he makes a mistake, I don't want us to miss it.'

We have no luck at all with the clothes. There's no traces from any of the victims or the crime scenes, even on the shoes. They've all been cleaned regularly. The surveillance fares no better. Travers seems to anticipate that everything he does will be watched and makes a point of doing very little. He doesn't even break the speed limit or park somewhere he shouldn't – nothing even remotely illegal.

And then someone leaks his name to the press, and

Clinton Travers is splashed all over the papers as the suspect questioned over the case. The whole thing's a mess, with the department trying to find out who leaked it without giving the media even more to chew on.

Travers appears to enjoy it. His shopping habits seem designed to provoke the cops. He checks out the knives in a couple of specialist hunters' places. A few days later, he picks up a parcel that looks like a mail-order delivery. Replacements for the ones we took. He restocks on condoms. He even goes looking for ski masks at sporting goods stores.

But he does nothing. At all.

The rapes stop completely. The papers eventually put forward a number of wild theories, none of which seem likely. To me, it's obvious that Travers is our guy and he's smart enough not to risk being caught. Every day that passes, the investigation dries up a little more, and I grow a little more frustrated at our lack of available avenues and at the waiting game we're being forced to play.

After a month of this, I get the recall to Quantico and my regular duties. Naomi and I go out for a last drink, and she finally makes good on her promise to take me to the Slaughterhouse, even though we don't have anything to celebrate.

After that, she sends me occasional updates, but in reality everyone's simply waiting for Travers to make the next move. Surveillance continues for a good while, and still he does nothing. Neither the police nor my superiors are especially pleased with the lack of progress, but I think both understand why we're stymied.

By the time the end of September rolls around and thirteen-year-old Marie Austen vanishes from the streets of Taunton, Clinton Travers is nothing more than a nasty, nagging sore at the back of my mind. The rancid taste of a criminal walking around free that surfaces late at night when I try to sleep. Cody Williams, a man whose guilt I'm equally convinced of – although I have even less on him than I do on Travers – is a far more immediate concern. We've still been unable to pin anything on him, and with the number of missing kids now standing at six, I'm getting more and more desperate to stop him before we lose any more. The local press is screaming for a successful end to the case, and the Bureau's hierarchy and the top police brass from the three involved states are only slightly less vocal. I can barely face phone calls from or to the victims' parents any more, asking for or supplying updates on our progress, such as it is.

Marie Austen was a bright, pretty young girl from a nice family. That's all I can remember about her, apart from the photo in the file. Too many of these and the details start to blur, to become one. Fade to interchangeable names, faces. 'A single death is a tragedy; a million deaths is a statistic,' as Stalin is supposed to have said. Right sentiment, but maybe the wrong scale, Joe.

Marie's now lying buried in an unmarked grave somewhere, a broken testament to her abductor's perversion, and I couldn't do anything to stop it happening. That I'm starting to lose feeling about these deaths is just adding to the sense of defeat.

The phone call I receive from Detective Sergeant Ed Frost from Hartford PD a few days after Marie's abduction only makes things worse.

'Agent Rourke, I know you're busy with other things, but I figured you'd want to know, seeing as you worked on this case with us.'

'Know what?'

'Naomi Carson was attacked last night. She's, well, not in a good way. We're doing everything we can, though. It looks like the same guy, so right now we're combing over the scene, and she's given us what information she could. It's not much different to the other attacks, but we're going to go over every goddamn thing we can if it means we'll get something that'll give us Travers.'

'What about the surveillance on the guy? What the fuck happened to that?'

'Agent Rourke.' He pauses, sounds uncomfortable, almost apologetic. 'It's been six months. We had to stop the watch on Travers.'

'Had to? What, you got a bunch of other multiple fucking rapists to worry about?'

'The department couldn't justify keeping it going without results. Naomi had done some occasional checks on him, but that's it.'

I can barely hear myself over the pounding, the blood surging through my veins. 'That surveillance kept him from doing anything. That's a goddamn result. Even if we couldn't arrest the guy, at least it stopped him attacking anyone else.'

'Look, I agree with you. I wish we could've kept it

going, but we don't have that level of resources. No one does.'

'Bullshit.'

'I wish to God we had maintained it, given what's happened to Detective Carson. That asshole won't get away with it. No goddamn way. Given the wait he's had, he might be cracking up.'

'Some chance.'

'It's true. He left a note for us. Hopefully, this means he's starting to get cocky, and that means he'll make mistakes. We're going to get the son of a bitch.'

Thump. Thump. Thump. 'What did the note say?'

'It's hand-written, and it says: "She is real cute, isn't she? Thanks for the introduction."'

Travers.

Chapter Eleven

When I download my emails that evening, one message stands out from the rest. 'ATTN: Ex-Special Agent Rourke – Case Information' is its subject line. I had been hoping for something funny or uplifting to take my mind off Williams, the bodies and everything else, but I guess I'll have to settle for this. It's a message with a sizeable attachment, and it looks like it's been run through an anonymizer.

Return-Path: unknown@unknown.com
Delivered-To: alex@r-garrett-assoc.com
Received: from unknown by mail.r-garrett-assoc.com
with SMTP
Message-ID: none
From: unknown@unknown.com
To: alex@r-garrett-assoc.com
Subject: ATTN: Ex-Special Agent Rourke – Case
Information
Message:

I hope the attachment interests you.
<<h_t_seg2.mpg>>

The attachment is an MPEG, a movie segment. As far as I'm aware, there's no way of embedding a virus or other nasty in such a file, and as this doesn't look like spam, I double-click on the title. Probably another piece of random craziness from one of Williams' supporters. Probably showing what'll happen to me if I don't leave him alone. I get ready to hit the delete key.

But I never push it.

The footage opens suddenly. No fade-in, no sense of an introduction. The cut is abrupt. A dark-walled room lit by a halogen bulb in a professional lighting stand to the right of the picture. I can see the edge of what looks like a window on the left; just a sliver, but enough to see the light leaking through the pane. The frame, like the walls, seems to be bare wood, dark in colour. The room is devoid of decoration. No pictures on the walls, no carpeting over the boards. It hardly looks as though it's regularly occupied.

In the middle of the shot, maybe six feet from the window, is an iron-framed bed with a faded pale-blue striped mattress on it, wedged against the far wall. No bedclothes. The frame has started to flake, losing some of its black paint to show grey beneath, stark in the halogen's glare.

A naked woman hangs by her wrists from a roof beam running across the room. Steel handcuffs run from one hand to the other, looping through an eyelet of metal cable lashed around the beam. I can see her pale skin is rubbed red and raw. Late teens or early twenties, at a guess. Thin, unhealthily so. Tousled blonde hair hanging down to below her shoulder blades. She's swinging round as the cable twists. Her head's thrown back, and she's thrashing against her bonds.

As the camera slowly moves forwards, the woman rotates fully so she's facing the lens. All the time, she continues to struggle and kick, and now I can see that her mouth's open and there must be no sound with the footage, because she's plainly screaming.

She sees the cameraman, draws breath, and starts yelling even harder. As her eyes widen and she pauses momentarily in her struggles, I get a mental flash of a photo on a mantelpiece eight years ago. A girl's face pinned like a butterfly under glass. There's a resemblance I can't deny, with an immediacy that only strengthens the connection in my mind, although I can hardly begin to believe it's possible.

The woman in the footage is Holly Tynon.

I can see red welts, hard to say how fresh they are, in places on her skin. Most are only small, finger-sized smudges, but there are a couple of longer, thinner lines. Maybe a dozen marks in total, although with the picture quality and the lighting, it's hard to say for sure.

No question who's responsible for them, though. The camera moves in so close that the only parts of Holly – if it is Holly, and I still can't quite believe it could be – in shot are her abdomen and upper thighs.

The cameraman's hand, reasonably strong but not huge or brutish, with a hairy forearm, no watch or tattoos, reaches forward and roughly squeezes her bare buttock hard. Pinches the skin roughly, then slaps her and sends her spinning again. She kicks and bucks against this treatment, and the camera shakes suddenly, lurching to one side and forwards. It whips back up in time to catch the man's fist slamming into Holly's gut. Her body quivers once, twice – winded and coughing, I guess – and she stops fighting.

For a few moments, the camera holds position, the man unmoving. He briefly pans up to Holly's face, obscured by clumps of blonde hair, eyes pinched shut, features hard to make out for sure. She seems to be crying. Then the camera pulls away, keeping her in frame for as long as possible, before losing her as the man moves past the halogen lamp.

The sudden drop in light plunges the picture into blotchy shadow. I can make out what could be the edge of something like a table, light glinting on an object or metal fixture.

A sense of movement, then we swing back quickly to Holly, stark white in the glare. She's looking up at the bonds holding her again, but is otherwise hanging limp. Head turns slightly in the direction of the cameraman and her expression starts to change.

The footage ends as abruptly as it began. The counter at the bottom of my MPEG player reads two minutes twenty-three seconds.

Chapter Twelve

The first thing I do is burn the file and the original email on to CD. No sense risking losing it if the power failed or the operating system wiped out on me. Then I play the footage again, pausing it at the moment the woman first seems to see the cameraman and stops to draw breath. Probably the best shot there is of her face. I dig out the picture of Holly from the FBI file and hold it up to the screen, side by side with the frozen features of the woman hanging from the beam. The low-res, pixellated image on the screen isn't as clear as I'd like. But I still see the resemblance, even with the years that have passed between the two. The shape of the nose. The eyes and the eyebrows arched above them. I can see it, but I don't know if anyone else will. Her parents, maybe, but there's no way I'd show them the footage.

I dial Tanya's number at the Boston Field Office and let it ring through to her voicemail. 'Agent Downes, this is Alex Rourke. It's, ah, nearly 9 p.m. I've just received something that could be of major importance for the Williams case, but it's going to need some kind of confirmation or analysis by the image lab. Please give me a call as soon as you get this message. Thanks.'

Hang up and try not to think of the possibilities. That there could be a chance that more of the missing girls are alive somewhere. That Cody Williams might be innocent. That I might have got the wrong man. Or that this is all just a highly unpleasant joke designed to make me think that way.

When I eventually go to sleep, my dreams are full of strange images. Holly Tynon stares at me with Clinton Travers' eyes, while Cody beats her with the butt of an old 9mm pistol until she dies, a bloody pulp. Then he turns the gun on himself, laughing hysterically as he pulls the trigger.

'You've got to be kidding,' is Agent Downes' response when I tell her about the email over the phone the next morning. 'Have you got any idea where it came from?'

'None. Anonymized email, blank sender information. It could've come from anywhere.'

'Jesus.'

'What do you want to do with it?'

'Bring it in,' she says. 'I'll take a look at it and we can decide where to go from there. If it looks like a fake, though, I'll treat it as such.'

'Sure.'

Downes' office is on the second floor of the FBI's building in Boston. The Bureau occupies a chunk of the vast Center Plaza office complex in the heart of the city. A sweeping, curved building of white stone surrounded by a flat expanse of brick broken here and there by ornamental flowerbeds. Inside, carpet tiles and fluorescent light strips. The whine of air-con, now blasting out heat to cover the fall chill. Impersonal fittings straight out of the Bureau's office catalogue, broken up here and there by little individual touches – a photo frame, a postcard, a fluffy mascot stuck to the top of the monitor. The latter, a lime-green frog about the size of a grape, regards me mournfully as I stand behind Downes, the two of us watching the footage.

When it's finished, Downes does the same as me, comparing a frozen still from the film with the photo of Holly.

'I don't know,' she says. 'I'm not convinced at all about this.'

'Looks like the same person to me.'

'It could be any blonde woman in that film.'

'There's a strong similarity there,' I say.

'I'm not as sure as you.'

'Look at the eyes.'

She shakes her head. 'I suspect someone's simply noticed that one of the snippets in their personal porno collection looks a little like one of the girls we're looking for and has sent it to you as a sick joke. It's not like the papers haven't been full of this case.'

'Could we do an age advancement on Holly's photo for better comparison? That shouldn't take long.'

'I think we'd better.'

She leads me up one floor and along a maze of

corridors interspersed with more open office space to a cubicle where a bespectacled woman in her forties, wearing a dark-blue trouser suit, sits at a computer putting together a report of some kind.

'Janice,' Downes says. 'Have you got a few minutes spare? I need a quick favour.'

'What is it?' Janice glances at me briefly, then back at Downes.

'I need an age advancement done, if you have a moment. It's a single photo which shouldn't need very much detailed adjustment. Not yet, at least.'

'Give me the photo.'

Janice scans Holly's picture and brings it up on screen. 'How much advancement do you need?'

'Seven years,' I say. 'She's thirteen in that photo.'

'Keeping the same relative body size? Any significant weight gain or loss expected?'

'No.'

I watch as the face on the screen morphs, flowing like mercury, shifting and pooling into a new, older shape.

'Hair?'

'Longer. Down to shoulder length. Worn loose.'

More changes on screen. Janice looks back at me. 'There. Done.'

The printer spools off a hardcopy of the image. Looking at it, thinking back to the face on the film, I'm even more sure that it was Holly in the footage. The thought makes me uneasy, suggesting at past mistakes and misjudgements that I can't easily live with.

Hold it down. Concentrate on the case.

'I still don't know, Alex,' Downes says, staring at the picture, as we walk back through the corridors. 'I don't know at all.'

'It's her.'

'You might be looking too hard for something that's not there.'

'It's her.'

We return to her office and she brings up the frozen still from the footage and compares the two. 'The quality of this film is so low that I think it could be anyone there, and we wouldn't be able to tell the difference. And the chances of it really being the Tynon girl . . . well, you know just how unlikely it is that a child kidnap victim could possibly be alive after all this time.'

'It still needs analysing. We might be able to sharpen up the image to get a better look at the girl. Maybe even learn a few things about where it was shot.' I frown. 'And besides, even if the chances are small, you've got to follow this up.'

'We got the guy, Alex. You know it and I know it. Once Cody was behind bars, there were no more disappearances. Three of his victims have already been found dead, and he's started to give you the locations of a couple of the remainder. Has he ever given you any reason to think any of the girls were kept alive?'

I stay quiet.

'Exactly,' Downes says. 'Even *he* hasn't floated the

possibility. I still say this is most likely to be the work of one of his supporters, who saw the news reports and decided to try to make it look like he might be innocent. They dug around for an old piece of obscure pornography with a blonde woman who roughly fitted Holly's description or, who knows, even shot some themselves, and sent it to you to throw you. That's all.'

'If that was the case, why not send copies to the newspapers, along with a letter saying what it's supposed to be? If they want Williams freed, they'd need media exposure for something like this.'

'Maybe they have. Maybe it just hasn't made it to print yet.'

'And maybe they haven't. Maybe it really is Holly.'

'And even if this footage is everything you think it is, it won't get him freed,' she says, tapping her fingers on the age-advanced printout. 'We never charged him with the abductions of any of those girls. He wasn't convicted of anything that involved them. We, and you specifically, had him for two clear-cut crimes — the murder of Clinton Travers and the attempted abduction of Nicole Ballard. Even if this film proves he had nothing to do with Holly Tynon, his convictions are perfectly sound, and he'll stay where he is.'

Hold my tongue for a moment, staying calm. 'OK, that's true. But if that is Holly in the film, we still need to find out what happened to her. Maybe Williams sold her into the kiddie porno trade, and she's been underground ever since, and someone had this in his collection and thought we should see it but didn't want to incriminate himself. Or maybe she simply ran away from home, and this is just a home movie she made last year with her boyfriend that somehow found its way back to me. Doesn't matter – we need to know. So do her family. If it's not her, it's not her. So be it.'

Downes nods slowly. 'OK. I'll pass the film on for image analysis and we'll see what, if anything, turns up. But it'll just go into the regular work queue. I'm not going to ask for it to be prioritized.'

'Why not?'

'Partly because I don't believe it to be genuine. Partly because I don't think we're likely to learn too much from it in any case. And mostly because even if it is genuine, Tynon's been alive for seven years after she disappeared, and so I see no reason to suppose she's going to be killed now.'

'What?'

'There'll be plenty of other, more recent cases, where analysis is far more urgent. They have to be given priority. This film will be examined, but it may take a while. In the meantime . . .'

'Can you imagine the media frenzy that'll result if this turns out to be real and we fucked up seven years ago? You can't let this slide.'

'In the meantime . . .'

'Unless you don't want anyone to think we botched the original case in case any of the shit sticks to you.'

'*In the meantime*,' she says again, 'I suggest you ask

Williams for everything he can tell you about Tynon and whether there's any chance she might still be alive.'

I'm not at all happy about it, but I guess I've no real choice but to accept her answers for now.

Fuck.

'OK.'

'I'm sorry, Alex. I didn't mean to jump on you like that.'

'It's OK. It's your call, I guess.'

'It is, but I shouldn't be jumping on you like that. Blame it on the stress or something.' She sighs and drops her shoulders, brightening suddenly. 'Are you free later on, by the way? I just thought that if you were, there's a new French place I'd like to try, and I did say I'd take you out.'

'Yeah, sure.'

'How's eight o'clock sound?'

I nod. 'Fine.'

I leave Downes' office with a copy of the age-advanced photo and a mind not even thinking about dinner or dating. Instead, it's fighting to come up with quicker solutions than those likely to emerge from the Bureau. At least, that part of it which isn't thinking about the unpleasant idea that Williams could be innocent of the crimes I've assumed he committed since we first met.

That part of it which isn't thinking of where that assumption took me, and what might have been.

And what was.

*

Dinner with Tanya Downes is a slightly uncomfortable affair, despite the pleasant surroundings of the French restaurant near the Common. Like going to the funeral of a vague acquaintance, seeing all the other mourners and realizing they have a lot more invested in this than you do.

Over warm goat's cheese salad, she tells me how she's hoping to make SAC before too long, if she can get a couple of major cases under her belt and make a name for herself. Then keep climbing the ladder, maybe become the first ever black woman to rise to director of the Bureau. I nod in all the right places and chase pine nuts around my plate with a fork.

Over grilled swordfish with herb-laced polenta, she tells me about her father, an accountant of unspectacular success until his death from lung cancer a couple of years previously. She tells me how she hasn't seen her mother in years, since her parents divorced. I keep nodding and briefly mention that my parents are both dead. I avoid going into details and concentrate on the last of the fish.

Over caramel cranberry tart, she tells me how she's always avoided settling down, raising a family, that sort of thing, to concentrate on the job, because she doesn't feel confident about managing both. I tell her I was the same. She asks me how I am now. I tell her I'm still the same, but the reasons have changed. She doesn't seem to know if I'm joking or not.

By the time we say goodnight, I'm pretty sure I

should never have agreed to the whole thing in the first place. I wasn't interested, so why say yes to dinner?

Because what else would I have done tonight?

Next morning, Rob looks up in surprise when I walk into the office. Nothing seems to have changed much. A few more 'in' tray items have become 'outs'. A few new ones have replaced them. My desk is still a mess.

'What's up, Alex?' he calls out. 'I wasn't expecting to see you back here for another few days to a week yet. I haven't heard anything about you breaking that Williams guy.'

'I found out yesterday that one of his victims could still be alive,' I reply, dropping into a chair.

Rob falls silent for a moment. Blinks once, twice. 'You've got to be shitting me.'

'I wish I was.' As I say it, I wonder why. Would I really prefer it if Holly had been killed all those years ago, like we thought then? Would that be better than having her alive now, after years of God-knows-what, to expose my mistakes for what they were? Mercy for years of suffering, or a sense of guilt on my part?

'Fucking hell.'

'Yeah, my thoughts exactly.'

'Who is it? Which girl?'

'Holly Tynon,' I say.

'So what happened to her? Where is she now?' Rob throws up his hands. 'I mean, how the hell is she still alive?'

'By the looks of things, she's being held by someone else.'

'After all this time?'

I nod. 'Yeah.'

'So Williams was working with someone,' he says. 'Must've been.'

'Yeah.'

'Or at least passing girls on to someone else.'

'Yeah. We screwed up.'

'You didn't have enough to get him on the murders anyway. That part of the investigation wasn't getting much anyway.'

'It was still our clusterfuck. No way we should be finding out about a surviving victim from a murder investigation that's seven fucking years old. And what that girl must've been through . . .'

He shakes his head. 'Christ, Alex. I don't know what to say to all this. Hell, is it even possible? Like you said, it's been seven years.'

'It wouldn't be the first case like this, but it'd certainly be a rarity. So yeah, it's possible.'

'How likely is it that he knows what happened to her?'

'Cody?'

'Yeah.'

I shrug. 'That, I don't know. He hasn't suggested anything like that before, so . . . I don't know. I can't even be sure that she really is still alive. I need to borrow Sophie to find out for certain.'

Sophie Donehan, our part-time intern and full-time college student, glances up from where she's sipping coffee and pretending to read something on her monitor as if she wasn't listening to everything we just said. Twenty-one and no longer the slightly freaky teenager she was when we first met, before she started college here in Boston. Black hair worn in a bob, no make-up at all – none needed with her complexion. Slim, sure of herself.

We sometimes find ill-at-ease male students hanging around in the foyer downstairs, waiting to pick her up out of work. Rob makes a point of doing his best to terrorize them. He has that sense of humour. She really should be doing an internship with the city police department or a similar body to help her degree, but she claims to prefer the private sector. Her marks don't seem to have suffered.

'I don't know what you'd all do without me,' she says, smiling sweetly. Her eyes are wide, alert. I guess she's pretty shocked by what she overheard, although she's doing her best to hide it. 'What do you need, Alex?'

'Your photographer friend.'

'Brandon?'

'Yeah. How good is he with digital pictures, do you think?'

'Taking or processing?'

'Processing. Someone else already took these.'

Sophie shrugs. 'I know he does a lot of photo manipulation on computer. So I guess he must know his stuff.'

'Do you think he'd be willing to do some analysis work for me? Clean up images, sharpen them. Look for details that might have been missed. That sort of thing.'

'I doubt he'll object,' she says. 'But is this, like, something the FBI should be doing? I mean, I don't know what it is you want, but if you're working with the Feds, and you've got something that needs looking at, shouldn't you give it to them?'

'Sophie . . .'

'I'm not saying you wouldn't, or that you haven't. I just wouldn't want anyone to kick down the door to Brandon's apartment and arrest him for withholding evidence or something.'

'Sophie,' I try again with a smile, 'the FBI are already working on it as well, but this could do with being finished as soon as possible, and I doubt they're going to get results soon. It's just image manipulation from a video clip I've already given them. That's all.'

'OK. Are you going to pay him?'

'Sure.' Rob coughs loudly in the background, but I ignore him. 'This might take a fair amount of effort. And the subject matter isn't great.'

'This would be the could-be-alive-but-still-captive girl you were talking about,' she says very matter-of-factly. 'How bad is it?'

'Nothing gruesome. No blood.'

'Uh-huh. What's wrong with it then?'

'It's got some violence in it, and there's what must've come after. But it's more the fact that it could be genuine that's unsettling. Of course, it might just be an S&M film that someone's using for a joke.'

'OK, I'll ask him.' She checks her watch. 'He should be in a lecture right now. I'll call him when he gets out. Is there anything specific you want?'

I shake my head. 'Anything that can be sharpened, magnified, picked out of the darkness. Any little detail at all. Tell him I can always meet up with him to go over what he can find out.'

'No problem.' Sophie smiles and changes the subject. 'How's it going at the jail?'

'Ask me again after today. So far I've heard a lot of things I'd rather have missed and not much of any use. How Cody'll react when I ask him about this film, I don't know.'

'Well, there isn't much I can do with that apart from wish you good luck.' She smiles. 'Talking to these people is much more your department than mine, Alex. Out of reach of us mere students. All I can do is offer moral support.'

'Don't knock it, I need it.'

There are no protestors outside MCI-Ashworth, and for that I'm glad. All the way here, I've been thinking about the person who emailed me the file, and I've found myself checking the rear-view mirror more than once. The last thing I would have wanted after that would be to be met by a pack of strangers, all staring at me.

I have to be given special dispensation by the

prison administration to take my laptop into the visiting room. I spend half an hour explaining the reasons why and waiting for them to check with the Bureau that I'm not likely to try smuggling anything to Cody.

When I make it inside at long last, Williams is sitting slumped in his chair. He looks sick and tired, worse than yesterday, and gives me a long, washed-out stare before dropping his gaze to the table again. One claw-like hand is draped around the drip-stand by his side, which rattles almost imperceptibly as his arm shakes. His skin is pale and stretched paper-thin.

'Morning, Cody,' I say, sitting down.

'Agent Rourke.'

'Have you had a chance to look at that map yet? Any details for me?'

He sniffs and drops the map in front of me. 'Maybe.'

'Maybe?'

'I think I know how I got to some places. Maybe.'

'I came out here for "maybe"? You'd be lucky to get me to answer my phone in the morning for "maybe", much less come out to a dump like this to talk to someone like you. I need more than "maybe", Cody. Or maybe I should give up on these little conversations and go home, and maybe you can go back to rotting inside.' I don't know if I mean 'in prison' or if I'm referring to the cancer.

'"Maybe" 's all I've got, Agent Rourke. Take it or leave it. Maybe you need it more than I do.'

I let that slide.

'How about you?' Cody continues. 'You been doing any thinking, Agent Rourke? Just maybe?' He smiles.

'I have, but not about what you're talking about. I want you to tell me about Holly Tynon again.'

This seems to confuse him. 'What about her? You want to know if I can tell you more about where I buried her?'

'Not exactly.'

'Good. I already told you, "maybe".'

'You grabbed her while she was walking home.'

'Right.'

'You took her, what, back to that cabin of yours?'

He pauses. A guarded look for a brief moment. 'Yeah.'

'You kept her there for a few days.'

'Uh-huh.' He still looks nervous, and I want to know why.

'Then you killed her, stuffed her body in a gym bag and buried her in some woods in a state park.'

'Like I said.'

'And you're sure about that,' I say. 'You're not confusing her with one of the others? Not just making this up, telling me what you think I want to hear?'

'Took that bitch, killed her, buried her in a bag.'

'So maybe you can tell me who this is?' I open the laptop, turn it round to face him. 'Because she looks to me like Holly Tynon, years older. I could be wrong, of course. But I want to know for certain what you did with her when you abducted her. No fucking maybes with this, Cody.'

Williams stays perfectly still for a moment, watching the video play itself out. Slowly, ever so slowly, his mouth cracks into a smile. A wolfish look breaks over his cracked lips.

'Well, now,' he says. 'That does make things interesting. Where'd you get it?'

'Turned up in my email yesterday. What did you do with the girl, Cody?'

He chuckles, fondly, or so it seems. 'Someone's been watching the news. That's real nice.'

'Who is it in that film?'

'What makes you think I'd know?' Carries on thinking, staring at the screen. The question is absentminded, softly spoken.

'You're the only one who can say for sure what happened to Holly, Cody.'

'Well, if that did happen to be her on this recording, and "maybe" it is,' he says, looking up from the laptop, 'then I certainly ain't the only one. Maybe I never knew at all.'

'Credit me with some sense. Even if all you did was pass her on to someone else, we both know it was you who abducted her in the first place. So stop dicking around and tell me, is that her in the video?'

'And if it was, you and your FBI buddies'd have to go find her, right? I guess that would be pretty fucking tough. Not much to go on in that film. Can't even see the guy she's with. Shame. She don't look good.'

I narrow my eyes. 'And if you know it's her, you'd know who she'd be with and where we'd find them. Can we skip the fucking around, Cody? What do you want in exchange for the information?'

Williams shakes his head, stifles a cough. 'Wrong question. I'm dead, one way or another. There's nothing that's gonna stop that, and so there ain't much anyone can give me that would really matter. Not that them dickwads I've seen outside would know that. Nah, the only question you *should* be asking is what *you're* willing to do to find that girl.'

'No, the question I need an answer to before we go any further is whether that's Holly or not, and whether I've got any reason to listen to your bullshit on this.'

'OK, Agent Rourke, I'll give you this one for free. She's changed, but I'd guess that was her. Surprised she lasted this long. I'll level with you, Agent Rourke . . .'

'Yeah?'

'. . . First off, I just wanted to fuck with you one last time. Y'know, give you the runaround, mess you around, fuck up your chances of finding them girls and make you look like a failure.'

'Nice.'

'It's all I've got left to me. I'd go happy to my grave knowing how the papers would be calling you a failure and shit. That'd be great.'

'I love you too, Cody.'

'But this,' he says, ignoring me and pointing at

the laptop. 'This changes everything. I never expected *this*.'

'So where is she? Who did you give her to?'

'Well, now, *that* ain't going to be free.' Williams smiles, exhaling in a blast of fetid air over his crooked teeth. 'How badly would you want to find her? How much can you sacrifice for her, eh? I've got nothing to lose here – I'm a dead man anyway. But what about you?'

I fold my arms. 'What do you want, Cody?'

'I want you to tell your other Feds that I was set up. I want you to admit that you framed me for killing Clinton Travers.'

I say nothing, sit still, keep staring at him.

'It's your choice,' Williams say. 'Nice easy one. You get to decide which is worth more to you – your career, or that girl's life.'

Chapter Thirteen

'So what's Williams playing at?' Rob asks. 'What does he want out of all this?'

We're nursing bottles of beer in a desperately trendy bar called Aqua. Busy, but not full. A crowd of identikit student types, indistinct in the spotlit gloom. Sugary spirit smell hanging in the air. Music playing just softly enough to hold a conversation. This choice of venue for a quiet evening drink came down to the place being within walking distance of both our homes, not its actual aesthetics.

'What do you mean?'

'Come on, Alex. You've been talking to the guy for long enough to have some kind of handle on him. Do you think he was always planning for the business with that video? What's the son of a bitch's angle?'

I take a swig of Bud. 'To start with, before he'd seen the video, this was all supposed to be a big joke for Cody. One last chance to get at me by lying about what he did with the missing bodies. Dredging everything up again.'

'He'd bother with that?'

'That's what he told me, and I've got no reason to doubt him. Not on this, anyway.'

'And then what?'

'He wasn't expecting to see this video, or that it'd get sent to me out of the blue. But he sure as hell knew what it was about as soon as he saw it.'

'You're so sure he was lying to you before, that the Tynon girl is really alive?'

'Yeah.' I think back to the look on his face, each little twitch, each flash of his eyes. 'Yeah, he was lying through his teeth, and he was enjoying it. That video changed his whole ballgame. Now he's got a far bigger carrot to offer me, and nothing to lose at all.'

'The guy *is* dying.'

'Yeah, and that puts him in a pretty unique bargaining position.'

Rob watches a couple of girls taking their pool shots at the table at the far end of the bar. 'So do you think you'll be able to get him to talk now? Figure the guy won't want to rat out whoever he gave the girl to, but none of them ever do.'

'And he doesn't want to either. I don't know how to get to him, though.' Another swig from the bottle. Conceal the half-truth behind the easy movement. Bury it, hide it. These little covering motions we all use to seal ourselves away, to avoid answering the awkward questions.

'Do you think he *could* give you this guy, even if you do break him? It's been a long time for him.'

'Yeah, I think he knows exactly where Holly is.'

'But he won't tell you.'

'No, he won't.'

One girl sinks the last ball, and her partner begins racking them up for a second game. 'What's going on between you and Williams, Alex?' Rob says, gesturing at me with his beer bottle.

'What do you mean?'

'Come on. We've been friends for a long time. It's pretty obvious the guy has a major problem with you, and it's obvious he thinks he's got something to gain by talking to you.'

'I told you, one last joke at my expense. I'm the guy who put him away.'

He raises an eyebrow. 'Which would explain a lot, but that's a pretty major fixation. Way beyond what anyone would normally show, even a backwoods psycho like him. What's he got against you, Alex?'

I finish the rest of my beer and gesture for another round from the barman. 'Williams was put away for killing Clinton Travers. He thinks I framed him for the murder.'

'Did you?' Rob doesn't hesitate.

It's a murky, unpleasant evening. An early nightfall and driving rain, and I'm watching myself drive from Massachusetts to Hartford. That's what it feels like, detached, floating somewhere behind my own head. My hands are white on the steering wheel, and I know that, down there, my mind, my *other* mind is full of Naomi Carson and the leer on Clinton Travers' face the last time I saw him.

In Hartford, I walk up the path in the rain, knock twice on Travers' door. More aware of my own actions, but still not wholly there. Still not sure exactly what I'm going to do.

When Travers answers my knock, it's obvious he's not sure what I'm going to do either. We head inside. I confront him, tell him I know what he did to Naomi and that he's finished. He laughs in my face. Taunts me. Aiming for a harassment lawsuit, maybe; I don't know.

I also don't know who throws the first punch, but I find myself laying into him. I'm wearing gloves, but the blows still hurt my fists. Hurt him more. He gets away from me, dives for a cupboard, comes out with a gun in his hands. It wasn't there during the search; he must've picked it up since.

I don't slow down. Grab him. Grab the pistol. He sprawls against the wall while I point his own gun at him.

Travers brushes the blood coming from his bruised mouth with the back of his hand and says, clear as a bell. 'What're you going to do, Feebie? You can't shoot me. You're already in so much shit for this – you're fucking toast, man.'

My mind is blank as my finger tightens on the trigger. His eyes go wide, and then I feel the gun buck in my hand, see the bullet punch a hole in his skull.

Mechanically, still blank, I check to make sure I've left nothing at the apartment that could identify me, then leave, back out into the rain, back to the car. Taking the gun with me.

I'm crossing the state line into Massachusetts when the reality of what's happened hits home. I snap back to full awareness, and I start to think of what the hell I'm going to do.

'Did you frame Williams?' Rob asks.
    'Yeah,' I say. 'Yeah, I did.'

Chapter Fourteen

'Jesus Christ, Alex.' Rob starts to say something else, then stops himself.

'In my years with the Bureau, that was the one time I stepped over the line, Rob. And don't tell me you've never had the same temptation, because we *all* do at some point.'

'We don't all act on them though, Alex. Jesus.'

I take a swig from the bottle. The beer is cold and bitter. 'I'm not proud of it, but that's the way it happened. And once you've crossed that line, you can't take it all back.'

Place the bottle back on the table. 'I just did what I had to do.'

Rob looks at me for a long while, measuring and reassessing me. Probably thinking back through all we've done over the years. Judging me anew.

'If we'd been able to build a case against either of them, I would never have snapped,' I say, trying to explain. 'But we couldn't, and I had one guy I knew was abducting and murdering little girls and another who was raping women right under our noses, including one of our own team, for fuck's sake.'

Rob keeps staring at me and I know he's playing me, the same way I've played dozens of people in interrogations down the years. But I can't help myself.' 'You get caught up in these things. I didn't think we were going to be able to stop them, and if we did, how many more people would be attacked and killed in the meantime? I already knew they were both guilty as hell, and I still do.'

Another swig of beer. 'Fuck, Rob, you should hear the way Williams talks about those girls. He's probably the nastiest piece of shit I've ever had to deal with. I'm glad he's inside and that he hasn't had the chance to kill anyone else.'

'Jesus,' he says again, this time to himself.

'Have you ever seen a dead child, Rob? In person. Right there in front of you.'

He shakes his head. 'No. Dead adults, sure.'

'It's not the same as a kid. You've got someone who's never done a damn thing to anyone because they haven't lived long enough. Someone whose future, all those dreams of theirs and their family's, will never come to be. It's not just someone who's been killed – it's someone who's never been given the chance to live. It's not the same at all. And when you've seen one, you can imagine the others . . .'

Rob stays silent for a moment, then orders us both another beer. 'How'd you do it?'

'When I went to confront Travers, he pulled a gun on me. We fought, I grabbed it off him. I shot him with it.'

'How'd you get Williams?'

'When Williams was arrested for trying to abduct

Nicole Ballard, I knew we'd get a warrant to search his house, so I made sure I had the gun with me when we went round there. I "found" it under some old blankets in his closet. I already knew that odds were he didn't have an alibi – Williams *never* did anything with other people outside work. The defence tried to argue that he had no motive to kill Travers, but even they couldn't argue with the ballistics.'

Rob raises an eyebrow. 'That was enough?'

'You don't have to prove motive, Rob. The guy was a known fuckbag already on the way to an attempted child abduction conviction, and he had no excuse for how the gun came to be there. Except that "the cops put it there."'

'And everyone claims that.' His voice is oddly quiet.

'Right. No one believes that story. Least not with just a public defender like he had.'

'So at the trial you put forward the theory that he shot Travers so he couldn't steal his limelight after Travers' name was leaked to the media,' Rob says. 'His attorney didn't pull that to pieces in court?'

I shrug. 'I got the impression he thought as little of Williams as I did. He made some effort to discredit the idea, but there's enough accepted background on murder as a form of attention-seeking that he didn't manage to sink it. The other theory we had for the prosecution was that Williams may have gone there to suggest to Travers that they team up, but that they'd argued and fought.'

'Thank Christ you didn't have to rely on that one.'

'Yeah. But like I said, you don't have to prove motive. It's all in the physical evidence.'

Rob shakes his head. 'Shit, Alex. I don't know what to say. It's no wonder he's pissed at you.'

'Trust me, I know that. I've carried the knowledge of what I did for seven years now. Damned near broke me completely.'

'And he wants you to give it up in return for telling you the truth about what he did with those girls. Shit,' he says again. 'What're you going to do?'

Holly Tynon's mother looks up at me with her blank, cold eyes and tells me her daughter's dead. Clinton Travers opens his mouth, blood trickling from his nose, and starts to say something as I squeeze the trigger.

I swallow the rest of the beer and order another. 'I'm going to hope something turns up on the analysis of the footage that can tell me where it was shot . . .'

'You're not going to confess?'

'. . . Failing that, I'm going to hope whoever sent me the first sequence sends me more . . .'

'So you're not going to confess?'

'. . . And I'm going to do anything else I can to trace its origin and find out what Williams really did with those girls.'

'But you're not going to do what he wants?'

The eyes of a missing thirteen-year-old girl stare out at me from under the lank hair of a grown woman, caught in grainy video. With it, the feeling of cold isolation and the sense of fate lost and locked away: the prison cell awaiting me if I do what Williams asks.

'I'm sorry,' I tell him. 'I can't.'

Chapter Fifteen

The next day, I spend an uncomfortable few hours at the jail, trying to persuade Williams to talk to me. But he sticks to his guns and won't give me anything more than vague hints that he knows what happened to Holly, and maybe the others too. So I give up with him and go to see what we've been able to find in the footage.

Grey clouds are deepening to murky ocean blue-black as daylight fades, and run-off sluicing from guttering high above hammers against Sophie's umbrella, falling around me in sheets of water. I'm about to push the bell again when there's the crack of the intercom coming to life.

'Brandon? It's Alex and Sophie.'

'Hi,' the voice says, muffled and distorted. 'Come on in.'

The door buzzes and we push through, doing our best to keep beneath the umbrella's shelter before Sophie whisks it inside after her. An empty cream-coloured hallway that smells of plastic and damp. Past the stairwell and elevator, a row of numbered doors, one of which swings open as I rub the rain from my hair and Sophie shakes out her umbrella.

Brandon's a lanky kid, somewhere over six foot,

with another inch of sharply spiked black hair on top. Pale-blue sweat pants and a baggy T-shirt with the slogan 'Don't Blame Me – I Voted For Kodos' and a picture of the alien from *The Simpsons* on it.

'Hey,' he says with a half-wave. 'Sorry – wasn't expecting you guys just yet. Halfway through eating dinner.'

'Sorry,' Sophie says. 'We tried to beat the rain by leaving early.'

'Heh. Looks like that didn't work out. It's like God's taking a piss out there.'

'That water you've got outside the front door did a fair bit of this,' I tell him as I pass into his apartment. 'That's got to be a real pain in the ass for you living here, walking through that every time there's a shower.'

'Broken guttering. I've been on to the manager about it, but he hasn't fixed it yet.' Brandon lets the door close, then leads us through to the front room of the cramped studio apartment. 'Sorry about the mess,' he says.

It's not as bad as he makes out. An unmade bed in one corner, a TV playing CNN on mute, a few clothes, books and other personal detritus scattered here and there. One wall is dominated by electronics – a stereo, stacks of CDs, a computer left on, its screen powered down, half a dozen peripheral devices and, tucked amid the bundle of papers on the desk, the edge of a laptop case. A track from the 'Goldberg Variations', slow and eerie, plays through the speakers.

A fluorescent tabletop lamp and the glow from the TV scatter harsh, flickering blue shadows.

Brandon scoops up a plate bearing a half-eaten pizza from the bed and sits in front of the computer. He gestures at the only other two chairs in the room and says, 'Have a seat. Where's this video you want me to look at?'

I hand him a CD. 'It's the only file on there.'

'What do you need?' He slots it into the drive.

'Anything you can pick out, detail-wise. The lighting's bad, so there may be things you can pick up by brightening the background. Anything you can find that's distinctive, or anything that was buried by noise. Or anything that would suggest this film is actually a commercial release that someone's using as a hoax.' The drive hums into life as the computer reads the disk. 'And you're OK with the content?'

'Worse things get posted online every day. To borrow a quote, "I've seen shit that'll turn you white."' Brandon shrugs and smiles. 'Course I don't generally try pulling it to pieces to see what I can find. But I still doubt there's anything in it that's worse than stuff I've already seen.'

He copies the movie file on to his hard drive and opens up three different programs, scattering them around his desktop so he can work with each simultaneously. 'By the way,' he says, as he clicks 'play', 'aren't the Feds supposed to be doing this?'

'They are. But I'd like to see the results first-hand, and it never hurts to get a second opinion. There's not even any guarantee they'll tell me what they find. They're not under any obligation.'

On screen, the camera slowly moves towards the girl hanging from the roof beam. She thrashes and bucks in total silence.

'Standard MPEG-1 compression,' Brandon says, eyes fixed in front of him. 'Doesn't seem to be anything weird in its encoding. No sound at all. Either the recording was made on a camera with no sound pick-up – which seems unlikely, unless it was set to mute – or the entire audio layer was stripped out afterwards. In any case, it ain't there.'

'Is there any particular reason why they'd do that?'

'No audio makes the file size smaller. If you wanted to stick this on the net, that'd make it easier to watch and download, and saves on your bandwidth. It happens quite a lot – porno samples, funny or nasty video clips on sites with a lot of traffic. There's less reason to do that if it's just one copy for email to you, unless they were worried about making it too large and having it bounce from your inbox.'

'So it might be existing footage that some joker's just pulled off the net?'

'Could be,' Brandon says, clicking on one of his subsidiary programs. It starts saving frames from the footage every few seconds, capturing each in a separate still image. 'But if I didn't want to be identified, I wouldn't want any risk of my voice appearing on video. No names, nothing to give it away. Besides, I don't recognize anything about this footage. Most of the classic clips do the rounds of the big compilation sites. If someone's grabbed it online, they found it somewhere obscure.'

'Yeah?'

'Yeah. And she's not a pro porn actress, that's for sure.'

'You know that many of them?'

He shrugs. 'Not my bag, but we live in the internet age. Figure it out.'

The woman starts crying, and the camera moves away, past the halogen lamp and into the darkness. Brandon checks the still images piling up in the window on the right of his screen.

'I don't know how much detail we'll be able to pull out of these,' he says. 'The footage is heavily compressed. You can see the edges of the blocks it's broken up into quite clearly in some of these. Mosquitoes too.'

'Which are?'

'Speckling, distortion, a kind of blurring where you have very sharp edges between light and dark areas. Common problem.'

'If anything had been changed – like her face, for instance – could you tell from differences in that kind of distortion?'

Brandon nods. 'Sure. I'll resample some of these stills. Any changes in tone, colour or level of distortion from anything that's been spliced in should stick out pretty clearly.'

A few clicks of the mouse and the woman's face

and the scene around her become progressively blockier and more heavily pixellated.

'It all looks even to me,' Sophie says behind me. I'm glad she sounds confident – I'm not entirely sure what I should be looking for. 'It all seems to match.'

'Yeah, the tone and colour's the same, and the overall quality and patterning of each block is consistent. Whoever she is, that's not a face someone's pasted in from elsewhere. That's the real her.'

I point at the stills taken from the seconds the camera stays in the darkness, looking at what could be the edge of a table with light glinting off something metallic. 'Can you lighten these up?' I ask. 'Maybe we can see what the camera's looking at.'

'Easily done. I'll do the same with any of the earlier ones where the background is visible. Something might stick out of the gloom.'

Brandon spends another hour playing with the images at his disposal, brightening, sharpening, resizing. At the end, he runs off printouts of the results and hands them to me.

'Sorry,' he says. 'Not much there, not with such a low resolution recording.'

I skim the results, passing them to Sophie as I finish with each one. The two pages that hold my eye for the longest are blown-up and brightened stills from the shots in darkness. Even through the digital noise, I can see a tabletop, what looks like a riding crop, a crude metal baton with wire running from one end, a couple of spare sets of manacles.

'Someone takes their shit seriously,' Brandon says. 'Wish I could tell you more about him.'

Sophie looks at the last of the pictures, then hands the whole bundle back to me. 'Are you going to go through it frame by frame just in case?'

'Yeah. It'll take me a day or two. I doubt there's anything else there – haven't seen any sign of it if there is. But you never know, huh?'

Half an hour after saying goodbye to Brandon, Sophie and I are sitting in Gattuso's, an Italian restaurant not far from the river. Not especially large, brightly coloured – pale-blue carpet, ash furniture – but this effect is lost in the subdued lighting the place uses after dark. A distant clatter of noise from the kitchens, murmured conversation from the tables around us. The aroma of garlic and tomatoes hanging in the air.

'Can I ask you a question, Alex?' Sophie says, laying her fork down.

'Sure.'

'Why is this thing eating at you like this? I mean, I know it was your case originally, and I know you think Holly's still alive. But you're becoming obsessed.'

I wonder whether to reveal all, tell her everything I told Rob, spill the lot for a second time. Let the chips fall where they may. But I know that would be crazy. Instead, I sigh and say, 'It was my case, and I thought I'd got the right guy. But if Holly really is still alive then I made a mistake, and she's paid for it with seven years of her life and God knows what kind of trauma. In the end, I'm responsible for that. I've shot, and killed, several people in my career.'

'Yeah, but . . .'

'People I've arrested have had families, innocents who'd only get to see their father or mother, kids or parents, on the other side of a sheet of glass for the next ten-to-twenty. But at the end of the day, I've only ever done that kind of shit when someone's done something to deserve it. Holly Tynon didn't, and the fact she's faced what's she's faced because of me and a mistake I made is killing me.'

She nods and fixes me with her wide eyes. 'The FBI don't believe she's alive,' she says softly. 'And if there was a mistake it was as much their fault as yours. That footage might just be someone's home porno video.'

'Agent Downes never had to face Holly Tynon's parents and try to find some way of telling them that their only daughter had in all probability been raped and murdered and was lying in a shallow grave somewhere. She never had to see the look in their eyes like their entire world had collapsed around them. She's confident, but can't be entirely sure, that Holly is dead. I can see the same odds, and all they mean to me is that there's a chance she's alive, a chance I never realized existed before now. So I've got to try.'

We eat in silence for a few minutes more. The cannelloni is good, solidly rich in flavour. The wine is also pretty good, although I'm no expert. Truth be told, I'm not paying much attention to either. Too much else on my mind.

Eventually, Sophie finishes her spaghetti and reaches for her glass. 'How are you, Alex?' she says. 'I never get the chance to ask at the office.'

'I'm OK.'

'You look thin. Really tired. Is anything bothering you, or is it just having to look at the old case again?'

I swill the remaining Merlot around the bottom of my glass before downing it in one and reaching for a refill. Sophie nods when I offer her one. 'It's mostly nothing or, at least, nothing unusual. Yeah, the whole Williams thing is a part of it. There's some other stuff as well that I can't talk about.'

'No?'

'No. But in any case it's mostly just, well, me, I suppose. I wouldn't expect you to understand it at your age.'

'You're thinking of going through a mid-life crisis then?' she asks with a mischievous look in her eyes, glinting at me from over her wine glass. 'You've already got the flash car, so I suppose you're halfway there already. Just need the ponytail and the twenty-year-old girlfriend.'

I smile. 'Hey, I've had the 'Vette for years. Way too long for it to be a vain attempt to recapture my youth.'

'And I don't think the ponytail would really suit you either.'

'Yeah, not my style.'

'Somehow I can't picture you with anything apart from the cut you've got now.'

'You should have seen me in my college years. My first year I had long hair, scruffy T-shirts, the works. Even tried a beard at one point. Well, I say "tried", but in reality I was just too lazy to shave.'

Sophie laughs, bringing her hand up to her mouth as she throws her head back. 'Please tell me there's photographic evidence somewhere. That I *have* to see.'

'I'm afraid not. Over the years, a series of unexplained thefts and fires have conspired to destroy as much of it as possible. And I'm not telling you where I went to college – no class or department photos for you either.'

'I'm working for a detective agency, Alex. I'm sure I can find out.'

I shake my head. 'I may have to resort to threats, bribery or extortion if you try.'

'If it's any consolation, I spent a month at high school walking around with this awful spiky punk cut.'

'Only a month before you came to your senses? You were lucky.'

'I found out how bad it was when the guy I had a crush on told me I looked like a porcupine that'd been struck by lightning in a paint factory.'

'Everyone's a critic,' I say, grinning.

'Yeah, I guess.' She fixes me with her eyes for a moment. The same intense gaze she's had since I first met her, but calmer now, adolescent growing pains all gone. Then she smiles. 'I'm glad you've lightened up a little, Alex, even if it's just for now. It's not good for you to let things get on top of you all the time.'

'Yeah,' I say.

After dinner, Sophie and I say our goodbyes and I head for home, the image of the woman's face in those stills never far from the front of my mind. Sharpened, image-enhanced, magnified as much as possible. Eyes wide, glassy, scared. And the more I think about them, the more I'm certain it's Holly who's staring back at me.

I'm in a long, high-ceilinged room. Red velvet wallpaper and wood panelling, dim bulbs in sconces way up on either side. A vast table of polished walnut sits at its heart, surrounded by high-backed chairs. I walk forward, into the light, head bowed. I can feel tears drying on my cheeks.

'You know why you're here,' Brooke Morgan says, as I reach the head of the table. A child sits in each chair, each wearing an oversized black gown. They're all watching me.

'We know what you did,' Abbie Galina says. Some of the girls have bruised faces, red-black marks around their necks. The hands peeking from the hems of the robes have purple welts and torn nails.

'You know what we want.'

I run my eyes over the faces staring at me. Holly Tynon is the only one missing. There are no empty seats.

A shuffling sound behind me, feet sliding uncertainly against the carpet. The scent of water, sweat. I brush my face with my fingertips, rub the tear tracks, and come back with red smears, drying blood still tacky to the touch. I know that if I turn round now I'll see Travers lurching towards me, skull shattered and bloody from the bullet I put through it. He's coming for me, and there's nothing I can do to stop him.

The dead girls watch, impassive, as I scramble on to the table and half-run, half-skid along its surface. At the far end, I try to jump down and run, but there's nothing there except a dark hole, and I fall as Travers starts shooting behind me.

Sit up to find myself fully dressed, on the couch, and the phone's ringing. At first I think it's still night, but the drapes are drawn and my watch says it's nearly eight in the morning.

'Yeah?' I say.

'Mr Rourke? This is Detective Sergeant Jack Gilbert from Hartford Police Department. Sorry to call you so early, but I was hoping to catch you before you left for work. I understand you're being kept busy at the moment.'

'That's OK, no problem. What can I do for you?'

'Just a courtesy call, really. Thought I'd give you the heads-up that we've had a couple of reporters call the last day or two, asking about one of our old cases.'

'The Clinton Travers rapes.'

'Good guess.'

'Only case I've worked in Hartford, Sergeant Gilbert.'

'Yeah. Well, they were interested in the whole saga really, but especially his shooting. Wanted to know what we found at the scene, things like that. How we linked it to your boy Williams.'

I keep my tone non-committal. 'Uh-huh.'

'Just thought you should know in case they come calling on you too.' The cop pauses, and I wonder how much of his build-up has been for effect. 'Not that I had much to tell them, just that there were signs of a struggle at the scene, and the guy's gun was missing. No prints, no usable trace evidence we could identify the intruder with. Some witnesses reported hearing a gunshot, but no one saw anyone leaving or arriving at the house.'

'Yeah, I remember. Too bad no one had kept him under surveillance.'

'Well, after what he did to Detective Carson, we would've nailed him before long. Guess we were just lucky your guy took such a dislike to him. Why'd you think he did that?'

'Williams is a fucking psycho, Sergeant Gilbert. Who knows why he does anything?' I sigh. 'Is that all? Only I've got to get ready for work.'

'Yeah, that's all. Just an FYI, in case anyone bothers you. Frank Sutherland from the, ah, *Herald News*, and Jason Curtis from the *Connecticut Post*. Take it easy.'

I hang up, trying to figure out if Gilbert was just making conversation, satisfying idle curiosity, or inferring he suspected what really happened. And if it was the latter, what he thought of it.

*

Winter, and a Boston courtroom. High ceiling, bathed in the blue-white glow of fluorescent strip lights. That wood-and-red-carpet school of decorating so beloved of the justice system's interior designers. The distant hum of the heating system, audible over the faint and muffled rustle of the crowd of people staring back at me. Each breath, each scrape of clothing on clothing multiplied a hundredfold, the white noise sighing of distant surf.

I'm sitting watching proceedings, uncomfortable in a sombre graphite-coloured suit. I've done my time on the witness stand, and I'm still hoping I didn't screw up my testimony. Out front, the prosecuting attorney, a woman maybe five years older than me, with a sweep of brown hair and a friendly, open face hiding her laser-like focus on the facts, has just finished her summing-up for the jury.

I told the court how Cody Williams may have felt so aggrieved at Clinton Travers' expansive press coverage that he felt he had to eliminate him before abducting Nicole Ballard, trying to ensure maximum exposure for his own planned misdeeds. I couldn't mention the other girls, because he's not on trial for what he did to them. I explained how, in interviews with Williams, he revealed himself to be an arrogant, self-aggrandizing monster who loved to receive the attention he felt he had been denied in his normal, everyday life. I ran through the state's preferred scenario for what happened on the night Travers was murdered, and explained Williams' role in the whole thing.

Now it's the defence's turn to sum up their case. Cody Williams' lawyer hardly seems thrilled at the job he's having to do – something about the eyes, no real emotion to them – but something drives him on. He's young, and from the looks of things knows that, unpleasant or not, this case is very high profile and the TV exposure alone could make his career. No one can say that Cody Williams abducted and killed all those girls, but everyone's thinking it, and there's been a regular media mob outside during the trial.

The attorney, whose name I vaguely remember being given as Luther Ellwood, pushes his glasses up the bridge of his nose as he reaches the climax, saying, 'The man you see before you is not the freak of nature, not the monster the prosecution would have you believe. Cody Williams is a good man, a decent man. He has never denied trying to seize Nicole Ballard, but he has shown throughout his testimony that he acted out of a misguided desire to protect her, having been so concerned about the stories in the media about these poor children. Irrational, certainly, but his motives were good. He is not a man deserving of your hatred, but of your pity. He is not a man needing punishment, but a man needing treatment and re-education. He is not a monster, but a decent soul who became caught up in events he couldn't fully comprehend.

'That is his only crime.'

For the next few days I stay in my apartment. I ignore every phone call that's not from someone I know.

The first evening, Brandon calls to tell me he's finished checking out the footage frame by frame.

'Sorry,' he says. 'Nothing much more there than what you saw last night. Your friends at the FBI might be more use, but I doubt it – I didn't see anything that might have helped, even if I'd been able to sharpen everything to photo quality.'

'What about any information buried in the footage itself – digital signatures, things like that?'

'If there's anything there, it was hidden by someone who knows more than I do. Which wouldn't be hard – kinda out of my usual department.'

'Oh, well. Thanks for checking – I appreciate it. You OK to look at any more that turn up?'

'Sure,' he says. 'No problem.'

He hangs up, and I sit in my armchair, thinking. There doesn't seem to be anything more to learn from the footage, and I still can't even be certain it's not something someone found online and sent to me for a joke. Some piece of random porno with just enough suggested menace to make it work.

But what if the reverse is true, and the film's maker attempted to sell his footage to commercial porn distributors, just to make an easy buck off something he was doing already?

I fire up my computer and start making a list of email addresses. A request for information, a few stills from the film, a suggestion of the seriousness of the crimes involved. A shot in the dark, but not much different to similar efforts we make in half the missing persons cases the agency handles. You have to try every possibility.

Over the following couple of days, a handful of people leave messages – mostly reporters with the same line of crap they were spouting before. Rob calls to make sure I'm OK. I ask him to let the jail at Ashworth know that I'm ill and won't be seeing Williams for a little while. Apart from that, I circle the wagons and barely move from my chair in the lounge.

Holly's picture stares at me from the coffee table, and I can't think of any other way of tracing her, no matter how hard I try.

I don't want to face Williams again – both of us are locked into our courses, our individual choices, and I see little chance of anything changing.

But I can't give up on her, not like I did all those years ago.

In the files detailing Cody's background, I find a mention of his first cellmate, Billy Perry. They shared for a couple of years before Perry's release, and his last known address was in Boston.

If Cody said anything after he was convicted, he said it to Perry.

But the problem is that he no longer lives at his last known address, and seems to have dropped off the radar entirely. I start chasing up every record I can find on Perry, calling everyone I can think of for scraps of information.

The only thing I can find of any interest comes from a friend in the BPD. At one point, three years ago, they suspected Perry was involved in loansharking for one of the city's mobsters, a guy called Gabriel Heller.

However, as far as the cops know, that's all over and Perry hasn't stuck his head above the parapet since. No one knows where he is.

On Tuesday, Tanya Downes calls. 'The image lab has finished analysing your video clip, Alex,' she says. 'I've got some stills they took from the footage, sharpened and magnified as much as they were able.'

'Do they show very much?'

'I'm afraid the results aren't especially impressive – too much data was lost in the video compression. I've compared them to age-adjusted pictures of Holly Tynon and I'm still not convinced. Any similarities are extremely vague. I'll email them to you anyway.'

I thank her even though I *am* convinced. 'Is that all?' I say.

'Is Williams being any more cooperative?'

'I haven't spoken to him for a few days. He wasn't giving me much, nothing to confirm or deny the truth of what happened to Holly or the other girls. So I left him to stew for a while. If he thinks he's lost the limelight, maybe he'll be a little more forthcoming.'

'You haven't heard?' She sounds surprised.

'About what?'

'Ashworth's management said they'd called you a couple of days ago – Williams has taken a major turn for the worse. The doctors can't give a definite figure, but they estimated his survival at days rather than weeks. You don't have time to let him sit things out,

Alex. If you can't get him to talk soon, we might never get a chance to do so again.'

I sigh. 'And the doctors have said I can still speak to him?'

'As far as I know, Williams himself hasn't ruled the idea out. If he's still strong enough to take the stress of an interview, and if he wants to see you, I'd guess they'll allow it. Everyone knows what's riding on this.'

'I'll talk to him tomorrow,' I say and hang up. I'm angry, at Williams for dying, at the Bureau for pushing me back together with him, and with myself, for not identifying his accomplice and the real fate of the girls they snatched back when it wasn't too late.

I turn on the coffee machine in the tiny kitchen, staying there until it's finished gurgling. I stare through the window as the rich, bitter aroma rises from the mug like sour incense. Night has fallen outside, and my apartment is silent save for the hum of distant traffic and the clawing of a guilty conscience futilely trying to escape, scratching behind my eyes, to undo past mistakes, to rewrite history.

Checking my email for the message from Tanya, I find that the stills she's sent aren't much different to those made by Brandon, and even on these the graininess and blurring makes it impossible to make out any fresh detail.

When I close her message, a second is waiting for me.

Return-Path: unknown@unknown.com
Delivered-To: alex@r-garrett-assoc.com
Received: from unknown by mail.r-garrett-assoc.com
with SMTP
Message-ID: none
From: unknown@unknown.com
To: alex@r-garrett-assoc.com
Subject: ATTN: Ex-Special Agent Rourke – Case
Information

Message:
You need to see more?
<<h_t_seg6.mpg>>

Chapter Sixteen

The video opens abruptly, much like the first, and seems to be cut arbitrarily, mid-scene, no sense of a natural beginning or pause in the action. No way of telling where it falls in relation to the earlier segment. Holly is lashed, spread-eagled, to what looks like another ancient iron bed with a bare mattress spattered here and there with old, dried stains and marks. In the harsh lighting of the footage, there's no way of telling much about them. A couple could be blood at a guess, but I can't be sure. Again, there's no sound. The room she's in could be the same as the first segment, but the bare wood walls and floor could just as easily be somewhere else in the building. No window in shot, nothing to give some idea of the surroundings.

For a moment, the camera lingers on Holly, panning up and down, her captor eyeing her up. She lies still on the bed, her only movement the rise and fall of her chest. She's breathing fast and shallow, afraid, maybe even sobbing.

The camera moves back a little and shakes for a couple of seconds, I guess mirroring the actions of the man behind it. Then forward again, right up to the bedside. Holly's head flicks towards it and she starts screaming soundlessly. The cameraman brings up a two-pronged metal fork wrapped with wiring. Not hard to guess what its intended purpose is. With something of a flourish, he snaps it downwards, riding-crop style, against Holly's midriff. Her whole body jerks as it hits, and when the cameraman raises the fork again there's an angry red burn on her flesh.

Twice more he brings the makeshift electric prod down on to her, holding it against her for longer each time. The last blow lands on her right breast, and when the fork is raised out of sight again, tears are pouring from Holly's eyes. Not even screaming any more, just weeping helplessly in the unearthly silence of the film.

The camera jerks slightly and changes position as the man seems to clamber on to the foot of the bed, positioning himself between her legs. The view zooms in on her crying face, and then the footage ends as abruptly as it began.

I go to the bathroom and rinse my face under the cold tap. Stare at my eyes in the mirror and try not to imagine the years of torture and abuse that girl has suffered. In some ways, I wish she had been killed all that time ago. In others, I hope she's never found, that I'll never have to face her parents once they know the full horror of what has happened, and those old wounds have been opened afresh.

Back at the computer, I send copies of the new footage to Downes and Brandon. With the latter email, I include a warning that what's inside is worse than before, and that if he doesn't want to examine it for me, I won't hold it against him.

Williams' eyes flicker open as I drop into the chair next to his bed in the prison hospital. His skin is the colour of milk gone sour, covered with a sheen of damp and the faint reek of a body going badly wrong. A machine off to one side monitors his vital signs. Next to it, a drip feeds fluids into his failing body.

'Not a pretty sight,' he says, voice hardly more than a mumble.

'You never were, Cody.' Wrong to speak ill of the dying, but I don't like him enough to care.

He makes a hacking sound that could be a chuckle. 'In a strange way I kinda like you, Agent Rourke. You're like the idiot kid brother I never had.'

'I'm touched.'

He closes his eyes again. 'Not long to go now, Agent Rourke.'

'I've got the champagne ready in the fridge at home.'

'And I'll be dead, and you'll never find that girl. Unless you pay the price first.'

'It's not her, Cody. The film was a fake. That girl was a porn actress called Shawnie Croft. We tracked her to a studio in Los Angeles, her and the guy who shot the film. I just came to tell you that we know it's all bullshit.'

Williams lurches into a semblance of life, tilting his head up from the pillow to stare at me. 'You're lying,' he says. 'That film was the real shit. I'd know her eyes anywhere. He always–'

He stops himself in mid-sentence, regards me coldly. 'Very clever, Agent Rourke. You nearly caught me with that one. But you didn't. You ain't getting nothing from me unless you admit what you did.'

I could try sticking with the bluff, but he's wise to it and I know it. 'That's not going to happen, Cody,' I tell him. 'And even if I did agree to it, knowing you, you'd break your end of the agreement.'

'Why bother?'

'Spite. Some feeling of revenge against me; you've already told me that's what you wanted. And there's the fact that you're an evil little fuckbag who's never done shit if there was nothing in it for him.'

A feeble smirk. 'Flattery ain't gonna get you anywhere.'

'You want me to believe you'd uphold your side of things, you've got to show me you can be trusted. Give me something to go on now.'

'As a gesture of good faith, you mean? I've seen this movie, Agent Rourke. I tell you a little something and you say that's good, but not enough, that you need more. And pretty soon you've got everything I know and you don't do jack in return. That ain't happening to me.'

I sigh and pinch the bridge of my nose. I'd love to choke the answer out of him, if I thought it'd work. 'Well, if you're wise to my plan, then you can just give me that first little piece and refuse the rest.

You've got as far as admitting you know who "he" is. Might as well go a step further.'

Williams says nothing, just lies there.

'Without some sign you can be trusted, I'm not doing a damn thing,' I tell him.

'It's all or nothing, Agent Rourke,' he says without looking at me. 'Which one of us has more to lose?'

Seconds, then minutes, tick by in silence. I stay sitting in the chair, watching the dying man in front of me. He doesn't show any sign that he's willing to say any more, and I'm sure as hell not going to give him the satisfaction of blinking first, so I stand to leave.

'I'm going now, Cody. Unless you want to play ball, this is the last time you'll see me. Make your mind up.'

The hacking laugh cuts the air again. 'Not the last time, Agent Rourke. I'll be seeing you in hell.'

Chapter Seventeen

In the warm, humid corridor outside, I call Downes to give her the news. 'We're getting nothing from him,' I say. 'He's clammed up for good. I doubt he ever wanted to say anything much to me in the first place. I think he just wanted one more laugh before he died.'

'Are you sure about this? I don't want to tell the families we've failed if you're not sure, or if this is just something you don't want to do.'

'I told you right at the start that if I thought it was going nowhere, or if I didn't want to talk to him any further, I'd walk away and there'd be no complaints from you or the Bureau. My conditions, remember?'

She sighs. 'I remember, Alex. I just don't want you jumping to a hasty decision on this if you're not a hundred per cent sure it's over. You know how important this is to everyone.'

'Trust me, it's over.'

'You're absolutely sure?'

'It's over.' The line falls silent for a moment. 'Did you get the second piece of film I emailed you? At the moment, those pieces of footage seem to be the best chance we've got of finding out what happened to Holly and the others.'

'I did, and I'll send it to the image lab just as we did with the first one. But I think you're wrong about them being the best chance we have, Alex; you know I don't believe the woman in the film is Holly.'

'It's not like you've tried to hide that, no.'

'Cody gave you directions to the place where he claimed he dumped her body. The locations he marked on the map, both for Holly and Katelyn, are very vague, but given what we know of his movements, the places he knew and would have felt comfortable hiding her corpse, we've come up with two reasonably solid search areas. Examination of the ground is due to start today.'

'You won't find anything,' I tell her. 'Not at the place he's supposed to have dumped Holly, anyway.'

'You don't know that.'

'I've spoken to the guy about it, and that convinced me.'

'We'd be fools not to look, though. Was there anything in the description he gave you that you didn't pass on, anything at all?'

'I don't think so.'

'The Tynon dump site is only a half-hour from Ashworth,' she says, after a moment's thought. 'Even if you can't remember anything else he may have suggested to you, I'd like you to go down there and see the ground for yourself with our team. Something might seem familiar from Williams' description – you're the only person who's talked to him directly, after all. Please?'

'We won't find anything,' I say again. 'That whole story of his was bullshit.'

'Do you really want to explain to the press why you didn't think it worthwhile checking out? Especially if you're wrong and we do find something?' she replies sharply.

'There's going to be fuck all there, and there's nothing I'm going to add to your search effort. And I don't give a fuck for the press either. You honestly think they'll say I should have been down there with a goddamn shovel?'

She sighs. 'I didn't mean to snap, Alex, but you know how much interest there's been already. We've been taking our share of flak as well, and I really don't want to face any more, from outside or within the Bureau. Please? It won't take long.'

'It's a waste of time I could be spending trying to find Holly Tynon. Alive. Sorry, Tanya, but I'm not doing it.'

'Jesus, Alex.'

The line goes dead. Something tells me I'm not going to be speaking to her again.

Stopping to fill up the 'Vette on the way back from the prison, I pick up a copy of the *Herald*. A couple of pages in, I see that they're still working on the Williams story. Digging deeper. Muddying the waters.

Beyond Reasonable Doubt?

Seven years ago, a Massachusetts man was sent to prison for life for a murder he always denied committing, on evidence that was less than overwhelming. Now, Cody Williams is dying in jail. A just fate for a convicted killer, or the terrible price of a miscarriage of justice?

It was a sunny October morning, and Shanya and Terry Owen had just walked their eleven-year-old son David to West Rise Junior High in Brockton when they heard a young girl screaming in terror. In a nearby side street, they found twelve-year-old Nicole Ballard struggling valiantly with a man who was fighting to carry her into a waiting van.

While Shanya called 911 on her cell phone, Terry rushed to Nicole's aid. He wrestled the man to the ground and managed to hold him there until the police arrived. Cody Williams had been caught red-handed.

At the time, the region was in the grip of a series of child abductions. Williams was, naturally, a suspect, and his home was searched. Police found a bracelet that had belonged to Kerry Abblit, one of the missing girls – a bracelet Williams would later claim he'd bought from a yard sale. No other traces of the children were found at his home, but police did find a handgun hidden in his closet.

This weapon would send Cody Williams to jail for the rest of his life.

The gun bore the fingerprints of an ex-con named Clinton Travers, a suspect in a series of rapes in Connecticut a few months previously, whose name had leaked to the media. Travers had been found dead at his home, shot in the face after an apparent struggle. Testing confirmed that it was this weapon that had killed Travers. Cody Williams had no alibi for the time of the killing.

Although he denied any involvement, he was charged with murder, tried and convicted.

At his trial, the prosecution alleged that Williams had been jealous of Travers' press attention and wanted him out of the way when he embarked on his own crimes. There was no evidence to support this beyond conjecture.

Key witness for the prosecution was the FBI agent leading the investigation into the missing girls, Special Agent Alex Rourke. He had spoken with Cody Williams during the early part of the investigation and had rated him among the main suspects. He also interviewed him repeatedly after his arrest.

Rourke's testimony was vital to the case.

Before the abductions began, Rourke had worked in New England previously. He had assisted police in Hartford, Connecticut, on the Travers rapes. Rourke had been present at a police search of Travers' home and had interviewed the man himself.

The Hartford rapes had, in fact, stopped for some time – possibly due to considerable police vigilance – before, on that fateful night, one of the investigators themselves, Detective Naomi Carson, was assaulted.

This newspaper has spoken with the police on duty that night, and with friends of Detective Carson. Speaking exclusively, Detective Sergeant Ed Frost told us: 'Yeah, I had to, uh, spread the word about what had happened that night. I called some of the team working the case, and a few of her friends – y'know, so they wouldn't hear it second-hand.'

'Did that include Agent Rourke?'

'Yeah. He'd worked with us, and I knew he was pretty friendly with Naomi. I figured he'd better know.'

'How did he take it?'

'He was shocked, I guess. And angry. If we'd kept up the watch on Travers, he thought it wouldn't have happened. Everyone took it hard, y'know.'

'Rourke was angry? Furious?'

'Yes.'

Travers was shot with what appears to have been his own weapon after a struggle around midnight that same day. The killer took the gun with them from the scene. It only surfaced again during the search of Cody Williams' house.

Police evidence logs show that after entering Williams' home that October morning, the man who found the handgun was none other than Agent Rourke.

Chapter Eighteen

'So where do you go from here?' Rob asks. I'm back in the office for the first time in what seems like forever. The kids are all out on assignment, and the place is empty apart from us.

'I'm not sure. I need to speak to people who knew Williams, maybe some of those involved in the original cases. See if there was anything we missed first time around, or if anything surfaced afterwards that was disregarded because we'd got the guy. And Brandon might still find something in the footage background, or the porn producers I've contacted might come back with something.'

'That's a lot of legwork.'

'Are you offering me the time off to do it?'

Rob rubs his chin and thinks for a moment before answering. 'Things are pretty quiet right now. We've had nothing major come in for the past few days, and the middling jobs Kathryn's more than capable of handling. If something does turn up, then obviously I'll have to rethink this, but for the time being, yeah, keep working on it.'

'Thanks, Rob. I appreciate that.'

He waves it away. 'If Holly Tynon really is still

alive, it's the right thing to do. In fact, if it'll save time, I'll help you with some of it.'

'Are you sure?'

'Yeah,' he says with a grin. 'The private sector's nice, and I wouldn't want to go back to the Bureau, but sometimes it's fun to do some real police work.'

We spend a couple of hours going through the Williams file and news reports before and since, listing everyone we can find involved in the case in some way.

From his prison days, there's always Billy Perry, of course. The problem is that he's still nowhere to be found. I make a note to have the agency chase him up through every conceivable channel, legit or otherwise. I'm not confident, but we've got to try.

Before his incarceration, Williams led a solitary life – few friends, just neighbours and the guys he worked with at Drill Hall Collectors' Autos. A bunch of customers he made deliveries to at the time of the disappearances, many of whom were contacted by the Bureau or the cops during the initial investigation to see if they had noticed anything unusual about Cody or his van. I very much doubt they remember too much about it now, beyond marking the incident as 'the time the Feds questioned me'. Even deeper background searching at the time of his arrest turned up little between the time he ran away from home and the year or so before he started snatching girls. He just seems to have appeared out of nowhere.

'What did this guy do – spend his teenage years in a goddamn monastery or something?' I ask aloud.

'A friend of mine became a monk once,' Rob says.

'From the Bureau?'

'No, back in Chicago.'

I raise my eyebrows. 'Not a place I would've thought was big on monks. The vow of silence ones?'

'That's Trappists. These were Benedictines,' he says, looking up from the notes he's reading. 'The monastery was someplace out in the sticks. Buttfuck, Iowa. Or Colorado. I can't remember which.'

'That's a pretty big difference, Rob. How many monks do you know?'

He shrugs. 'All these places look the same to me, you know that. In any case, he's not a monk any more.'

'No?'

'Not as far as I know.'

'Didn't like the prayers and the lifestyle?'

'Not that. He was only there for a year, so he was – what's the word? An apprentice? A novice? Anyway, whatever it's called, he was like a probationary monk, so he didn't have to take his vows until the end of that year. But he left instead.'

I think for a moment. 'Must be a strange life. Kinda dull though.'

'From what he said, it didn't sound too bad. They'd grow stuff and make things at the monastery, and him and another monk would sneak down into town with some of what they had, so they could trade it for booze to take back with them. Like college students in cassocks.'

'Strange world.'

Rob nods. 'You got that straight.'

Orange lamplight casts a copper halo over Boston. While I wait for an answer from Brandon's intercom, I notice something dark and strangely discoloured in the twilight on the damp-streaked wall by the door. Moss or algae, colonizing the water tracks left by the broken guttering above. A thin film of life clinging to the brickwork.

'Hey, Mr Rourke,' the kid's voice says over the intercom as the door buzzes to allow me inside. Brandon's waiting to let me into his place proper.

'Sophie got here a while ago. She just made coffee. You want some?'

'Thanks,' I tell him, and step into the apartment. Nothing much seems to have changed from my last visit, except the TV is now playing something from the Sci-Fi Channel, again with the sound turned down, and some of the scattered clothing seems to have moved around. Brandon's T-shirt reads 'Every time you masturbate, God kills a kitten.'

Sophie's in the kitchenette, nursing a mug of coffee with both hands. Fleece hoodie, hair still a little wind-blown, even though she's tied it back. She moves into the main room to let Brandon reach the kettle. 'Hi, Alex,' she says. 'I had a look at the recording while I was waiting. It's much worse than the first one, isn't it?'

'Yeah, it is.' I take off my jacket and throw it on the bed. 'I hope that's as bad as they get. And I hope we find the guy soon.'

Brandon hands me my coffee and sits down in front of his computer. 'I don't know how much help this is going to be,' he says. 'Same as the last one, there's not much on this.'

'Show me what you've got.'

'Sure.' He starts working the mouse. 'Look, I'm sorry it took me a while longer to work on this one.'

'That's OK.'

'Had a bunch of other stuff to deal with. Boyfriend trouble, a break-up to get through.'

'Really, it's no problem. Just glad for the help.'

Shots of Holly caught in freeze frame fill the screen. Stills grabbed from the footage. Mouth open, mid-scream. Body straining against the restraints as the blows rain down on her. Some have been magnified, some recoloured or retouched in an attempt to bring out smaller details.

'The coding is exactly the same as the first segment,' Brandon says. 'And again, the audio has been stripped out. But it's not from the same recording as the first one.'

'How can you tell?'

'The resolution's different. And the colour balances have changed as well. While it could be that he altered settings on the camera for the different lighting when he moved rooms, I doubt it. More likely this is a separate recording.'

'And you're certain it's another room?'

He nods. 'From the direction the floorboards run, and from changes in the floor-to-ceiling height. And like I said, there's the lighting as well – probably more than one source and at lower intensity than in the first segment.'

'That's interesting, but it doesn't tell us much,' Sophie says.

Brandon shrugs. 'No, true enough. But it's a little more detail. I've also been able to estimate your guy at around five-seven to six foot tall. And he has short hair. Well, I suppose it could be long, but if so, it's tied back. And he doesn't wear glasses.'

I raise an eyebrow. 'How do you know that?'

'Remember what I said about the light sources being different?' He switches pictures. 'Look at this. When he changes position, you can see a faint shadow on the wall behind the bed.'

He's right. Image-enhanced, magnified and with the light levels changed to accentuate the darker patch, there's a clear shadow of the guy. Blocky in the low resolution, but distinct. Medium build at a guess, and I think Brandon's right about the hair.

Sophie frowns. 'Won't the distance from the lamp to the guy make a difference to the size of the shadow? How can you tell how big he is?'

'I showed it to one of my old roommates. You can also see the two posts at the foot of the bed in the shadow. Beds come in pretty standard sizes, so you can guess how far apart they are in reality and compare that to how far apart they are in the shadow. Then you know how big the guy is in perspective compared to his shadow. It's rough, but it sounded pretty sensible to me.'

'Nice work,' I tell him. 'Damn nice work.'

Brandon grins a little sheepishly. 'Apparently, the light is probably around nine feet from the foot of the bed. So the room's at least fifteen feet across. Of course, if it's a wall light that's casting the shadow, the room's *exactly* fifteen feet across.' He shrugs. 'Again, not very useful until you're standing in it, but you wanted to know as much as possible.'

'Well, at least if I find the place and fancy doing some interior design while I'm there, I'll know what amount of carpet to bring with me. Are there any other identifying features you could find on the guy?'

'Nothing,' Brandon says, shaking his head. 'His hand's in shot a few times, but I couldn't get any detail out of it that we didn't already know. Nothing distinctive there that I could see at all.'

The ugly weather that's plagued Massachusetts all fall is in full force as Rob and I drive south to catch up with Williams' old associates. Oily black clouds lash the windswept earth beneath them with iron-hard needles of water. The incessant hammering on the roof of the 'Vette is like ball bearings shaken in a steel drum. Mid-morning, and, like the rest of the traffic, we've had to turn our headlights on just to be seen in the downpour. It doesn't look like easing, either.

'Are you sure you wouldn't rather have stayed in the office this morning?' I say to Rob.

'Look at it this way, if something comes in around town it'll be someone else who has to handle it. Let them get soaked.'

'We might not have it any better.'

'Hell, we'll be in a car half the time. Might even get coffee off one of these people.' He runs his hand through his hair. 'And if it's still like this by tonight, you can give me a ride home and I won't have to walk it. This way's a damn sight better all round.'

'If you say so.'

'As it is, I'm gonna have to check the attic space when I get in. Pretty sure we've got a leak somewhere on the roof.'

An eighteen-wheeler roars past, heading back to Boston, and the 'Vette's windshield temporarily fogs over with a million flecks of grit-laced spray.

'Teresa's on at me to talk to the neighbours about it. She reckons it might have happened when they were doing some work up there last month. Not that it makes any difference.' He smiles grimly. 'Hey, maybe we'll get lucky. One of these guys might have become a roofer, and we could persuade him to fix it for me while we're here. You think they do calls to Boston?'

'Threaten to set Teresa on them, and they'd come out to New York.'

'I'll keep that in mind.'

The smaller towns we've been passing through, empty and locked away behind the curtain of rain, begin to merge into the outskirts of Fall River as the highway crosses the dull grey expanse of Taunton River. Before long, we're passing through the town's New England mix of old and new buildings, and Rob's checking the street map in front of him.

Waiting at a stoplight, I glance down the road to the right and, through the streaks of water on the glass, see a guy in workman's overalls bundling a young girl into the back of a white van. I yank the window down as quickly as possible, half ready to jump out of the car. The man is loading decorating materials, paint, tools and some sort of tarp into his van. Nothing more.

'What is it?' Rob asks, as I wind the window up again.

'Nothing. Thought I recognized someone, that's all.'

He shrugs and settles back in his seat. 'Light's green, Alex.'

'Oh, yeah.' I slip the 'Vette into gear and pull away, flicking a brief look at the white van as we cross the intersection. The workman is closing the rear doors and scurrying around to clamber in, out of the wet.

Drill Hall Collectors' Autos is an old building of crumbling brick bordered on two sides by a concrete forecourt spattered black here and there with old oil stains. An engraved slab of pitted marble halfway to the roof reads 'Drill Hall – 1914', without giving any clue to who it was a drill hall for, or when it ceased to serve its original purpose. A couple of ribbon windows so covered in grime that they appear an opaque yellow look out on the street. The trunk of an ageing brown Mercedes is protruding from the huge warehouse-style main doors, half concealed by tattered foot-wide strips of industrial plastic, there to keep the worst of the weather out, swaying in the wind.

We park on the forecourt. Rob opens the door and locks his umbrella into place before swinging out of the 'Vette. I make do with turning up the collar on my jacket and making a beeline for the body shop. Inside, an old guy with scruffy white hair and a bristling moustache to match, dark-blue overalls smeared in oil and engine grease, is swigging coffee and chatting with another man, who I take to be the owner of the car. Maybe a few years older than me, short brown hair, in a thick fleece coat and sturdy boots. The hood has been popped, and both of them are staring into its recesses as they chat.

The car owner sees us enter and says, 'Well, I'd better get going, Pete. My ride home should be here soon, and I might as well pick up some groceries before that.'

'Sure thing, Jim,' the old man says. 'I'll give you a call when it's ready. All depends on whether it needs a new gasket or not.'

'No problem. Take it easy.' With one further glance

at the two of us, the car owner steps through the plastic strips and out into the rain.

Pete waves us over and goes to get a refill from the battered coffee machine in the corner of one of the workbenches. 'What can I do for you guys?' he asks.

'Mr Marshall? My name's Alex Rourke, and this is Robin Garrett. I was wondering if we could talk to you for a few minutes.' Rob folds his umbrella again.

'I know who you are, Mr Rourke,' he says. 'I recognized you from the TV news. So I guess you want to talk to me about Cody Williams.'

'That's right, yeah.'

Pete nods. 'Figures. You guys want coffee?'

'Sure.'

He looks over at the machine, then yells to the small office in the far corner of the room, 'Hey Joey! Wash a couple of cups and bring them out here, would ya.'

A moment later, a young-looking lanky guy emerges with a couple of coffee mugs still dripping with tap water. He looks briefly at us, then heads back into the office.

'So what do you want to know?' Pete asks, once his employee has vanished again. 'Been years since it all happened, but once you know what the guy working for you did, the whole thing sticks in your mind.'

'We've read over your original statement back from the time of Cody's arrest,' I tell him. 'But there's some questions that were never asked back then, or if they were, they were only touched on briefly. Can you remember who Cody would have been friends with?'

Pete puffs out his cheeks and strokes his moustache. I take the opportunity to sip my coffee. Not bad. 'Well,' he says, 'I don't remember him having much in the way of friends. I suppose you could count me and the other people who worked here back then. Bob Hawkins, Mark Laine and Leila Alford. Now it's mostly just Joey, although Leila still does twenty hours a week. Haven't seen either of the other two in years, though.'

I look across at Rob, who nods. We've already got those names on our list. 'How about people who would have visited here regularly – neighbours, suppliers, people like that? Anyone who would have known him from that kind of contact.'

'Well, we've got a bunch of different suppliers. I don't remember any of their people being especially friendly with Cody. In fact, I doubt he would have been here half the times they showed up, not if he was out on a delivery.'

From the corner of my eye, I see Rob scribbling in his notebook. 'What about regular customers?' I ask. 'The people he would have seen more than once on deliveries and repairs.'

'Well, that's the thing – if the job's done right, the car's fixed, and he wouldn't see the same customer again. He only worked here for just over a year, and I'd be surprised if he saw any of them more than twice. I suppose if there'd been one particular problem car – which does happen now and then – he might have done a bunch of call-outs for it. I'll check for you.'

Pete heads into the office and I hear the metallic rattling of a filing cabinet drawer opening, muffled conversation.

'I'm not hopeful,' Rob says, keeping his voice low. 'If there'd been anyone obvious, I think old Pete would've remembered straight off.'

'We might get lucky.'

'We might, but don't bet the farm on it. Could be Pete himself.'

'No,' I say, shaking my head. 'His build's wrong. He's not the guy in the video.'

I finish the rest of my coffee, as the old man returns from the tiny office with a large, heavily worn and clearly well-thumbed ledger-style notebook in one hand. He shakes his head as he flips it open and starts running his finger down the entries inside.

'This is the work book that covers most of the time Cody worked here,' he says. 'As far as I can see, I don't think there was anyone he dealt with more than once or twice. We had ... uh ... let's see, a 1967 'Cuda needed four visits to get it fixed properly, but Mark handled that. Apart from that, I can't see any repeat addresses worth noting. We had a bunch of regulars in for servicing, minor repairs, but like I said, I doubt Cody would even have been here for a few of them.'

He hands the book to me. The writing inside is cramped and spidery and faded with time, but it's readable. 'You can borrow that if you want,' he says. 'I don't have much need for it unless someone wants to audit me and check a real long way back.'

I hand him a business card. 'Thanks, Mr Marshall. Give me a call if you need it for anything and we'll get it back to you.'

'Any time. If that son of a bitch did do all them things, least I can do is help you guys with whatever you need.'

Back in the car, Rob turns to me and says, 'So where now?'

'Laine was the one that moved to . . .'

'San Diego, if the background check was right.'

'OK, so no point worrying about him at the moment. And as he's moved cross-country, I wouldn't make him for Cody's accomplice anyway. Shifting Holly quietly – I don't see it. Let's try the other two co-workers, then take a look at Cody's house, and his neighbours. Hopefully, some of them lived there back when he did.'

Bob Hawkins is out when we call on him, and while Leila Alford is pleasant and open with us, she can't add anything, just confirms what Pete told us.

Williams' old house looks even worse now than it did when I first saw it all those years ago. The boxy front yard is full of yellowing weeds running almost to waist height. One of the front windows is boarded up. I can see a handful of roof tiles sticking out of the gutter from where they've slid further up. A weather-beaten sign for 'Rainbow Realty' proclaims that the place is for sale, but I doubt it's attracting many buyers.

'Was it always this nice?' Rob says, behind me.

'No, not always. It doesn't have Cody Williams inside it any more, and that's a serious improvement. Let's talk to the neighbours.'

'You don't want to go poking around in there? I know how much you like run-down buildings.'

I smile faintly. 'Yeah, but that one was picked over inch-by-inch by the crime scene team back when we arrested him. If there was any evidence there they missed, it's probably been destroyed by whoever's lived there for the past seven years.'

All the first neighbour can tell us is that he moved in long after Williams went to jail, and that there used to be an elderly couple who lived in Cody's house until they died a year ago.

The neighbour on the other side of the property is a little more helpful. 'Yeah, I lived here back then,' he says. 'Used to work for a printing company not far from here. Retired now, of course.'

'Do you remember much about Cody Williams? What was he like as a neighbour?'

The old man scratches his head. 'Well, I didn't see much of him. Kept himself to himself, and with the two of us working, I hardly saw him.'

'Did anyone ever visit him?'

'No, no. Never saw anyone, not that stayed any-way. But he was always going out, though. Must've had somewhere to go, because he'd always be heading off in his truck not long after he'd come back from work. And at weekends. Now I wonder, of course. Knowing what he was doing. Probably spent all that time looking for those poor kids to take.'

I glance at Rob. 'And you never knew where he went? He didn't say anything at all, not even in passing?'

'No, no. And I didn't see any reason to pry. Man may have been going to tap-dancing lessons for all I knew.' He chuckles roundly at his own joke.

We thank him and make our excuses. On the way back to the 'Vette, I turn to Rob and say, 'Either he was meeting with someone, or he had somewhere else he used to go on a regular basis.'

'How about where he stashed the girls? Didn't he say something about a place by Lake Stevenson?'

'Could be. But from the way he described it, there wasn't anything there he had to prepare in advance. Why spend all that time in an empty hut?' I leave the shelter of Rob's umbrella and drop into the 'Vette. He strides round to the other side and follows suit. 'No,' I say, 'my money would be on his accomplice, and stalking the girls. Find out what the other guy likes, and then try to track one down for him.'

'It still doesn't bring us any closer to finding him, though.'

'True. Let's try some of Williams' customers.'

The few we've been able to trace and who are in when we call aren't able to add anything to our knowledge of events. Some don't remember Williams at all, and those that do only recall him in terms of the time they met a murderer, a story to be told to drinking buddies and spouses, the details long since warped by years of internal Chinese whispers. None of them seems like a good make for Williams' partner, and I don't get the impression that any of them are lying. There are still a few names left on the list, but I'm not optimistic.

When I drop Rob off at his house back in Boston, he leans back in through the open car door and says, 'So where do you want to go from here, Alex? Start with the investigators tomorrow?'

'Yeah, I reckon so. When I get home, I'll go over the work book we got from the body shop just in case there's anything interesting there. But failing that, yeah, let's try the investigators.'

'Hope one of them has something we can go on, because otherwise we're damn short on leads.'

'Yeah, I know. But nothing ventured, nothing gained.'

'Sure. Goodnight, Alex.'

An hour going over the work book, and I've got a couple of names and addresses scribbled down. The first is a guy Cody visited twice to carry out small repairs and replacements. After that, the customer switched to coming down to the body shop himself, and carried on doing so for a few years after Cody's arrest. The second client looks like he moved house during Cody's tenure at the body shop, so his address changes for the last two of four separate visits Cody made to his home. I guess this change in details is why no one noticed him before. He doesn't seem to have used Drill Hall Collectors' Autos since the arrest, either.

I'm skimming the book again just in case I've missed anything when the phone rings.

'Alex,' Tanya Downes says when I pick up, 'I thought you should hear this from me.'

'What?'

'Cody Williams died half an hour ago.'

Chapter Nineteen

It's a cold, dreary morning. Grey sky, clouds heavy with promised rain. I stand on the turf by the side of a pauper's grave, looking down at the simple wooden casket in front of me. The priest drones through his expected eulogy, but it's by the numbers and his heart isn't in it. He gives the standard blessing because it's tradition, nothing more. I'm the lone mourner present, and the priest never knew his charge. Not like I did.

Cody Williams is lowered into the ground by men who only knew him through the papers, if at all, and whose presence here is due solely to the paycheck they expect, no sense of duty or moral obligation.

I'm not even sure why I'm here. I hated Cody, I'm glad he spent the final years of his life in jail, and I'm happy he's dead. But like it or not, he was a part of my life, and he's gone. He has no family, no friends, no one who wants to mark his passing apart from the FBI agent who ended up framing him for murder because he couldn't think of another way of stopping him. Not even the media are here – now he's dead, Cody's a historical story. His burial means nothing.

'Ashes to ashes, dust to dust,' the priest says, and nods at one of the guys on burial duty. 'All yours, Terry.'

The gravedigger glances briefly at me, then begins to shovel dirt into the hole while his master heads off in search of a hot cup of coffee and more important church matters.

I look down at the grave and wish Cody hadn't held out on me until the end, wish he'd given up his accomplice, told me where to find Holly. My confession is no longer called for, my secret safe for the time being. But how much suffering would Holly have been spared if I'd talked to him in those last hours, if I'd given him what he wanted?

The world's a better place without him, but I can't help thinking Cody could have gone a long way to redeeming himself if he'd wanted to.

'Goodbye, you batshit-crazy son of a bitch,' I say to empty air.

As I pick my way between the burial markers, a thin, reedy drizzle begins to fall, fog with gravity. If anyone watches me go, I don't care. Let them watch.

'Is that Alex Rourke?' The voice is deep, the accent heavily Californian. A radio is playing in the background, tinny pop leaking in over the receiver. I can hear it over the noise in the office around me. 'This is Nathan Sheffield from Hot Steel Productions in LA. You sent me some stills of a girl you were looking for.'

I try to remember which one of the various porn companies I sent the stuff to this is, but I can't. 'Yeah, that's right.'

'You might be in luck. I think I remember this one. Have you got the video these pics came from? Could you email it to me? I'll know for sure if I can see the film.' He reads off an address.

'No problem.' I juggle the phone, pinning it between ear and shoulder, as I dig out the footage and send it to the guy. 'Shouldn't take too long,' I say.

A minute or so later, he says, 'Uh-huh. Got it.' Another couple of minutes pass. 'Yeah, yeah. This is the one I'm thinking of. Knew it looked familiar.'

'You must have a good memory,' I say, genuinely surprised.

'It helps in the trade. I don't want to end up paying for a scene I already own the rights to, and it's always handy to know who the upcoming talent is.' I hear him tapping on a keyboard. 'Let's see, it would've been about six months ago, I think. Some guy out east sent me a CD with samples of his films, wanted to know if I'd be interested in buying his stuff for distribution.'

'Does that happen a lot?'

'Yes and no. There're regular performers and smaller-scale operators, whose work my company distributes, but I know most of them in person. But occasionally we get amateur submissions, mostly people looking to make a quick buck from their private home videos of them and their wives or girlfriends.'

I raise my eyebrows. 'Seriously?'

'We don't often take them — they're usually too

poor quality. This is more specialist stuff, but the roughly filmed look works for some BDSM scenes.'

'BDSM? I know S&M, but I've never heard of that one.'

'Very similar. Bondage, Domination and Sado-Masochism,' he explains. 'Not something I sell a lot of, but there's a steady market for it. All net-based, not worth bundling on to DVD, as it's not something I specialize in. Anyway, this guy sent me the samples he had and I decided to offer him a deal – standard amateur rate, nothing major. But I said before that I'd need to have all the paperwork straight to meet my USC 2257 requirements.'

'Uh . . .'

'Never heard of it?'

'It's not really my field.'

Sheffield chuckles deep and low. 'No kidding. It's a federal requirement for proof of identity and legal age, things like that, which I'd need to keep records of.'

'OK. Paperwork to stop people using underage girls in their films.'

'That's right.' He seems to want to explain himself a little. 'I run a strictly legitimate business, Mr Rourke. It's an industry like any other, and everyone I work with has to follow the rules to the letter. No exceptions. I'm a professional.'

'I never thought otherwise,' I say. 'What did the guy give you for your records?'

'Nothing. I never heard back from him. I figured either he couldn't give me the documentation, or he got a better offer from someone else, or he had second thoughts about the whole thing. It happens.'

'Or he wasn't on the level with what he was offering.'

'Exactly.'

'I don't suppose his face was anywhere in the sample material he sent?'

'No, I'm pretty certain it wasn't. From what I remember, everything was the same kind of POV shot used in the film you sent me. No way of telling who's behind the camera.'

'You don't still have the CD he sent you?'

'Again, sorry, I don't. It's policy never to hang on to anything from an unverified source. The last thing I need is to find out some girl in a video someone's sent me is underage and end up in court myself for possessing child pornography. That CD will have been thrown out long ago,' Sheffield says. 'Aha, here it is,' he says. 'Contact information. You got a pen?'

'Yeah. What've you got?'

'No phone number. Postal address is a PO Box in Berwick, Massachusetts.' He rattles off the details he has, such as they are.

'What name did the guy give you?'

Sheffield clicks his mouse a couple of times. 'Richard Goddard, according to this. Whether it was his real name or not, I couldn't say. He claimed the girl's name was Violet, but *those* are almost always fake.'

'I thought the guys who made porn all went for pseudonyms like Max Woody.'

He laughs loudly and with genuine warmth. 'Yeah, some do, Mr Rourke. It's kinda silly, but some parts of our market expect it. Not every male performer or producer does, though. It's much more common with the girls.'

'Yeah?' I say.

'The puns are even worse for them.'

'Do you still have his email address?'

'Sure. It's goddardproductions@hotmail.com.'

I know I can't ask the Hotmail administrators for the user information on that account, not without a warrant. And in any case, the guy probably used fake information when he set up the account. Unless he told them the truth for some reason. Somehow, I doubt it.

'No actual email from the guy, though.'

'That's right,' he says. 'He sent his stuff by post. That must just have been with his details. Shame, really.'

'What do you mean?'

'We had a problem with nuisance email a couple of months ago. Someone feeding me all this shit about the evils of sleaze, threats, all kinda sad. Turned out to be a woman somewhere in the Midwest. But to find where to send the nasty "stop doing this or we'll take you to court" letter, we had to find out who it was.'

'You traced her?' I ask.

'Yeah, got an expert in to help us out. Turns out the email's header includes a number which corresponds to the place it was sent from. Like, for this Goddard guy, it would show where he was accessing Hotmail from. You just check who owns the number online.'

'Like a reverse phone-number lookup.'

'Yeah,' Sheffield says. 'Just like that. We were lucky with out moralist freak – she was with a small company which helped identify her when we explained that she was harassing us.'

'Did she stop?'

'Yeah.' He laughs. 'I hear she wrote a pretty rude letter to our lawyers, but that was the last we heard of her.'

'And I'd need a message from Goddard to try the same thing on him.'

'That's right. If I had one myself I'd pass it on to you, help you find the guy.'

I smile. 'That's OK. If he gets in touch with you again, or you get any similar footage from a similar source, could you call me, Mr Sheffield? I'd appreciate that.'

'Nath,' he says. 'And yeah, that's no problem at all. Glad to be a help. Good luck, Mr Rourke.'

Berwick Post Office is a blocky modern building with plate glass framed in blue steel running most of the way along its front, presumably there to give passers-by a good look inside and leave them with the impression that the US Postal Service can be trusted with their packages. It also affords me a far better view of the interior than I'd normally expect on surveillance jobs. From the tables outside a coffee shop across the street I can see the three rows of locker-like post office boxes on the right-hand side. They're separate from the main section of the building, and it's easy to distinguish between those who have come to check their boxes and customers on other business. I have direct line of sight to PO Box 14, the address used by the would-be porn peddler. I've got no idea whether it's still in use by the same guy; all I can do is watch and hope. Perch across the street each day with a newspaper or paperback, hope he checks the box fairly regularly. Closing time means freedom to leave my position. A cheap motel room, take-out or bar food, trashy cable TV and warm beer.

Three days I do this, and the staff are beginning to give me strange looks, slightly uncomfortable with the stranger who seems to have taken up residence at one of their tables, all day, every day. One girl strikes up light conversation whenever she passes my table and the place is quiet. Her name's Chantel and she's a dropout from U-Mass who's trying to become a graphic designer. My name's Andy Hames, and I'm a writer hanging out at a coffee shop, waiting for inspiration. It was the best excuse I could come up with at the time, as bizarre as looking for creativity at a generic Starbucks clone sounds. I hope she hasn't seen any of the news reports on Williams or my trips to the jail. If she knows I'm bullshitting, she doesn't show it.

During this time, I watch dozens of people entering and leaving the post office. Men, women. All ages, all types. Box 14 remains unopened. Then, just when I'm thinking I'll have to get a laptop from somewhere to keep up my pretence any longer, my prayers are answered and my hopes dashed at the same time.

Light traffic in the mid-morning sunshine and another uneventful day. Chantel's doing her rounds, and my brief conversation with her, and the boredom of three blank days spent staring at the far side of the street, distracts me more than it should. By the time my eyes and attention have wandered back to the post office, there's someone standing by the open door to Box 14.

A man, height and build don't look anything out of the ordinary. Dark, puffy jacket, baseball cap pulled down low. Sunglasses, I think.

Three days' worth of caffeine jolts through my system and I nearly vault out of my chair in surprise. Just about hold back the urge; I don't want to draw attention to myself before I know who this guy is and where he's come from. Nevertheless, I sit bolt upright, one hand clenched on the arm of my chair, as I watch him leaf through a couple of pieces of accumulated mail before closing the box again.

There's a good ten or eleven cars parked in the bays in front of the post office. No way to tell which could be his. My own is round the corner. Close, but I don't know if it's close enough.

The guy walks out through the sliding doors and back into the sun, keeping his face shaded by his cap. I'd guess somewhere into his fifties, which fits with what I know, senior enough to order Cody around back when they were snatching girls, but apart from that, I can't make out any more about him. I hold my coffee up at mouth level, hoping this'll disguise the fact that I'm staring at him.

He unlocks a dark-blue station wagon, fairly old, and opens the door. Glances up as he's about to drop inside, and sees me. That momentary pause as I feel the eyes behind the sunglasses meet mine, that hesitation in his movements as everything tenses up.

Fight or flight.

I drop a twenty on the table for Chantel and snap out of my seat.

He vanishes into the station wagon and starts the engine with a roar of throttle. I'm running for my car as he whips it out of the bay in reverse and hits the gas. As it passes me, I catch a flash of blonde hair, a glimpse of a woman's face from the passenger seat. Eyes glint once in the sun, the same eyes, the same face as in the footage.

Holly's eyes, Holly's face.

She looks at me in surprise and, for a second, everything else slows and freezes, the world closing to a tunnel between the two of us. She opens her mouth as if she's about to say something, and then everything rushes back inwards and the station wagon accelerates away.

I make a half-hearted attempt to get the plate, but it's impossible to do while running and I only catch the first couple of numbers before it's grown too small to see.

By the time I've reached my car and pulled away in pursuit, I'd guess he's got maybe a mile on me. But he was heading west out of town, and the main highway doesn't have too many turns between here and the state line. He's heading into upstate New York, almost certainly.

Unless it's all a trick to lead me away from his real home, of course.

I burn up the highway. Fifty, sixty, seventy, eighty. Flash past regular traffic like the devil's after me. The roadside fades to a green-brown blur and my eyes strain from reaching towards the horizon, desperate for any sign of my quarry. Despair slowly sets in as the miles roll past and I can't find him. Took a turning somewhere, hid the car back in town while he was out of sight, I don't know. But he's not out here. I've lost him.

And Holly.

All the time I was sitting there, drinking my coffee and talking to Chantel, watching the guy inside the post office, she was in a car across the street. At any point I could've saved her just by walking over and getting her out.

She was there, right in front of me, and I did nothing. It could all have been over.

But it's not, and maybe she's in even more danger

now the guy knows how close I came to him, and all I can do is go back to Boston knowing I've blown my main lead.

It's probably too late, and he'll probably be long gone, but I want to do something, anything, that feels like I'm still close on Goddard's tail before I go back to fruitlessly tracing anyone involved in the Williams case with Rob.

I fire up my computer and think for a moment. What to send the guy to elicit a response from him. I don't know if a ruse might work and, if so, what sort, or if he'd respond better to another nasty shock to match seeing me in Berwick. In the end, I try both. First, I set myself up for a free email account and send him a message claiming to be from a newly established porn producer interested in his material. Then I open my regular personal email and start typing.

From: Alex Rourke <alex@r-garrett-assoc.com>
To: goddardproductions@hotmail.com
Subject: Holly Tynon
Message:

I'm coming for you.

Chapter Twenty

The first of the cops who worked on the girls' disappearances is a barrel-chested guy with an unruly mass of greying hair and a smile that looks just a little forced when he welcomes me and Rob into the room. A reasonably nice suit and a neat and tidy office. A photo on the shelf to the right of his desk shows him with his arms around a plain but happy-looking woman and two young children. Seven years ago he was a sergeant in Providence PD and helped handle a fair chunk of the canvassing work carried out in the wake of Holly's disappearance. Now he deals with insurance claims for auto accidents.

He runs through the sort of people he remembers speaking to during door-to-door, but straight away we know we're not going to get anything useful from him. Memories grow dim, and these can't have been that thrilling to start with. Another day, another job, another set of questions to ask another set of anonymous faces.

Our second port of call was a uniform beat cop back in the day, now a detective with a glass-walled cubicle office in Providence Police Department's squad room that smells of pine air freshener and black coffee. All business. A short woman a couple of years younger than me, in a neat trouser suit and subdued blue shirt. A sharp, direct demeanour with the suggestion that she doesn't suffer fools gladly.

Or for very long, it seems.

'Anything I noticed I would have included in the reports,' she says bluntly, after we've explained the purpose of our visit. 'And anything I dismissed at the time I've long since forgotten. I'm sorry, gentlemen, but I think you've had a wasted trip.'

The next name on our list is the one I know best. I haven't seen Detective Frank Hall since I washed my hands of Cody Williams.

Times have changed. Frank's home is a basement apartment in downtown Providence, well away from the city's commercial and college districts. The building is a three-storey brick structure that I guess was last renovated the best part of thirty years ago. The gutter lining the path to the front door is full of old cigarette butts, and a broken pram lies overturned on the straggly front lawn. Through the unlocked door, we follow cracked linoleum steps down into a narrow, fetid corridor splashed yellow by the overhead lamps. The air smells of old cooking and other people's sweat.

I can hear a TV playing from behind the door to apartment B when we go to knock. 'Are you sure this is the place?' Rob asks, hand poised over the woodwork.

'I think so. Only one way to find out.'

It takes a while for Frank to answer the door, and when he does I'm not even a hundred per cent sure it's him. His hair's mostly gone, apart from straggly tufts that form a rough belt starting just above his ears and running around the back of his head. His nose looks to have been broken and re-set slightly out of joint somewhere down the intervening years, and his skin is blotchy and dry. He's wearing a grubby white T-shirt and a ragged black jogging top, both of them with holes at the armpits, and a pair of scuffed shorts. He's thin, worn out.

But the most striking thing about him is the smell. The sickly-sweet reek of cheap alcohol surrounds him like an invisible fog, made worse when he opens his mouth to say, in a voice gone scratchy and broken, 'Yeah? Do I know you?'

Rob looks to me for some indication of how to proceed. In all honesty, I'm not entirely sure myself. 'Hi, Frank,' I say. 'Alex Rourke. Haven't seen you in years.'

'I don't remember.'

'Holly Tynon? The girl abducted not far from here.'

Something stirs in his yellowing eyeballs. 'Yeah, Rourke. Fed, right?'

'That's right.'

'Yeah, I remember. C'mon in.'

He leaves the door open, and we follow him into the poky studio apartment, lit by a naked bulb in the centre of the main room and a couple of windows looking into the trash-spattered concrete trench that surrounds the building. A portable TV is playing some game show or other in one corner of the room, faced by a single sagging brown armchair. A matching couch squats beneath the windows, half-covered by old newspaper and dirty laundry.

The floor of the room holds my attention, though. Apart from a few well-worn paths, from bed, to chair, to kitchen, to bathroom, the place is carpeted in empty Colt 45 cans. There must be hundreds of them. Here and there – mostly by the bed and chair – there are fresh cans in opened crates or six-packs.

'Drink?' Frank says, dropping into his armchair.

'Thanks, no,' Rob says, staring at the detritus. 'Too early for me.'

'Fair 'nuff. Have a seat. So, how you been, Alex?'

I join Rob in trying to find a clear perch on the couch. Neither of us wants to move anything if possible, just in case something worse lurks beneath. 'I'm fine, Frank. Not in the FBI any more these days.'

'Same here – quit the department.'

'Yeah?' I say, trying not to make it sound like that was obvious from his surroundings. Trying to find a polite way of asking him, *What the fuck happened to you?* Not easy when my natural instinct is to grab him by the shoulders and say, *For God's sake, man, you were a good cop last time we met. How the hell did you slip so far? Can't you see what you've become?* 'What made you quit?'

'My wife, Tricia, left me.' He takes a swig from the

213

opened can next to his chair. Blinks once or twice, like he's trying not to cry. 'Got a phone call at work one day, saying she was gone. Packed her stuff. Said she'd met someone else. Totally, well, y'know, floored me.' Another swig, a lopsided nod in our direction, but he's not meeting our eyes. 'I mean, I had work and all, and sometimes something would hit you, like the one we worked on about the girl. But never often, and I always treated Tricia right. Treated her real well. I loved that woman. I dunno. Came out of the blue. Divorce didn't seem to matter much when that came around – pretty insignificant next to her leaving. And I, I dunno, I didn't cope well.' He raises the beer can to illustrate his point, looks almost apologetic. 'I haven't coped well since.'

'That's rough, man,' Rob says. 'Always happens when you least expect it. I know – I've been there.' Which I know is bullshit, but he says it like he means it, and Frank doesn't seem to pick him up on it.

'Thought about finishing it all, y'know? Bunch of times. Not like I've got much left. But I never tried it.' He sniffs and drains the rest of his beer. 'She still sends me Christmas cards. Can you believe that? No idea where she is now.' He trails off into silence, lost in thought or trying to force his errant emotions back down into the comforting morass of old alcohol and empty memory.

'Frank, how much do you remember about Holly Tynon, and what we did when we were trying to find her?'

'Plenty, sure.'

'Do you remember anything or anyone strange – at the time or since then – connected with the case in any way? Something you might have noticed at the time, but which didn't seem important back then?'

He scratches his face with grimy nails. 'Shit, Alex. I mean, it was all pretty strange. Thing like that makes people act crazy. Had people keep volunteering to search and stuff. Had people saying all kinds of things, like they'd seen her, or they knew where she was, and it was all bullshit. Didn't deal with them myself, but I know we even had a few fuckers saying they'd taken her, or they wanted to, or they were going to take more. Crazy stuff. It all got checked, I think, 'cos you've got to, but they were nothing but freaks. More of them when the guy went to trial. Saying we should kill him for what he did, or that we were lyin' bastards who'd got the wrong man. More crazy shit.' He shakes his head. 'Poor fucking girl.'

'Did any of those people stand out, do you remember, Frank?' I ask. 'Any who seemed to be more knowledgeable than the others, or more vocal in what they were asking? Or any that were just plain creepier than the rest?'

'I'm sorry. I didn't deal with them, not myself. Just heard the stories from the others. Only time I saw any of them was outside the courthouse, and there was only a few of them. One guy gave me a flower.'

'A flower?'

'Yeah. Think he was nuts. Or strung out on something. Said something about God. Some religious vengeance kick. "God loves those who send sinners down to hell," or something. I don't remember too clearly.' He sniffs again. 'Was gonna say it's sad when people get that way. But I guess that sounds kinda stupid coming from a mess like me.'

I shrug in a way I hope looks friendly. 'True, though. Was he the only one you remember?'

'Yeah. The rest would be in the files, I guess, from when we checked them out. But I don't know if any of them were anything much. Apart from that, can't think of anything else from that case. Poor fucking girl.'

'Yeah.'

'Poor fucking girl.' His head droops a little, and I guess his mind is back wandering the fuzzy halls of remembrance again. I don't think we're going to get much more from him. I glance at Rob and stand to leave.

'Well, thanks, Frank. I appreciate your help. We'd best be going.'

''S OK,' he says, and clambers unsteadily out of his chair. 'Whatever. Good to see you again. Old times.'

'Yeah.' He shows us to the front door. 'Take care of yourself, Frank.'

'Sure,' he says, without any conviction at all. 'You too.'

We head back down the stale corridor towards the stairs, watched most of the way by the shell of a man behind us. Out in the open air and away from the cloying atmosphere of the basement, I puff out my cheeks and say, 'I don't believe that.'

'He certainly wasn't what I expected. Was he a friend of yours, back then?'

'No. I knew him from the Tynon case, and he seemed like a good cop – handled the family with a lot of sensitivity, knew the job, and didn't play the jurisdiction game once with us. A real professional.'

I look at the broken remains of the pram as we pass by. In the near distance, a group of four or five kids are taking it in turns to push each other down the road in a shopping cart. 'He came up to see me during the trial. He wasn't testifying or anything – as we couldn't pin any of the abductions on Williams, we couldn't use evidence from those cases – but he showed up on the day I started my testimony just to wish me luck and say that everyone from his department was rooting for us. I appreciated that.'

'It's a nice gesture.'

'Yeah. He seemed pretty solid, plenty of confidence in himself. I can't understand how he got like he is now.' I think for a moment about what I just said. 'Well, I can understand it a little, just from my own situation. I know how hard it is to lose something that means so much to you. But even so . . .'

Rob nods and stays quiet.

*

The rest of the afternoon passes in a sea of old interviews and statements from the case records.

'Well,' Rob says, after what seems like forever ploughing through the paperwork, 'all the nutjobs who the cops had to check out sound like exactly that – nutjobs. There's nothing in the ones I've read so far to suggest any of them actually knew a damn thing about the abductions. A few of them they never managed to trace, but none of them revealed any details that weren't in the press, and most of them were plainly just totally whacko.'

'Yeah?'

He nods. 'One guy here claimed to have already snatched a dozen girls and needed Holly to make his "perfect thirteen" with which he could summon Satan to earth and gain immortal life. He probably felt pretty damn stupid when the next girl went missing.'

'Sounds like if he was going to feel stupid about anything, he would've done so a long time ago,' I say. 'I've got a similar picture from the ones I've looked at as well. I don't think there's going to be anything in them.' I glance out the windows at the darkened sky stained orange by the street lights. 'It's late. Let's head for home.'

Rob nods. 'Fair enough. Drop me at your place. I'll walk the rest of the way.'

Boston is cloaked in damp blackness. Haloes surround every light, circles of hazy neon hovering against the night, angelic moths to each and every flame.

Plenty of traffic, as always, but quiet, muted somehow.

I swing the 'Vette into my resident's parking space and kill the engine. Check I've got everything, and climb out of the car. The air outside is cold and sharp.

'Are you still going to be working with me tomorrow?' I ask Rob, as he adjusts his coat and plunges his hands into his pockets, out of the chill. 'I didn't notice what came in at the office.'

'Yeah, I should be. It all looked pretty quiet to me. Are you planning on trying to talk to Williams' repeat customers?'

I nod. 'Next on the list, yeah, unless anything else comes up.'

'Worth a try, isn't it. Might get lucky – one of them could be the guy we're looking for, and we can go home heroes of the hour.'

At the back of my mind I hear journalists asking me why we didn't find Holly seven years earlier, why we abandoned the search for her. I hear them asking why we were so sure Cody was the guy who took her. I picture the look on her parents' faces as their daughter is returned to them, in God only knows what kind of mental state, seven years too late.

'Something like that,' I say.

'Well, anyway, see you tomorrow.' He turns to go, then stops, eyes fixed on my apartment. 'Alex, your door's open.'

I follow his gaze. True enough, the door is hanging a couple of inches ajar. It's hard to tell from here, but I think I can see the lock wrenched and twisted.

There's a glow coming from a couple of the windows. Unsteady, moving. Orange.

'Is that what I think it is?' Rob says.

Fire.

Chapter Twenty-One

I don't answer him, but run up to the busted door. There's a definite smell of smoke coming through the gap in the frame, but I can't feel any heat.

'You're not seriously going in there?'

'We don't know how bad it is, and there's things I want to make sure are OK,' I say. 'Call 911, tell them there was a break-in as well as a fire, so it looks like arson, and get the neighbours out of the building, just in case.'

Rob looks like he's considering arguing, but he doesn't try to stop me as I push through into the hallway. Smoke hangs like thick fog up around the ceiling, but the air's not too bad lower down. It's pretty obvious that it's getting worse, though.

The door to the front room is open, and I can see my notes and papers scattered on the floor. Anything that could be opened, anything that could be thrown around, has been. I can't see anything obvious that's been stolen – the TV and stereo are still present, and although the monitor's been knocked over, my computer hasn't moved. Nevertheless, the place has been trashed.

I don't even try the kitchen – I can hear the hungry roar of flames from the hall, and the smoke is at its thickest and blackest where it creeps past the doorframe. The only extinguisher I own is in there. Life's funny like that.

I tug the bottom of my shirt up, over my mouth and nose, and head deeper into my home, knowing even as I do it that the gas system could blow completely, or the kitchen ceiling could give way and drop the building's upper floors on to me.

I'm not going to salvage the case files. The Bureau has copies. Instead, I run into the bedroom. It hasn't been trashed like the front room, although the contents of my closet are on the floor and my drawers are all open. I hunt around for the things I came for, that I couldn't handle losing, and stuff them into my pockets. Sentimental things, the kind that are more a symbol, a trigger for your memory, than valuables in their own right. A framed photograph and a pack of similar pictures. A broken necklace.

By the time I've returned to the hallway, my eyes are streaming and the smoke's too thick to see far. Up ahead, I can hear uncontrollable coughing. Rob is leaning against the wall near the kitchen and looks ready to collapse.

I grab him by the arm and haul him outside as fast as I can, trying not to breathe in. When we get out to the open air – the fresh, clean, lovely open air – he starts to breathe more easily, but it's pretty obvious he's got lungs full of smoke.

'Thought . . . you'd got . . . trapped . . .' he manages to gasp, laid out on the grass. 'Went . . . in . . .'

'Thanks, Rob. You're an idiot, but you're a friend. I was in the bedroom. The air was better there.' My throat feels like I've inhaled ground glass, and my eyes are still watering, but I don't let him know that.

He tries to answer, but seems to give up in favour of remaining conscious. I try to make him as comfortable as possible, but apart from that, there doesn't seem to be much I can do. I check to make sure the apartment's gas has been killed at the meter and that the neighbours are all aware and out of the building. They gather in the parking lot and on the grass. A few ask me about Rob.

The magnitude, the reality of what's happened – or what may have happened – starts to sink in while I wait for the ambulance and fire department to show up. I've been shot at before. I've been punched. On the arrest of one fugitive, while I was with the Atlanta field office, I was even deliberately hit by a moving car. But my home has always been safe.

Until now.

I reach into my pocket for a cigarette. The lighter is just flaring into life when I realize the irony of what I'm doing and put the damn thing back in the pack.

The fire department arrives just ahead of the paramedics. I give them a quick rundown on events, and they haul ass inside the building to deal with the flames. An ambulance shows up for Rob, and he's stretchered away. The paramedics don't seem too worried by his condition, smoke inhalation, they say, so I hope he'll be OK. I call Teresa and let her know everything that's happened before riding with Rob to Beth Israel Deaconess Medical Centre.

The ambulance blasts through the city streets, rattling with every crack in the concrete, every resurfaced crosswalk. The paramedic in the back puts an oxygen mask on Rob and tries to keep him still. They offer me one as well, but I don't feel too bad. I think of the email I sent, trying to draw out Goddard. I see flames gutting my home. I see myself, lonely and exposed. And guilty. The haloes around the lights outside look like hazy, burning eyes, staring, judging.

'Your husband should be fine, Mrs Garrett,' the young-looking doctor in spotless whites says to Teresa. Rob's been away for tests and examination somewhere in the depths of the hospital for nearly an hour now, and I've been keeping Teresa company in the waiting area. She looks tired and drawn, still wrapped tightly in a winter coat. Normally she's a bundle of energy with a sharp wit and a sharper tongue. Not now. 'We'll need to keep him here for observation, but there should be no lasting effects. He just needs oxygen and rest.'

'When can I see him?'

The voice is strong and steady, but there's a pleading, the wide darkness of fear in her eyes. I've known Teresa for years, and I've never seen her like this. But then again, I've never seen anything happen to Rob before.

'In theory, right now, I think. But he'll probably be unconscious until the morning at least, so you might want to get some sleep.' He smiles. 'Best not to stay up all night, only to nod off the moment he wakes up tomorrow. I'll go find out what room he's likely to be put in, and I'll see what we can do to make it comfortable. You might have to make do with a couple of chairs and a blanket, though.'

'Thank you, Doctor,' she says. 'That's really good of you.'

She watches him head off through the double swing doors, then turns to me and says, 'Who did it, Alex? Who nearly killed my husband?'

'I'm not sure, Teresa.'

'You can guess, though.'

I nod. 'Yeah. Yeah, I can. Cody Williams' friend, the one who's been holding Holly Tynon for the past seven years. At a guess, he wants me either scared or out of the way.'

'You get him, Alex. You make sure he never does anything like this again. Eight years I've been married to Robin, and I've never had any reason to worry about him.' She lowers her eyes, looks away. 'He could've been killed tonight, Alex. You both could. When you called me, I didn't know what to think. I was so afraid it was ... that you were trying not to worry me, that it was worse than you were saying.'

'I wouldn't do that.'

'I know, I know. I just . . . you get him, OK, Alex? I never want to worry like that again.'

The doctor waves Teresa in through the doors, and she follows him, hand brushing my shoulder in farewell as she goes. I stand there for a moment, thinking about what she said. As I turn towards the hospital's main entrance, a cop in a suit, badge hanging from his top pocket, makes his way through the doors and heads in my direction.

'Alex Rourke?' he says. 'I'm Detective Jack Connell with Boston PD. We need to take a statement from you, to find out exactly what happened and what you saw at your apartment. Are you feeling up to that?'

'Yeah, I'm fine. Feels like I've smoked a whole lot, but that's the worst of it.'

'In that case, if you could come with me to the station. You want a lift or have you got a car?'

I shake my head. 'No, it's back home.'

Head outside to his car. The night smells of snow and the long slide into winter. Further down the vehicle bay, beneath the harsh lights of the apron roof and the red and white glare of an ambulance's emergency strobes, a team of paramedics rushes a gurney from the back of their vehicle and run towards the doors to ER. A bag of plasma rattles above the body strapped to its surface. A neck brace and a shock of scruffy black hair. I catch a brief glimpse of the guy's bloody face beneath the oxygen mask and he looks like Clinton Travers.

'The Fire Department put out the blaze pretty quickly,' Connell says as we drive through the near-deserted streets. 'The last I heard, they didn't think the damage was too serious. If the structure's still sound, you might be able to move back in once it's been repaired. You got a place to stay tonight?'

My eyes snap back from the streetlit blackness beyond the glass. I'm tired, weight of fatigue dropping on to my shoulders like lead snowfall. 'I hadn't thought about it. Should probably sort something out.'

'You got any friends or family you could go to for a couple of days?'

'No. Not this time of night, anyway.'

Connell nods. 'There's a Yellow Pages at the station. Make a call to a motel or something when we get there, find somewhere with a room.'

'Thanks.'

The D-4 District Station is a modern brick building, three storeys, solid and well-built. An odd arched portico on one corner of the street, giving the entryway a church-like appearance, some throwback to the concept of sanctuary, I guess. It mirrors the towering form of the Cathedral of the Holy Cross opposite, a bulwark illuminated by spots in the ground at its feet. The same trick we'd pull as kids, holding a torch at the bottom of our faces as we told ghost stories. Exaggerating the shadows, throwing our ideas of scale off kilter to intimidate and enthral. The lights in most of the station windows are still on, the cold blue-white of fluorescents unfiltered by blinds or curtains. The colour of work, business. A colour no one ever has at home.

Down a short, echoing tiled corridor to an open-plan squad room. Connell finds a copy of the Yellow Pages and gets me a coffee while I find a hotel with a spare room for tonight. Then I tell him what he needs to know about me, and everything Rob and I found when we reached my apartment. The place turned over. The busted lock.

'Do you have any enemies, anyone with any reason to want to do this to you or to your property?' he asks, once he's finished typing up what I'm saying.

'You mean anyone I could put a name to, anything like that? No, not recently.'

'No one you've encountered through work? You're a private detective, right?'

I nod. 'Yeah, but I can't think of anyone specific we've worked on recently who would've gone as far as torching my home.'

'How about from your FBI days?' he says.

'I can't remember any arsonists. I suppose anything's possible, but it doesn't seem very likely.' I shrug. 'Someone's got a grudge against me, that's for sure. And there's a bunch of people who I suppose might have had something to do with this – old friends of a guy called Cody Williams, say, or the people trying to get him released from jail who've hassled me in the past few weeks. But I can't think of anyone I know for sure would be a good make for a suspect.'

Connell stops typing and looks up at me. 'Oh, you're the Cody Williams guy. Yeah, I saw that on the news, along with those idiots outside prison. Why didn't you mention it before?'

'I've worked unpopular cases plenty of times. And the kind of dipshits who call you up to hurl abuse at you are usually restricted to phoning because they're not the sort to go any further – cowardliness or fear of getting caught keeps them at a distance. None of the ones who called threatened to kill me, not from what I remember.'

'Well, we'll have a check on your phone records to see if we can find them and question them, just in case. What about these friends of Williams you mentioned – anyone in particular?'

'No one obvious I can think of. He didn't have many friends.'

And maybe that's all it'll turn out to be, I remind myself as I lie back on the scratchy sheets at the Jefferson Lodge. Some whacko nutball tries to torch my place in revenge for me hassling an 'innocent man'. Another decides to send me snippets from his porno collection he's tried hawking to half of California that happen to feature a girl who looks a lot like Holly Tynon. Cody latches on to the idea and tries to use it for leverage against me.

That's a whole lot of coincidence. I'll stick to my theory for the time being.

A morning of cold and bitter rain. I pick up some grapes on the way to Beth Israel to see how Rob's doing, not because he likes grapes, but because I know he'll appreciate the humour in the tradition. I also leave a message with Jean at the office so she knows what's happened and not to expect either of us in for the time being.

Rob's awake when I get to his room. Eyes looking a little red and raw, but otherwise unharmed. And he's off the oxygen. Teresa is by his side, nursing a cup of coffee. By the sounds of the conversation they're having when I come in, he'll be going home in an hour or so.

'Hey, Alex,' he says, as I wander in. 'Some night, huh?'

'You could say that. I brought something to keep your strength up.' I drop the grapes on the table next to him.

'I was hoping for an apple Danish and a cappuccino.'

'Don't knock it – they're packed with vitamins. How are you feeling?'

'Like I've smoked the whole of Cuba. But not bad, considering. Next time we're messing around with a burning building, I'll leave you alone. Your lungs take it a whole lot better than mine.'

Teresa laughs. 'You would too, you chicken son of a bitch.'

'I thought the injured hero was supposed to be treated with great sympathy and have every need pandered to.' Rob rolls his eyes. 'I'm hurt. I don't have to take that sort of thing.'

I sit down on a spare chair and help myself to a grape. 'I see I needn't have worried.'

'Yeah, it's nothing. I'll be back at work tomorrow. How bad's the damage to your apartment?'

'I don't know yet. I picked up the 'Vette from the lot on the way to the hotel last night, but the place was sealed off. The cops said the fire wasn't too bad, so I might be lucky. Hopefully I'll be able to pick up some spare clothes and stuff there later today.'

'No chance they've caught who did it yet?'

'Not that I've heard. I suppose one of the neighbours might have seen something, but the cops aren't likely to say much about it unless it leads somewhere.' I shrug again. 'I spoke to Jean earlier, by the way. Let her know what happened and asked her to explain the situation to the kids and any clients who get in touch. I told her there was nothing to worry about.'

'Real stupid you'd have looked if you got here to find there'd been complications and I'd died in the night,' he says, grinning. Teresa purses her lips but keeps quiet. 'Anyway, you'd better get to work. Keep the kids in line until I get back tomorrow. Though I know you want to keep on Holly Tynon.'

'Yeah, if that's OK with you.'

Rob nods. 'Sure. Just be careful, Alex. Whether

they meant to or not, whoever you're looking for could've killed you last night. They're not fucking around any more.'

Chapter Twenty-Two

The place smells like morning at Scout camp. Old smoke, damp firewood, traces of whatever food was on the fire the night before. Except that now those stray scents are from the drapes, the work surfaces, the ceiling tiles in what remains of my kitchen. The acrid hit of burnt plastic. The wet dog undertone of carbonized wood. A complex mix of subtle flavours from food that cooked off in the heat.

The detective from the Fire Investigation Unit adjusts his hard hat and says, 'The inspector said the structural damage is repairable. Place should be fine with a bit of work.'

'Uh-huh.'

'Must be weird, seeing it like this.'

I nudge at the soot sludge by my feet. 'I guess. But it's only a place. It's not like the family farm's just gone up in smoke taking my ancestral heirlooms and all my worldly possessions with it.'

'Fair enough,' he says, shrugging. He turns and heads past me, in the direction of the front room. 'People take it all sorts of different ways. Knew a guy once drowned himself in the Charles River when his family's home went up. I never did understand why – while they'd lost almost everything, they were staying with friends, and a big cheque from the insurance company showed up a couple of days later. People are strange.'

'I guess.'

'Anyway, speaking of worldly possessions, let's do what we came here for, see if anything's missing.'

The room looks like a crime scene. Strange impression to get from my own home, but it has that frozen feel to it – a little window on events from the past, which no one witnessed apart from the perp and that we can now only attempt to piece together from the signs he left behind. Although everything in it is mine, and I recognize it as such, it's from a distance, one step removed, like looking at a photograph of the real thing.

Papers – notes from the Williams file, other stuff I'd found out on the search for his accomplice – lie scattered on the carpet, the boxes that once held them upended on the couch. Shelves of CDs, books and a couple of stray houseplants that were barely clinging to existence anyway are strewn across the floor by the TV. My computer screen is lying face down beneath the desk, with a drift of scattered CDs on and around it. A couple of them are snapped, and I can see traces of forensics chemical fuming where the cops presumably looked for finger- or shoe-prints on the broken plastic.

'So,' the detective says, 'does it look like there's anything missing here? Valuables, personal items?'

I scan the debris. 'I don't think so. Not valuables,

anyway. I don't know if anything's been taken from the files I had.'

'Well, take a look through them once we've gone over the rest of the apartment. It might be that it was thieves, and they found what they were looking for elsewhere.'

He doesn't sound convinced by his own suggestion. I'm not either. We check the rest of the place anyway. The bedroom seems to have been briefly searched by the intruder, but even though I can't shake the nagging feeling that there's something different, even allowing for the place being ransacked, I can't think of anything obvious that's missing. Even my gun is still in the drawer where I left it. If it was thieves, they were looking for something pretty obscure.

Back in the front room I start picking through the scattered papers on the floor, rebuilding the files, checking their contents. Most of the original material seems to be intact, if a little crumpled.

'Nothing,' I say. 'Nothing missing that I can see.'

'Nothing at all?' He looks baffled.

'Not that I've noticed. If anything's gone, it's minor stuff.'

'There's absolutely nothing missing or different?'

'Apart from my kitchen being a burned-out wreck? No, I can't see anything that's changed.'

Next day finds me in Worcester and at the home of Brian Tucker, the first of Williams' old regulars who were never checked during the original investigation.

Back in the day, he had a couple of visits from Cody and then switched to taking his car to Pete's body shop directly. I'm not too hopeful of finding anything, but I've got to try.

Tucker lives in a fairly sizeable house set above and some way back from the road. A pair of old elms overlook the drive and cast a thin shadow on the sidewalk in the clouded light. Tucker's 1970 Oldsmobile Cutlass is sitting at the top of the driveway and looks newly washed. I leave the 'Vette by the kerb and head up to his house.

'Cody Williams?' Tucker says. 'That guy off the news?'

'Yeah.'

'*He* was the guy who used to fix my car? Seriously? Christ, I never knew it was him.'

Through the door behind him I can see clean, modern décor. Cream walls, a polished pine staircase. A couple of framed art prints in the hallway. The place smells of air freshener and something cooking in the kitchen.

'I've never even heard Pete talk about it,' Tucker says. His eyes are wide and he seems genuinely surprised. 'Not in all the time I've known him. Not any of his other regulars either. We've chatted about plenty of things over the years, but never that.'

'No?'

He shakes his head. 'No, never. It's not the kind of thing you'd ever forget. I mean, the things that guy did . . .'

'It's a strange world, Mr Tucker. You never think you'd meet these people, but someone has to at some time.'

'I suppose so. But still . . . I'm sorry, Mr Rourke, but I don't think I'll be much help to you. I just don't know anything about him, certainly not after all this time.'

He smiles a little ruefully. Tucker is maybe five eight, well-built without being too stocky, a few years older than me. He'd be a fit for the guy in the footage, but then so would a lot of people. I seriously doubt he'd be able to keep Holly here, in a neighbourhood like this, and do those things to her without someone hearing or seeing something. If it was him, he'd need to have a second property somewhere. I make a mental note to run a full background check on him when I get back to Boston.

'Well, thanks anyway, Mr Tucker. If you do remember anything, my number's on my card.'

'Sure,' he says, and waves as I amble back down towards the road.

Next stop finds me at an old farmhouse near Ayer in northern Massachusetts, home to Ben Joyce, at least according to the notes in front of me. A few straggly trees line the dirt track running up the hill. Apart from that, it's empty pasture all around. The main building lurks just below the ridgeline, grey stone with a battered wooden barn next to it. In between the two, I can just make out a burgundy station wagon. Either he's got rid of the 1965 Impala he owned back when Cody worked for Drill Hall Collectors' Autos, or it's in the barn. No sign of life, but with the windows reflecting nothing but the gloom of the sky above, that's no surprise. I slide back into the 'Vette and take the track up to the house.

Joyce is peering at me through the window by the door as I climb out of the car, parked in the yard in front of the two buildings. Through the lace curtain I can make out a thin, gaunt-looking face with wide, staring eyes. A flash of grey-white hair above them, catching the light as Joyce pulls away from the glass. I walk up and knock on the door.

For a moment I think he's going to act like he's out and ignore me. Then I hear a board creak inside the house and the door opens a fraction, just wide enough to admit his grizzled face. Stale, unheated air drifts past him. He's wearing a threadbare grey sweater and jogging pants.

'Yeah?' he says.

'Mr Joyce? I'm a private detective. I was hoping you could give me a couple of minutes of your time to answer a few questions.'

'Is this about Martha?'

I raise an eyebrow, try to stay open, friendly. 'Who's Martha?'

'My ex-wife. This isn't about her court case?'

I continue to look politely blank.

'Her drugs bust? You got some questions about

it?' He wipes his nose. 'Can't help you. I haven't spoken to her in months. Only found out about the arrest 'cos her goddamn lawyer tried asking me for bail money. Told him she could go fuck herself.'

'No, it's not about that, Mr Joyce. It goes back a lot further than that. I understand you used to own a '65 Impala.'

'Yeah, but I sold it, what, five or six years ago now,' he says. He still hasn't opened the door any further. 'It was the divorce. I needed the money to pay my attorney's bills afterwards. Goddamn wife.'

'Uh-huh.'

'Never had the money to buy another one. So whatever happened to that car, it wasn't my fault.'

I try a smile. 'When you owned the Impala, though, you had a number of repairs and replacements carried out by someone from Drill Hall Collectors' Autos.'

'Yeah, that's right.'

'Do you remember the guy who worked on your car?'

Joyce looks blank for a while, thinking, or so it seems. I watch his face carefully, looking for any sign that he's readying a lie. His eyes glance up, away to the left, and he purses his lips, exhaling over his front teeth. 'Young kinda guy?'

'That's the one.'

'Don't recall much about him, to be honest. Saw him a few times, but I can't even remember his name.' I'm not sure, but I think he's telling the truth. 'We never talked about much. Just the car, that was about it. He might've asked about my job, maybe. But I ain't sure.'

Wasted journey. 'Did he ever say anything about any friends, places he liked to visit, anything like that?'

'Don't think so.'

'Well, thanks anyway.' I sigh, then decide to try one more thing. 'Before I go, could I ask a favour? Kinda long time on the road, and I was wondering if I could use your bathroom.'

Joyce looks me up and down for a moment, eye-balling me suspiciously. 'Sure,' he says, and hauls open the door. The hallway beyond is covered in threadbare lilac carpet and lined with dusty prints of watercolour landscapes. It's also plastered – no bare wood panelling here. 'First door on the right, under the stairs.'

I drive away from Joyce's farmhouse knowing that he isn't the one, as much as I'd wished otherwise. Even ignoring the difference in interior décor, his build isn't big enough to make him the guy in the footage. He's a loner, but that's no crime.

I finish my journey back to Boston under skies now darkened into night. Sit in my hotel room and write up a few notes, then head into town to check my email. Still no reply from Holly's kidnapper.

Dinner is a Tex-Mex place in the North End. Chicken in a fiery tomato sauce laced with plenty of chilli, salad with garlic dressing, It's a good meal, washed down with cold Mexican beer, and I feel better for it. I've just paid the check and hauled on my jacket when my cell phone bleeps to signal an incoming text message.

Mr rourke. Have info 4 u. Come 2 house. Must talk. Urgent. -brian t

I try calling Tucker back on the number at the bottom of the message, but I get no answer at all, so I'm left wondering what's so urgent or so secret that he couldn't have told me before I left his place earlier today. Guess I have no choice but to head back to Worcester if I'm to find out.

Cutting through the traffic on the myriad feeder roads leading to the main highway, I spot a silver Taurus that seems to be mirroring my moves. I speed up, he speeds up. I make a couple of experimental turns, he follows. The roads are busy, and there's a lot of people heading for the I-90 the same way I am, but everything about this car screams 'tail' to me.

The last intersection before the interstate, I hang a right and almost immediately turn again, this time into a strip mall parking lot. The Taurus follows and pulls up just shy of the lot entrance.

When I stride back towards it, the driver guns the engine and roars off down the street. I don't get a look at him.

They must know I was heading for the highway, and they might try watching for me on the I-90. I avoid it and take minor routes as far as Natick. There, I pull into a gas station within sight of the I-90 off-ramp – might as well fill up the 'Vette while I'm stopping, after all – and try once more to call Tucker. The phone rings, but again there's no answer. I leave him a voicemail anyway, telling him I'm on my way. Pay for the gas and a fresh pack of Marlboro, then I hit the road again. This whole meeting is worrying me. Tucker's silence, the sudden change in his tune. Whoever that was in the Taurus. I'm not entirely sure what I'm getting into. I'm glad I've got my Colt with me. If this is someone's idea of a trap, I'm damned sure I'm not going to be caught easily.

Worcester is a web of lights in the blackness, the faint glow from the city reflecting dimly off the clouds above, just enough to give a roof to the night. The traffic in the city centre thins and fades as I turn east, away from the loop the highway cuts through the heart of the sprawling town. There's been no sign of the Taurus behind me since I lost it at the strip mall.

Tucker's street is quiet. Lights are on in most of the houses, but the 'Vette is the only vehicle on the road. A glow comes from the lamp on Tucker's porch, and the same from one of the ground-floor windows. There's no sign of movement as I climb out of the car, even though the engine noise must've told him I'm here. Above me, the bare trees rasp in the wind.

I see the first sign that something is wrong as

I approach the front door. It's hanging maybe half an inch ajar. I want to reach for my gun, but this isn't my house. Instead, I stalk up to the door on the balls of my feet and listen hard for any sounds within.

'You've got to help me, Doctor. You've got to get me out of this place!'

'But Michael, we are helping you. You belong here. Don't you remember?'

'I'm not crazy! For God's sake, man!'

'You murdered your wife, Michael.'

The TV. No other sounds. I nudge the door open further and call into the house. 'Mr Tucker?'

No answer. I push the door in all the way. The bulb's dead in the hallway, but light spills from the doorway into the front room. A faint glow comes from the kitchen at the far end of the corridor; oven clock, maybe, or an open fridge.

'You can't keep me here! I don't belong! I don't!'

'I'm sorry, Michael.'

'I DIDN'T KILL HER! I couldn't. Could I?'

Move inside, and Brian Tucker is lying on the carpet in a pool of blood. The beige walls of the lounge are spattered with crimson here and there, and there's a bloody handprint on the corner of the coffee table. The print isn't shiny in the light. It's had time to dry. I check quickly for a pulse, but Tucker is long gone and cold. A couple of stab wounds in his back, and I'd guess more on front.

I have time to mutter, 'Jesus fucking Christ,' before

something hard hits me in the back of the neck like a cartoon anvil dropped from a rooftop and the floor crashes up to meet me.

Chapter Twenty-Three

Swimming drunkenly in a sea of pain, I barely register a couple more blows driven into my ribs. The carpet smothers one cheek like pins and needles, I'm seeing bright lights fuzzily through swirling frosted glass and there's a roaring in my ears.

Over it, I can just make out one voice, slow and distorted like it's coming from deep underwater, saying, 'He's out. You make the call, then we can report back to Mr Heller.'

Another voice replies, 'Let's get the fuck outta here. Small towns, dunno how quick they'll be. Do it from the car.'

A third voice says, 'You'll never see free air again,' but I'm pretty sure that's just the TV.

Then I black out.

The two men are gone a couple of minutes later when I force my eyes open and fight to stand. My knees feel like rubber and my head is full of loose wiring. I can't feel my neck at all, but my limbs seem to be working, after a fashion, so I figure nothing's broken.

Tucker's body is next to me, his one outstretched arm flung out towards me as if it doesn't want me to leave. As my vision wanders unsteadily over him, I see something dark in his clenched right fist. It looks like a glove, black leather. A little worn and starting to show threads. Exactly the same as a pair that was in a drawer in my apartment.

It's my glove in a dead man's hand.

Was it still there when I checked the place with the arson detective?

I don't remember.

My heart quickens, adrenaline cutting through some of the molasses that fill my head. As I lurch to my feet, I catch sight of a knife, barely visible where it's been dropped under the couch. The murder weapon, I guess. It looks like one from the set I have in my kitchen.

I'm being set up.

In the distance, a siren's wail briefly cuts the air. Clearing traffic. Racing to the scene. We heard a violent argument, Officer. Suspect found at the scene. Evidence of a struggle.

I want to grab the knife and the glove so the cops won't find them, remove them from the scene. But if I take too long, if they're closer than I think, if they catch me and I'm still carrying them, I'm finished. And every second I spend trying to decide only makes it more likely.

Fuck.

Fuck.

Fuck.

I take a huge gulp of air and force myself to move. Reel shakily outside, pulling the door back to its original position, and jog down to the 'Vette as best I can. Fumble the key in the ignition, try to concentrate on making it go. Not go anywhere much, just *away*.

Blue lights are coming into view in the distance behind me as I ease away from the kerb and get the hell out of Dodge.

You get found with a dead body, signs that both of you were in a fight, your prints on the weapon that killed him, then you're screwed. Case closed. Even if the two guys who were there left traces, there's no need for the cops to check them. They already got the killer, so who cares about the details?

On the outskirts of Worcester, the sick feeling in my head suddenly flushes out, migrates south. I pull over to the side of the road and throw up all over the shoulder.

I have to make the cops work the scene, hope they find something from the real killers. I have to figure out what I'm going to do about all this and where the hell this leaves me.

And I have to find out what the *fuck* all this has to do with Gabriel Heller.

Chapter Twenty-Four

I don't stop again until I'm back in Boston. Nerves feel like lines of ice, everything taut, ready to snap. I am, or will be, a murder suspect, and I don't know just how far they've fixed things to make it look like it was me.

Fuck.

I try to gather my thoughts, concentrate, figure it all out, at the hotel, but I'm too on edge. Panicking. Not thinking straight. I need to calm down a little, look at this rationally. I pack up my meagre things and stick them in the trunk, then drive to a bar a good half a mile away.

Perched at the counter, one bottle of Bud sunk and another on the way, and Billy Idol's 'Rebel Yell' drowning out the conversations of everyone else in Bailey & Munroe's. I've only ever been in here once, and that was a year ago. Damn near anonymous.

Some guy – Jack or Jock or something – has latched on to me. Slouched on the next stool, speech to match his posture, a good three or four beers over the line where he'll remember anything the following morning. I'm not sure if he's mistaken me for an old friend, or if he's just in the habit of picking strangers to yammer away at. I let him talk, act like I'm listening, and I think.

'. . . and 'cos I hadda brother who'uz in the business, y'know – doin' the same thing – I tol' him I'd . . .'

The murder weapon may have come from my kitchen, but I don't know how much there'll be on it to link it to me. And I can't imagine any cop thinking I brought a knife all the way from my gutted apartment just to kill some stranger. Unless they think I did it deliberately just so they'd think it was someone else . . .

I clamp down hard on that line of reasoning. Start looking for double- and triple-bluffs and you're on the short track to paranoid madness.

'. . . You been there before, 's right? Have you 'ver been there? Course you have. Loadsa times – alla time, right? So . . .'

My prints will be on the front door, where I opened and closed it, and if they think to check there, on Tucker's neck. But nowhere else, which will surely look strange if it seems the killer wore gloves the rest of the time. Of course, it wouldn't be the first time a murderer's made that kind of mistake. And they might just assume it was a lousy wipe job. Or that I just hadn't touched anything else.

'. . . 'n this wuz a coupla years 'go, so this wuzza big thing . . .'

Having my glove in the victim's hand is bad. I'm no OJ – that thing will fit me. But can it be traced to me? It's not as though it's monogrammed or anything. It's possible there'd be some kind of hair or other trace evidence on the inside, but otherwise it might be all right. I doubt anyone would even remember I owned a pair like that. That might be wishful thinking, though. And who knows what other trace stuff there is that'll link back to me.

The girl tending bar gestures at the bottle, but I make a 'still drinking' gesture, as does my drunken companion, and she goes away again. The jukebox switches to Iggy Pop's 'Gimme Danger' and I have to stifle a laugh.

'. . . 'S right! That's 'xactly what I said. 'S no *way*, I said, yer can . . .'

The cops probably also have whatever bullshit description the killers used when they made the call. That'll tie in with the prints and the knife when they start following the chain. But they won't be able to find the person who made the 911 call, and that in itself will seem strange. Plus point for me. And there's no motive for me to kill Tucker. I hope.

Of course, there was no great motive for Cody to have killed Travers, and they still locked him away based on the physical evidence. Happy thought.

Equally, I have no idea what motive Heller has for getting involved in all this. Unless he's Goddard, or protecting Billy Perry, or there's another Heller in the city with goons ready to kill on his order, but they all seem unlikely.

'. . . So I figured, fuck 'er, y'know? No one wantsa . . . a . . . a . . . bitch, thing, like that . . .'

Apart from the tenuous suggestion I'd heard about Perry working for him once upon a time, I know

Gabriel Heller from the news, and from stories cop friends have told me. He was one of the 'honest businessmen' involved in the free-for-all in the North End's mob scene after the Hal White debacle a few years back. Boston's Mafia, never huge, had cut themselves half to shreds in an internal turf war and were losing ground to the Asian gangs, the Russians and just about everyone else. Then one of their big competitors from South Boston, this Irish guy called Hal White, turns supergrass and finds himself a couple of dodgy Bureau agents to look after him and help do his dirty work. The thing runs for a couple of years, getting dicier and dicier, and eventually comes crashing down when White gets cold feet and goes on the run. The whole bloody mess comes out, the Bureau's chasing its own tail with his handlers, the Irish gang scatters, and the mob in the North End is in absolute tatters. Leadership's dead or in jail, no one trusts anyone else, and the organization collapses as everyone decides to stake out their own piece of the pie.

Heller was one of them. Carved himself out a bunch of business interests, a gang all of his own, and a police investigation into his activities that fell apart when they tried to use evidence obtained in breach of his constitutional rights. Big goddamn mess, and the Boston PD haven't been able to touch him since. I heard a year or so ago that someone tried to kill him but shot up his brother Jack and his wife by mistake. What I've heard from the cops is that Heller's been cautious ever since, kept out of the public eye.

It seems pretty obvious now. His men steal some things they know they'll need from my apartment and use the fire as cover. They follow me the first time I go talk to Tucker and wait for me to get home. Then they kill him, send me a message from his phone, plant the evidence and wait for me to show up to complete the picture for the cops. Caught red-handed at the murder scene. Stabbed to death following a struggle. The Taurus doesn't seem to fit, but maybe they wanted to be sure I was coming. Maybe he was someone else entirely.

None of which explains why Heller would kill Tucker and frame me. Nor why he'd do it for God-dard, which seems like the only explanation. Unless he's staggeringly rich, it can't be for the money – Heller has more than enough of his own. Maybe they're friends. Maybe Heller knows who he is and where I'd find him.

'. . . an' I haven't 'ver seen her since – not, like, in years – not 't all. An . . . an' . . .'

I think about turning myself in. Going back to the hotel and waiting for the call, or the knock on the door. Ride out the music and hope the evidence isn't enough to send me to jail.

Hope. Right.

Wait around in a holding cell for days, get bail, don't get bail, months before a trial, maybe have the Travers case dug up again and the whole thing go to shit, and all that time Goddard's free to kill Holly, move her, hide her again, cover his tracks. And all this, everything I've been through, will have been for nothing.

Heller is in Boston.

Perry is likely to be in Boston, and might know Heller.

Whoever was in the Taurus followed me from Boston.

Any of them, and especially Heller, could give me Goddard. Give me Holly. I gave up on her once before. Let her go. And she paid for it in ways I can't even begin to imagine.

I can't let it happen again.

Then I'll face whatever's coming to me. Just let me get her back. Let me make up for the mistakes of seven years ago.

The drunk claps me on the shoulder and drains the dregs in his glass as he lurches unsteadily off his stool. ''S good t' see you, Jack,' he says. 'Funny, funny, shit that. You take . . . take care, yeah?'

'Yeah,' I say. I don't know if he even hears me as he stumbles towards the door.

I drive the 'Vette over to my apartment and park it in my space. It's a surprising wrench to leave it like that, but it's just too distinctive to stick with if I'm trying to lie low. I sling my bag over one shoulder and walk the few blocks to the office. Drop a sealed note for Rob through the door, explaining what's happened and asking him to get in touch by email if he needs me, then head down the ramp into the parking garage.

Less than a minute later, I'm driving out of there in the company's car. I'm placing a lot of trust in Rob. If the shit really does hit the fan and the cops come to ask him questions, there's nothing to stop him telling them I've taken it, and then everyone'll be watching for it. But I've got no choice – I can't rent a car without drawing the same heat, and I can't buy one this time of night.

In Natick, west of Boston, to make it look as though I've left town, I max out my daily withdrawal limits on every piece of plastic I own, then wait for midnight and the reset, and do it all again. Cash only from here on in. Switch off my cell phone as well; can't have them tracking me that way. Tooled up as best as I can, I head back into town for an uncomfortable night in the car and an uncertain morning to follow after.

Wake up with a jerk, a deep, throbbing pain in my neck where my head is scrunched up against the window, probably a hangover from the punishment it took last night. I'm parked at the back of a cracked and tumbledown lot that must've originally been a building of some sort; a single structure, a bar occupying what would have been the corner of the block, is the sole survivor of whatever stood here before. Dawn is rising over Boston, and the city is slowly coming to life.

Through the windshield, I can see traffic moving on Ellis Avenue. Delivery trucks making their morning rounds. Early shift workers. The first overly keen cubicle jockeys heading for work an hour or two before most of their colleagues, trying to get that pay rise, make that promotion. Or maybe just correct the mistakes of yesterday before the boss shows up.

A young couple walk past. Hair still damp from the shower. His clothes a little more creased, an extra day's wear. Hands clasped together, leaning into each other. Smiling with the unfamiliarity of it all, still adjusting to each other. Going for coffee, breakfast, a cab home, or not.

I watch it all with a strange sense of dislocation. As if there is more than just a simple pane of glass between me and the city. A physical fracture or disconnect of some sort, separating us on a deep, primal level. As if I'm looking at the world through a stranger's eyes.

Knowing I've crossed some invisible, intangible line. Crossed into another land where there is no law to rely on, no safety net to catch me if I fall. Where I'm alone in a sense I find hard to quantify.

First order of business is coffee. I tug my baseball cap down, collar up, just another guy trying to stay warm on a cold morning, and head for the nearest Starbucks. Buy an anonymous coffee and a muffin from the anonymous store, take it back to the car.

Next, a place to stay. I wait for the morning rush to burn itself out, then go find a hotel. Cheap, inattentive staff, cash rates. Little chance of anyone calling the cops for anything short of a dead body showing up in reception. Somewhere even the slightest police presence would probably cause its residents to vanish into the night like rats from the proverbial doomed vessel.

The Heart of the Fens Hotel fits the bill nicely. The name's an outright lie – the place sits on Bridlington Street, right on the boundary between the Fens and Roxbury. From the outside, it looks like someone's moved an old Soviet apartment block to Boston, given it a crumbling brick façade and hung a non-functioning neon sign from the corner near the manager's office. The inside lives up to the expectations created by the outside. Peeling boiled-cabbage-green paint speckled with dark spots of mildew, old carpet, terrifying furnishings, and the smell of air that hasn't seen an open window in a long, long time.

If I had to pick a place to die from a heroin overdose, this would be it.

It's ideal. I pay for the next few days up front, and by the time he's finished telling me where the parking lot is, the manager's eyes have already glazed over with the haze of disinterest and selective amnesia that comes with the job. Drop my stuff in my room, check to make sure I can get out in a hurry if needs be. The building's pretty quiet – at the moment anyway. With luck, if someone comes for me, I'll hear it. Then, in the tiny en suite bathroom, I shave my head with my electric razor.

No use looking like my description when the cops release it, which they will.

On Milton Avenue, there's a blocky brick building whose high, empty windows hang darkly over the street like glassy tombstones. In the early 1900s it was a linen factory. One day a fire broke out in the stacks of dry cloth, and twenty-three workers trapped inside were burned alive.

Now the shell of the old building is a pool hall for lowlifes to play games in dead women's ashes. A petty crook and sometime cokehead called Angie tells me she doesn't know where Heller is. 'Saw him once,' she says, as she tries to justify my fifty bucks. 'At Metro's, way back. Think he probably sold after that thing with the cops. Dunno where he hangs out now.'

Tom Vine thinks he's talking to Rob. Tom used to be a delivery driver with a sideline in hauling things over state lines without bothering with taxes and paperwork. Our agency did some work for his lawyer when one of his employers tried to charge him with theft. He doesn't know where Heller is, either. 'But shit, Mr Garrett,' he says over a crackling phone connection, 'you don't want to get involved with him. Gabriel Heller's a mean son of a bitch. Paranoid too. He thinks you're messing with his business and he'll . . . well, you see what I'm getting at.'

'Why you asking me abou' Heller?' asks a youngish pimp and pusher called Thierry that Tom recommended I speak to. We're in a fearsomely trendy coffee shop near the river, a maze of bright orange couches and a haze of mochaccino steam. He's sitting with a couple of either hangers-on or minders. I'm not sure which, but they don't look like much. 'Why would I say anything to you? I don' care if you are a frien' of Tom's. That gets you nothing. Even if I could tell you anything, which I can', I wouldn'. You get away from here.'

This is how it goes with just about everyone I can think of who might be able to help. Two days playing deadbeats and dead-ends. After this, I figure I might as well have a look at Metro's; even if Heller did sell the place after his arrest, the management might have a number for him. Nothing else seems to be working.

Heller's old nightclub is a windowless concrete block squatting on an unwelcoming street corner. Walls painted all black, starting to crack and crumble, with double steel-bound doors. Like the sacrificial temple of some long-lost cyclopean civilization thrust up through Boston's crust.

No flyers posted on the walls, a bare minimum of graffiti – both a good sign; either it's well-cleaned, or people know not to mess with the owner. No answer to my hammering on the door – not such a good sign; no use finding the place if they won't talk to me. I give it one more try, then circle the building, looking for a service entrance. The back doors are almost identical, and identically shut.

Another minute's battering at the main entrance is eventually rewarded. One door opens a crack and a bald guy with a face like a grizzly with a sore ass says, 'Yeah? What?'

'I'm looking for Gabriel Heller.'

'Never heard of him.'

'He used to own this place. Maybe still does.'

The door opens further so the guy can loom properly. He has a body to match the face – thick, heavy. Punching it would probably be like hitting a sack full of lead. 'Dorian Robertson's the manager here,' he says. 'He runs this club. Who the fuck are you?'

He doesn't look like the sort of guy to follow the news. 'Brian Tucker,' I tell him. 'Mr Heller and I have a matter we need to urgently discuss.'

'Told you, I never heard of him.'

'Maybe you could ask your manager if he has a number I could call Mr Heller on. I'm sure *he'll* have heard of him.'

'Maybe you could get lost.'

'Maybe Mr Heller would appreciate it if you'd be more helpful. I'm sure he wouldn't want our business together delayed.'

The guy glares at me for a second, then vanishes back inside the club, letting the door thump closed behind him. I stand on the street corner in the cold. Some passing traffic at the next intersection along, but this dead block might as well be something out of a Western, emptied before the gunfight at high noon.

'What can I do for you, Mr Tucker?'

A blond guy in a good suit, no tie, is in the doorway. About my age, an inch or two taller, wiry. Eyes like chipped marbles, sizing me up. This must be the grizzly's handler. If he recognizes Tucker's name, he doesn't show it.

'Mr Robertson?'

'That's right.'

'I need to speak to Gabriel Heller.'

'So Jerry tells me.'

'I was hoping you could help me.'

He shifts his balance, weight on to his back foot. 'Mr Heller no longer runs this establishment.'

'But he used to. Maybe you have a phone number for him, or the name of one of the places he still runs.'

'What's your business with him?'

'He wants to talk to me. We have some urgent things to discuss.'

Dorian shrugs. 'If he wants to talk to you, why hasn't he contacted you?'

'He tried a couple of days ago. But his messengers left before they could tell me where to reach him.'

'How careless.'

I smile. 'Quite.'

'Well, Mr Tucker, I'm busy right now, but I'll have a look, see if I can find some contact details for him later today. Where can I reach you when I have them?'

'I'm a busy man too, Mr Robertson. How about I give you a call later, see if you have anything for me.'

He nods, hands me a card. 'Of course. If I find anything I can't give you over the phone, maybe you could drop by again and pick it up.'

'Sure. Whatever.' I don't smile. 'Speak to you later, Mr Robertson.'

I hear the door close behind me as I walk away.

'Police have released details of a man they wish to question in connection with a murder in Worcester two days ago. Brian Tucker, fifty-two, was killed at his home late on Monday night. Police want to speak to Alex Rourke, a former FBI agent, in connection with the murder.'

Cut to that same footage of me and Downes walking into MCI-Ashworth on that first blustery morning. The anchorwoman continues speaking in voiceover as it replays twice and freezes on my face. 'Rourke was in the news recently when the FBI brought him in to speak to convicted killer Cody Williams in jail at the request of the families of his suspected victims. Rourke's efforts – controversial in some quarters,' she says as the picture cuts to shots of the protesters outside the jail, 'failed, however. Detective Perigo from Worcester Police Department said that Rourke may still be in the Boston metropolitan area or elsewhere in eastern New England.'

Cut to still photo. Tucker. The picture looks a few years out of date. Professional job, probably one he'd use for the office, something like that. 'Brian Tucker was a successful and respected property developer who had lived in Worcester for over twenty years. Police do not yet know why he was murdered.'

She turns to her fellow anchor with a broad smile. 'Tom,' she says.

I stop paying attention. Lie back on the bed with my stomach a cold, hollow pit. Nothing makes you feel like a wanted man like being plastered all over the news. And knowing that anyone or everyone you meet may have seen it as well. A city full of hungry eyes, every one of them watching you, following every move you make. Remembering, reporting.

And somewhere out there, Goddard. Did he put Heller on to me? Have they been following me? How do the two of them tie together? Knowing that Goddard's paid such direct attention to me, and to removing me from his path, I feel like I could touch him – walk round the corner tomorrow morning, find him sitting drinking a coffee, wake up in the night to see him pressed up against my window. But I can't picture him. He's formless, intangible. A ghost. A creature of smoke. An illusion.

Two days of being on the run. Two days of keeping to the hotel except to talk to lowlifes in shitholes or on the phone. The rest of the time spent gnawing on my nerves and jumping whenever I hear a police siren in the streets nearby. It's like waiting for a really important phone call – the results of a biopsy or a blood test. You're constantly strained to breaking point, worrying about every noise outside and every footstep in the corridor, trying to cover every possibility. Picture every outcome. Imagine every possible ending.

Is it any wonder that most criminals on the run get caught when they do something stupid, let their guard slip, go out drinking or take in a movie, some other normal social activity, and someone recognizes them? Just because they wanted to feel like part of the human race again.

It's because cabin fever sets in quickly. You start going stir crazy. Because you're left with no one to talk to about your situation, no one but yourself, and all you can hear is the sound of your own thoughts scratching at the inside of your skull and your own heart pounding with fear. You're utterly, totally alone, and there is no one that you can trust not to turn on you. Like being a spy in a foreign land, except that no one trains you for it, and you don't have some organization of fellow spies watching out for you back home. No support. No one to turn to. No one to care what happens to you, and an entire world against you. And everything I do, everyone I speak to on Heller's trail only ratchets the risk up another notch.

I try to shake off this feeling before it sets in hard, and to kill time before I call Robertson. He should have had a chance to speak to Heller; with the way he acted there's no way he wasn't connected. I go for a walk in the rough direction of the city centre and the harbour beyond, to find a payphone, make arrangements.

I used to love this city at night.

The curious mix of old and new as you near the

financial district and the Common. The winding streets of the old core of Boston. Weathered brickwork, iron railings. That feeling of age, solidity, continuity. Like returning to the house you grew up in, it has a sense of permanence and comfort, even when you're bitching about its faults or cursing your fellow inhabitants. The sense that it's as much a part of you as you're a part of it.

Now it smells of cold water and empty air, and feels so delicate and fragile that I could send the whole thing crashing down with one wrong glance. As if the cracks in the paving and between each brick of each building are widening like fault lines, slowly tearing themselves to pieces before my eyes.

Four women spill out of a bar on Chambers Street, mid-joke, faces raised in laughter. The air momentarily flushes warm and carries the scent of beer casks from inside and perfume from the quartet. The girl at the back, quieter than her companions, glances at me as we pass, her eyes still smiling from the joke before. That brief meeting of gazes, the same primal judging and measuring trick our animal ancestors were pulling millions of years before. That tiny fraction of time between one footstep and the next, enough to meet, fall in love, fade and part before we vanish from each other forever. Life in microcosm, repeated a million times a day all over the city. A tiny fragment of us dies and is reborn with every passing glance. With every footstep we are remade.

Those moments fall less frequently to me now. I

find myself lowering my gaze, not making contact with anyone. Imagining the dark glittering of dozens of eyes on me everywhere I go.

Picturing every passer-by stopping behind me, thinking, 'Don't I know him from somewhere? Didn't I see him on TV earlier?'

Waiting for someone to shout my name.

Waiting for the sounds of pursuit.

This feeling grows infinitely worse on the couple of occasions a police cruiser rolls past. I *know* I'm just another night-time pedestrian and they're not even looking at me, but I still feel the urge to dive into the shadows, and I still find myself thinking nonchalant thoughts as if they can somehow read my mind. At one intersection, I see two beat cops standing on the street corner. I cross over rather than walk past them.

By the waterfront, within spitting distance of the Long Wharf and the ugly upturned hull-like shape of the Marriott which protrudes from its centre, I find myself walking through sparse crowds at a miniature fairground set up on the wet paving stones. Lights from the half-dozen or so rides cast long, shimmering lines of colour on the harbour water and the city's regular sounds are drowned out by piped music, rattling machinery and the occasional voice of a child somewhere within the neon whirl.

I find a payphone by the harbour railings and make the call.

'Mr Robertson.'

'Mr Tucker.'

'Have you found that information I was looking for yet?'

'Maybe, maybe,' he says. 'I've got a package that might help you. Come down to the club and you can have it.'

I think, where Heller's guys can wait for me in comfort. I say, 'That's quite a walk and I don't have a car.'

'The city has many fine taxi companies.'

'I've only got the change for one ride and I have to get home again.'

'I pity you, facing such a dilemma.'

'I have a better idea,' I say. 'Have someone drop it with me. I'll be near the entrance to the Long Wharf Marriott. Don't take too long, either – it's almost my bedtime and I'll have to go home.'

After I hang up, I figure I have at least fifteen, twenty minutes before anyone shows up looking for me. I buy a couple of hot dogs from a vendor and find a spot from where I can see the Marriott to eat them, looking out over the water.

I picture diving in, letting my lungs fill. Wash away all the problems. The ultimate solution.

What a fucking mess I've made of all this, I can hear myself thinking. Like eavesdropping on my brain arguing with itself. *Everything. Holly gone, maybe already dead, Goddard free, Cody laughing at me. And when they catch me, everything'll come out. The whole lot will come crashing down.*

If the water has any advice for me, it keeps it to itself.

Stand there a while after I finish my snack dinner, mind empty. Check my watch and see that it's time to get into place, although I can't see anyone hovering near the hotel doors just yet. I turn away, back towards the bright lights of the fairground.

I'm weaving through the rides when the cop sees me.

Chapter Twenty-Five

Ambling past the stalls with a beat policeman's gait. A few yards behind him, hurrying to catch up, his partner carrying two newly bought cups of coffee. For a brief moment, his gaze shifts over me, and I lower my eyes, try to look inconspicuous, as I turn away from him and keep walking.

Inside, my mind's turning somersaults. Did Robertson or Heller tip them off? Are they here for me? Are his goons waiting nearby, or is Robertson genuine about letting me speak to Heller?

Past a half-dozen people waiting by the side of a spinning-teacup ride. All quiet behind me, and maybe he didn't recognize me.

I hear the 'Hey!' as I'm approaching a cotton-candy stand.

Don't flinch, don't speed up. Don't run. Crowds will always look at a running man. Instead, with thin lines of raw adrenaline pounding through my veins, I make a right, between the teacups and the cotton candy. I jog across the road through a narrow gap between passing vehicles.

'Hey! Stop! Police!' from behind me, as I dodge between a bus and an oncoming Chevy. Keep walking, briskly, without looking back. The traffic noise doesn't let up until I'm almost at the corner of the restaurant opposite the fairground. Then I hear horns, cars stopping. I picture the two cops holding them up, hands outstretched, eyes darting my direction, trying to keep tabs on me as they cross in my wake.

I dive into the alley that runs next to the restaurant and, safely out of the way of the general public, run like hell.

I sprint down the canyon between buildings, cut left where the alleyway turns, and slam on the brakes about a yard from where it spills out on to the street beyond. I can hear the echoing *rap rap rap* of running feet from behind me as I walk briskly away and manage to hail a passing cab.

The two cops emerge, out of breath and staring hungrily around, as I close the door and the taxi pulls away in the direction of North Station. Plenty of civilian traffic, but no squad cars following. From the station, a second cab takes me to a spot four blocks from the hotel.

The night's grown colder, and this part of town's far quieter than the centre. The adrenaline rush from the waterfront has long turned sour, and although my ears jump at every little noise around me, it's a deep sense of tiredness and a longing for sleep that fills me most.

The taxi's just about vanished from sight when a

black BMW cruises past me at speed and skids to a halt by the sidewalk a few yards ahead. Three big guys in suits jump out, two of them carrying guns and all of them looking at me.

Chapter Twenty-Six

For an eternity that lasts a fraction of a second we do nothing but stare at each other. Six eyes boring into mine. Hard as steel. Unflinching.

Then I'm vaulting over the chainlink fence next to me and pounding across the parking lot beyond. One of them shouts, 'Fuck!' and I hear the fence screaming in protest as they climb after me. No one shoots.

Skid round the side of a darkened convenience store, hoping for a back way off the lot. Running footsteps echoing in the night air. A car engine, probably the BMW, the other end of the building. Past a couple of dumpsters, and I hear a woman's voice suddenly cry out, in anger or protest. The deep rumble of a man replying, tone heavy with threat.

Between the back wall of the store and a sedan of some kind, a girl I guess to be a hooker is arguing with a big guy in a sports jacket. He has one fist raised beside his head.

'Victor, you fuck, I paid you everything I owed. You give the rest . . .'

Her voice dies suddenly as she sees me running towards them and the back entrance to the park-ing lot. Victor is about to say something pertinent, probably about minding my own business, when the BMW rounds the far corner and screeches to a halt, lights blazing. He shuts his mouth again. A fourth guy in a suit pops up from the driver's side of the car with a gun in his hand. I can hear the other three behind me, see the hooker's shocked eyes flicker past me to the pursuing pack.

The maths say I either surrender or get shot. Or one, then the other. That I'm not going to make it off this lot without dealing with the suits.

The maths say, if I try to charge the guy by the Beamer, him or his friends will start firing.

But instinct says they haven't shot me yet, so they want me alive. Which might give me enough of an edge.

Victor is obviously slower on the uptake than everyone else. He stares at the suits, then rounds on the girl and yells, 'You call the cops? You fucking bitch!'

She doubles up and collapses to the ground as Victor slams his fist into her stomach. 'Fucking set me up!'

The BMW driver's eyes skip in his direction, and by the time his attention is back on me and the gun, I'm crashing full tilt into the car door, all my weight behind it. The door rams him back into the frame with an ear-grating crunch, and his gun goes skittering into the darkness.

I'm going to follow up with a kick to the head, but as he drops, he's making horrible roaring, rasping noises with each laboured breath, like a lung's gone or his throat's crushed, and I just can't do it.

Then someone punches me in the kidney like a kick from a horse and I bite gravel. A couple more blows, one to the base of my spine, one to the thigh. They hurt like hell, although the pulsing agony from the first one still comes through strongest. Someone huffing and swearing above me. My arms balled behind my head and my still-bruised neck. Somewhere upstairs, someone's saying, 'Hey, easy there.'

Kick. 'Fuck easy. Look what he did to Jack.' Kick.

'One piece, remember, the boss said.'

'He'll live.' Kick. I try to twist round, get into a position where I can catch the guy's foot, haul him off balance, maybe fight back.

'Mr Heller wants to have a word with you,' the third suit says. 'He's not —'

There's a *pock* like someone banging two bricks together, and the voice cuts out. A wet gurgle and the taste of copper on the air, and he collapses to the floor next to me with a hole in his throat.

Past the slumped form of the driver I see a figure moving. A man's silhouette picked out for a second as he steps beyond the thin pool of light cast by one of the dim security bulbs at the back of the store. Coat flapping behind him as he dances towards us. Movements smooth, an eerie grace. An uncertain target in the dark. He swings his outstretched hand up and round like he's casting a rose into an invisible audience. There's another two *pock*s from the gun in his fist, and something wet hits the asphalt behind me.

The third suit, the one who'd been kicking me, finally frees his gun from his jacket and whips it up at the approaching figure. I take the opportunity to punch him in the balls. He drops, and the look of surprise is frozen on his face as another two bullets slap home.

I rise to my feet, wincing at the pain in my back. I'm amazed to see, over by the wall, that the pimp, Victor, is oblivious to what's been happening around him. He's standing over the girl with his fist raised again, face twisted with rage. Locked into his own anger. Caught up in the thrill of violence.

He never gets the chance to do anything further, because I kick out the back of his knee. Follow up with a punch to the side of the head as he falls backwards and crunches to the asphalt with a grunt of pain. Almost immediately he lunges upwards, reaching for something in his jacket pocket, but I drive my knee into his nose with a snap of cartilage, and he drops again, out for the count, blood already pouring down his face.

Behind me, the man in the trenchcoat says, 'We've got to be making tracks, Alex.'

I look past him, at the carnage. 'Who the fuck are you? What the fuck is going on?'

'Save it for later. At the moment, I'm your friend. We need to get this cleaned up. Then we can talk.'

He steps back in the direction of the BMW. I

look down at the girl, who's realized the beating has stopped and is looking around her with tear-streaked eyes. Her face is already going red in a couple of places. She gasps at the unconscious form of Victor.

'He was trying to keep more money than you owed him?' I ask.

She nods and manages to get to her feet, still shuddering to draw breath. 'He said . . . interest. But I need . . . Who are you? What's happening?'

I start going through Victor's pockets. 'Right now, I'm asking myself the same question. I'm not Victor, which I guess is good for you.'

He has about seven hundred bucks loose in one pocket, and a money clip in another with what looks like at least three grand. In his jacket, I find a slightly battered Beretta. It's loaded, but there's no sign of any spare clips. More for show than anything else, I guess.

'Is . . . he . . . dead?'

'No. Broken nose, but he's just out cold. You OK?'

'Short on . . . breath, but I'll be all . . . right.'

'You got kids, boyfriend, any family?'

She shakes her head uncertainly.

I pocket the gun and toss her the money. 'Then take this, get a cab, throw your stuff into a bag and get on the next train out of town. Raise kids. Open a flower store. Have a good life. Just get well away from this one. And forget everything that happened here.'

She stays silent for a moment, then very quietly says, 'Thanks. Why do . . . I mean, why did you do all this? I mean, with the cash and all.'

I shrug. 'I need the karma. Go.'

She scurries away with a last downward glance at Victor. I turn to face the BMW just in time to see the guy in the trenchcoat put a bullet between the eyes of the wheezing suit I crushed in the car door.

Chapter Twenty-Seven

He sees my expression. Says, 'What? You gonna complain? You gonna call the cops? To clear away the rest of these assholes and sort out this mess I can't leave 'em alive. Get fucking real, Alex. You're not in the Boy Scouts any more. These people were going to kill you.'

I think about drawing Victor's gun on him, but everything's starting to hurt big time, and I'm in no condition to start another fight. 'Who the *fuck* are you?'

'When we're away from here,' he says, and hauls the dead suit round to the BMW's open trunk. The others must already be inside. He looks some way younger than me. Mid to late twenties, maybe, but worn down. A ragged mop of bleached hair, equally ragged face a shade too pale to be completely healthy, trenchcoat over cargo pants and a T-shirt. Battered sneakers. Leather gloves.

'What are you doing?'

'Amazing the amount of room there is in these things. When you don't have to leave breathing space, anyway.'

'What?'

'Parking the car some place out of the way. The

harbour maybe, away from anyone much. It'll be a few days at least before they're found, and by then it's just another mob murder.'

I just stand there and stare at him, baffled.

'Who's that?' he asks, pointing at Victor.

'Some pimp who was having an argument back here when I showed up.'

'He alive?'

'Unconscious.'

The guy reaches into his coat and pulls out a pistol. Overly thick barrel. One of those integrally silenced ones; I guess the noise it makes is because he's using ordinary shells, not subsonic.

'Whoa, whoa,' I say. 'You're not going to kill him too. He's unconscious.'

'He's a witness.'

'He's a shitty little pimp. You think he's going to report any of this? To who? He'll wake up, know he got caught up in something beyond him, and be fucking thankful he wasn't killed. He won't care about anything else.'

The guy hesitates for a moment, fixes me with watery blue eyes. 'You said he was arguing? Who with?'

'A girl.'

'A girl?'

'A hooker. I gave her the money he had and told her to get out of town.'

He shakes his head. '*Another* fucking witness, Alex? What were you thinking?'

'I was thinking I'm not about to start murdering everyone I meet. I was thinking I'm not some fucking psychopath, and I was thinking this isn't a fucking war zone. She's got nothing to tell anyone, he'll be glad to still have his fucking kneecaps, so we're done. Unless this place has CCTV watching its parking lot, in which case we're fucked.'

'Only inside the store.' The guy shakes his head, seems to think for a second. 'Help me find my brass, then we can go.'

'Won't someone spot the bloodstains?'

'Behind the back of a convenience store?'

I consider that. The guy smiles.

'It'll have turned dark by morning. Look like motor oil or brake fluid. No reason to think it's blood unless we leave brass for them to see.'

He starts scanning the ground for shell casings. I try to at least look like I'm helping, all the while keeping one eye on the stranger. He moves quickly, eyes skipping fiercely over the asphalt. His head snaps up at every sound from the street beyond, meerkat-like. A minute of this, occasionally stooping to collect a casing, and he's finished.

'I'll take the BMW,' he says. 'You follow in my car.'

'And if I don't?'

'Who do you think Gabriel Heller will blame for killing his men? If the cops get wind of it, do you think they'll believe some story about a stranger in a long coat shooting them out of the blue?' He tosses me a set of keys. 'And you drive off in my car and I'll report it stolen.'

I think about my options. I don't have many, and I still want to know who this guy is. 'Fair enough,' I say.

'It's parked out front,' he says, and disappears into the BMW.

A silver Taurus is skewed across the gravel near the main entrance to the parking lot. It looks identical to the one that tried to follow me to Tucker's on the night he died.

Inside, the car's seen better days. Half a dozen empty Coke bottles on the floor, other trash, snack food and bits of paper. The interior's scratched, busted in places. It smells like an old dog in a men's locker room.

The BMW rolls past me, and I swing into position, line astern. The guy drives cleanly and carefully, no speeding, stops at every stop sign, obeys every light, always uses his turning signal. We head east until we hit the harbour. Along one of the wharfs dotting the edge of south Boston, we find a couple of unused warehouses with a cracked 'FOR LEASE' sign on the fence outside. The guy pops the chain on the gate with bolt cutters from the trunk of the Taurus, and parks the BMW between the two buildings, just like a regular visitor. Then he joins me.

'Job done,' he says. 'They won't be found for a while.'

'What now?'

'Now, we talk. I'm hungry. Let's find somewhere to eat. You like Moroccan?'

I nod. It seems like the thing to do. 'Where to?'

'Theater District. I'll give you directions.'

The place looks like the cantina out of *Star Wars*. Dark alcoves, domed ceilings. An orange lamp in the centre of each table the only light. The guy stays quiet until the food arrives.

'Kris Vine,' he says between mouthfuls of couscous. He's chewing like he hasn't eaten in a week.

I crack open a *tajine* pot. 'How do you know me?'

'You were talking to Cody Williams. I saw that on the news. But more than that, you're looking for Anderson.'

'Anderson?'

He looks at me. 'I don't know what he'd be calling himself today.'

'The guy Cody was working for?'

'Yeah, that's what I guessed. His old crew all broke up, twelve years ago, something like that.' He takes another forkful of grains. 'You're looking for him, that I know. I don't know what Cody told you.'

I don't rise to that. Chew for a moment, pause for thought. 'You seem to know a whole lot about all this. How come?'

'Do you know where he is?'

'Not yet. How come you know all about him?'

Kris stares at me, hard, unreadable. 'Anderson grabbed me before he found Cody,' he says. 'I was his first.'

Chapter Twenty-Eight

You're a twelve-year-old boy, son of a store clerk in Queens, New York. Your neighbourhood's poor, but it's got pride. People keep their buildings clean, they sweep their steps in winter, kids go trick-or-treating at Halloween. Your mom tries to bring you up a good kid, and you do your best to make her happy. One day you're walking to school.

It's a beautiful fall day. The trees are starting to turn properly, and the streets are peppered with red and gold. You're breathing cool, fresh air, different to the baked lungfuls of summer. It's a good day to be alive. You're thinking about the friends you're going to see later, about the homework you haven't done and the excuses you'll use to cover it. You're wondering if Mom will be making cherry pie tonight like she promised she would.

Then the black car pulls up next to you and the guy inside flashes you a badge and says he's a cop. He asks you your name, and when you tell him, he nods and says he's been trying to find you. Your mom's been in an accident, he says, and you have to come with him so he can take you to her. The badge looks just like the ones off TV.

You climb into the back of his car and he drives

off. The car's very big and it smells of leather. The cop doesn't drive you home, or to the nearest hospital. He drives you across town, away from your neighbourhood, to parts of the city you don't know.

When you start freaking out, he tells you he's not a cop. He tells you his name is Mr Anderson, and he and his friends have kidnapped your mom, and if you don't want anything bad to happen to her, you'd better do everything he says. You keep staring at the people in passing cars, hoping one of them will see that you're in trouble and will help you out. Call the real cops. But they don't notice you, or don't notice that there's anything wrong. And you're all alone with this man, and there's no one to help you.

The car pulls into the driveway of a brown house. The man walks round and opens your door, and tells you not to try anything because he'll hurt Mom if you do. He walks you in front of him all the way into his house, and he closes the door behind you. The house smells of lemon air-freshener and fried onion.

The man takes you upstairs to an attic room, which is empty apart from an old rusty bed and a bucket. There's one window looking out, but it's small and it's locked. You ask the man where Mom is, and he just laughs and says he doesn't know, but you won't be seeing her again. And he forces you on to the bed and does things to you.

That's how it goes for the first few days.

No one hears you when you try calling for help.

No one hears you crying alone at night. You're closeted away, the outside world forever lost to you. Trapped in a nightmare place where there's nothing but the man and his desires, where if you resist in any way at all he just hurts you more as punishment, something that only adds to his enjoyment. If you're good, he sometimes gives you little treats, like candy bars or clean clothes. They seem like a big deal for a moment, until you think of what you've done to 'earn' them. He acts like you should be grateful he's taking such good care of you. Every time you eat a candy bar or slurp your Pepsi, it's like you're betraying yourself. Giving up hope.

Then his friends start showing up and taking their turns with you.

'Friends?' I say.

'Anderson had a little circle of friends,' Kris says.

'A paedophile ring?'

'Something like that. There were six of them, including him. It was like a club night or something. The "Gang of Six", I always thought of them as. Motherfuckers. They weren't always all there, but it was like a group meeting, all arranged, I'd guess. I don't think any of them ever showed up unannounced.' He gulps his orange juice and orders another from the waiter. I get another beer.

'And they were all in on what was going on?' I stop myself from saying 'abusing you'. I don't know how he'd react.

Kris nods. 'Hell yeah. Sometimes some of them would just like to watch, but they all had their turn sometime. They were all guilty.'

'I'm guessing you knew who they were. Or you found out since.'

'Yeah, I knew. I caught enough names, overheard enough conversation. Like I said, it was like club night. They were relaxed, enjoying themselves. Anderson was the one I knew the least about. He was always careful. You say he's calling himself Goddard now? Here in Boston?'

I shake my head. 'I don't think so. He's still got links here, though.'

'Heller,' Kris says.

'Heller was one of the Gang of Six?'

'Yeah. Back then, I think he was just a thug for the local mafia. Mid-level tough. That sort of thing. He's grown since then.'

'Gabriel Heller? Jesus. So he's a friend of Goddard's.'

'I don't know about that,' Kris says. 'Not these days.'

I finish the last of my *tajine*. 'They fell out?'

'They all did. Because of me. And because of Cody Williams.'

'What?'

'One night, Anderson brought this other kid home. Some poor runaway he'd found. He treated him the same way he treated me when he first arrived – saying the same thing about how trapped he was, blah blah

blah.' Kris scratches his head, looks away. 'When he'd finished with him for the night, he locked him in the attic with me, and told us if we even looked at each other he'd punish us for it.'

'But you didn't obey,' I say.

'I was good at looking scared and obedient and everything by then, I guess. I can't say how strange and exciting it was to see someone else, someone in the same shit I was in, someone I could talk to. But I hid that excitement until Anderson was long gone. The kid was just crying, for hours and hours. But he talked to me a little when he calmed down. He said his name was Cody Williams. About the same age as me, no idea where he was or what was going to happen to him – to us. I didn't tell him what to expect.'

Kris must see something register on my face when he says this because he adds, 'What was I supposed to do? Make him more afraid? Let that fucker know we'd been talking? It wouldn't have helped him anyway. Nothing we could do, not against Anderson and not against the others. Fuck it, you know?'

'So what happened then?'

Kris finishes the last of his drink. I make the universal airborne scribbling motion that means 'check, please'. He says, 'Anderson seemed to be real taken with the new kid. Almost forgot about me. He spent hours . . . with him downstairs. The rest of the gang all had their fun too. I guess they found Cody was more obedient, or easier to manipulate how

286

Anderson wanted, than I was. Even with the act, they must have figured I was resisting them. Cody even fell for the whole "little treats and candy bars" trick. I could see it in him. That was a real treat for him. Like a whipped dog suddenly being given a fresh bone by its master. Fucking scary. I had a bedspring free, and when they were with him and I was alone in the attic, I was using it to cut out some of the wood around the lock on the small window.'

We fall silent as the waiter arrives with the bill. I pay cash. 'No one noticed?'

'Maybe Anderson believed his own bullshit about how trapped we were. Maybe he was just caught up with Cody. Anyway, that was all I thought about. Getting out. Away from *them*. Took me a couple of weeks, then I did it. I got out, ran, disappeared into the city as fast as I could.'

'You didn't try to take Cody?'

'He was downstairs when I did it. I needed him to be a distraction so I could get out.' We stand to leave. 'He wouldn't have come anyway, I don't think. He was too scared. Too much in their control. But after I escaped, they had a witness on the loose who could identify them. So Anderson went into hiding someplace else. The gang broke up and had nothing to do with each other again, and no one saw Cody until he showed up years later.'

'How do you know?'

'I had a rough few years. I was one fucked-up kid. Imagine it.'

We leave the restaurant and step back into the cold night air. The streets are quiet and it's getting late. Places are shutting down. Bars are still open, but subdued. I can taste rain.

'Did you go to the cops?' I ask.

Kris shakes his head. 'Craig Warren. Member of the Gang of Six. Also a lieutenant in the NYPD. New York's Finest. I was terrified if I did, he'd find out and find *me* again. I can't explain how much I dreaded that. No cops. In fact, I couldn't even look at a fucking cop for months after that without hiding in case they were looking for me.'

'So you had a few rough years, and you've, what, been tracking them all down in turn?'

Kris says nothing, which I take to mean I'm right.

'If you wanted these guys so badly, but you were scared of the cops, why didn't you try getting in touch with me or the Bureau when we were working on the Williams case? You must've known we would've had nothing to do with the NYPD.'

'I had good reasons at the time.'

'Good reasons?'

'Yeah.' He nods. 'Good reasons.'

I let it go. 'What about now? Why follow me? And how did you know where I was or what the hell was going on this evening?'

We reach the car. Kris unlocks it, slides across to open the passenger door for me, turns the heater on.

'What?' he says.

'Why follow me?'

He shrugs. 'I've been hoping you were going to find Anderson. That's why I sent you those video clips.'

Chapter Twenty-Nine

I stare at him, unable to believe what I just heard. '*You* sent those? Where the hell did you get them, and what the fuck do you know about them?'

'There was another member of the gang, lived out in Buffalo. He must have still been in touch with Anderson, because I found those clips on his computer, maybe a year ago. I couldn't find where he was or anything, just an email address I never got an answer from. But I hung on to the clips, because of who they'd come from. Then I saw on the news you were working with Cody, and they started showing pictures of those girls, and I knew it was one of them in the film. I knew you'd want to find Anderson or Goddard or whatever the fuck he's called now, so I sent you the videos.'

'Why the hell didn't you just call me and speak to me? You could have told me everything back then and maybe I'd already have found Holly. Fucking hell.'

Kris glares at me, eyes stony. 'Would you have listened? Or would I have been just another crank call? You must have been getting them, right?'

'Yeah, I got some.'

'So that's what you'd have thought, right?'

I don't answer.

'Exactly. You'd have deleted the things and forgotten all about it. Or even if you hadn't, you'd have wanted to speak to me, the cops would have wanted to speak to me, and I can't fucking have that. Understand?'

'I guess,' I say.

'So I sent you the clips, and I followed you. You finally spotted me that night you left town. After you lost me, I went back to your hotel and waited until you came back. Tracked you all the way to that shithole you're staying at now, and I've been keeping an eye on you since. Especially when you went looking for Heller. I've been after him a while now, but he's been untouchable.'

The Taurus steers a lonely path through streets fogged with electric light. I don't know where Kris is going, but I guess it's the hotel.

'Speaking of Heller, how did his guys find me tonight? For all I know there's a welcome party waiting in my room when I get back.'

'They were watching you at the waterfront. Then when you took off, they followed around the block and watched you get into the cab. They stuck with you when you changed, and tailed you all the way until the second cab let you out.'

'How do you know all that?'

'I was doing exactly the same thing, only I hung back behind them when I saw them after you. You're a popular guy, Alex. Everyone wants to know where

you're going.' He bares his teeth. A smile, of sorts.
'Look on the bright side.'

'There's a bright side?'

'There's always a bright side, you look hard enough.'

'I was right about Heller knowing something,' I
say. 'And that he still has something to do with that
nightclub.'

Kris nods. 'And he probably doesn't know where
you're staying. Unless his guys called it in before they
grabbed you. You should be safe a while longer.'

'Probably.' I roll my eyes, reach for a cigarette.

'Probably is about as good as guys in our position
get, Alex.'

Our position. I think of the car with a trunk full of
corpses. A parking lot covered in blood. Victor's gun
in my pocket. A child-abusing gangster hunting me,
and somewhere his former buddy holding Holly
prisoner.

Some position.

We pull up by the Heart of the Fens Hotel. Kris
hands me a crumpled piece of paper. Says, 'That's a
number you can reach me at. Get some rest, see what
else you can find out tomorrow. Call me with what
you get.'

'You don't want to check the hotel for more of
Heller's guys?'

'They won't be here. And I've got things to take
care of. Don't worry about giving me your number;
I'll call the room if I need to talk to you.'

I don't bother asking how he knows which room

is mine. I get out of the car and watch it make a right at the next intersection and disappear. The streets are an empty black grid with me, alone, at their centre. I eye them for a moment, then walk into the hotel, half-expecting the lobby to be crawling with Heller's thugs.

It's not. Empty, dimly lit by a couple of sputtering uplighters. From somewhere behind the manager's office I can hear a TV playing. Ride the elevator up to my floor, and the only noise I hear when I step out is the muffled sound of a couple having sex a few rooms down from mine. My door's locked, and when I step inside, the place is empty. Without turning the light on, I cross to the filthy window and look out at the street for a sign of Kris's car or anyone else watching the hotel.

No one's there.

Despite that, sleep is patchy. All the bruises I've suffered tonight and in the past few days are coming through with a vengeance, and it's impossible to get comfortable for very long. Every once in a while, I wake up with a start. The building settling, down below hearing range, or a sudden noise in the distance that's gone by the time my brain's snapped awake.

Some time past three in the morning, I figure I might as well get out of bed and take care of Victor's gun. All the way to East Boston I keep an eye out for any sign of the Taurus or any kind of tail, but the roads are deserted. I bury the gun on a patch of wasteground not far from the airport, digging through rubble-strewn soil under the orange glow of the city sky. Wiped thoroughly for prints, along with the shells and magazine inside, and wrapped in plastic. I'll collect it if and when I need to. Under the circumstances, I don't want to run the risk of being caught with a weapon used for God knows what, and push comes to shove, I still have my Colt for emergencies.

Next morning, the incident with the cops at the fairground sees me back on TV again, albeit only a brief segment on the local news. No mention of a car full of dead gangsters showing up at the dockside. No mention of Victor or a mysterious fight in a parking lot late at night. Just that police believe Rourke could be in the Boston area, now here's Sarah with the weather.

And the weather is: rain. The heavens open and nothing seems to close them again. It just won't stop.

When I check my email at a phone a few blocks north of the hotel, I have a message waiting for me. I don't recognize the address, but the 'freaky-studentkid' label and its content tell me it's Sophie. Rob must've told her what happened after he got my note.

> Still looking for Billy Perry through channels. Had one lead that might be useful though. Guy called, said he was his old parole officer from way back. Says Billy was living at an apartment in the North End. Address is down below.

Red Breast says to call, needs to talk. Been kinda grouchy recently. More than usual, I mean. Not sure why.

Good luck, and keep in touch,
– S ×

For a moment the 'Red Breast' thing throws me, until I get the 'robin' connection and realize she means Rob. I offer a silent prayer of thanks to her, copy down Perry's details, and sign out before calling Rob.

'Hold on, hold on,' he says, before the word 'hello' has barely left my lips. I hear the sounds of doors opening and closing, then his voice takes on a tinny, echoing quality.

'You're taking this in the toilets?'

'Shit, Alex, do you really want me talking about whatever you want to talk about in front of Simon or Liz? You want them becoming accessories as well?'

'You told Sophie.'

'Sophie guessed straight away. She's smart like that. Wouldn't leave it alone. You know what she's like.'

'Yeah, I know what she's like,' I say. 'She's a good kid. The others probably know as well.'

'But I don't want to confirm anything and then have them suddenly get guilty about helping you. You want them telling all to the cops?'

'Good point.'

'And while I'm making them, how about I point

out that you've put me in a seriously bad position here? I just want –'

'Rob, I'd prefer to do this face to face,' I say. 'You got a while free to meet up?'

'Maybe. We're coming up on lunchtime and everything. But first, I just want you to tell me – did you do it? Really?'

'No, I didn't.'

He pauses for a moment, then says, 'Where'd you want to meet?'

'Craigsdown Park, there's a bench by the pond, west side.'

'I'll be there in half an hour. And I'll bring lunch. Might as well look the part.'

Chapter Thirty

I spend a nervous thirty minutes in the park, circling the area around the pond, trying to identify anyone who might be watching me. Cop or otherwise. The bench I've chosen is about as good a location as I can come up with. From here it's possible to watch both the nearest entrances. Doesn't stop someone climbing in over the fence past the trees behind me, but at least if they do I'll know the escape routes are clear.

Under the cold iron skies, the park is almost deserted. The ground is sodden and the gravel paths swamped by standing water. Even the pond's jumbled surface is lapping over the edge of its concrete banks. But still, each of the few visitors passing beneath the blanket of rain, every jogger, every businessman taking a shortcut somewhere, every lone mother hurrying home with the groceries could be something more. An undercover cop, part of a surveillance team. One of Heller's people. One of Goddard's.

I tell myself it's stupid, that I'm only a suspect, not a known criminal, not an escaped convict. Hell, not a spy in wartime Europe. But I can't help feeling these stray twinges of paranoia.

If Kris is still tailing me, I haven't seen any sign of him. Nothing since he left last night, vanished back into whatever shadows he's been lurking in for the past twelve years. If his story's true.

The thought that if any of the people hunting me are out here then at least they're getting the soaking of a lifetime is small comfort.

By half-twelve I'm staring at the pond with water trickling down the back of my neck and running in a stream from the peak of my baseball cap. Then I see Rob, huddled beneath an umbrella, sloshing his way towards me from the eastern entrance, a bag from Walker's Deli and two plastic coffee cups wedged rather precariously in his free hand. I wait for him by the bench, observing him, watching for movement in the background, alert for any sign that things aren't entirely kosher.

He stops ten feet from me, looking old and tired, wrapped up in his dark overcoat.

'You couldn't have gotten us into all this back in the summer, could you?' he says.

'Yeah. Real sense of timing.'

'Or are you just trying to add pneumonia to your list of problems?'

I laugh, although the joke isn't a great one.

'Did you do it, Alex?' he asks, for the second time today. 'Did you kill him?'

'No, like I said.'

'No?'

'How can you even think I would, Rob? How long have we known each other?'

He runs his eyes over me briefly before turning to glance at the water. The rain rattles from the umbrella's canopy. 'I'm beginning to wonder whether I've ever known you, Alex.'

'What's that supposed to mean?'

'It was just the other day when you were admitting killing one guy and framing another for it. You've crossed that line, and it's not something you can ever take back. What's to say you wouldn't cross it again?'

'How many times did you pull your gun in the Bureau?'

'Once. Fired off half a clip, without killing anyone. Not even sure if I hit anyone, come to that. And I don't mind admitting I was crapping myself the whole time.'

'So don't talk to me about what it means to kill someone.' I sit down and rub my face with wet and frozen hands. 'I'm not having this argument, Rob. Either you believe me, or you don't. Either you accept that in the years you've known me, I've never been the sort to do this kind of thing, or you ignore all that, say "fuck it" and walk away. I didn't kill Tucker. Hell, even if I had, you think I would've stabbed him to death? And then dropped my own goddamn kitchen knife at the scene? I've got a brain, and a gun, for Christ's sake.'

He sits down next to me, doing his best to cover

both of us with the umbrella's canopy, and passes me one of the coffees before reaching into the bag and producing a sub.

'Cream cheese, pastrami, pickles, hot sauce,' he says. 'Figured you could use something with a bit of bite to it. I like the new hair, by the way. Makes you look like an escaped mental patient, or a member of the Russian Navy.'

'Thanks.' I make a start on the thing, trying to keep it in one piece. Rob's on the standard BLT.

'We got something on Perry,' Rob says. 'Might help you out.'

'Yeah, Sophie sent it to me. That's why I called you, remember?'

'Dammit. I must be getting slow in my old age. Give it a couple of years and I'll be forgetting what day it is or where my pants are.' He smiles grimly. 'She's good, Sophie. Guessed that you'd left me a message straight away.'

'Not too hard. Me and you have been friends for a long time.'

'Yeah. Yeah, we have.' He sighs, and I wait for him to get round to saying what he came here for. 'How's the case going, anyway?'

'Some good, some bad.' Keep it vague, I tell myself. Telling him about Kris probably wouldn't make him think more highly of me. 'I think the guy who's got Holly is in a town over in New York State. Perry might be able to give me something I can use to narrow the search,' I say. 'Maybe Cody gave him

Goddard's real name, or described where he lives, or something.'

'And the bad?' He tears a huge mouthful from his sub.

'You don't want to know about the bad.'

'I saw you on the news.'

'That wasn't the bad. That wasn't even close,' I say.

'I don't want to know about the bad.'

'Told you.'

'Is there anything else you need from me?' he says after a moment's chewing time. 'You've already got the car, right?'

'Does anyone else know about that?'

'No.'

'If they ask . . .'

'If they ask, I've got it.' He jabs the air with a strip of bacon. 'Or one of the kids has got it. Or it's in for repairs. Or my in-laws are holding it hostage in revenge for my failure to provide them with grandchildren. The one thing that definitely *hasn't* happened to it is that you've got it.'

'Thanks, Rob.'

'Just don't write the damn thing off. I'm going to be real pissed if all this comes out because of an insurance claim. So what else do you need?'

'Keep my emails so I can check them over the net like I said in the note. I can't do that if you've already accessed them from the office. I'm still hoping Goddard could come back to me, and if he does,

I need to know about it. It'll also give people a way of contacting me if they need to.'

'No phone?'

I shake my head. 'Don't want my cell traced, or anyone to know where I'm staying.'

'Fair enough.'

'If anything comes up on Perry, or anything like that – any of the old leads we were working before – drop me a message and let me know.' I finish the last of my lunch and light up a cigarette.

'Still on the case.'

'Can't work it from inside a cell,' I say, staring at the pond. For a moment, there's a break in the rain and the surface suddenly flattens and stills, a mirror for the sky, the trees on the other side. That sense of disconnection, everything flipped, a reflection of the world I normally inhabit. 'Have the cops been in touch with you yet?'

'Yeah,' Rob says, nodding. 'Two detectives dropped by first thing the morning after to ask if I'd seen you. Perigo and Morton. Either I just caught them on a bad day, or they're always jerks with an authority complex.'

'Great. A couple of hardasses.'

'Like concrete. They've called once or twice to check on me, but I've kept quiet.'

I shrug. 'I guess I'm lucky this is Worcester PD's case.'

'They are Worcester PD. Specially assigned to liaise with Boston on Tucker's murder.'

'Shit.'

'In your favour, at least having no suspect straight away meant they processed the scene properly. All right, they found you through the evidence, but if your guy dropped anything himself, they'll be looking for him too.'

'Guys, plural. *If* they dropped anything.'

'Why'd you think they killed Tucker? Did they just do it to get you, or did Tucker know something for real?'

I shrug. 'They grabbed that stuff they left with the body before I'd even been to talk to the guy. My guess is they wanted someone they could kill and leave me to take the blame. Get me out of the way. Tucker was just their first opportunity to do it.'

Rob crumples his trash into a ball and weighs it thoughtfully in one hand. 'These guys, did you get a look at them?'

'No, I was pretty out of it. I heard them, but that was about it. Why?'

'I told you Perigo and Morton came to see me, and they're the cops on the case. But yesterday afternoon we had another visit from a couple of guys who called themselves Harvey and Andrew. If they were cops, I'm a goddamn ballet dancer.'

'What did they want?'

'Wanted to know if I knew where you were,' he says. 'Same answer as before. But they had that feel to them. Body language, whatever. Threats, that sense of violence. Tough guys, or at least they thought they were.'

I think of Gabriel Heller and the corpses in the BMW's trunk. 'Not cops.'

'They weren't even dressed like cops.'

'No suits?'

Rob shakes his head. 'Only time those two would've worn a suit would be in court. Shirts and jeans, and neither of them expensive. Boots too. One guy was big, one smaller. The smaller one had a scar on his face. Looked like someone had rammed a broken bottle through his cheek.'

'And this was yesterday afternoon?'

'Yeah. You know them?'

'No, and that's what's bothering me.' Heller must have teams of people out looking for me. Day shift and night shift, at least. Maybe these two were the ones who killed Tucker for him. He must really want me badly.

'They didn't say why they were looking for you.'

'I don't suppose they left a number in case you changed your mind?'

'No. Their kind never do.'

'Guess there's no point having a cell phone when most of your friends are in the slammer.' On the far side of the pond, a bedraggled crow is paddling in the flood, occasionally pecking at flotsam by its feet. 'Look, Rob, I'm sorry I got you into all this.'

'It can't be helped.'

'Yeah, it could have been. I was expecting the cops, but not everything else. I just hope it'll all be OK once I've got it all figured out.'

He sighs. 'Me too.'

We sit there for a few moments more. I finish my coffee, then say, 'Spit it out, Rob.'

'What?'

'Something's on your mind. It's been bothering you since you got here, it was the reason you wanted to speak to me, and it's still bothering you even after everything we've talked about. So what is it?'

'Yeah, yeah, I guess.' Another sigh. 'I guess there is something. Look, Alex, some of the clients have been . . . well, they've been asking . . .'

I nod. 'They've seen the news.'

'Yeah, they have.'

'And they know I work with you.'

'Yeah, they do.' He drops his head.

'And they've been getting a little twitchy about employing a company with a murder suspect on their books. I know it's only "police want to question", but for just about everyone that's the same thing as "think he did it".'

'Yeah, that's about the shape of it.' Rob's voice is so low I can only just make it out over the rain and the *spack spack spack* on the umbrella. 'Some of them are saying they're not sure about taking us on. They never say why, but they ask about you, and it's pretty damn obvious. We've lost out on a couple of jobs, and there's a few more who are nervous. And it's getting worse the longer this goes on. So . . .'

'Yeah.' I nod.

'I'm sorry, Alex . . .'

'Yeah.'

'I've got to let you go.'

'Yeah.'

'It's just hurting the business too much. I'm really sorry. I know things aren't exactly easy for you at the moment . . .'

I shrug. 'I pretty much knew it was coming, Rob. It's not like I'm earning anything at the moment anyway. And you've got Teresa, and four other people working for you, and they suffer when work suffers.' I smile. 'You've always been good to me, Rob. You gave me a break when the Bureau had given up on me, and I still appreciate that. You're a good friend.'

'I don't feel much like one. In fact, I don't know how I feel.' He tries a smile back. 'I'll sort out some kind of severance pay for you – that should keep you going for a while.'

'Hang on to it for the time being. If this goes on much longer, I'll need it in cash. They'll be watching for ATM activity.'

'Sure, sure.'

'And you will keep my email account open? I need it right now.'

He nods. 'Of course. I've got to do this to keep the company going. I don't want to screw things up for you any more than I have to. Hang on to the car for as long as you need it. And if you need us to do anything for you, same as now, just get in touch. We'll sort something out.'

'I will do.' I glance up at the clouds. 'Hell of a day for all this.'

'Hell of a day.'

'End of an era. You'd best get back, Rob. No sense sitting around here in all this for any longer than we need to.'

'It might not last forever.' I don't know if he's referring to the rain or to my exile from the agency. 'It's got to clear up some time.'

I smile and shake his hand. 'Take it easy, Rob. And thanks for everything.'

'Good luck, Alex, and keep in touch. I'll see you when all this has blown over.'

We part company and walk off in different directions, and with him go the last vestiges of my normal life, leaving me cut loose, adrift, free.

Alone.

I explain what's going on to Kris in the parking lot of a video store a block or so north of Perry's apartment. The neighbourhood's like a Victorian industrial ghetto. Buildings like tall dark sweatshops. Streets overlooked from all sides, gloomy, walled-in. The scent of broken dreams on the air.

'You want me to keep an eye outside,' he says.

'Right.'

'You're expecting trouble?'

I shake my head, say, 'Not really, no. Rob didn't seem to think there was anything odd about the information.'

'So why leave me outside? Why have me here at all?'

'I don't want you following me up there and spooking Perry, and the only way I can be sure you won't is if you know what to do.'

He shrugs. 'I wouldn't spook him.'

'OK. I don't want you coming up there and putting me in the middle of another fucking bloodbath. How about that? Perry could give me Goddard or Heller or both. This is important.'

'Whatever. You want me to hang back, I'll hang back.'

He winds up his window. The conversation seems to be over, which suits me fine. I walk down the street to Perry's building, eyeing the area up as I go. Looking for anything amiss, anything that doesn't belong here. A car too expensive for the neighbourhood. A guy loitering nearby with clothes that haven't worn in yet.

I see nothing.

The inside of the building mirrors the streets outside. Drab brickwork, and one gloomy stairwell that wraps around a central elevator core. A bank of mailboxes with apartment numbers but no names. The smell of dog hair and bug spray. Perry's apartment is at the end of a short corridor on the third floor. No sound from the neighbours' places, but I can hear a TV playing in his.

I knock and the door swings all the way open, held by a big guy in a suit jacket and polo shirt. An identical twin stands by the wall opposite him, watching me, while a third man is sitting in an armchair facing the doorway with a gun pointed at my face.

Chapter Thirty-One

'Good afternoon, Mr Rourke,' he says. 'Please come in.' His voice is gruff but cultured; he must be a well-mannered tough. Close-cropped greying hair and a bristling moustache, like an ageing army sergeant major in a five-thousand-dollar suit.

I could try running, but with the corridor behind me, shooting me would be the proverbial fish-in-a-barrel situation. So I step into the room and let one of the twins close the door behind me.

There's no sign of Perry in here, and it looks like the apartment hasn't been occupied in a while. I feel like an idiot.

'My name is Mr Norton, and if you so much as think about stepping out of line here, I will shoot you,' the man with the gun continues. His eyes are flat and cold, and if he wants it, I know I'm a dead man. He probably wouldn't even blink before pulling the trigger. 'If you're lucky, I may only take one of your knees as a warning first. If you're not, or if you threaten either me or my employer, I will kill you. My employer wants to speak to you, so he'd like you alive. But he doesn't want it enough to give you the chance to mess us around again, so you won't get that chance. You're a smart man, Mr Rourke. You should know the odds here.'

'Who's your employer, Mr Norton?'

'Like I said, you're a smart man.'

'You work for Gabriel Heller?'

Norton nods, but doesn't take his eyes off me. Behind me, I can feel the twins lurking over each shoulder. 'I'll be taking you to see him, Mr Rourke. And you'll be coming along quietly, and you'll behave yourself.'

He says this with a clarity and calmness that leaves me in no doubt that he'd happily make good on his threats if I do otherwise. Some people are all bluster when they say things like that. You learn to spot them easily enough. Norton isn't one of them. He has an air of absolute finality about him.

'That's fine, Mr Norton. I want to talk to your employer too. There're things we've got to discuss.'

'I'm sure. Lawrence here is going to search you for weapons, and then we'll go to see Mr Heller.'

Without a word, one of the twins begins patting me down. My Colt's in the car back by the video store, so he's out of luck. Part of me wonders if that's all that'll ever be found of me – an empty car and a loaded gun.

Norton and the twins take me back downstairs and out to a waiting Opel. It's a few years old and dusty. A guy in a battered jacket and a baseball cap is behind the wheel. I think maybe I saw him standing further down the street on the way here, but now I know these guys wouldn't look out of place in this neighbourhood because chances are they *own* this neighbourhood. Or enough of it to pull this kind of stunt. I can't see Kris or the Taurus anywhere.

'Do you like ballet, Mr Rourke?' Norton asks, as we cut across town.

'I've never been.'

'You should, I think. The precision of the routines. The grace and elegance despite the physical hardships. The sacrifice the dancers make for the sake of art. It's beautiful, yet tragic, as even the best have only a few short years at the peak of the profession, and their reward could be a lifetime of pain.'

'You sound like a major fan.' Stating the obvious, but there's not much else to say to that.

Norton nods. 'You could say that. If you get the chance, the Kirov Ballet is performing *Sleeping Beauty* at the Wang Theater for the next month.'

'It's good?'

'Breathtaking, Mr Rourke. Breathtaking.'

'I'll check it out if I get the chance,' I say.

The car lapses into silence for a while. Squeezed in the back between the twins, I'm in no mood to try starting a conversation on my own. I'm trying to watch the streets, see where we're going. Somewhere between plotting an escape route and sampling as much of what could be my final journey as I can.

Eventually, we swing into a narrow alleyway and pull up next to a set of red loading-bay doors. We get out in formation, and Twin Number Two rolls them open. Norton gestures for me to step inside. The car pulls away as I walk into the concrete cavern of the garage beyond. The three of them show me through a side door into a small storeroom with a single chair in it.

'Take a seat, Mr Rourke,' Norton says. 'Mr Heller is a busy man, so I suspect you'll be waiting here a while. Lawrence will be outside should you need anything.'

I look at him and the twins, once more weighing up the odds and my chances of making a break for it. I don't see it happening. Norton is back out of reach and the other two are built like wrestlers. So I do as they say and step into the storeroom. The door thuds shut behind me and the lock ratchets into place.

I'm trapped in a windowless concrete box sur-rounded by killers, wanted by the police, cast adrift by my only friend, I'm an accessory to a multiple homicide, and I'm still no closer to rescuing a girl I was supposed to have saved seven years ago.

I sink into the lone chair and drop my face into my hands.

Chapter Thirty-Two

The place must be a club of some kind. Not Metro's – this is a different building – but after the first three hours alone in the storeroom, I can definitely hear bass thrumming through the walls. Either Heller's busy, or he likes making his 'guests' sweat a little before he sees them. Or maybe he's just deciding what to do with my body after they put a bullet through my skull.

The door is heavy steel, and the only other opening is a tiny grate-covered drain in one corner. I figure I might as well test Lawrence a little and hammer on the door.

'Whatcha want?' comes the muffled reply. He doesn't open it.

'The bathroom.'

'I ain't your fuckin' nursemaid. Hold it or piss yourself, I don't care.'

Which leaves me with nothing to do but wait. I perch on the chair and scuff my sneakers against the concrete. Tiny patterns in the dust. Works of art for the short on entertainment. It's that or listen to my brain listing all the ways I've screwed up in the past, and that way lies madness.

It's gone nine in the evening by the time I hear

voices murmuring outside and the lock is shucked back. Both twins, and Norton standing between them. 'Mr Heller will see you upstairs,' he says.

They lead me a couple of floors up a back staircase, out of the way of the club's patrons and regular staff, and out behind a bar in what looks like a private function room of some kind. Lamplit tables in shallow alcoves, all painted up to look like some kind of tropical ocean scene. Coral reefs and kelp. It looks hideous. A balcony to the right stands on the flat roof of the floor below, looking out over the harbour. The French windows leading on to it are closed and probably locked, but I bear it in mind. Along with Norton and the twins, there are three other guys in the room. Two of them in position near another set of doors, which I guess lead down to the club proper, and one heavy-set guy maybe a year or two older than me, in a very expensive suit, sitting at a table by the side of the room.

A TV set above the bar is playing the evening news on mute. I have no idea what the anchor is saying, but they're showing Rob's picture on the screen.

Behind me, Norton says, 'In you go, Mr Rourke.'

I ignore him, keep staring at the screen. Cut to the outside of a hospital. Cut again to shots of emergency vehicles outside Rob's house. Police, paramedics. Someone putting up crime scene tape. I catch sight of the words 'critical' and 'brutal assault' on the news ticker before Lawrence pushes me forwards.

The guy at the table stands up.

Heller. I recognize him from the news stories back when he was arrested. His expression is unreadable, but he doesn't look too friendly. He waggles two fingers at me, waving me over. The fucker's put Rob in intensive care and he's acting like I'm here to arrange a fucking car loan.

'I bet you wish you'd never got involved with all this,' he says. A thick New York accent untouched by his years in Boston. Robert De Niro with a bad throat and a couple of Valium. 'You're in seven kinds of shit, Rourke. Sit down.'

I take a seat, and he nods at my escorts. Norton and the twins walk away to join the rest of the gorillas.

'Mr Heller,' I say, fighting the urge to jump over the table and squeeze his throat until his eyes pop for what he's done to Rob.

'You have any idea what you're into?' He keeps his voice low, hard to hear over the bass from downstairs. 'You must do, smart guy like you, else you wouldn't be asking about me.'

'You tried to frame me for murder, Mr Heller. Until then, I had nothing to do with you.'

'And if things'd worked out like they should've, you wouldn't have nothing to do with me now. You're a resourceful man, Rourke. You've dodged the cops so far, and I had a buncha guys watching you and they all vanished.'

Think, fuck you, you piece of shit. Say, 'Everyone

wants a vacation this time of year. They probably went to get some sun.'

'I'll bet.'

'So you set the cops on me, and had people after me, and now you want to talk to me, Mr Heller. Why the change in tack?'

'When it became clear how resourceful you are, it struck me that you might not be just some dumb jerkwad who fell into something that didn't concern him. I want to know what you know.'

'Couldn't get any information out of my partner, you fat sack of crap? That why you're asking me?'

I must say this just a little too loudly because I hear Norton or one of the gorillas move at the back of the room. Heller waves them back into position and fixes me with eyes like a shark. 'What the fuck are you talking about? Fuck would I want with your partner?'

'Rob's in hospital right now with God knows what done to him by your guys. I saw it on the news coming in here.'

'My guys?'

'Your guys went to the office to talk to him the other day. He told me. He didn't give them what they wanted to know, so you had them come back later and beat the shit out of him until he talked.'

'*My* guys haven't been near your goddamn office,' he says, jabbing his finger at me. 'Fuck would I need anything from him? Only time we talked to him was to set up your meeting with Mr Norton, and that was a phone call.'

'Harvey and Andrew. One big, one little. Little one's got a scar on his cheek. Your guys.'

Heller looks behind me and calls out, 'Norton! Two guys, Harvey and Andrew, little and large. One with a scar on his cheek. They ours?'

'No, Mr Heller. We have an Andrew, but he's currently out of town. We don't have anyone by the name of Harvey working for us.'

'There you go, Rourke. Not my guys.' His voice drops again. From the look on his face, like I've offended him by even mentioning it, instinct tells me to believe him. Instinct could be wrong, of course. And if it wasn't Heller's people looking for me, and Heller's the one tied to Goddard, who the hell were they?

'If they did whatever to your friend because of you,' Heller says, 'then maybe you're in even worse shit. You got a lot of enemies, seems.'

'Yeah. Seems.'

He lets me digest the information for a while. He seems to be enjoying the confusion I'm feeling.

'So you want to talk to me, Mr Heller, and find out what I know about . . .'

'Who it is whose affairs you've interfered with. Everything you know about him.'

I nod. 'Which is interesting, because I want to ask you the same thing. And I'm guessing that what I know is right, or else you wouldn't have your goon

318

squad way over there where they can't hear what we're saying.'

'Is that so?'

'I guess it's the same in the real world as it is in prison,' I say with a smile. 'No one wants people to know they've got a thing for little kids.'

For a moment, I think he's going to snap and kill me on the spot. His eyes bulge, his nostrils flare and he seems to be biting his tongue like it was a piece of prime rib.

'Your guys wouldn't like it if they found out, would they, Mr Heller? I bet some of them have families of their own. Shit, I expect you like to act like a respectable family businessman yourself. They'd turn on you real quick if they knew what you like to do to children.'

His expression's stony enough to mine for granite. 'What do you know about him?'

'Anderson, or whatever his real name is? You know his real name?'

'If I did, he'd be dead by now.'

'He had a couple of little boys he kept at his house when he lived in New York. One of them was a scrawny kid called Cody Williams. You and him and a bunch of other guys used to get together to take turns fucking them.'

He shows no reaction this time, says, 'Continue.'

'And then one of them escaped and you boys all went your separate ways. Anderson moved, you came to Boston to become part of whatever operation this is, and you never saw him or the kids ever again. Not until we busted Cody for snatching little girls.'

'Williams told you all this? Little fucking loudmouth. We should've shut him up years ago.'

I don't correct him. 'You used to know Billy Perry too, right? I imagine you must have been tempted to ask him about what Cody talked about.'

'Haven't seen him in ages either. Not since he shacked up with one of my girls in Roxbury. Hey, Norton,' he calls out. 'Who was the piece of ass quit working to start a family or some shit with Billy Perry?'

'Di Marco, Mr Heller. Gwen Di Marco.'

'Was she cute?'

'I honestly can't remember, Mr Heller.'

Heller looks back at me with a smirk and lowers his voice again. 'That's all that Billy Perry means to me. He never said anything about Cody, and I never asked. If he'd have known something, I'd have killed him. And you don't need to find him to find me, because I found you first, Rourke.'

I shrug. 'If you were worried about me finding you through Perry, you'd just have killed him. You wouldn't have tried to frame me, and you wouldn't have known this had anything to do with Anderson.'

'I hadn't thought about that son of a bitch in years, until a few days ago I got a phone call. The voice at the other end told me that you'd been sticking your nose in business of his and how you should disappear and the whole thing should be forgotten. And if I didn't there were photos of me that would reach the wrong hands. So I decided to have you put away for murder. Discredited and disgraced. Then I could go after Anderson to stop that shit happening ever again. *No one* blackmails *me*.'

'You guys took *photographs*?' Kris was right; they really did treat it like being golfing buddies. Christ.

Heller shrugs, changes the subject. 'So what'd you know, Rourke? Where's Anderson?'

'I don't know.'

'You don't know.'

I shake my head. 'I thought you might. All I know is he's calling himself Richard Goddard, at least to some people, and he's out there. Probably living in New York State, but I'm not sure.'

'Why're you looking for him?'

'I'm putting something right I should have fixed when I busted Cody Williams.'

Heller's eyes bore into mine. 'And that's all you can tell me about him?'

'Yeah.'

He glances past me, says, 'Then we're through here. Norton! I'm done with him.'

I turn to see Norton and the twins walking towards the table while the other two gorillas watch on. Norton reaches inside his jacket without any sign of emotion whatsoever and levels a pistol at my head. The barrel is a deep black pit in front of me swallowing all available light and I feel myself slipping inside as I wait for Norton to pull the trigger.

He never gets the chance, because Kris's first bullet blows a hole in his skull the size of a squash ball.

Chapter Thirty-Three

He comes through the door a blur, hand already outstretched, and kills Norton before anyone even knows he's there. A taut smoothness and efficiency in his movements. Not trained, but focused and wired, living only for the job in hand. Face blank like a poker player, pale and withdrawn. Death, come on his white horse.

The two gorillas near the door drop before they've finished turning. Then time slams back up to speed like a kick to the face and all hell breaks loose. The twins grab at their weapons and dive for opposite sides of the room, firing as the air fills with noise, dust and the *spacker* of brass hitting the floor.

Heller slumps in his seat, and I think for a moment that he's been hit, but then I realize it's just disbelief at what he's watching. I hit the boards and roll for cover as the deadly chaos roils around and overhead in a cordite haze.

I see Lawrence collapse like a marionette with all its strings suddenly cut as a bullet punches out the back of his spine. I can't see the other twin from where I'm lying, but then the firing cuts out just as suddenly as it began.

The *thum thum thum* bass from downstairs bleeds

back in and there's the feeling like we're emerging from the farmhouse cellar after the tornado has passed.

The two gorillas by the door have almost matching bullet wounds punched up from jawline to the peak of the skull. Lawrence's spinal fluid is slowly seeping into the blood on the floor like condensed milk, and the other twin's face is a bloody mess. I can feel cold patches of wet on my face that used to be Norton's brain.

Kris seems to be unscathed. He walks up to Heller, reloading, and brings the gun up to the big man's temple. I see his hand shaking, and he seems to be on the verge of tears. 'Do you know me? Do you know me?' he says.

Heller looks blank, mouth twitches in what could be a 'no'.

'You know me. You must know me. You know me.' Like a mantra.

Heller just says, 'Sorry.'

'Look at that cute little face and that ass! Hey, I can't wait for my turn! Damn, boy, you gonna scream for me!'

His eyes widen, and I see that Heller recognizes the words, even behind his fear and confusion.

'Scream for me,' Kris whispers, and pulls the trigger.

Gabriel Heller expires all over the tacky ocean décor of his nightclub, as his past sins finally catch up with the present. I can't find any remorse for him.

Kris doesn't look at me, just says, 'Let's go.'

We leave by the same back staircase I was brought up. I can hear the music pulsing away behind the wall, the club apparently oblivious to the shooting of its owner. I wonder how long it'll be until he's found.

The silver Taurus is parked at the end of the alley. Kris hands me the keys and tells me to drive, anywhere, then slumps into the passenger seat and begins to sob uncontrollably.

In a late-night grill somewhere near Atlantic Avenue Kris calms down enough to drink coffee. I can't tell if the place is one of those Fifties-themed ones, or if it just hasn't been redecorated since those days. The staff look old enough to have been working here back then, but I'm not curious enough to ask, and they don't pay us any attention beyond taking my order. I plump for burgers, coffee, just like regular people, and find a corner booth. I'm not hungry, but the food's still pretty good.

Beyond that, I can't say. Between Heller, Rob and the cops, my mind's all over the place. Even while I'm watching Kris to see which way his mood will flip next, my eyes stray towards the counter in the hope there'll be a TV there and I can find out how Rob's doing and what happened to him.

There isn't one.

Kris says, 'I need to ditch the car.'

'What?'

'Heller's guys might have seen it following you, or outside the club. I should ditch it.'

'You think they'll come after us?'

He shrugs, goes to pick up his cup and then thinks better of it. 'Might be too busy fighting over his cash. On the other hand, they might want a show of revenge or something. He tell you where Anderson was?'

'He didn't know. He told me where another guy who knew him and Cody was, and maybe he'll be able to help. I'll go see him tomorrow.'

'Why'd he want you?'

'He had a phone call,' I say. 'He was blackmailed into getting me off Anderson's, Goddard's, trail. He hoped I knew where to find him so he could go kill him. Did any of his people see you on the way in?'

'His people? In the club, maybe, yeah. I couldn't get in the back way. Yeah, I should ditch the car. Get some new clothes too. I can't be seen like this.'

I finish my coffee. 'You do that. I've got some things to take care of.'

'Things?'

'I have a friend in hospital. Maybe I can get to see him.'

Kris shakes his head. 'If he's a friend, the cops will be watching him, waiting for you. And you're outside visitor hours. You'll be obvious.'

I want to make sure Rob's OK. I want to comfort Teresa, to let her know things will be all right and he'll come through fine, just like before, after the fire. I want to be there for my oldest friend.

I should be able to do those things, but I can't.

I'm cut off from that world now. In this world, someone I care about could die, and I couldn't even attend the funeral. I wouldn't even be able to pay my respects properly.

'Jesus,' I say.

'Yeah.'

'But there are other things to do. You sort yourself out, ditch the car, do whatever you have to. I'll call you in a day or two and let you know where we stand.' I don't say that I just don't want him around right now. From abuse victim to killer to emotional wreck; I can't handle it on top of everything else.

'Sure,' he says. 'I'll be around, Alex. See you in a couple of days.'

Outside, I try calling Teresa from a payphone, but there's no answer, and the voicemail cuts in. I hang up without leaving a message. I catch a cab back to the vicinity of the hotel and walk the rest of the way, eyes and ears straining for anything that could be some kind of pursuit. But the streets are quiet and it's just my imagination and fears cannibalizing my nerves.

In my room I turn on the local news, hoping for a story about Rob and what happened to him. Instead, I catch the second half of someone's pet exposé on me. The pictures are the same stock footage from the Williams case and my prison visits, cut with various talking heads.

I collapse on the bed as a woman's voice washes over me. '. . . *Attention has begun to turn to the killing of*

Clinton Travers in Hartford and the conviction of Cody Williams for the murder.'

A keen, hawkish guy in a suit identified by the caption as a civil rights lawyer says, 'When you look carefully at the evidence against him and take into account the circumstances in which it was obtained, the case against Williams could be less solid than thought at the time. While I'm not saying there was any impropriety on the part of the investigators, the possibility that the physical evidence on which Williams was convicted could have been tampered with does make it harder to claim "beyond reasonable doubt".'

Someone off camera asks, 'If you had been defending Cody Williams at the time, do you think you could have won the case?'

'Yes, it's possible,' the lawyer says, nodding with an air of informed gravitas. 'The status of the evidence, the lack of a clear motive for the crime . . . it all adds up.'

The interviewer says, 'Of course, the motive they *couldn't* give in court was that Williams had killed Travers because he was stealing media attention from the string of child murders Williams was committing.'

'He was never charged with those murders, so it's disingenuous to bring them up. Building the case for him as a criminal shouldn't be based on something for which he was never charged. The same goes for anyone facing prosecution.'

'Do you think there's any chance his conviction could be posthumously quashed by the courts?'

The lawyer gives one of those knowing little shrugs that says, 'You and me both know what the answer to that is.' 'If it did go to court, it might be possible. But that would be for the court to decide.'

Cut back to the stock footage, stills and the woman's voiceover. '*In the meantime, the FBI may be re-examining the conduct of their agents involved in the Williams and Travers cases, with attention focusing on former Special Agent Alex Rourke. Rourke's former partner Jeff Agostini is now a senior agent with the FBI's Office of Professional Responsibility, the arm of the Bureau responsible for monitoring the integrity of its agents.*'

This makes me pay attention again. Agostini has changed since the days when I knew him. Older, obviously, but with age has come an air of seniority and authority he never possessed as an agent. His outward energy has gone, replaced with an apparent easy coolness. I don't find it entirely reassuring.

'If the Bureau decides it wants to look at those cases,' he says, 'I'm sure they'll be very thorough, and I'm personally confident the investigating team will be exonerated. I certainly never saw anything untoward while working on the Williams case, and I'd be very surprised indeed if there had been anything going on in secret. These people were professionals with no reason to do the kind of things you're suggesting.'

The voiceover says that Agostini's superiors seem

less sure, although they have yet to launch a formal investigation. I don't know how much of that is media bull or whether someone in the Office of Professional Responsibility really is considering a look at the Williams case.

Cut to an old guy in a suit, sitting behind an artificially neat desk underneath some FBI memorabilia. He says, 'Of course, we're monitoring the situation, and if we see any reason to examine the prior conduct of any of our agents, then we'll take the appropriate steps.'

The same interviewer as before asks, 'So you're saying that if someone shows you any sign at all that the evidence against Cody Williams had been tampered with in any way, you'd launch an inquiry?'

'Absolutely.'

'And this inquiry would also include former agents – particularly Special Agent Rourke?'

The suit nods. 'Of course. Rourke was our lead investigator on this case.'

'What kind of sanction would anyone found to have tampered or falsified any evidence face?'

The suit says, 'I couldn't comment – that would be for our legal team and the court system to decide.'

Depending on what they found, prison for messing with evidence, or a murder charge, I think.

Cut back to the voiceover, this time speaking over the most recent picture of me. '*And what of Rourke himself? The man responsible more than any other for the conviction of Cody Williams is currently wanted for questioning by police in Worcester regarding the murder of local business-man Brian Tucker . . .'*

I fall asleep before whoever's speaking can reel off another list of my crimes, both real and imaginary. I don't hear the program finish or find out if Rob or Heller are on the news.

Chapter Thirty-Four

Perry's girlfriend lives in a small house on the south side of Roxbury, or so the phone book tells me. Old brickwork, wooden fittings, all starting to show the cracks of age. A small and desolate front yard covered in short yellow grass and windblown leaves. Smeared windows, keeping the interior fogged. Much the same as the rest of the neighbourhood.

A woman somewhere in her mid-twenties answers my knock. Short, blonde hair worn pinned up at the back of her head, old T-shirt and jeans. An air of boredom.

'Yeah?' she says. She talks like she's chewing gum, even though she's not.

'Is Billy in?' I smile, like we're old friends and he'll be just dying to talk to me. Inside, I'm hoping none of Heller's people who knew I'd been looking for Perry have come calling before I got here. Her manner suggests nothing unusual's happened so far.

'Who're you?'

'Al. Al Garrett.'

'Are you a friend of Billy's?'

I shrug. 'I'm a friend of a friend, so I guess so.'

'Wait here.' She disappears inside the house for a moment. Then Perry comes to the door. He's getting tubby, going to seed. Head shaved and chin grizzled, both not entirely unlike my own. Shirt untucked, barefoot.

He says, 'Who're you, what do you want?'

'I want to talk to you about an old buddy of yours, Billy. Nothing serious – I just need to know the kind of things the two of you might have chatted about way back when.'

'Who?'

'Cody Williams.'

He looks at me closer and says, 'Fucking hell.'

'Just a quick chat, Billy, that's all.'

'You're the guy off the news. The guy that was talking to Cody.'

I nod. 'Yeah.'

'You got any idea how much I *don't* need this? I'm out of all that now.'

'Just a few minutes of your time, and I'm gone.'

He sighs and steps aside to let me into the house and out of the rain. His girlfriend is hovering just down the hall by the stairs. From the uncertain look she's giving me, I can't work out if she's just nervous about inviting a soaking wet stranger into her home, or if she heard what Billy said about recognizing me.

The house is pretty neat inside. Nothing special, but she seems to like it tidy and as comfortable as possible. It smells of laundry detergent. The TV in the front room is showing last night's ballgame highlights. Billy kills the sound and gestures to one of the chairs. His girlfriend closes the lounge door behind us and leaves us to it.

'Have a seat. What you want to know? Been years since I knew him, so I'm not making no promises.'

'Sure. Did he ever talk about what he did?'

Billy shrugs. 'If you mean all them girls and stuff, no, never. Probably didn't want word to get around. Or get overheard and end up on charges for it. He wouldn't say nothing about that, even when this big bastard was going to kick the shit out of him in the showers.'

'Not at all? How about people he knew on the outside?'

'Friends?'

'Yeah,' I say. 'Friends, family, anyone that he knew. He never struck me as a particularly social type, so there can't have been many of them.'

'He talked about you. He *really* hated you.'

'That's not very helpful.'

'OK, OK.' Billy holds up his hands in the way that half the criminals in the world do when they want to say 'I'm cooperating. Really, I am.' 'He never said much about it, but there was something. It was like, how some people when they're inside will talk about their wives outside, or about where they want to live when they get out. Like moving to Florida, or buying a bar or something.'

'So Cody had something like that in mind.'

'No, this was all before, in the past. Happy memories, I guess,' Billy says. 'He'd talk about some guy like he was his dad, or an older brother. Y'know, someone who'd taken care of him, who he'd looked up to.'

'What did he say about this guy?'

'Nothing very specific. He'd only really talk about it to himself, almost. Comforting, I suppose. Something about living in some place in the mountains. About doing stuff together. About teaching.'

'The guy was a teacher?'

Billy shakes his head. 'No, like, how your dad would teach you to ride a bike. That kind of thing. Not schools. And I remember Cody had these scars on his back. I asked about them once and he said something about a mistake, doing something . . . or not doing something . . . or not doing it right . . . Shit, I don't remember how he got them.'

'You don't know what it was he'd done, or he was supposed to have done?'

Billy shrugs. 'How the fuck should I know? They could've been going fishing or . . . raping a . . . a busload of nuns for all I know. He never said. That's all I remember.'

'He never said the guy's name?'

'No.'

I frown. 'Didn't that seem odd?'

'Cody was a goddamn nutcase with a thing for little girls. How much fucking odder do you want?'

'Did he say which mountains, or where he was when all this happened?'

Billy shrugs. 'He never said. Catskills, Green

Mountains, White Mountains. Could've been any of them.'

I wait for a moment, just in case Billy's going to add anything more that floats up from the depth of memory, but he stays quiet.

'That's everything?'

'Cross my heart.' Billy stands and waves a hand at the door. 'I think you should be going, Mr Rourke. I'm an honest citizen these days, and you're trouble. Get going and leave me alone.'

I'm not keen on staying long in a place where my identity is known anyway. Anonymity is almost the only protection I've got, and the urge to crawl back into hiding is a powerful one. I wedge my hands in my pockets and step back out into the rain. Billy's door slams shut behind me.

Two blocks away and closing, I can see blue flashing lights.

For a second, I stand and watch the cars approach. Streamers of rain caught in the air, like looking through a field of grey grass stalks. Three cars – one unmarked – scything through them. In my mind's eye I can almost see the dark shapes of the men behind the windshields, poised, eager for the chase. I can practically feel their hunger.

I sprint across the street and into a narrow alleyway between houses. Some way inside its welcoming shadow and shelter, I hunker down behind a trashcan and watch as the cars screech to a halt outside Billy's home.

The girlfriend has the door open before the two guys in trenchcoats have even finished crossing the front yard from their unmarked car. She must've called them; I can see that their arrival isn't coming as a surprise to her, and they're not treating her like someone who's potentially harbouring a fugitive.

The two detectives form a kind of little and large pairing. One is taller and blond, maybe in his early thirties. Pointed jaw, face to match. A serious scowl. The second is shorter and fat, with a nose that looks like it's been broken at least once and probably more than that. He has maybe five years on his partner.

Detectives Perigo and Morton, I presume.

They talk with the girlfriend for a moment, and I see the tall one swearing. Billy comes to join them in the doorway. They speak to him, and he shrugs, shakes his head.

I'm about to leave my hiding place when the tall cop turns to look in my direction while his partner asks a final couple of questions. He runs his gaze over the street, the houses either side of me, and the alley itself. For a second I can almost believe our eyes lock, and suddenly the shadow of the buildings and the cover offered by the trashcans are stripped away and I'm helpless, pinned, trapped in his stare. Certain I've been spotted. That it's all over.

Then he looks back and calls to his partner, and

the feeling passes. As they walk towards the cars to give orders to the uniforms to search the area, I retreat further into the alleyway until I judge it safe to turn and run.

I don't stop for two blocks, where I do my best to vanish into a shopping mall for an hour or so, grab a coffee and a bagel like a normal citizen, then taxi back to a spot a few blocks from the hotel. I'm wondering whether or not I should move, switch places. Wondering how long it'll be before someone identifies me.

Then I wonder, if I move, will the manager at the next place spot me straight away? I could be better off staying put. Hunkering down. Doing nothing. And, in the end, I know it's just a panic reaction. Twice now I've nearly been caught. It's just the adrenaline wearing off.

On the bed is the newspaper I bought this morning. No mention of Heller's death at all, but it's open to the brief story inside about Rob. Apparently, unidentified intruders attacked him when he came home from work yesterday. Teresa found Rob in a pool of blood. They beat him badly enough that he needed six hours in an operating theatre last night, and, according to the paper, he's still in a critical condition. Normally, they'd say, 'critical but stable'. I wish they did now. And I wish there was something I could do about it.

The cops are looking for two men, no descriptions

given. Forensics, maybe, or the vague recollections of a neighbour who saw them leave. Nothing was taken from the house, and they don't have a motive as yet. At least, not one they're talking about. It has to be the two guys who came to the office, Harvey and Andrew. Again I think about calling Teresa or Sophie to find out how he's doing, but I don't dare.

Out there are cops and psychos and Goddard or Anderson or whatever the fuck his name is and Holly and I want it all to stop.

I want to find her and have it all over with, just so I can rest. Once she's safe and sound and no longer out there, in danger, none of the rest matters. It's over.

I'm just afraid it'll never happen.

This fear becomes all too horribly real that evening.

Chapter Thirty-Five

For most of the day I sit in the hotel room, trying to calm down and get my thoughts in order. In the evening I flick the TV on, slowly relaxing as more and more time passes without the cops showing up at my door. It's then that the late news makes my heart jump into my mouth.

TV chopper shots of a riverbank covered in scrub. Guys in overalls working the scene. '. . . Police have sealed off a section of the Charles River this afternoon after the body of a young woman was found in the water. A spokesman for Boston Police Department said they were still trying to identify the woman, described as being in her late teens or early twenties, slim build, with blonde hair. They are treating her death as murder, although no details have yet been released. Anyone who was in the area of the Larz Anderson Bridge last night, or who has any information at all should . . .'

It's Holly and I know it. I'm too late.

Or at least, that's what my brain is still screaming at me an hour later. Pressed up against the damp brickwork at the corner of the mortuary, hidden just a few yards from the staff entrance, waiting and listening in the cold.

The door's a heavy fire model, safe and solid, locked from the outside to anyone without a security card. The public entrance has a guard on it, and I can't see any other easy way in. Windows are all firmly shut against the weather and I don't know if breaking them would trip an alarm. So I'm left with nothing to do but wait. Inside, that cold sick feeling, a gut full of clammy jelly. The unshakeable certainty that everything's gone wrong, that it's all over, that I've failed.

That she's dead.

Half an hour, and finally I get my chance. A woman steps, yawning, into the parking lot and walks towards her car without a backward glance. The door's heavy and secure, but it's very slow to close. While she's still digging her keys out of her bag, I slip through before it shuts.

Inside, yellow linoleum flooring, fluorescent lighting to match and the sharp scent of disinfectant. The hum of ventilation and the dead air of empty corridors. The soft-focus desolation of a 1950s insane asylum. No security on this entrance – I guess because it's not used except by workers, no stray members of the public.

I'm only one turn into the building, nothing but blank closed doors to what I guess are supply closets or utility rooms, when I hear voices. A stairwell cutting into the corridor to my left, footsteps tip-tapping down towards me. A man's hand visible on the guard rail only a floor up.

'. . . So he's shown them this home movie of one of these dead students, and they're all real jumpy; you can see it in their eyes, right? And he tells them . . .'

Nowhere to hide in the corridor ahead.

Three steps from the turn halfway up the flight of stairs. *Tip-tap.*

Two. *Tip-tap.*

Nowhere to hide in the corridor behind.

One. *Tip-tap.*

No way of knowing which way they'll turn when they reach the bottom.

I dive into the narrow space beneath the steps, the little cubby-hole they create and overshadow. Wedge up between some kind of electrical junction box and a couple of old equipment trolleys, try my utmost not to knock any of them and make a sound, hold my breath and grit my teeth against the adrenaline.

'. . . So they're absolutely freakin' *shitting* themselves, right? They're all hugging each other and a couple are crying and saying what an experience it all was . . .'

I will my bones not to creak. My teeth not to grate together. My lungs to hold until they're gone. If sheer concentration was enough to force people away from me, these guys would be blown through the concrete and halfway across the city.

'. . . And then he walks outside while the credits roll, out to the TV van, and the dead girl is sitting in it, and she's not dead and the whole thing was a fake. I swear, man, that's clever . . .'

The voices fade as the men walk away.

I exhale slowly and count to twenty before emerging from my hiding place. They've gone, and the corridors are empty once again.

Not far down, I find a door marked 'Locker Room' held open by a janitor's cart. From inside I can hear someone humming tunelessly, but the sound is faint and distorted.

I risk a glance. There's no sign of the cleaner, presumably out of sight behind the central row of lockers. On top of these, just another part of the usual locker-room clutter, I can see what looks like a discarded set of blue medical coveralls, crumpled and forgotten.

Think for a second, then scuttle across the room and gently slide them off the lockers, ears taut for any change in the janitor's humming or the swish of his mop on the tiles. I catch the tinny strain of music playing through earphones and figure I'm safe so long as he doesn't finish that side of the room and come round to mine.

The blues smell stale, but look clean enough. I can wear them over my shirt and jeans without it looking too weird, but the jacket's right out. Carrying it will look strange as well.

There's a roll of clear plastic trash bags on the janitor's cart, and what looks like a set of tear-off work sheets. Just about official enough to pass as generic paperwork. I wrap my jacket in one of these plastic sacks with the form clearly visible on top and tuck the package under one arm. Just taking some dead guy's coat for analysis. Passing it on to the cops. Bringing it back from a lab somewhere. Whatever.

The unseen janitor launches into a new song as I leave.

I turn the last corner before the mortuary itself and come face to face with a guy in full security uniform and a look of pure determination on his face. Our eyes meet, and I freeze.

'Hey,' he says. I swallow and blink. 'You don't know where Dr Kendrick is, do you? He's not in his office, and I'm damned if I can find him.'

'Uhm . . .' I reply. 'He's not in his office?'

'No, hasn't been for a while.'

'That's the only place I can think of he'd be around now,' I say, trying to look thoughtful. 'Sorry, no, no idea.'

'Ah well. Doctors, huh? You see him, could you tell him we need him at the front desk?'

'Sure, sure. I'll do that.' I attempt a friendly smile and hope I'm not sweating too hard. The guard certainly doesn't seem to notice, as he stomps away, shaking his head.

The morgue itself is mercifully empty. Cold and damp. The slabs in here are all unoccupied and the screens are rolled back. It doesn't look like it's currently in use by any of the place's medical staff, but since someone could walk in at any minute and change all that I can't hang around. I find the chart that lists the identities of those stored in each freezer and scan the names until I see a 'Jane Doe' in #11.

The drawer rattles harshly as I haul it open to reveal the bluish naked form within. A young blonde woman, skin blotched and distorted but intact – she can't have been in the water too long – with a mass of stab wounds to her chest and abdomen clear against the clinical autopsy cuts. Face bruised and swollen, lips split.

It's not Holly.

After all this. It's not her.

She's alive. She's still out there.

A flood of relief as the cold dread lifts from my gut. Tinged, maybe, with a bitter and guilty twinge of disappointment. That if it had been her, it would at least mean her suffering was over. Or that I could give up on her.

I close the drawer and get the hell out of the building.

The next morning at the hotel, they come for me.

Chapter Thirty-Six

Multiple car engines, running fast, from the street outside. I look through the window to see the blue and red flashes of the strobes, see the cars screaming to a stop in front of the hotel, Perigo and Morton in the lead, and I know they're here for me. The manager saw me on the news and squealed. Some eagle-eyed beat cop spotted the car. It doesn't matter.

I've got to get the fuck out of here.

Grab my bag, left packed for just this eventuality, and run down the corridor to the stairs. Floating up from the bottom of the stairwell, I can already hear pounding footsteps and cop voices.

I run up, taking the steps two at a time. Stick to the outside, stay out of sight of those below me. Hope my sneakers don't make too much of a sound, at least, not over the noise they're making.

My only hope of getting away relies on not being seen. You can't outrun the radio, or the cruisers below. Anyone spots me while I'm running and the trap will close ahead of me. It always does.

Thud. Thud. Thud.

At the top of the stairs, my desperate prayers are answered. As I'd hoped, there's a door marked 'Roof – Maintenance Only'. Given the state of the hotel, I doubt it sees much use. Try it first – locked – then lean back ready to kick it in. It's not padlocked, thank Christ; if it was, I doubt I could force it open. The internal lock shouldn't be as tough. I hope.

I wait for a second until I hear the crash as the cops plough out of the stairwell five floors below and rush towards my room. Pray the echoes will mask my own noise, and kick the door to the roof with all my strength.

The wood around the lock splinters and snaps, and it flies open.

I'm not a Catholic – not even a believer – but I still get the urge to cross myself.

The roof is a flat expanse of galvanized sheeting, slippery in the continued rain, peppered here and there by odd protuberances. Bumps and vents for air conditioning, drains and aerials. I sprint down to the far end, trying to use them to break line of sight to the door behind me. A couple of times I come close to losing my footing entirely.

There's a gap of about ten feet over a narrow alleyway to the adjacent building, and a drop of about the same from this roof to the next. It's doable, but it'll hurt on landing.

No choice, and no time to mess around. I throw my bag over, give myself a decent run up, and hurl myself out over thin air. Gravity tugs me downwards and I have a sudden moment of panic.

I'm not going to make it.

I'm going to fall eighty feet on to solid concrete.

Then my feet hit the rooftop, all the air is knocked from my lungs and I roll to a halt with every joint aching and my head spinning.

Expecting at any moment to hear someone shout my name, running feet behind me, a gunshot, anything, I pick myself up and run along to the far end of the building I'm now on and look for a fire escape.

It takes forever to reach street level, and I drop the last ten feet on to a dumpster, but there's still no sign of pursuit. Trying to look as normal as possible, I head out on to the street beyond and do my best to lose myself in the city, burrowing in like a worm into an apple, vanishing into the anonymous mass of humanity.

The boardwalk looking out over Fort Point Channel is almost deserted in the constant rain. I risk buying hot dogs and a Coke from a street vendor and eat them looking across the water at the airport.

I'm running out of options. I've got no idea where Goddard is, and no obvious way of finding him unless I can somehow tempt him out of hiding. I've no car, not much cash and I'm exhausted and battered from jumping around on the roof and everything else the past few days.

And there's nothing else I can do but keep trying for Holly's sake.

I'm still not at all sure about him, but I call Kris from a payphone. Say, 'The cops raided the hotel. I need a place to stay.'

'Sure. I'll pick you up.'

Kris is driving a blue Acura. I don't ask him where he got it; I don't want to know if it's stolen. Judging by the minimal amount of trash on the floor and back seats, he hasn't had it long or done much with it yet.

The trip is calm and he hardly says a word. There's no trace of whatever emotion overtook Kris after killing Heller.

He currently lives in an apartment in Brookline. A low, cramped beige limbo that even the city's rats would ignore, figuring they deserved something better. It's not as bad as Frank's alcoholic hovel, but they obviously both went to the same school of housekeeping.

But beggars can't be choosers, and I thank him when he points me in the direction of the couch.

'You need anything?' he says. 'There's a store down the block. How much did you leave for the cops?'

'Some soap, dirty socks and a load of trash. I kept everything else in the bag.'

'Nothing that could tie you to anything?' The flash from his eyes makes it clear he means 'tie you to me'.

'Nothing.'

'Good. They didn't track you from the hotel?'

'If they went up to the roof it was long after I was gone.'

Kris nods, and some mental gear shifts deep inside. 'I'll get food, smokes. I'm going to the store.'

'Sure.'

He lets himself out, leaving me alone in the apartment. From the state of it, I could almost believe he was using it for a stakeout. Don't worry about clearing out the trash, don't make it a living space any more than you need to. You're not living here, you're just inhabiting space while you work.

Here until you leave.

Here to go.

On the windowsill are a couple of oily rags and some boxes of ammunition. A small toolbox on the floor beneath. A pair of greasy pizza boxes wedged behind the sole armchair. Muddy shoeprints everywhere.

There's a good three or four empty quart bottles of orange juice waiting next to a refuse sack in the kitchen. A fridge with the remains of a dozen different types of snack food and candy.

And on top of it, a plastic baggy containing pure white pills.

I'm not certain what they are, but at best guess, my only ally is wired on amphetamines, maybe something worse.

Jesus fucking Christ.

How much of what he's told me could be magnified by speed paranoia? Is this what's behind his weird moods, or are they something else entirely?

I hear a key turn in the apartment door. Put the baggy back on top of the fridge.

'Hey,' Kris says, coming into the kitchen with a brown grocery bag. 'Looking for something?'

'Coffee,' I say with a smile. 'I could use a pick-me-up.'

'Cupboard above the kettle. I don't have any milk.'

When evening comes, I tell Kris I'm going out for a while to check some things, and go find an internet connection. First I look up Lieutenant Craig Warren, NYPD. I get a slew of old news stories.

Police hero slain in own home.

Hero cop murder.

One of NYPD's finest brutally beaten and shot in his own home. No apparent motive. Police suspect a revenge slaying.

No mention of anything to do with abusing children. As far as the NYPD is concerned, he was a senior officer and a good cop. His murder was never solved, but since his killer is currently shadowing me, all that does is confirm what I know.

What I don't know is who Kris Vine is.

But I can find out. I doubt the cops would be keeping tabs on the accounts the agency holds with various background check services and records databases. If they are, I'm about to trip every alarm they have.

I start tracing the lines of Kris's past. Following the little strands left by his passing. The stray records, the notations, names, dates, places. The where and when of it all. There's very little from his childhood.

Nothing in the news about a child by that name going missing.

Nothing about an abduction.

By itself, maybe not surprising. Old news, so it's less likely to be in the available archives. It's no cause for doubting his story by itself.

The reasons he took his time going after the Gang of Six are more worrying. For a period of nine years until the summer before last, Kris was in and out of asylums. I can't tell what he was in for, but it must have been something serious to require such continual treatment.

For most of this time, he seems to have had no permanent address and no employment either. Wandering here and there, either as part of whatever work – I'd guess petty crime from the way he acts – he had, or tracing the other members of the Gang.

I'm relying on a revenge-obsessed killer with a history of mental health problems and an amphetamine habit for help. And I'm relying on him for information and to understand who Goddard is, or was.

And I can't be sure how much trouble any lies he's told have got me into. Nor whether or not I can trust him not to turn on me once his private vendetta is over.

I walk back to his apartment, watching my back every step of the way. I want a drink, but I can't do anything that means losing control while Kris is around.

'You look like shit,' he says, when I get back. 'No luck with whatever it was?'

'Not really.' I notice that the baggy on top of the fridge has gone.

'It happens. We'll get him tomorrow.'

I sit down and try to hide the fact I'm less than keen on getting Goddard at all with him around. That I may have to find a way of ditching him and striking out on my own again.

Then an email I receive the following morning blows all my plans to tatters.

Chapter Thirty-Seven

'Did it say who they were?'

I shake my head, light a cigarette. 'No. Heller's guys, maybe, or the ones who beat up Rob. Fuck.'

'Fuck,' Kris repeats. 'When did they grab her?'

'It didn't say. From the time it was sent, I guess yesterday evening.'

WE HAVE YOUR GIRL SOPHIE, the message said.
YOU WANT HER TO LIVE, COME TO TRENT CHEMICALS,
KING'S ROW.
ANY SIGN OF THE COPS, SHE DIES.
YOU'VE GOT THREE DAYS.

The apartment is wreathed in cigarette smoke and stale air. Kris is perched on the edge of the couch, fingers nervously playing with each other. I'm glaring through the window, as though a solution will appear on the glass if I concentrate on it hard enough.

So far, all I know is that if these sons of bitches have hurt Sophie in any way, I'll kill them.

'They're going to be waiting for us,' Kris says.

'No shit. Wait.' I hold up a hand to cut him off before he can object to me snapping at him. 'They're going to be waiting for *me*. They probably don't know about you.'

'You sure?'

'If they're playing it this way, they don't know where I am now and they weren't able to find me before, otherwise they'd have done the same to me as they did to Rob. They'd have dealt with me days ago.'

'*If* they're the ones who attacked him,' Kris says. 'If they're Heller's guys out for revenge, they'll know you had help.'

'We'll have to hope they're not.'

He shrugs. 'Even if they're not, the surprise won't last long. You got a gun?'

'Yeah,' I say. Kris looks like he's ready to dive out of the door and go to war with these guys without a second thought. 'But let's see if we can get a look at this place first, find out what we're up against.'

Trent Chemicals is a derelict refining plant that was only half-finished when its owner went bankrupt. The site is in the middle of dead industrial wasteland overlooking the Atlantic south of Boston, an elephants' graveyard for steel dreams turned to rust. The area is flat and deserted; Sophie's captors will be able to hear any approaching vehicle well before it gets to the factory. We leave the car half a mile away and finish the journey on foot.

We have a good view of Trent from the collapsing canning plant next door. Most of whatever processing machinery was originally on the site seems to have been stripped away, probably to pay its creditors, but a couple of huge concrete factory buildings, dark and blocky, remain. The nearest of them has a raised sub-section at one end lined with broken windows. The old plant offices, I guess.

'That's where they'll be,' Kris says.

'Yeah.'

'High view, watch the road coming in. About as good as they're going to get on that site.'

He hands me a pair of binoculars bought on the way out here and I scan the shattered building for signs of life. Most of the windows are empty, and much of the place appears to be open plan, but on the top floor, far northern end, I see a drift of pale white smoke. A cigarette. Just visible beyond, a man sitting a few feet in from the window, looking out over the approach to the plant. I can't see what he's wearing or what he's carrying, but he's slouched. Looks like an attempt to get comfortable.

I point him out to Kris.

'Can't see anyone else.'

'Any lights would show up for miles here; these places don't have electricity. If they're holed up inside for the nights, they must have to stay somewhere out of sight of the windows.'

'Keep watching. They must change shifts at some point.'

For nearly three hours we wait, staring across a couple of hundred yards of dead ground in the rain. Then, at long last, Kris says, 'We've got movement.'

'Where?'

'A second guy's come to take over the watch. I didn't see where from, but I guess the first guy's going to go back that way.'

He passes me the binoculars in time for me to catch a glimpse of the two men together in the gloom. The newcomer must be a foot taller than the first, and much heavier set.

Little and large. The guys who attacked Rob.

The conversation finishes, and the short one walks out of the room and vanishes from view. He eventually reappears from a stairwell two floors down in one of the open plan offices and makes his way through a door into a back room. He doesn't come back out.

'Got them,' I say. 'And I think there's only two of them.'

'Where?'

'Two floors down there's a back room. Best guess, that's where they're keeping Sophie.'

'If they're keeping her at all. If she's alive,' Kris says.

I almost hit him. The urge is there, the sudden flush of rage and sheer bloody-minded unwillingness to consider the possibility that he's right.

'Doesn't matter,' he continues, oblivious. 'Either way, we go in and get them. If there are only two of them, they can't be watching the back of the building. They must be expecting a car.'

'Maybe. Maybe there's no back way in.'

'Maybe. Only one way to find out.'

I concede him that. 'So we try to sneak round there without the guy upstairs seeing us, and then . . .'

'Then I suggest we split. I'll go upstairs, maybe over the factory roof, and nail the watchman before he knows we're there. You go for the downstairs and get the other guy. That way we don't have one of them free to do whatever to your friend as soon as they know we're in the building.'

'It'll be tricky without knowing the layout of the place. Timing could be a problem.' I shrug. 'But then, we've got no way of communicating, and the whole thing's guesswork anyway.'

Kris nods. 'It's as good as we'll get. Wait until night?'

'Blundering around an unfamiliar factory in the dark? When they could have night-vision equipment, and we definitely don't? No, I don't like that idea. Let's just give them an hour or so to get comfortable and dozy, get round the back and go for it.'

The downpour doesn't let up at all. I'm soaked in the time it takes to scuttle across the southern side of the canning-plant lot, keeping its bulk between us and the watching eyes in the Trent offices.

The chainlink that marks the southern border of these derelict units is peppered with climbing weeds and windblown trash. Maybe two feet of solid vertical cover, and better than nothing above that. I hunker down and move as quickly as I can in a half-crouch along the periphery, checking through the weeds every now and then to see where we are in relation to the offices. Once we're within sight of the back of the building, I check its crumbling face for any sign that they're also watching the rear.

Nothing. No one.

Only the top two floors of offices are visible above the factory roof, and they're almost windowless on this side. Maybe the view wasn't great with all the refining pipework in place. There's a huge sliding door on the ground floor open maybe a few feet. Inside, it's dark, but I can make out the front of what looks like a pickup truck. No movement there.

'Looks clear,' I say to Kris.

'There's a ladder leading to the roof on the rear wall past the gas tank. Keep to what's left of the piping and head for it. We can get upstairs that way.'

'How do we know the roof's in any condition to support our weight?'

'We don't. There's a gantry up there. Otherwise, stick close to the walls. It'll be strongest there.'

I swing up and over the fence, feeling the blood pounding through my system. I'm expecting to have made a mistake. That there's someone watching us. A shout of alarm. A rifle bullet through the spine. Sophie dead upstairs.

What I get is a shoe full of muddy water on the other side and a twenty-yard dash to the nearest cover. We follow a low concrete enclosure as far as we can, then break across another ten-yard stretch to some rusting pipes.

I keep scanning the factory, but nothing's changed. No sign that they know we're coming.

From the pipes to a pile of brick rubble, and from there to the back wall of the factory and the ladder up. Kris taps me on the shoulder and whispers, 'Hope you have a head for heights.'

I don't answer, but climb. The rungs are greasy with the rain, and the drab olive paint on them is cracked and crumbling, revealing the rust underneath, but the ladder seems pretty sound. I make it to the top, a little out of breath, and glance down at the lot below.

I'd guess it's around seventy feet, but I'm not sure. All I know is that it's far enough to kill me if I fall. The wind up here tugs at my hair and presses my freezing cold, wet jeans against my legs.

The maintenance gantry running across and along the roof is in a worse state than the ladder, but it holds. I dash across as fast as I dare, then down to where the top couple of floors of offices jut from the corner of the building. Pop my head up to the nearest window long enough to see a bare room beyond the empty frame, then back down again.

I point at Kris, then gesture upwards and nod. *Remember, you go after the guy upstairs.*

He nods and gives me the thumbs-up.

We haul ourselves in through the window. I draw my Colt and flick the safety off. I wish I had a silencer like Kris. Wait by the door, listening for any sounds of movement inside, then open it and check the view.

A short corridor dividing two open office spaces, other rooms like ours dotted along the back wall, and there, the stairwell. The place smells of mildew, and the only sound is the wind howling through a dozen shattered holes in the structure.

We split at the stairs. Kris creeps up to the top floor, and I edge my way down a level, watching the turns below me as best I can. The door below is missing, giving me a clear view down to the room the little guy vanished into earlier.

Still no sounds and no sign of movement.

With the wind outside whipping itself into a frenzy, I creep to the door, gun out in front of me.

Still nothing.

I hold my breath, count to three, calm and steady, then throw open the door and swing into the room. Sweep the corners with the gun, finger taut on the trigger, ready to drop the smaller guy before he can even blink.

Sophie's handcuffed to a radiator at the back of the room, with a strip of duct tape over her mouth. She looks roughed around, but not badly hurt.

The little guy isn't here.

From upstairs there's the sudden roar of a shotgun blast, and a moment later Kris starts screaming.

Chapter Thirty-Eight

I run across the room, trying to keep one eye on the door behind me. Tug the tape from Sophie's mouth – to her credit she doesn't cry out – as a second blast from the shotgun splits the air. I bunch the chain on the cuffs up as high as possible, away from her hands, and shoot through it, aiming out the window so I don't end up killing us both with a stray ricochet.

'Where's the other one?' I ask Sophie.

'Don't know,' she gasps, and flings her arms around my neck, crying.

I drag her out of the room. It looks like one guy has been bedded down here to keep an eye on her while the other's on lookout duty. A couple of sleeping bags, a camping stove, food and water.

The corridor's empty. I keep Sophie cradled in one arm as she clings to me, and cover the stairwell with my gun. Still no sign of the little guy.

Hit the top floor and break out into a T-shaped corridor. At the far end, the room being used as a watch post. I can see the top of someone's head sticking out of the doorway, hear whimpering.

I try to watch the doors to the other rooms I pass as I make my way there, but it's impossible. Too many angles, only one gun.

The lookout post is a mess. The big guy is the one lying in the doorway. He has a pair of bullet wounds to his chest and most of his face has been blown away. By his hand, a bloodied hunting-knife. Kris is slumped, sitting against one wall, covered in blood and gripping a semi-automatic shotgun in one hand. He must have fought it away from the guy. His pistol's lying on the floor some way away. He has a gaping hole in his gut, probably from the shotgun, and half a dozen slash wounds to his arms and face. One eye is gone, just a mass of blood and ichor, vanished beneath a vertical cut running from his scalp down to the top of his cheek. He's alive, conscious enough to be in pain, but he's a mess.

Sophie screams at the sight of him, then stops, starts hyperventilating.

'Kris, Kris, can you hear me?' I say.

I want to lay a hand on his shoulder, show him I'm there, that there's someone with him through all the pain. But I don't have a free hand, and I have to watch him suffer alone.

He whimpers, stop-start breathing, the agony from his chest and the need for air fighting it out.

'Kris,' I say again.

I can barely make out the words, but it sounds like he's saying, 'It hurts . . . it hurts . . . God . . . God . . . hurts . . .' Tears begin rolling down his face, and he stops talking.

I hear the stairwell door open and lean out far enough to see the smaller guy staring in utter horror at the corpse of his friend, face white. He sees me, his mouth opens like he's about to say something, and then he dives back inside. I lurch forward to follow, but Sophie tightens her grip and cries, 'Don't leave, Alex! Don't leave me alone!'

Behind us, Kris has gone silent.

Caught in a moment of indecision. The raw urge to hunt down the small guy with the scarred face, to find out who he is and make him pay for what he's done. The petrified look on Sophie's face, red eyes pleading with me not to go.

Fuck.

'I won't, Sophie, I won't,' I say. Pocket my gun and hold her, comfort her as best I can.

Downstairs, the faint roar of the pickup's engine revving. It rockets away from the factory like hell is following after.

Sophie begins to calm down after ten minutes or so, once she knows she's safe now and the other guy isn't coming back. 'They didn't do anything, they didn't do anything,' she tells me, as fragments of her story come out at random. 'They hit me a couple of times, but they didn't do anything else. I think . . . I think they wanted to, but I pissed myself, and they didn't want to come near me after that.'

'That's good, Sophie. That's good thinking.'

I check Kris, but he's dead. In a way, I wish I could have asked him the full truth about his past, to know just how damaged he'd been. Somehow it would have given his death more meaning if I could have understood his life better. But I don't know why that should be.

The dead kidnapper in the doorway has a wallet on him along with the usual personal crap. A New York State driver's licence for Andrew Byrne of Lorville, NY. An ATM card, but no credit and very little else. A shade under a thousand bucks in cash.

I walk Sophie back to Kris's car. She doesn't ask me about calling the cops and I don't talk about it. Someone will find the bodies eventually, but it'll probably be put down to a drug deal or something gone wrong. There's nothing much there to trace back to either of us.

Harsh, but I can't do anything more.

'Sophie,' I ask, once we're driving away, back to Boston, and she's on a more even keel. 'Did those guys say who they were or who they were working for? The big one was Andrew and the other was Harvey, right?'

'They were brothers,' she says. 'They were asking me if I knew where you were or how to get hold of you. I'm sorry about telling them your email . . .'

'No, no, you did the right thing.' I try a smile. 'If you hadn't, I wouldn't have known where to find you.'

'Who was the other guy? Was he with you?'

'His name was Kris. He was a friend, I guess.'

'I'm sorry,' she says.

'Stop apologizing, Sophie. None of this is your fault. So why did Harvey and Andrew want me?'

'They talked about it. They were going to kill you. They were working for someone who'd hired them to do it, but they hadn't been able to find you before . . . well . . .'

'Before the Tucker thing.'

'Yeah,' she says. 'So they tried to track you down. They said they were the ones who'd put Rob in hospital. The big guy, Andrew, he seemed to enjoy talking about it.'

I swing the car into a rest stop and buy us coffee and doughnuts from the drive-through. We sit in the rain, and I watch some of the colour return to Sophie's cheeks while she eats.

While I sip my coffee I'm trying to figure out what's going on. I know Goddard blackmailed Heller into framing me, so why would he hire the brothers to kill me as well? Unless he was hedging his bets by having both, it means that someone else wants me dead. Damned if I can think who, though.

'So someone hired them to get rid of me. Did they say who?'

Sophie shakes her head. 'No, they only ever called him "him". But they were planning to threaten him for more money.'

'A double-cross.'

'Yeah. They were going to blackmail him for more cash, or kill him if he didn't pay up.'

Which means they weren't professionals. Not for any length of time, anyway. Thugs, maybe, given their first shot at murder. If word spread that they

366

did that kind of thing to their employers, they'd never last.

'Did they say anything about anyone else? Did they have anyone in Boston that they knew?'

'No, I don't think so,' she says. 'I don't think they'd even been to the city before.'

I drop Sophie at her home in Cambridge. I don't like the risk, but I walk her to the door of her studio apartment and help her check there's no one waiting for her. She says she'll find a friend to stay with for a couple of days until everything's back to normal again, and I stay long enough to make sure someone's coming over to look after her.

'I'm not going to tell anyone about what happened,' she says. 'I don't want the cops to be chasing you even more. And it's all over now, isn't it?'

I nod. 'Yeah. I'm going to track down Harvey and whoever hired him. You'll be perfectly safe. I don't want you, or Rob, or anyone else getting hurt any more because of me.'

She smiles and hugs me tightly without saying anything.

I wait outside in the car until I see Brandon climb out of a cab and hurry up to her door, then I pull away from the kerb. I wish I could see Rob before I leave the city but that's not possible.

According to their background checks, Harvey and Andrew Byrne look to be regular small-town toughs, aged forty-one and forty-three respectively. A few convictions and charges between them for assault, extortion, conspiracy. Suggestions that they've done that sort of work for hire. Both of them have addresses in Lorville, neither has a regular job. Harvey's last steady employment lasted six months and came to an end two years ago. He was a driver for a haulage firm in Albany. Before that, another gap of about a year to some short-term warehouse work. The same pattern repeats all the way back. The same with Andrew. Listed family members amount to only one, apart from his older brother – his wife Jackie, no details on her.

The brothers were small fry. No one would've hired them unless they knew their reputation locally. If it was Goddard who did it, then he's a local too, and I'll find Holly in Lorville.

And Harvey will know where she is.

I copy down his details, then drive out to the waste ground where I buried Victor's gun.

Chapter Thirty-Nine

Waiting in a queue of half a dozen cars while traffic cops clear a jack-knifed truck from the road up ahead, hoping they have no reason to look at me or the car. High hill country on the state boundary, wooded, dotted with small towns. The dive down into the Hudson valley to come, then the Catskills proper.

I'm wondering how I've got into this situation. How far over the line I've gone.

How far over it I'm still to go.

I have lunch in the small town of Eastbridge. A diner by the name of Charlie's House. Decent place, the scent of fresh coffee and doughnuts. Quick service by a local girl with a nice smile and a breezy manner. From my seat by the window I can see down the main drag all the way to where the Hudson curls past the promontory on the far side of the river. Trees almost bare, fall marked by their empty branches. For a moment, I wonder what it'd be like to retire to a place like this, to be able to forget about everything and relax, withdraw from the world. To leave it all behind, forever.

Then I figure that's all just horseshit.

We all indulge our little dreams, our momentary fantasies. A life, a fate, considered, given form and then cast aside in moments. These ten-second destinies. These heartbeat dreamworlds. We paint our future in lies, and sometimes we're foolish enough to believe them.

But not today.

I finish my coffee and quit the diner, leaving a decent tip for the waitress. Walk back into the present and cold reality.

Across the river, I drive along highways twisted by the folds in the land, the upthrust slopes of the Catskills, forested and dark. Shreds of dark grey cloud, the tattered remnants of someone else's rain, scud across pale blue skies, with darker weather promised by the eastern peaks. Pass through a couple of small mountain towns, clusters of buildings gathered around the road. Half an hour of this, maybe, and I see the sign up ahead welcoming me to Lorville.

The first thing I see when I arrive is a cemetery occupying maybe a couple of acres running up the slope to the right. A boarded-up chapel sits on the opposite side of the highway, a curling notice pinned to its doors – something telling people to look elsewhere for salvation would be my guess. Then the first waves of housing and small neighbourhood stores. Blue-collar homes running in belts up to either side. It's a minute or two until I hit the town centre and a few square blocks of small businesses and chain stores.

There are a few people out and about, but whether

it's the oncoming rain or something else, the only ones I see smiling are a couple of kids playing tag with each other as they follow their mom along the sidewalk.

I cruise past the address I have for Harvey. A narrow, boxy house whose small, widely spaced windows, black against the pale walls, remind me of a prison. There's no sign of the pickup truck in the driveway, but over the back fence I can see laundry hanging out to dry. Someone's home, or they'll be back.

With a bit of luck, Harvey will be back later. If not, I can talk to his wife. I drive off in search of somewhere to stay.

The Discount Motor Lodge is a two-storey building shaped like a horseshoe around a central parking lot. Low-grade rooms with cable TV and sheets that smell like cheap washing-powder. A radio alarm clock running twenty minutes slow and without a working alarm function. I pay cash, do nothing to draw the attention of the staff. I can't afford to be discovered, not with Holly so close I can almost touch her.

The roof over my head sorted, I drive a few miles out of town on the main highway, north and south, and look at a couple of the larger side roads feeding off it. Now and then, a gravel track will wind up into the mountains, vanishing into the trees. A few have a signpost or hand-scrawled board indicating the eventual destination of these trails – isolated houses, tiny settlements, old industrial property. Many are entirely unmarked. I can see thin streamers of white smoke rising from the woods somewhere up towards the ends of a couple, the only signs of human activity I've seen.

Looking into the forest, hoping for some clue as to the whereabouts of Goddard, I wonder if he's up there somewhere, staring back. Standing on his porch, or gazing through his kitchen window, out through the trees. Aware on some subconscious level that I'm here hunting him. A crazy notion, but one I can't help harbouring for a moment. It passes when I wonder what he'd do to Holly if he knew I was here.

By the time I drive past Harvey's house for a second time, the day is heading for dusk. The rain hasn't arrived, but the clouds have sunk even lower and a thick blanket of grey lies heavily over the mountains, sealing off the valley in which the town sits like a vast dark curtain. The forest with its thinning brown and yellow leaves casts the place in sepia, all the colours draining out in the dim half-light.

Harvey's pickup is in his driveway.

I drive slowly past, then pull into the parking lot of a closed sporting goods store at the end of the block. I can't confront him in his house. In full view of the neighbours, with his wife inside, on his home territory.

I want to, but I can't.

But a guy like Harvey has to go out. A bar, a pool hall, some kind of regular haunt. Maybe he goes hunting up in the woods. I get as comfortable as I can in the Acura and wait for him to move from his house.

My neck's aching and every joint is stiff by the time eight o'clock rolls around and Harvey emerges in a puffy denim jacket and strides out to his truck. He pauses by the door, running his gaze over the street around him, then climbs inside and fires up the engine, apparently satisfied that he's safe.

I slip my car in gear and follow him across town to a decrepit bar, apparently nameless as the sole neon sign simply reads 'BAR'. He parks up and disappears inside without a second glance. I weigh up my options, but figure it's best to see if he's alone. I pull my baseball cap down as far over my face as I can, and glance quickly through the door before stepping inside.

Frosted glass windows, unpleasant brown carpet. A long counter broken in two by a single large pillar decorated with posters and flyers. The smell of spirits, stale breath, past nights out on the town. A jukebox playing Bruce Springsteen.

Harvey has met up with three other guys, similar ages and similarly dressed. The quartet are heading out back towards the pool table. As far as I can tell, they're not paying any attention to anyone else.

I buy a Bud and bury myself in the anonymous gloom of a corner table. In the mirrored glass on the far wall, I can see the four playing pool. There's only one way in or out of this place, apart from a fire exit that has one of those seals that trips an alarm when broken. Harvey will have to leave the way he came, and hopefully he'll leave alone. With this lighting and the way I'm sitting, there's no chance he'll spot me unless he walks right up to me.

I settle in to watch. I'm contemplating a second beer, when a woman comes over to my table, waves a cigarette and says, 'Hi. I don't suppose you've got a light, do you?'

She's maybe five or six years younger than me, brunette, with a kind of desperate leanness about her. Not especially attractive, but not a buck-toothed crone either.

I make an attempt at a smile, but my heart's just not in it, and my eyes constantly flick to the mirror behind her. She probably thinks I have a tic. 'I thought we weren't allowed to smoke in here.'

'I like doing things I shouldn't.' She makes a more promising effort at a grin, but her eyes give her away. 'I'm Mary, by the way.'

'Alex.'

I don't offer her a seat, but she takes one anyway. 'What brings you to this shithole? Don't think I've seen you around town before.'

'Work.'

'Yeah? What kind of work are you in?'

'I'm a pet psychiatrist.' She looks blank. 'Joke I saw in a film once. I'm a claims negotiator for an insurance company.'

'That a joke too?'

'I'm afraid not.'

Mary's eyes flick down, around. Thinking, measuring. In the end, she seems to decide that work's pretty much a conversational dead end. 'How long are you in town for?'

'I don't know.'

'You want another drink?'

I consider telling her to fuck off and leave me alone, as she doesn't seem to be getting the hint. But it'd only draw attention. I sigh. 'Sure.'

Another bottle of Bud duly arrives, along with an identical twin for Mary. 'Where are you from then, Alex?'

'Kansas City.'

'Wow. You have come far. First time out east, away from the big city?' Mary smiles, shifts in her seat, brushes the neck of her bottle with her fingertips.

'No,' I say, shrugging and taking a swig of beer. 'I've spent a fair amount of time in the north-east.'

'Oh, a regular visitor?'

'I wouldn't say that.'

We lapse into silence for a moment before Mary launches into what I hope will be a last-ditch bid to win my interest and telegraph her intentions. 'So, are you married? Wife back home in Kansas? Something like that?'

The question makes me smile, just for a second. 'No, nothing like that. No wife, no kids, no dog.'

'Were you ever married?' She takes a mouthful of

Bud. 'I had a husband, but he died in a car crash five years back.'

'Sorry to hear that.'

'I'm not. Son of a bitch was a mean drunk and a sober asshole.' Another swig from the bottle. 'If it hadn't been a Mack truck that got him, I would've done sooner or later. So, ever married?'

In the back, Harvey's racking up the balls for another game while one of his friends goes to the bar. I look back at Mary. 'Yeah, I had a wife once. Met in college, we were married a few years. Then she left me for someone else, some guy she met through work. Feller made eyes at her and off she went, hardly a second glance. I guess that's how it goes, huh?'

'I guess.' Mary smiles, and it looks genuine. 'But I suppose that's all in the past now.'

'It is,' I say, and take the opportunity available to me. 'But not far enough in the past. I'm sorry, Mary. Maybe I'm reading it wrong, and you're just being friendly. But maybe not. And you seem like a real nice woman. But I'm just not . . .'

'I understand,' she says. 'You seem like a nice guy, Alex. If you feel like buying *me* a drink anytime while you're in town, I'd like that. We can leave it at that.'

She gets up from the table with a smile and walks away. A part of me feels guilty for my earlier hostility. Misjudgement, an error in reading character. Maybe, maybe not. In the end, it doesn't really matter.

I was just a part of her own ten-second destiny,

her heartbeat dreamworld. Passed over and forgotten in no time at all.

Maybe an hour later, Harvey says goodbye to his friends and leaves the bar alone. I give him ten yards' head start, then follow.

We're the only people out here in the dark, but he doesn't seem to register my steps crunching across the parking lot behind him until he reaches the door of his truck, and by that point I'm almost on him. He wrenches at the handle, and I elbow him in the gut, hard and fast, then kick him into the closed door with a hollow thud as he doubles up.

I whip Victor's Beretta out and press it against his temple. 'Harvey Byrne, I presume,' I say. 'You need to talk to me. Or you're dead. Your choice.'

'You're *him*,' he says. The colour has drained from his face, and the old scar on one cheek stands out, pink and glistening in the distant lamplight.

'The guy you were hired to kill, yes. Now let's talk about who hired you. Get in the truck.'

He doesn't argue, and climbs inside. I follow, keeping the gun trained on him.

'Who hired you?' I say. 'Why?'

'Just some guy.' He hugs his stomach, wincing at the pain. 'Just some guy. He called Andrew and said he'd heard we'd done that kind of thing before. We had a meeting and he told us about you.'

'Had you done this kind of thing before?'

He shrugs. 'Once, by accident. We were only supposed to hurt this chick, scare her out of town. And then this guy a few months ago. We got paid to do that one.'

'Who?'

'Just some fag from out of town. But that was all.' He snivels, whines. He sounds like a goddamn six-year-old who's been caught stealing candy. Even twists his face up like one. 'It was all Andrew's idea. He was the one said we could make a lot of money doing it.'

'All Andrew, huh?'

Harvey sniffs raggedly, eyes pinching at the pain in his gut. 'He just told me what we were doing, and I just did it. It was never my thing. Always his. I just did what he told me.'

'And with big brother dead, you came running back out here to hide and hoped it would all go away, huh? So who hired you for that last time?'

'Some guy, called himself Mr Goddard. He was going to pay us six grand for you.'

'But you and Andrew were going to stiff him for more money, and kill him if he didn't do what you wanted.' When Harvey looks at me warily, I say, 'The friend of mine you tried to use as a hostage told me you'd been talking about it. Who was the guy?'

'I *told* you,' he whines. 'Goddard.'

'Who was he, Harvey? Description, address, phone number. How were you supposed to tell him you'd finished the job? How did you contact him and where did you hand over the cash?'

He looks at the gun in my hand. 'I've got his phone

number. And I know where he lives. Someplace out-side town.'

'Where?'

'An old house up one of the dirt trails on the highway north of town. Maybe a mile and a half, on the left. It had a couple of posts at the bottom, like there used to be a gate there. He was old, older than us. Brown hair.'

I let his voice trail away into silence for a moment. 'And he told you to kill me. Did he say why?'

Harvey shakes his head. 'No. Just who you were and that you were in Boston. He told us to keep going when you were on TV for killing that guy.'

'It was you and your brother who put my friend in hospital.' A statement, not a question at all. When Harvey stays quiet, not even meeting my eyes, I add, 'Why?'

'Andrew thought he knew something more than he was telling. But all he knew was that you were still in the city. Andrew said we had to shut him up.'

'And you just went along with that.'

A nasal murmur that could be a yes.

'And then you abducted a young girl to use as bait, and you went along with that as well. You never thought, "Well, shit. This can't be what decent people do." Do you know Gabriel Heller?'

Harvey looks blank. Shakes his head. 'Who?'

'You never heard the name?'

'No.'

The cab of the truck falls silent again. Then Harvey

says, very quietly, almost ashamed, 'You killed my brother.'

'No, I didn't. I would have, though. Happily, for what he did.'

'Does that mean you're going to kill me too?'

Chapter Forty

I think of Holly's face staring out of the screen at me through tears of pain. Rob lying in a hospital bed with God knows what chances of pulling through. The look in Teresa's eyes the last time I saw her, and how much worse it must be for her now. Sophie's frightened gaze when I found her chained up inside the refinery. Kris gasping out his life in a pool of blood.

Harvey had a hand in all these things. Protecting Goddard. Hunting me down. Targeting my friends. And until I showed up, he felt no remorse at all.

Everything about pulling the trigger would feel right. He's earned it, he deserves it.

But I can't do it. Not in cold blood.

'No,' I say to Harvey. 'I'm not going to kill you. Not right now.'

He glances at me, eyes wary.

'You know who your employer is?' I ask. 'What he did? What you were helping protect?'

'No. You owe him money or something?'

'He likes to abduct little kids, fuck them and kill them, Harvey. He's been getting away with it for years, and you've helped cover this up. You're going to have to live with that.'

Harvey swallows hard and I can see from the look of surprise and revulsion on his face that he had no idea what Goddard was doing. What he was involved with. I've seen the look before. That sense of disgust is why paedophiles are kept as separate as possible from other prisoners in jail. For their own safety.

'Get the fuck away from me, Harvey. Don't ever let me hear about you again.'

I climb out of the truck and leave him sitting there.

Back at the hotel, I grab a few hours sleep and wake just after dawn. Harvey has given me Goddard. Find him, and I find Holly. I leave as soon as it's light and go looking for his house.

It doesn't take long.

The track is narrow and the trees grow over it like a vaulted roof. The rocks and mud that make up the trail have well-worn tyre ruts in them. The air is close and thick, but cold, the cloud barrier above looks so near I could touch it. Empty trees rattle all around me, but that's all I can hear apart from my own heartbeat.

When I see the woods beginning to open out up ahead, the hole hacked out of them to accommodate Goddard's home, I leave the track and begin stalking quietly from tree to tree as I continue uphill.

The house must be sixty or seventy years old at least. Two storeys, all in heavily weathered, sturdy wooden boards. Unpainted, dun-coloured. A lean-to at one side of the building is occupied by a stack of firewood, while a similar extension at the back is home to what looks like a generator and a diesel tank. The house's windows are dark, empty. No lights on. No smoke rising from the chimney. No car parked out front.

I draw my gun and move to the back of the building, keeping low as I cross the empty space between the last of the trees and the rear wall. Risk a quick look through the glass set in the back door. A deserted kitchen area. Pretty basic, old equipment, a single large table at its centre. All wood, same as the exterior. I can see a small collection of crockery waiting to be washed. Probably more than enough for one person, but it's hard to say for sure.

I try the door, but it's locked. Hoping once more that there really is no one home, I knock out a pane of glass next to the catch for the window and open the casement. The splintering noise sounds loud enough to be heard from town.

Inside, the house smells of woodsmoke and old cooking. I sweep up most of the glass with my gloved hands to make it easier to clear away when the time comes to leave. The floorboards creak almost imperceptibly beneath me as I head through the kitchen and into the hallway beyond. There's a door beneath the stairs – closet space, or a basement entry – and rooms opening up from either side by the front door. I head to these first. In one, a bare bones set of furniture facing an old TV and VCR in one corner.

Against the far wall are stacks and stacks of magazines and video tapes.

Brutal Domination – Japanese bondage special! Bend Her, Break Her!

The videos include a couple of commercial porno titles, but most are marked solely by date and a varying sequence of letters which I can't decipher, but which I guess is some indication of their content. I'd rather not find out for sure.

The room opposite is the boxy bedroom where the second piece of footage was filmed. The bed is there, absolutely unmistakable, and there are plenty of scuff marks on the floor where either more furniture or equipment used in the filming has been dragged in and out.

Leave the room and back out into the hallway. To my surprise, the basement door is unlocked. A narrow flight of steps leads down into a dirt-floored space lit by a sole naked bulb hanging from the centre of the ceiling. Hooks have been driven into the beams; one has a pair of manacles hanging from it still. In the centre of the room is a low, large table, like a bed without a mattress. There are various fixture points built into it, and the whole thing looks like it can be lengthened or contracted like a workbench. I could be wrong, but I'd guess that it's a kind of homemade rack. Its surface is pock-marked and covered in stains.

I have to stop myself trying to imagine their origins.

In the far corner is another homemade contraption, about the size and shape of an isolation tank, or a coffin, with a pair of iron bolts securing its lid. Shelves packed with cardboard boxes run down the wall next to this last contraption. Amongst the unpleasant-looking devices there I can see Goddard's makeshift electric prod with a car battery next to it. I can see what look like girls' clothes in a couple of the boxes that are open. Hard to say whether they're long-term storage or something used more recently. I saw Holly in that car outside the post office, so he must allow her to dress. Another box, tucked at the back and thick with dust, has what looks like old, very old, boys' clothing. As I head down the stairs, I pass a piece of paper tacked to the wall.

'SLAVE CONTRACT'. At the bottom there's a jerkily scrawled signature. It's too badly written for me to make out anything but the final 'y'.

The air down here smells rancid. A mixture of sweat, urine and other acrid odours. It gets worse when I open up the 'coffin' to make sure it's unoccupied. It's lined with dark brown carpet, which again is marked with old stains. The fibres are worn thin in places, and from the shape and the impressions left in them, it looks to me like this is where he keeps Holly. At the head end of the box, blonde hairs sparkle in the light from above.

Feeling ill and angry in equal measure, I shut the lid again and head upstairs.

The first door I come to on the landing leads into a cramped room with a computer in one corner, along with cables and equipment which I guess allows Goddard to transfer and edit his video footage. There are also a couple of shelves of books – normal paperbacks for the most part, but amongst them I find *Psychological Torture in the Korean War, Mental Chains – the Willing Slave, Identity Breakdown and Nazi Brainwashing* and a handful of similar titles. Tucked into one, I find a dozen or so photos of different girls, all of whom look twelve to thirteen. Recent photos, on modern equipment.

With only room for one 'guest' here, Goddard seems to have been scouting for replacements for Holly.

Also present is a small collection of spares for the lighting and set-up rig he was using in the films he sent me. Leaning in one corner is an upside-down placard. The text on its front reads 'LIBERTY BEFORE DEATH'.

I think back to the crowd outside MCI-Ashworth. To the figure in the anorak waving this sign at me as I drove past. Every time. Staring at me with that faint smile on his lips.

From here I move through to what is clearly the location of the first piece of footage, a long, broad space that looks like it might once have been two rooms, knocked through and enlarged into one. Undecorated wood, same as the rest. A second bed, similar to the one downstairs. No ceiling beneath the ridge of the roof above, just the bare joists. There are still two halogen lamps up here, along with a video camera on a tripod pointing at the bed. A hostess trolley to the right of the room holds a variety of tools. Unpleasant, metal contraptions for the most part. Restraints. Pliers. A cigarette lighter and a screw with a soot-blackened head. A makeshift whip made of steel cable.

A side door leads into a surprisingly well-decorated bedroom. A lilac carpet, kept almost spotless. A double bed, spread with a beige duvet with tiny purple flowers on it. A dresser and closet which look to be made of oak. In the closet is a collection of men's clothes. There are more men's clothes in the dresser drawers. Tucked at one side of the top drawer is a Smith and Wesson revolver and a box of shells. I look at it for a second, but leave it where it is.

In the bottom drawer there's a very old-looking shoebox. Notes and photographs. Guys looking at the camera, smiling. Guys with one young boy or another held in front of them. Kris. Cody. The Gang of Six taking it in turns to abuse them while the others watch. Names, details of jobs or family lives, phone numbers. Out of date, but I guess it wouldn't be hard to find any one of these guys in a pinch. In the notes, Heller is described as a 'gangster' and a 'killer'.

On top of the dresser is a pair of framed photographs. Both look like they were taken years ago, that washed-out colour of old film, further fading from spending a long time out in the light. One shows a scrawny boy, can't be more than fourteen or so, with windblown brown hair, blinking into the sun behind the camera. He's in a T-shirt and shorts, an adolescent suntan. Summer vacation somewhere. His arm is around the shoulder of a girl a couple of years younger than him. Wavy blonde hair, similar kids' summer clothes, one hand held up to shade her eyes.

The second photo is of the girl on her own, a close-up of her face. Smiling, innocent. There's a definite resemblance to the boy in the first picture, something about the eyes. Brother and sister. Barely visible at the bottom, 'Lucy' is written in faded pencil.

I slip back out of Goddard's bedroom to check out the film in the camera. I want to see if Holly is still alive. I've made sure there's a tape in there, and I'm just about to switch the machine on and see what's on it when the sound of an approaching car engine cuts through the silence.

I scoot over to the corner of the room from where I can see both doors, gun in hand, and wait.

The car comes to a halt and the engine dies. I hear the front door open and footsteps in the hall. Two people, both starting up the stairs. One set fades along the landing, the second heads towards me.

The door opens, and Goddard walks into the room, heading for the camera. Five foot seven, medium build, looks around fifty-five. His hair's chocolate brown and has a faint greasy shine. Clean-shaven, pallid skin. He's wearing a heavy green jacket and jeans splashed with tiny specks of mud, and carrying a package under one arm.

He doesn't notice me until I step forward, level my gun at the back of his head, and say, 'Hello, Richard Goddard. Or is it Anderson? Or whatever other names you use?'

Chapter Forty-One

He stops what he's doing and freezes for a moment before saying, very calmly, 'Alex Rourke.'

'Right in one.'

'And can I ask what you think you're doing here?'

'You know the answer to that already.'

He sighs. 'Kill me, rescue all the prisoners I'm keeping here, hope you don't get caught by the cops. Or maybe you'll find someone else to pin the crime on like you did with poor little Cody.'

'That's basically it, yeah.'

'So why,' he says, slowly turning to face me, 'are we having this conversation? Shouldn't you have pulled the trigger by now? Or do you want to find out what I've done, or who I am and why I've done it?'

'I know what you've done. I know what you did to Cody, and how you turned him into your own pet monster. You tried to do the same with another kid called Kris, but he escaped. Once Cody was doing what he was told, you sent him back out into the outside world to snatch little girls for you. Was that your sister's photo in the bedroom? Holly's just someone to play out your fantasies about your sister, right? Someone you can torture and abuse to your heart's content.'

Goddard's eyes narrow. 'You found Kris. Little prick.'

'Right. And I talked to Gabriel Heller after you tried to have him kill me. So I know enough about you. I don't know why or how you started going after kids. I guess there's some sob story or other behind it, but I don't care what it is. Someone like you, who gives a fuck about "why"?'

'I've had nothing to do with Gabriel in years.'

'That's not what he says.'

'Are you going to take the word of a man like him?'

I roll my eyes. 'Am I going to take the word of a man like you?'

'I've got no reason to lie. You're holding a gun to my head.'

'Neither did he. He was holding one to mine,' I say. 'Face it, Goddard, you just like trying to mess with people. You love control, and you love lies and fantasy. You fucked and killed a bunch of kids. Dress it up with whatever bullshit justifications you like, you did it because you're a sick fuck. Just like every single other sick fuck. I spent years dealing with guys like you. There's nothing about "why" that I haven't already seen a hundred times, and there's nothing about the "who" that I give a damn about.'

He smiles without humour. 'So I'll ask again, why are we having this conversation?'

I smile back at him. 'Because I don't like shooting people in the back.'

The door through to the master bedroom clicks

open and Holly walks in. The long T-shirt she's wearing drapes loosely over her shoulders and her hair is hanging in untidy strands around her face. In her hands, held unsteadily out in front of her, she has Goddard's gun.

'Holly,' I say. She looks at me, confused, wide-eyed. A hint of recognition, but I don't know for what. 'Holly, put down the gun and go wait in the room next door.'

Goddard glances at her. 'Lucy, you know what to do.'

'I'm not going to let you kill him,' she says to me, and sights up on me with the pistol.

'Holly, you don't know what you're doing. I'm here to set you free and take you away from all this. I'm a good guy.'

Goddard smiles. 'She won't listen to you, Alex. She's my Lucy. She'll do what she's told, just like Cody used to, once I'd educated him. She's mine.'

Holly blinks once, twice and flexes her grip on the gun. I keep mine pointed at Goddard.

'You tried to do to her what you did to Cody? Make them into what you want by doing all that shit to them?'

'I educated Cody. I brought him up like a son.'

I don't smile. 'Some father.'

'He never complained. And neither does Lucy. She's mine.'

Holly nods, says, shaking, 'He takes care of me. He loves me.'

'Do you remember your parents, Holly? Your

mom and dad, back in Providence? They've been missing you. They want you to come back to them.'

'No, I've got to stay here. I don't want to leave. I can't.' She shakes her head violently. 'You can't make me.'

'Don't you want to see them? They want to see you, Holly.' I try to reconcile everything I know about Holly the girl with what I'm seeing now. Strange how she still sounds like a kid even though she's an adult. An adult who's pointing a gun at me and who looks shaky enough to fire the thing for real.

'I . . . I don't have parents. I've got my owner and that's all I want. All I want.'

I think back to the 'slave contract' downstairs and swallow my anger. 'Do you remember your friend Tina, who you went to see on the night you were grabbed and put into that van? Do you remember that, Holly?'

She stutters, glances at her captor. 'What? No. I'm Lucy. I'm Lucy. Stop calling me that. I'm Lucy.'

'I'm here to help you, Holly.'

'You were supposed to leave us alone. You should be in prison, or dead. That gangster was supposed to kill you. You shouldn't be here.'

'What did I tell you, Alex?' Goddard says with a smile. 'She's mine, and she's never going to leave me.'

'Like the others?'

'Others?'

'The other girls you had Cody grab for you so you could take your pick. So you could find the one that matched what you had in mind the best. They didn't leave you, did they?' I glance at Holly. 'You killed them because you were bored with them, ditched the bodies and started again.'

Goddard shakes his head. 'They weren't worthy. I haven't had to do that in a long time.'

'Why did you keep snatching girls if Holly was the one you wanted, Goddard? I mean, if she was so perfect, then why keep Cody out there grabbing them off the street? He wasn't sure about you then, Holly, and that hasn't changed.'

She shakes her head. I notice she knows I'm talking about her without calling her Lucy. 'You're lying. You're lying.'

'Don't you remember him bringing other girls home? Or leaving this house to go and examine them, to see if they fitted what he wanted better than you did? He's always had an eye out for someone who'd suit him more than you, Holly. You shouldn't stand by him. He doesn't deserve it. Or you.'

'Lies, Lucy,' Goddard calls to her, as she bites her lip. 'This man is just afraid and angry. He wants to hurt both of us, and he knows you won't let that happen. He just wants to confuse you so that he can kill me and then turn on you. You'll do what I say, won't you?'

Holly's wide eyes flick between us, but she keeps the gun pointed at me. 'I . . . of course, yes, of course.'

'Does Holly know you were planning on replacing her?' I say. 'That she was getting too old for your fantasy? You like young ones, don't you Goddard? And you were looking for a young girl to take her place.'

I see her eyes flick towards him again.

'That's crap,' he says. 'Don't listen to him, Lucy.'

'There are pictures of the possible replacements on your bookshelf, tucked into your books on brainwashing. If you want to see for yourself, Holly, go and take a look. I won't do anything.'

'It's a trick, Lucy.'

'No trick. You never cared about her, of course you didn't.' Beads of sweat are making my eyes itch. 'You just wanted her to match the fantasy in your head, all this Lucy shit. That's what you care about, not her. How long before you found yourself an excuse to kill her?'

'No, no. I just wanted . . .'

'Maybe you'd pretend to yourself that I'd forced your hand and that you had to get rid of her? But deep down, you just want a reason to be finished with Holly. You're already looking for a new Lucy.'

Goddard shakes his head as I continue. 'And living out here, killing Holly and ditching her body wouldn't be hard. You were going to start again. You don't want her any more.'

'That's not . . . no, it's all a lie! Lucy!' Goddard's voice grows increasingly shrill.

Holly's upper lip trembles and a tear trickles down her cheek. 'You don't want me? What did I do wrong?'

'He never wanted you, Holly. He just wants the fantasy you represented. Now he's going to get that from someone else.'

A second tear, and a third. Holly lowers the gun a notch and turns to look at Goddard like a child facing an angry parent. 'I did everything I was told like a good girl. Why?'

'It's not your fault, Holly,' I tell her. 'It never was. Everything, it's all his fault. You never did wrong. He doesn't deserve you.'

Goddard catches her eyes, and I can see him weighing the change in her mood and previously servile attitude. He must know he's losing her, that things are slipping out of his control. A moment of judgement, preserved in utter stillness, and then he lunges at her, arms outstretched, grabbing for the pistol.

He never makes it.

My first bullet catches him in the shoulder, sets him spinning as he tumbles. The second blows out the back of his head. Spray of red over the camera equipment and the wall behind him. He crashes to the floor in a bloody heap, so much dead meat.

Holly screams, a wordless cry of grief and rage. Her watery eyes watch him fall to the floor, wide with horror and loss, like a child watching her father gunned down in front of her, her doubts and anger at him utterly overwhelmed as she realizes he's gone. She's still howling, tears pouring down her face, as she snaps the revolver up in front of her, features twisted by fury and the burning wish to see me dead in revenge for what I've done to him.

Her finger tightens on the trigger, and I act on instinct. Another kick from the gun, and a hole blossoms in Holly's chest as the bullet punches clean through her heart.

She drops without firing a shot.

The scream is still on her face, and her eyes are wide, staring at me from where she slumps on the floor. The same innocent eyes that looked out at me from her photograph all those years ago, in a different world, a different life.

Chapter Forty-Two

I stand there for a minute or so, frozen in place, the smell of gunpowder, sharp and acrid, wafting past me as I stare at her corpse and try to come to terms with what I've done.

Break them down, build them up. Teach them they're worthless and then give them little rewards. They'll adore you. Stockholm Syndrome, reprogramming, call it what you like.

Something Holly said before she died comes back to me. '*You should be in prison, or dead. That gangster was supposed to kill you.*'

Holly was the one who called Heller, told him to deal with me. Goddard was telling the truth when he said he hadn't been responsible. He wanted to get rid of me, and that's why he hired Harvey and his brother. But he didn't think of blackmailing his old criminal buddy. And when Heller described the call he received to me, it didn't sound like he was having a conversation with a former friend. It sounded like a threat from a stranger, out of the blue. Heller didn't know who Holly was, but she knew who he was and everything about him from the old days. She must have read Goddard's notes, seen that Heller was a thug and a killer, and figured she could use him.

She did it to protect Goddard. He had that level of control over her. She wanted to keep her master safe from me.

She killed for him.

The son of a bitch remade Holly just as he remade Cody, to serve him. And both of them loved him because of it.

Died for him because of it.

If I hadn't staked out the post office, if she hadn't seen me looking for them, would she still have acted this way? Would Tucker still be alive? Or Kris? Every action, every choice, with a thousand consequences pinwheeling from them.

I get to work on the scene. Fire a few rounds from Holly's gun, and a couple more from mine, a random spray to make it impossible to be certain who shot what into whom if and when the scene is discovered. I leave the Beretta by Goddard's hand. As far as the world will be concerned, the two of them fought when Holly found out his plans. These things happen. I leave the window open, relying on wind and weather to help further obscure any stray trace evidence, then head downstairs.

I use duct tape and a plastic bag to seal over the broken windowpane to make it look like it happened accidentally and they'd repaired it as best they could. I take the broken glass with me, to be dumped in the woods well away from the house.

Outside, the wind has picked up a little, but there's still no sounds apart from the trees rasping against each other. No car engines. No police sirens. No indication that anyone knows what has just happened.

Holly Tynon died seven years ago. Everything she was, the core of her personality, was broken down and rebuilt by Goddard to fulfil a role in his own personal fantasy life. The girl I shot was a living ghost whose life was endless abuse and torture and whose personality was a construct of the monster who kept her as his slave.

At least, that's what I tell myself.

I didn't just kill the nineteen-year-old girl I'd come all this way to save, to restore to her family. To make up for my past mistakes. To repair everything I did wrong in the name of doing right.

After all's done, I still don't know who Goddard himself was and what started him off, and I probably never will. I guess he started by abusing his sister, or at least fantasizing about it. It's the only way to explain his obsession with her years later. Maybe their parents found out, maybe they were separated, or maybe she died. It took him a while to have the confidence to find a surrogate that he could grow in her image, to do with as he wanted. First he practised his technique on Cody and Kris, secure in his circle of friends. Only when he could distance himself from the abductions did he send Cody, his shadow, out to find him a new Lucy.

Exactly why he chose Holly, and exactly what happened to the other girls Cody abducted for him beyond them 'not being worthy', I don't know. Someone will be out walking, or they'll be digging the foundations to a new highway, and they'll find another pathetic bundle of child's bones and rags, and another name will be crossed off the list.

Maybe Cody could have been saved if he'd been willing to confide in someone when he was arrested, or even later in prison, some time before the end. He wasn't born the way he was, but made that way. I don't believe in God, but I do believe in redemption.

With all I've done, I have to.

As I drive away from Lorville, most of what I have is guesswork, supposition. But that's the way it goes in these cases. We never know all the details, and even if we know the reasons behind them, we can never understand. Men like Goddard are an alien species, and all we can do is look on in horror. We can catch, but never cure or comprehend.

When I get back to Boston, I wipe down the Acura and leave it in a mall parking lot, feeling suddenly empty.

I have nowhere I can go.

I have nothing to do.

Think for a moment, staring at the world from behind a glass wall, a partition that exists only in my mind, separating me from them, the light from the dark. Then I take the long walk down to the harbour and call Teresa.

'How's Rob doing?' I ask her.

'*Alex?*'

'I wanted to see him at the hospital, but I couldn't. How is he? How are you?'

'He's awake, and they say he's getting better. Alex, Alex, what happened? What did you do?' Her voice chokes like she's fighting tears.

'Nothing. I didn't do anything. Someone tried to frame me for killing Tucker. Someone else wanted me dead and went after Rob. I'm sorry, Teresa. I'm sorry.'

Sobbing from the other end of the line.

'When you see Rob, tell him I'm sorry. I'll come see him if I can, if that's all right. But I never thought it would go as far as it did. I'm sorry.'

She sniffs hard, pulls herself together. 'You can see him. He'd like that. I'd like that.'

'Thanks, Teresa. I will. Now I have to go.'

'Take care, Alex.'

I hang up, then make a quick call to my lawyer, explain to him where I am and what I'm doing. He's not happy, but he sounds confident about our chances of beating anything to do with Tucker. He doesn't ask me anything about Heller, or Kris, or Heller's dead henchmen and the deaths at the abandoned refinery. All that murder and pain and grief. Blood and fear, all in the past. I guess no one knows I was involved in any of it.

But I do.

I lean on the railings, and wait by the water's edge for the cops to finally catch up with me.

My life was just an elaborate lie, a dream painted on glass. But that dream is now irrevocably broken and through the cracks I can see the darkness inside.

The trouble is, when I look at it now, I can't tell which side of the glass I'm on.